Return to Widows Hollow

J. Helen Elza

Also by J. Helen Elza

Rosemillion

Remember fairy tales?

They're back…

Acknowledgments

My sincerest thanks and gratitude to the many great folks who shared in creating this book:

Becky Moser for being afraid to tell me but telling me anyway. The result is in your hands.

F. Warrick Crawford for being there.

Pat McGlone for your enthusiastic support and for staying glued to your chair start to finish.

Gerry Simpkins, my go-to writer for always having answers when I have questions.

Attorney George L. Partain for your help with West Virginia Family Law.

Travis Dewitz for your outstanding photos that make me *feel* and for the perfect cover photo

Todd Anderson, for your endless talents, hard work on the content, the cover and the re-designed website.

Prologue

Rose McKinley gripped the wheel of her cherry red 1970 Chevy C10 pick-up with white knuckles.

She had driven treacherous roads before but Highway 10 in Southwestern West Virginia was different.

Straining to see through the relentless rain, she crept along the twists, turns and hair pin switchbacks at twenty-five miles an hour. She had fishtailed and spun out twice already.

Even though she was hours late arriving at her friends' home in Wolf Laurel Creek, she wasn't going to take any chances on this slick icy road.

She had come too far in her twenty-eight years to let icy roads defeat her now. She could hear the whispered reminder in her father Joseph's voice. "We's survivors, Pick! We ain't no hillbillies like them folks in town calls us. We's mountaineers and survivors!"

And Rose had survived. By age sixteen she had lost both parents, her father to the miners' curse, black lung, and her mother to the ravages of a stroke that had left Isabel McKinley with a twisted body and twisted speech.

Losses like these had proven enough to destroy the strongest of survivors, but there had been more, much more.   There were siblings, four of them, and no breadwinner, no father returning home from the mines with scrip or a paycheck, no mother returning from her domestic labors with magical stories and fairy tales.

There had been only Rose whose first venture to the city to find work had proven to be a near fatal one.

Lost in a blizzard and freezing in a threadbare jacket, she would have surely perished.   But God answers prayer.

Rose twisted the diamond engagement ring on her finger.   He had placed it there.   He had found her near-frozen body and had saved her.   Now he had waited for years to marry her.   That truth alone was fairy tale enough.

Klaus Janssen Vandeventer, Jr., Jan, could have chosen any debutante or wealthy heiress he wanted from his gilded inner circle of world class breeders and horse enthusiasts.

But he had refused them all and over his friends' protests, had chosen her.   He had pledged his love for her repeatedly but Rose had refused.

She had been an impoverished, illiterate orphan with three brothers and a sister to feed and support.   The townspeople called her hillbilly, she and others who were born on the wrong side of the tracks in one of Appalachia's most desperate and decimated regions.

Rose could see him in her mind's eye, his compassionate blue eyes, his blonde hair and dimpled face, his taut muscles straining to control one of the magnificent animals that had made his family name, Vandeventer, famous.

He could have run but Jan had elected to stay. He had been there for the announcement, right there on the courthouse steps where a fairy tale, Isabel McKinley's fairy tale, had forever changed Rose's fate.

Rosemillion, the tale of a beloved child whose angelic singing and love for neighbors and kin turned bleakness and despair into an enchanted garden, was just a fairy tale, her mother's fairy tale.

Or so Rose had believed. It was to be their meager legacy, her own, and that of her siblings, Jimmy Joe, Willie, Buddy, and Olivia.

Neither Rose nor her family had been prepared for the enormity of that inheritance. Rosemillion had banished the nightmare and saved them all, Rose, her family, and her close-knit community, Widows Hollow.

It was the fairy tale that had closed the doors of poverty and illiteracy and opened the doors to education, freedom, and prosperity.

Pick McKinley, the name sounded so strange to her now, had rejected Jan's advances. He was after all a registered blue blood and she a mutt mama dog with a litter of pups and not much else until that day on the courthouse steps.

Rose braked for yet another precarious switchback and then smiled to herself. She had finally said yes, had accepted his ring and had promised herself to her ruggedly handsome, defiant and determined, fiancé, Jan Vandeventer.

She had difficulty believing that so many years had passed since that day. So many things, so many lives had changed, but the wait was almost over. She would help her friends Suzanne and Bennett Gardner who had volunteered to help their friend Mustafa establish a medical clinic here in the mountains of West Virginia while she waited for Jan to come home from the war.

Soon she and Jan would return together to Widows Hollow to her family and to his. If she could make it a few more miles up this icy mountain all the nightmares of their lives would be behind them.

Navigating the icy treacheries of Highway 10 in the rainy pre-dawn darkness, Rose had no way of knowing that the real treacheries, the unfathomable nightmares, lay just ahead, up the mountain and around the hairpin curves for her, and in the killing fields of Vietnam for Jan.

Would Rose McKinley and Jan Vandeventer return together to Widows Hollow to become man and wife at last? Or would the nightmares that await them on two separate continents forever alter their fates?

For

My Treehouse Ghost

Thanks for the motivation

And a special thanks to my editor

Jim Elza

Chapter One

Wolf Laurel Creek, West Virginia
February 27, 1972

"Suzanne, will you quit pacing? Rose is all grown up now. She'll call if she has trouble finding us."

"Bennett, she doesn't know these roads. They're bad enough in good weather. They're deadly in ice. She should have been here hours ago."

"Are you forgetting that she grew up in Widows Hollow? Remember those roads?"

"Yes, but that was Kentucky. This is West Virginia. She's on Highway 10, also known as The Most Dangerous Highway in America."

Suzanne knelt on the sofa, cupped her hands at her temples and pressed her forehead against the window. She tried to peer into the darkness through a driving rain but it was useless. She could see nothing. She heaved a sigh and retraced her steps to the fireplace and to the smoldering embers of a fire.

"Suz, you're making me nuts!" Bennett Gardner dropped the newspaper he had been reading. He rose from the sofa knowing that he had to tread lightly here. Suzanne could be tough as nails if she needed to be, but she could also dissolve into a puddle of tears for reasons he might never comprehend.

Unable to sleep, Suzanne had crept downstairs to wait. She had not been alone long for her husband, Bennett, who could read his wife like a Dickens' classic, knew that she was worried and that she would likely torment herself with worst case scenarios until Rose arrived safe and sound. As a husband Bennett was a rare and quick study.

Suzanne had taught him that while logic and reason motivated most men, women labored under no such obligation. In a whirlwind of emotions, they could sprint from fury and frustration to purring passion faster than most men could blink.

Bennett walked a fine line when it was obvious to him that Suzanne was on her emotional roller coaster. He did not judge, he did not condemn, and he did not try to match fury for fury or silence for silence. He waited. When the

2

mood swings and crying jags passed, she would reward him with the love and passion that he had yearned for all his life.

Suzanne's concern was justified this time. Rose had confided through tears that she had not heard from Jan in almost a month. The Vietnam War was winding down, the remaining troops returning home. Jan's last letter had been optimistic, filled with his plans for their wedding and for their new life. Rose had heard nothing since that letter.

Now Rose was long overdue. The weather had taken an abrupt turn for the worst and she was driving in it.

"Suzanne, quit worrying. It's dark out. You couldn't see through this downpour if it was light. Tell you what, if you'll stop pacing, I'll get us another cup of coffee. We can snuggle and watch the sun come up and maybe that'll keep you from wearing a rut in Mustafa's hardwood floor.

Suzanne heaved a sigh. She crossed her arms and flashed her husband a lop-sided grin. "Am I that bad?"

"We're gonna have to replace Moose's floor. Look at that rut." With a coffee cup in each hand, Bennett nodded to the floor beneath Suzanne's fuzzy pink slippers. "See?"

Suzanne glanced at the floor. "Bennett Gardner!" With a scowl she pinched the spare inches of flesh above his waist. She would have gladly bitten him on the back of his neck, but she could not reach Bennett's neck in her bare feet.

Doctor Bennett Gardner, 6'6", dwarfed his doctor wife who stood 5' 6" in heels.

Suzanne wrapped her arms around Bennett's waist and padded after him into the kitchen.

"Is that passion I'm feeling? I hope, I hope, I hope." Bennett placed the cups on the countertop and turned to Suzanne with an impish grin.

"Oh, no you don't, Buster!" Suzanne flattened her palms against his chest and gave Bennett a playful shove. "Get those green, come-hither eyes off me and pour that coffee right now! We have company coming and a community that needs doctors. No time for hanky-panky this morning, so get your cute little butt in gear and quit playing around."

Bennett's lips went smiley. "God, I love it when you say I have a cute little butt. See, you want me, I know you want me." Bennett fluttered his eyelids.

"Dr. Gardner, I have you," Suzanne said and tapped the two-carat diamond on her finger, "And we have...."

Bennett melted. Suzanne was so irresistible with her petite frame draped in a sleep shirt and with her long black hair tumbling loose down her back. "Shut up and kiss me," he said.   He locked his arms around her waist, lifted her off the floor and crushed his lips to hers.

Suzanne returned his kiss with the same passion that had ignited their marriage years earlier.   She adored her tall, handsome, green-eyed husband and the adoration was mutual.

Suzanne had been engaged to another when she and Bennett met at Ashford County Hospital in Kentucky where they both had worked as interns.   But fate had intervened when Suzanne's former neighbors invited both Suzanne and Bennett to an informal Christmas gathering.

It was at this gathering where Dr. Bennett Gardner learned that Dr. Suzanne Claiborne had delivered an abrupt and fatal blow to her engagement and where the two good doctors shared one playful kiss that had ignited a fire between them that continued to this moment.

Bennett felt Suzanne's soft lips touch his and his pulse quickened.   He tightened his arms about her waist anticipating a few moments of heated passion.

Suzanne kissed him with a fiery kiss, buried her fingers in his curls and yanked.

"Ouch!"   Bennett shot Suzanne a pained look and rubbed the back of his head.

"Ssshhh," Suzanne said with a giggle and then pressed a finger to her lips. "You'll wake Mustafa."

Bennett puckered his lips in a pout. "Aw Suz, I thought I was gonna get...."

"Lucky? Too bad for you, you wake Mustafa already!"

Bennett and Suzanne glanced up in surprise. Their friend Mustafa stood in the kitchen doorway yawning through a scowl.

"Oh, Moose! We're sorry!" Bennett exclaimed, trying hard not to giggle. "We didn't mean to wake you."

"A likely story." Moose's words were distinct and heavily weighted in his Eastern Indian accent.

He bounced his eyes between Suzanne and Bennett who stepped quickly apart. "But I am awake now so if you could hanky-panky somewhere other so I could get to coffee, I appreciate very much."

Bennett slapped Moose on the back. "Let me get it, Moose my man," he offered. Bennett stepped to the counter and filled a cup with the steaming brew.

"Where's mine?" Suzanne pushed out her lower lip in a pout.

"I don't get any, you don't get any," Bennett crowed. He made a comical face, shrugged and raised flat palms in the air.

Suzanne giggled but stopped short. Mustafa was staring at her chest.

"I don't do mornings." The words printed on Suzanne's oversized tee shirt sounded funny in Mustafa's thick accent.

Suzanne glanced down at the shirt. Her cheeks turned a bright crimson. The shirt's thin fabric did not adequately cover her otherwise naked body, particularly when she and Bennett shared mornings with their Pakistani Muslim friend, Dr. Mustafa Dhingra.

Noting Suzanne's embarrassment, Bennett turned a sober face to Mustafa. "Don't need an x-ray machine to see through that shirt, huh, Moose?"

Slow to comprehend, Mustafa knit his brows and then he turned crimson.

"Bennett Gardner!" Suzanne cried.

Bennett laughed. "Now you're even. Moose is embarrassed, too."

"You are a donkey's behind!" Mustafa growled.

Suzanne darted past him and up the stairs to the bedroom that she and Bennett shared.

Bennett shook with laughter. "You know, Moose, "donkey's behind" sounds so much better with a *Mooslim* accent. It's almost like a compliment."

Mustafa repeated "You are a donkey's behind. And that is no compliment. And I do not have a *Mooslim* accent." He feigned a scowl at Bennett. "And this coffee is horrible."

"Drink up. It'll grow hair on your chest," Bennett quipped, straight-faced, knowing that Moose had to slowly run the English through his head before the words sank in.

Mustafa kept silent for a moment and then he shot Bennett a contemptuous glare. "Donkey's behind!"

"Come on, Moose, it's freezing in here! Let's add some fuel to that fire." Bennett sipped his coffee and led the way to the living room.

This was Mustafa's house. Like most in the seventeen villages that spilled down the narrow mountain hollow known as Wolf Laurel Creek, it had been built by the mining company in the twenties or thirties or as early as 1912 when the first rail spur had been laid in the hollow by the Chesapeake and Ohio Railway.

Coal community cabins were tiny, stark identical frame structures first built as company rentals to miners.

Throughout the coal-mining region cabins like these stood rotted and fallen to ruin.

But for the local miners, shifts that had once paid one or two dollars' worth of scrip now paid as much as fifty dollars per shift.   In Wolf Laurel Creek where the continuous miner and outward migration had reduced the local population to one third that of the twenties, moderate prosperity showed in home improvements and new additions.

The former coal camps had become close-knit neighborhoods where a sense of security and pride now prevailed.

Mustafa's house was one that had been transformed. The original single story frame dwelling was now a brick two story that boasted three bedrooms, two baths, a modern kitchen and dining room, living room with a large stone fireplace and a covered porch that stretched across the front of the house.

Mustafa had replaced worn linoleum with hardwood floors.   Colorful rugs scattered throughout complimented the muted tones of the wallpaper that covered the walls. The house was cozy and tidy for the most part.

Medical supplies and equipment that had been stored upstairs in the spare bedroom had been moved into the living room and dining room to make a place for Rose.

Bennett and Suzanne had come to West Virginia to help Mustafa establish a medical center for locals who fell through the cracks, the people who did not qualify for state aid, yet needed but could not afford health insurance.

Mustafa, like many other foreign-born men and women, had taken advantage of the U.S. Government's offer of a free medical school education, a green card and permanent U.S. residency in exchange for a four-year stint as a doctor in a depressed rural area.

No one could deny that the fringes around Wolf Laurel Creek, the Appalachian coal-mining community in West Virginia's Highlands, were as rural and as poverty stricken as any to be found in America.

Mustafa had graduated med-school with honors and had completed his internship. Now he wanted to give back to the community and to the country that had made it possible. But the going had been tougher than Mustafa expected.

The people of Appalachia were a paradox. They could be both warm and hospitable, but could be equally suspicious and distrusting. Mustafa had felt welcomed to

Wolf Laurel Creek as a neighbor, but as a doctor the people had given him a wide berth. They had their doubts.

Mustafa's accent did not help matters either. Many of the locals complained that they could not understand him. The people were suspicious by nature, the area, depressed. Too many families in the nearby communities lacked sufficient money for food, much less medicine and doctors.

Mustafa had become disheartened. The task was overwhelming for a single foreign-born doctor so he had asked Bennett and Suzanne for help.

Their response had been immediate, positive, and enthusiastic. In turn they asked their friend Rosemillion McKinley to come and visit and to help them ready the clinic.

Bennett removed the fire screen. He took a polished brass poker from its stand and rearranged the smoldering logs.

"I will get more wood," Mustafa offered.

"Let me get it, Moose. It's too cold out there. I'm dressed and you're still in your jammies."

Bennett replaced the poker and strode across the room. He pulled open the front door and whistled at the pounding rain. "Geez! It's coming down in buckets." He switched on the porch light, darted through the door, and loaded an armful of logs from a stack in the corner.

He returned to the fire, spilled the logs from his arms, and coaxed the embers into a colorful blaze.

"Your friend, she is late?" Mustafa asked. He gathered up the newspaper sections of the *Charleston Gazette* that lay strewn on the coffee table and headed for the trashcan in the kitchen.

"I'm afraid so. I hope she gets here soon, Suzanne's going nuts."

Mustafa glanced to the outer darkness and shook his head. "This rain been coming for three days. We never see so lot of rain. We cannot get to mountains until rains stops. More lost time we do not afford."

"Cheer up, Moose. We've made some good progress and we've only just started to recruit."

"What is recruit?"

"Ask for help. Beg for volunteers."

"We do not supposed to beg, you boron!" Mustafa cried. Looking perplexed, he scanned the coffee table and a corner reading table. "Did you take my coffee?" He narrowed his eyes at Bennett.

"Yeah, I threw it in the fire. See?" Bennett pointed to the fire.

Mustafa waved a finger. "You will not get me again with that one," he said, and then added "Moose is learning." He refused to look to the fireplace.

Knowing Bennett's penchant for practical jokes, Mustafa searched under the coffee table and among stacks of medical books and supplies that spilled across a desk to the right of the sofa.

While Moose's back was turned, Bennett took the man's coffee cup from the fireplace mantel, slid it by its handle onto the fireplace poker, and placed it in front of the fire.

Moose squeezed his brows. "I cannot find it."

"Look in the fireplace," Bennett insisted with a grin.

Mustafa picked up a yardstick from the desk and turned to Bennett. "I will not look in fireplace," he said, but the temptation was too great. Despite his resolve, he glanced at the fireplace and saw his cup.

"How you ever become doctor is mysterious to me!" Mustafa huffed and smacked Bennett with the yardstick.

"I cheated. A lot," Bennett said with a grin. "Want some more coffee?"

"Yes, thank you, but I get another cup." Mustafa absently scratched his cheek with the end of the wooden yardstick.

Bennett laughed and reached over the fire screen to retrieve Mustafa's cup. "Youch!" He yelped. The hot cup burned his fingers.

"Serves you good," Mustafa said with a grin.

"That's *Serves you right*, Moose."

Mustafa raised the yardstick to take another swat at his leering friend when he saw headlights through the window.

"Somebody is lost or your friend, she is here."

Bennett sucked his burned fingers and flapped his hand in the air. "Woo, that really burned!" He crossed the room, kneeled on the sofa, and peered out the window. "Somebody's lost," he said.

"How you know that?" Moose asked. He was on guard now and was not about to take anything that Bennett said seriously.

"Because it's a dame, need I say more?"

"What is dame?" Moose asked, curious. He joined Bennett on the sofa.

"That's not a dame, that's Rose! Bennett Gardner, quit antagonizing Moose and help her in before she drowns." Seeing the headlights from upstairs, Suzanne had hurried down. She wore jeans, a white turtleneck, two socks and one boot. She waved the other at her grinning husband.

"Killjoy!" Bennett snatched a hooded jacket from the coat rack near the door. He threw it around his shoulders and with his head bent, ran outside into the pouring rain.

He tugged open the door of Rose's pickup and raised his jacket over his head to shield her from the downpour.

"Rosie Mac! Welcome to Wolf Laurel Bog. It's sloshy out here, watch your step." Bennett took Rose by the hand and helped her from the truck.

"I need to get my…," she began.

"Fanny inside before we wash away!" Bennett cut in. "I'll get your things when that dove shows up with the olive branch." He wrapped an arm around Rose and, huddled together under his jacket, they raced for the porch.

"I see you haven't changed a bit," Rose said with a laugh.

"Hair's thinner, waist is thicker, other than that, I'm good as new," Bennett replied.

Suzanne held the door and smiled a smile wide as the State of Texas. "Oh, Rose, Sweetie! I'm so glad to see you and I'm so relieved to know that you're still in one piece!"

"Let me have your coat. You come over here and soak up some of this heavenly heat. Was it horrible? Driving Highway 10 in this weather? Have you ever seen anything

like it? Under the best of circumstances, that road's a
nightmare, but in this freezing rain, I've been so worried.
I can't tell you how happy I am to see you safe and sound!"

Bennett winked at Rose. "My girl's wound up like a
two day clock. She'll settle down in a minute."

Suzanne made a face and after a moment she speared
Bennett with her elbow.

Rose took off her coat and raked her fingers through her
long, spiraling red hair. She smiled at Suzanne and
glanced at the sparkle of the engagement ring that Jan had
placed on her finger before she replied.

"The drive was a nightmare, one that I would not
recommend to the faint hearted." She bit her lip and
continued. "But all I had to do was to think of Jan. He's
the one who is in danger. He's the one who risks his life
to save others. He's my hero and he'll be home soon. No
icy mountain is going to keep me from being there to greet
him!"

Rose said it with a smile, a smile that Suzanne
suspected required some effort. Rose twisted her ring and
then added "Thank God, he'll be home soon."

On impulse, Suzanne hugged the tall, elegant woman
again, and then held her at arm's length. "You look
wonderful, Rose! I think you grow more beautiful with

each passing year. But, enough of that. I know you must be exhausted. We…" Suzanne fell silent to stare at Bennett.

He behaved like a conductor waving a baton. Keeping his arms stiff, he raised his hands waist-high and extended his pointer fingers. He jabbed a finger at Mustafa and then nodded to the man.

Mustafa smiled at Rose. "Welcome to my home. I am Mustafa." He cut his eyes to Bennett. "Some friends call me Moose." He extended a hand to Rose. "May I get you coffee?"

Rose said with a nod "Thank you. That sounds great!"

Bennett smiled a smug smile, dipped his chin and aimed a pointer finger at Suzanne.

"Oh! Where are my manners?" Suzanne cried and smacked her forehead. "Mustafa, Rose, I am so sorry! Rose, of course, this is Mustafa. Mustafa, this is our friend Rosemillion McKinley, but we call her Rose."

"So they've been told," Bennett chided.

Suzanne added with a scowl "And this is my tacky husband, Bennett, who better fly into that kitchen and return with some steaming hot coffee if he knows what's good for him!"

Rose returned Mustafa's smile. "I've looked so forward to meeting you. Suzanne and Ben tell me they've never met a more dedicated doctor. I look forward to helping you in any way I can."

Moose lifted his chin in mock arrogance. He tilted his head in Bennett's direction. "If Suzanne speaks of me, you may believe. If Bennett speaks, I am not so realizing."

Bennett laughed. "I better speak for you, Moose. Here in America, that sentence goes like this "If Bennett speaks, I am not so sure.""

"Grow high, Bennett!" Mustafa huffed.

"Up, up and away...," Bennett pretended to watch balloons drift upward and sang a chorus from the Fifth Dimension's popular 1967 hit song.

Mustafa rolled his eyes and shook his head at Bennett.

Rose had looked forward to this visit. Now she felt certain that she had made the right choice in coming. She expected the playful bantering between Suzanne and Bennett. Their relationship was and had always been a rare and wonderful one. They were much more than man and wife. Suzanne and Bennett were best friends.

Mustafa was the surprise. He was nothing like the stereotyped immigrant-doctor that Rose had envisioned.

She had expected a short, bespectacled, olive-skinned man with a slight build and no-nonsense demeanor whose social skills were limited to a bedside or clinical setting.

She was more than a little surprised. Mustafa stood 6'2" with a solid, square build. He was constructed of pure muscle that stretched from his ankles through his broad chest and shoulders.

His thick, black, collar-length hair framed a strikingly handsome face with deep-set black eyes fringed with curling black lashes. Despite the cold, he wore ivory linen pants and a linen tunic with loafers and no socks.

"Soup's on." Bennett returned from the kitchen carrying a tray laden with four cups of aromatic coffee. He centered the tray on the coffee table and then playfully slapped at Moose's hand. "Ladies first Moose!"

Moose shot back "This is no soup, Beanie. This is coffee."

Suzanne giggled. "Very good Moose! Keep the boy straight!"

Bennett stuck out his tongue at Moose behind the man's back.

"And you Suzanne, I have a few words I want to speak to you." All hints of play had disappeared from Moose's face and from his voice.

Bennett rolled his eyes and poked his tongue in his cheek.

Moose ignored him.

"Well?" Suzanne held her coffee suspended in her hands, waiting.

"You do not tell Moose truth. You tell me your friend from Kentucky Mountain is pretty woman. She is no pretty. She is beautiful."

Rose blushed at Moose's unexpected compliment. Compliments had been rare in her early life. She had never gotten used to them.

"I agree with you Moose, she is beautiful," Suzanne said and patted the sofa. "Rose, come, sit. Tell us how things are going at home."

Bennett sat cross-legged on the floor in front of Suzanne. Mustafa sat beside Bennett.

Rose sipped her coffee. "Great coffee and I was so ready for a good, hot cup."

"Moose thinks it stinks," Bennett quipped.

"Shut up Beanie, nobody want to hear about Moose. Let your friend speak, she is guest here."

Bennett accepted Moose's jibe with a grin and turned to Rose. "So Rosie Mac, tell us what's going on at home."

Rose pulled a hand to her face. "Where do I begin? There's so much to tell. Of course everybody sends their love and best wishes. They all miss you." She brushed at a wayward curl as she continued. "Things are changing so fast, I can hardly keep up myself."

"Olivia graduates from high school this spring. I think she and Willie and Buddy would sleep in the barns if we'd let them. They love the horses so much. I never dreamed they would become skilled so quickly in caring for them."

Moose wrinkled his brow. He directed his gaze at Suzanne. "She has children who sleep in barn?"

Suzanne laughed. "No, Moose. Rose has no children but she did raise her sister and three brothers. Their parents died when Rose was sixteen. She was oldest so she raised them."

"How old are they now, Rose?" Bennett asked.

"Buddy's twenty, Willie is twenty-two, Jimmy Joe is twenty-six and Olivia is eighteen."

"I can't believe they're all grown up," Bennett said, shaking his head. He looked at Mustafa. "As Rose was saying, her younger brothers, Buddy and Willie, raise thoroughbreds at home on Rose's horse farm."

They had a great teacher, Rose's father-in-law-to-be, Klaus Vandeventer. Klaus is a famous breeder known all over the world. Klaus and his family raise some of the finest racing horses that money can buy."

"What's Jimmy Joe doing?" Suzanne asked.

"He's building. He loves building like the other boys love raising horses. He has his engineering degree. Now it's official. He's a design-builder. I think he's remodeled every home in Widows Hollow and just recently, he completed some spec homes in Ashford. In last year's Parade of Homes, he made a name for himself. People love his designs."

"And how are Klaus and Olga?" Suzanne asked. She swatted Bennett who had tied her bootlaces together.

Rose's face turned serious. "They're fine, but they're worried. They haven't heard from Jan, either. We're hoping it's just the mail, you know, with the war." Her voice trailed off, she furrowed her brow. "Maybe the mail is just slow."

Suzanne felt a tug of apprehension. No news from a war zone in a month was not good news. Rose's concern showed in her face.

Hurrying to change the subject, Suzanne asked, "And how are Mama John, Jimbo, Mule and the family?"

Rose had to smile. Mama John was the closest thing Rose had to a mother after her own had died. Rose adored the sweet old black woman, her husband, Mule, and their tribe of kids. Rose loved Mama John better than she loved anyone on earth with the possible exception of Jan.

"Mama John? Oh, she's wonderful! Olga keeps her busy baking for the folks in Ashford and Mule still makes the best jerky in all of Kentucky!"

Rose let out a sudden gasp. "Oh, that reminds me, I have fresh bread, a basket of fried chicken, and all the trimmings in the truck. You know Mama John wouldn't let me leave home without enough home cooked *vittles* to feed half of West Virginia."

Bennett wasted no time unfolding himself from the floor. "Yeah, and I know Mama John's cooking!" He bounced his brows at Mustafa. "And, my little *Mooslim* friend, you are in for a treat!"

Bennett stretched his lanky frame, noticed the light outside the window, and reached a hand to Suzanne. "Hey, daylight! Looks like another rainy day. Oh well, if you'll make another pot of coffee my love, I'll go fetch the goodies and bring in Rosie Mac's stuff."

Bennett gave Suzanne a peck on the cheek and then headed for the door.

Suzanne and Rose gathered coffee cups and continued their conversation. They had a lot of catching up to do.

Mustafa followed Bennett. "I help you, O.K?"

"No thanks, Moose, no need getting your jammies wet!"

Bennett darted out the door with Mustafa close behind. Without warning, Bennett suddenly reversed himself and then shoved Mustafa backward. Sheer horror twisted Bennett's face.

Pushing Mustafa he screamed. "Oh my God, Moose! Rose! Suzanne! Run for your lives! Run for your lives! Get in the truck now!"

Chapter Two

Suzanne and Rose exchanged mute, disoriented stares in that few seconds that the brain requires to shift gears from a lazy Saturday morning of hot coffee shared with good friends to a sudden and unannounced foot race with death.

The sounds of shattering china preceded the women's flight into the living room where, like a man gone berserk, Bennett ripped coats off their hooks and, without a backward glance, threw them to Suzanne and Rose.

"Bennett, wha…." The alarmed women raised their arms to deflect the flying coats and then caught them with disbelieving stares.

The look on Bennett's face frightened Suzanne as he herded the women out the door like a longshoreman shoving thugs.

Frightened and bewildered, Suzanne demanded "Bennett! What are…?"

Bennett cut her off with a howl. "Get in the truck, Suzanne! Just get in the truck, now!"

Bennett's chest heaved. "Rose, where are your keys?" He demanded. Fumbling an arm into his jacket sleeve, he shoved the women before him.

"They're in the tr…truck," Rose stammered.

Furious with Bennett's indefensible rudeness, Suzanne stomped across the porch beside Rose. "Bennett Gardner, there's no excuse, no excuse…."

Over the cab of Rose's truck Suzanne glimpsed the advancing wall of Black Death and screamed. "Oh, my God! Oh, my God! Run, Rose, run!"

Fear froze the women in their tracks but their screams continued.

Mustafa panted toward them. "Get in truck! Go! Go!" He grabbed for a handhold on their coats, found it, and shepherded the women through the ankle deep swamp that had been his yard. With a backward glance at his house, Mustafa shoved Suzanne and Rose through the open door of the pickup.

With his jacket half-on, Bennett jumped behind the wheel, slammed the door closed and twisted the key in the ignition.

Rose landed awkwardly on top of Suzanne.

Mustafa squeezed in over baskets, boxes and luggage. He slammed his door with a shout. "Go Bennett!"

Bennett jerked the gearshift into reverse, stomped the accelerator, and, blasting the horn, sped onto the narrow road that divided the hollow. He rolled down his window and screamed. "Run! Run for your lives!"

Bennett ground the heel of his hand on the horn. The horn emitted its loud ominous bleating over Bennett, Suzanne, Rose and Mustafa's screams, "Run! Run for your lives!"

Bennett steered the pickup at break neck speed through rising, swirling water bare minutes in advance of the twenty-foot wall of black, liquid death that careened down the narrow mountain valley behind them with the explosive force of an avalanche.

The foursome's frantic shouts and the urgent bleating of the horn roused people at the upper end of the sixteen-mile valley of Wolf Laurel Creek in Logan County, West Virginia.

With heavy lids and lulled reflexes, the citizens that populated the sixteen communities that lay scattered along the narrow valley stumbled to their doors and windows, men, women, and children, some dressed, some undressed, all slow to comprehend that death was at the door.

The water, 132 million gallons of it, weighted with tons of black coal sludge and debris, crashed down the mountain and through the hollow.

The breathing, belching mud wave took corners like a bobsled in a trough, careening from one side of the valley to the other, crushing, destroying, or wiping clean everything in its path.

Too soon the people were in it. The killing waters swirled at the feet of people in nightclothes, barefoot children clad in underwear, mothers with babies in their arms, sons and daughters carrying and piggy-backing their elderly parents.

Cars and trucks raced to any outlet that led up the sheer rock cliffs and out of the path of the flood.

"Bennett, she's not going to make it!" Suzanne screamed.

The careening water crashed over a woman with a baby in her arms, forcing the woman to let go the hand of a second child, a toddler.

"Bennett, stop! We help her!" Mustafa threw open the door and waded into the woman's path.

Rose and Suzanne jumped into the rising water and desperately tried to follow the little girl that the waves tossed about like a rag doll.

Mustafa folded his body and like a hockey goalie, he spread his arms and legs to prevent the woman's being swept past him. He caught her by the shoulder just as the crashing wall of water ripped the baby from her arms.

Mustafa would hear the woman's screams in his nightmares for years to come.

He groped in the black murk and caught a blanket corner. The screaming infant spilled from the blanket. Mustafa thrashed the water and with one huge hand he snatched the infant. He pressed the slippery baby to his chest and fought to keep his footing long enough to haul mother and baby to safety.

With their arms locked to form a human rope, Suzanne and Rose caught the little girl and carried her choking and screaming to her mother in Rose's truck.

This steaming wall of deadly liquid was more than water. It was filled with coal dust and other solid materials that had compacted together into a mud wave.

Setting off one explosion after another, the roiling flood shot through the smoldering slag and raised mushroom-shaped clouds high above the valley. It threw huge splatters of mud hundreds of feet up to the narrow road where a few late shift miners walked home from the mines.

The flood was like a living thing. It absorbed everything in its path and soon carried more than a million tons of waste in its raging current.

It erased Spurgeon. It didn't grind the community into piles of rubbish, but hauled everything away with it, homes, trailers, rail cars, community centers. It scrubbed the ground bare as effectively as a thousand bulldozers.

Tears streamed from Bennett's eyes. A woman screamed for him to save her husband, her Henry, whom the water had swept away.

"Henry! Henry!" Bennett cried. He fought the current and dodged debris that pummeled him now like gunfire.

"Henry!" Bennett filled his lungs with air and screamed into the roaring din of the lost and dying. He realized that if he could save Henry, Bennett's time was up. If Bennett did not get the truck to higher ground immediately, he, Suzanne, Rose, Moose and the others who had climbed into the bed of Rose's pickup would become victims themselves.

Bodies rolled and spun in the crashing waves, tossed between rooftops, railroad ties, cars, trees and bellowing livestock. Blackened bodies, bodies everywhere, struggled in their human frailties against the steaming, suffocating water.

Bennett raised his blackened face to Heaven and bellowed. "Henry!"   Then, "God! Please!"

Bennett flailed the water like a madman.   He twisted his body with his arms stretched out from his sides like a human propeller.   A flash of white caught his eye. Bennett snatched at the white gauze.   Like tissue, the thin fabric ripped free of his grasp.

Bennett groped again.   A leg.   A knee.   Bennett clawed to hold on and clenched his fingers around the slimy flesh and bone.   Two skeletal arms shot out of the water and wound themselves around Bennett's neck.   A blackened face with a scraggly beard followed.

"That's my Henry!   That's my Henry!"   The woman screamed.

Mustafa lost ground in the surging water, but he fought it and with sheer determination, made his way in inches to Bennett to grab one of Henry's hands.   Together, Moose and Bennett pulled the gasping man through the powerful current and to the truck.

Moose jumped into the back and sat with his legs spread and hanging over the tailgate.   Clutching Henry beneath his arms, Moose reared backward and hauled the choking man into the truck.

Henry's wife collapsed in tears. Her Henry was safe.

Bennett closed his eyes. The darkness amplified the sounds, the roar of the water, the screams, and the terror. Boom! A thundering explosion shook him. The flood took out an electrical transformer. Now the wails would echo through this Death Valley in complete darkness.

Bennett wiped his eyes on his sleeve and plowed through the water to the driver's side of the truck. He yanked open the door, climbed behind the wheel, and gunned the engine.

The truck churned water but gathered speed up the gravel road that led to the top of the rock cliff behind the little village of Brighton.

There, Bennett, Suzanne, Rose and Moose jumped from the truck. Huddled together in the freezing rain, they watched, wet-eyed, mute and helpless, as the horror continued.

Chapter Three

Three days later

There were the fragile, those who could not comprehend the enormity of such human suffering and loss. These shuddered and dropped in silence to the floor.

And then there were the lost, the men and women who shuffled slack-jawed, staring with vacant eyes, forever locked in the void of shock. These former neighbors and friends would never again venture into a post-flood reality.

One of them beckoned now to Rose. Despite the ice cold touch of her fingers on Rose's arm, the woman smiled. "Hit didn't get my Amy, Merciful Jesus, hit didn't get my baby. See? My Amy's right here, she's gonna be all right!"

The woman, clad in a neighbor's bed sheet, smiled serenely and offered a battered, rubber doll for Rose's inspection.

The water swirled at the woman's feet.

"Watch out!" Rose screamed. She flinched at the sound of a deafening boom! The electric power station exploded, hit by the avalanching wall of black sludge. She wanted to cover her ears but the numbness prevented her.

"Run for your lives! The dam broke!"

She watched the water as it tore toward her. It smashed like a tidal wave against one side of the hollow and then it leapt across houses and churches and loaded coal cars to smash into the rock cliffs on the other side.

Suddenly Rose's icy body warmed. There was a blaze, a bright, fiery blaze in the middle of the water! *BOOM*! Another explosion, this followed by thick black smoke and debris, flying debris.

People in strange costumes screamed and ran. They ran through the smoke with their bodies bent close to the ground. Rose strained to see, but she couldn't make out their faces. Then she saw him. Jan!

He smiled at her, smiled that beautiful deep dimpled smile.

"*RAT-TAT-TAT-TAT-TAT*!"

"Jan! No! No! Jan!"

The flood was not an act of God. No, the thirty foot wall of raging black death that virtually wiped off the map

Prater, Largemont, Coleta, Lucasville, Spurgeon, Katy, Lakeville, Rogers, Oakmont, Beacon, Fremont, Raceland, Argollite, Cleary, Karnes and Brighton, the sixteen towns scattered along the seventeen mile stretch of Wolf Laurel Creek was the result of a coal mining operation's move to save money.

Rather than dump the tons of water that were required daily to wash coal, the mining company began to store the waste water behind a slag heap. The slag heap grew from a mountain of coal waste and debris into a makeshift dam. The dam rose high enough to contain a hundred million tons of water.

It was wide enough and strong enough to support the forty-nine-ton bull dozers that mine operators drove across the top of it many times daily.

On the morning of the flood, one of the dozer operators reported to the company supervisor that the dam felt spongy. He suggested that the residents of the sixteen communities scattered below the dam, down the narrow, snaking, hollow known as Wolf Laurel Creek, be warned to evacuate.

The coal company supervisor advised that no such warning would be necessary.

The dam collapsed.

There was no power or telephone service to the area and both roads and railways were impassable. The explosive force of the slag filled water was powerful enough to uproot railroad tracks and twist them like pipe cleaners around trees.

The raging water destroyed homes and businesses, demolishing them as effectively as bombs, while scraping the landscape of some of the communities so barren that even the topsoil was removed.

Wolf Laurel Creek was cut off from the outside world for two days. In freezing temperatures, the survivors were stranded without communications, water, or power. The flood took the food supply and the local grocery stores that provided it.

Thousands of the homeless crowded into the school gyms and other emergency shelters. Some were taken in by kin outside the flood area and some by neighbors whose homes had escaped the ravages of the flood.

Mustafa was lucky. His home had survived undamaged and for the past two days had seemed more like a barracks than a home.

Mustafa, Suzanne and Bennett had taken in families and sole survivors, as many as could possibly be crowded into the modest house. There, the friends had willingly shared food, water, shelter and all of the necessities that they possessed.

Water had to be hauled down the frozen mountainside in buckets by men on foot since the hollow was impassable to all motorized vehicles. Food was rationed until emergency supplies began to arrive, first by helicopter, then through emergency relief organizations.

The strong worked in shifts, filling the water buckets, stoking the fire, preparing food, and comforting the weak, the broken and the disabled.

Beds were offered and refused. Wretched in their despair and grateful beyond words, the survivors dozed sitting upright with their backs against the wall or with their heads resting on the shoulders of kin.

Suzanne and Rose crept among them, taking care not to disturb those who slumbered, no matter how briefly. They quietly took sleeping infants from the arms of   mothers who battled to remain alert, but succumbed in the end to woeful exhaustion and fitful sleep.

Bennett and Mustafa tended the injured and kept watch, alerted by sudden shrieks to the clamoring of men toward the door; men desperate to rip open the door and shout warnings to their neighbors. "Run, run for your lives! The dam's broke!"

Bennett and Moose gently turned the men by the shoulders and led them into the kitchen where the traumatized survivors would be comforted by hot coffee and compassionate souls.

Only yesterday the displaced survivors had gone, relocated to the emergency shelters in schools and churches to await temporary new quarters in designated mobile home communities that HUD would provide.

And now, alone at last, Suzanne and Rose looked forward to returning, as much as possible, to normal.

"The nightmare again?" Suzanne asked. Concern showed in her eyes above the dark circles that resulted from her multiple sleepless nights.

She placed a steaming mug of coffee before Rose and then took one for herself. "Oh, Suzanne, I'm so sorry for waking you! I keep hoping it'll go away but it doesn't."

Rose looked tired even though she had slept fairly well alone in her bedroom for the first time in days. She had come down for coffee at Suzanne's insistence but hadn't mustered sufficient will power to change out of her pajamas.

Rose wore her long red hair pulled back in a neat ponytail. Her face looked freshly scrubbed. With no make-up her pale skin glowed. Her green eyes looked bright and alert and despite her age, Rose looked to Suzanne like a beautiful child. But, Suzanne noted, the dark circles under Rose's eyes made Rose look like a beautiful, troubled, child.

"Sweetie, don't apologize to me. It's going to take some time. We were all there, remember? None of us are strangers to nightmares anymore. This isn't something that's going to go away any time soon."

"We have to remember that we're the lucky ones. We have everything to be grateful for. These people lost everything, their loved ones, their homes and belongings. They even lost their way of life."

"For the flood survivors, nothing will ever be the same again. They can't return to what they had before. It's gone forever."

"You and Ben and I, we will return home. Our loved ones and our homes are still right where we left them. And eventually Moose will move on. Unless something happens to change his mind he'll start his own practice in a metropolitan area somewhere."

Suzanne took a sip of her coffee and smiled. "Ben's getting so attached to Moose, I think Ben's trying to persuade him to settle in Ashford so that they can continue to antagonize one another."

Rose had to smile at that. "I don't blame Ben, Moose is an incredible man and he's a great doctor. You all are. You work so tirelessly and give so much of yourselves. I don't know how you manage. You've gone without food and sleep and it looks like you've lost weight, too."

Suzanne interrupted with "And that didn't hurt any of us!"

Rose laughed aloud. Suzanne hadn't changed. She remained just as optimistic and vibrant as ever. This morning her black silky hair hung loose behind a red headband. She was dressed in a green sweatshirt and jeans and as always, Suzanne was there offering Rose comfort and support.

It was true that Suzanne, Bennett and Moose had had their share of nightmares. It was also unlikely that anyone who had witnessed or survived the flood slept as peacefully now as before. The horrific images would not go away. The screams and cries of the victims tore their way into the soundest of sleep.

The coffee pot had rarely been empty of hot coffee since the flood. More often than not, a good portion of every night had been spent here at the table. Some talked while some listened and all remembered.

With a glance at the stairs it suddenly occurred to Rose that she and Suzanne were alone in the house. Had the men been present, they would most likely be here at the table drinking coffee too.

"Where's Bennett and Mustafa? You usually leave when they do."

"Not today!" Suzanne stretched her arms above her head and spoke the words with relish.

"This is my day off, or at least, it's the day that I'm taking off. Ben and Moose had a meeting with the other area doctors. After the meeting they're going over the mountain to help with the smallpox immunizations. They're hoping to immunize every flood survivor against typhoid."

"I volunteered to go along but Ben ordered me to stay home and relax." Suzanne swept her eyes over the kitchen cabinets and then she said with a chuckle "I think what he meant was, go get some groceries and feed me a decent meal."

"Suzanne, I can do that! I'd be glad to. Why don't you let me do the shopping and you stay here and relax?" Rose reached for Suzanne's cup and then stepped to the counter to the coffee pot.

"Thanks, Sweetie, but I'm afraid to be alone with myself right now. I think that if I don't keep moving and going, I'm not sure what I feel." Suzanne's words came out in a whisper. She wrapped her hands around her coffee cup and fought the tears that spilled from her eyes.

"Oh, Suzanne, don't!" Rose cried and hurried to Suzanne with a hug.

Suzanne pulled a tissue from a box on the table. She wiped at her eyes and then continued. "I'm convinced that we could have done more! Somehow, someway, we could have saved more of them. But we didn't know how! We did everything we knew to do, but that damn black sludge! Even when we could get it out of their eyes and noses and throats, the damage was already done!"

"Once it got into their lungs there was nothing we could do to save them. We had to watch them suffocate! Over and over, so many of them! God, I feel so angry and ashamed and helpless and guilty!" Suzanne slammed her fist on the table and then she dropped her head on her arms and sobbed.

"But Suzanne, look how many you did save, you and Bennett and Moose. If the three of you hadn't been here, right here in this house when that water came down, who knows how many more lives would have been lost?"

"Without you and Ben and Moose, hundreds of these people wouldn't be here today! Ask yourself why, every time we open the door, there's another package on the porch. We all know the packages are from the survivors."

"They're grateful and they want to show it. They credit you with saving their loved ones. These brave, wonderful people will never forget all that you did. They knew that you couldn't save everybody. No one could have saved everybody!"

Rose slammed her fist on the table.

It startled Suzanne. Rose looked so angry, so defiant, so determined to absolve Suzanne of any feelings of guilt.

Suzanne rolled her eyes above her crossed arms to peek at Rose.

Rose remained standing at Suzanne's side, her face rigid, her eyes flashing, her temper flaring.

"Whoa there, Mama! This table can only take so many punches!" Suzanne said with a giggle to her red-haired warrior friend.

Rose propped her backside against the table. Coffee sluiced from the cups but Rose laughed.

"Hey, if we ever go into combat I want you on my side!" Suzanne said through her laughter to Rose. Suzanne wiped at the spilled coffee with a tissue and then added "You fire right up, don't you?" Smiling and anticipating a reply, Suzanne raised her eyes to Rose.

The red haired warrior had vanished. She had been replaced by a tormented waif.

Rose's transformation stunned Suzanne. "Rose? What?!"

Rose dropped her eyes to stare at her exposed forearms. The hair on them was standing. Chill bumps covered the surface of her skin. Her lips began to quiver and inexplicably, she burst into sobs.

"Combat…. It wasn't costumes. It was uniforms, military uniforms! The nightmare. It was Jan! There was shooting. And a fire! Jan's been hurt. Oh God, Suzanne! Jan's been hurt!"

Suzanne toppled her chair backward in her rush to grab Rose.

"Rose, Jan's okay! We would know if he was hurt, Sweetie! You've had a rough week. Like everybody else's around here for forty miles, your nerves are on edge. Don't pay any attention to that nightmare. It's just your…."

The ringing telephone interrupted the conversation. Suzanne squeezed Rose's shoulder and then hurried to answer the phone.

A look of horror swept over Rose's face. Sobbing loudly, she backed away from the phone.

"Hello. Yes, this is Suzanne. I'm sorry, I can't understand you. Could you please repeat that?"

Klaus Vandeventer gently took the phone from his wife Olga. She had tried to speak but was prevented by the grief that overcame her. Tearfully she waited, holding hands with her husband who spoke into the phone.

"Hallo. Hallo? Could I please speak with Rose?" The voice was unsteady, the words broken.

Rose took the phone.

"Hallo, Rose?" This is Klaus. I am so sorry to have to call you with this news, but Army notify me and Mama today. Dey tell us, dey tell us dat Jan, our Jan, he ees missing in Vietnam…."

Chapter Four

Life delivered news that Rose McKinley could accept and news that Rose McKinley refused to accept. She refused to accept that Jan was missing. He might not be present among his fellow warrior-heroes, he might not be present in their camp, in their tents, but her Jan was not missing.

Rose could not know the details of Jan's whereabouts in the jungles of Vietnam, but she was certain of one thing- Jan Vandeventer was alive and he was making his way home.

Rose could not tell you how she knew but she knew. Perhaps it was a learned trait common among those born and raised in remote regions where communication devices were limited or non-existent.

Whatever it was, the trait served mountain people. The unspoken, unbidden knowing served Rose. It presented her with images in her mind that assured her that Jan was alive, that he was mobile and free of constraints.

He could be injured, that was a possibility, but the bond between them remained alive and active. Rose could feel it as surely as one felt an engaged telephone line. If Jan were gone, that line to him would ring as hollow as a disconnected phone.

Following Klaus's call with the news, Rose had cried of course. She and Suzanne had stayed up late with the expected discourse of *what if* scenarios.

In a bigger pond of conflicting ideologies, beliefs and expectations, Rose might be viewed as vain, looney, heartless, or downright uncaring.

But in the small pond of Wolf Laurel Creek, West Virginia, and in the even smaller pond of friends in Mustafa's house, Rose's knowing was met with acceptance and understanding.

Mustafa, maybe not so much. But over the years, Suzanne and Bennett, through shared experiences with Rose, had come to accept Rose's knowing as one of the undeniable mysteries of life.

Rose's heart sank. She hadn't had the courage to look outside much less walk outside since they had returned to Mustafa's house following the flood.

The news regarding the flood's devastation was staggering and the worst was not over yet. In 45 minutes the flood had claimed more than 125 lives, had left 3 victims unidentified, 7 missing and another 523 people injured.

It had demolished, swept away, or reduced 502 houses to piles of splintered rubble, destroyed 1000 cars and trucks and left 4000 of Wolf Laurel Creek's 5000 inhabitants homeless.

Rose fortified herself with a deep breath. She checked her coat pocket again to be certain that she had Suzanne's shopping list. Feeling the folded paper in her pocket, she pulled her hood over her head and then stepped outside.

Rose squeezed her brows and narrowed her eyes. The noise in the hollow was deafening. Helicopters hovered overhead waiting to transport victims to any local hospital that could receive yet another victim of what would become known as the worst flood in history.

Rescue squads from nearby counties, the West Virginia State Police, Red Cross, the Salvation Army, and the 3rd Squadron,107th Calvary of the West Virginia National Guard from Williamson scrambled about in Jeeps, trucks, and buses volunteering help and assistance in any way they could to the cold, hungry, displaced residents.

In Lucasville, the midway point of the 17-mile Wolf Laurel Hollow, Guardsmen operated end loaders and bulldozers to reroute Wolf Laurel Creek away from the tons of debris and twisted metal that had once been the homes, cars and personal possessions of the people of the community.

Rose stepped from the porch and walked slowly toward what remained of the area's business center.

The stench from the bodies, river bottom mud, coal slag and piles and piles of burning debris triggered her gag reflex. The air was heavy and filled with black smoke.

She looked to the top of the mountain above Mustafa's house. Nothing remained there but barren soil. The trees, and but for a lone structure here and there, the houses and the churches were gone.

Further down the hollow nearer to where she walked, National Guard trucks were lined up one behind the other. Young guardsmen in sand colored uniforms and boots labored in the back of the trucks handing out blankets and bottled water to the shivering survivors.

Rose overheard bits of conversation between two wet and muddy soldiers who passed a cigarette back and forth between themselves.

"Yeah, the governor said those 158 folks that were missing from Largemont were found this morning. All of 'em made it over the mountains to safety." He said that the people from Lucasville figure we'll find at least 15 bodies in that mountain of debris there. West Virginia's got over 400 of us here from the Guard searching for victims and that ain't nearly enough."

"The first search detail just reported and Colonel McCallum said there's near total destruction." The soldier nodded to the top of the mountain. He continued with a frown. "He said there was 37 houses up on that 2 ½ mile stretch near the top. Ain't nothin' there now. Ever bit of that land is wiped clean. The top soil's gone all the way down to bedrock."

The second soldier shook his head. "I ain't never seen nothin' like it and don't care to never again!"

The young man pointed to scattered houses that had sustained major damage. "The Colonel said we got to search the rest of these houses this afternoon and paint red X's on the ones that ain't safe and then we got to bulldoze 'em."

The soldier handed off the cigarette to his buddy. He whistled and then signaled with a wave to a nearby group of people that walked hand in hand.

"Uh, if you folks would just step that-away please," he said, pointing. "It ain't safe to be in this area. We're trying to clear it now and maybe find more survivors."

A grim-faced woman dressed in a nightgown and a coal miner's jacket walked between what appeared to be her husband and her son. Her hair was tied in a scarf and she wore men's shoes that fell off her feet time and again because they were sizes too large.

"Survivors?" She cried. "There ain't no survivors! Them of us what ain't in the morgue is just as dead as them what are!"

The tall, stooped man to her right was dressed in ragged jeans that were too short by inches. His jacket with its broken zipper was threadbare. It flapped about him in the wind. He gently pulled the woman against his shoulder. "Hit's all right, Mama, we'll find 'im, we'll find 'im and he's gonna be all right!"

The young boy to her left dropped his head and sobbed.

High-pitched, frenzied shouts drew Rose's attention from the devastated family to a young guardsman further down the hollow.

"Oh, my God! Jeezus!" He jumped from the end loader he had been operating, folded himself beside it and vomited. With his left hand he waved to the pile of debris that he had been clearing. "Colonel! Colonel McCallum! They's dogs in there, dogs in there with the bodies! Oh, Jesus, Lord! Get them dogs out of there!"

A heavy-set man in a sand colored camouflage uniform barked to his driver from the passenger side of an open Jeep. "Get up there!"

Spinning mud from the Jeep's tires, the driver wasted no time following McCallum's orders.

McCallum jumped from the jeep, pulled his .45 Smith and Wesson from his holster and fired it over the dogs' heads. The hungry canines scattered.

McCallum looked up the hollow to the Guardsmen who unloaded water and blankets. He placed two fingers in his mouth and executed a loud, shrill whistle.

"Connor! Hayes! Get some body bags and get over here! Get these people over to South Morgan Elementary. The Red Cross has set up a temporary morgue there."

The Captain glanced at the half-eaten bodies that lay wedged between rock and iron in the pile of rubble. "Be careful with them!" He barked and then added softly in a voice that was choked with emotion "Just be careful with them."

Tears fell from Rose's eyes. She had witnessed death and sorrow all her life, but never anything of this magnitude. Everywhere she looked people were hurt and crying. Their faces were blank, their eyes hollow.

They were cold and hungry and lost. They just wanted to go home but had no homes to go home to. They just wanted to wake up and find that this was a nightmare, nothing but a nightmare.

Rose couldn't shake the feelings of guilt that assailed her. These people had lost everything and she was walking past them with a grocery list in her pocket on her way to buy food for a nice hot dinner that she would share tonight with Suzanne, Bennett and Mustafa.

What were these people going to have for dinner? Would they have dinner at all? Where would they sleep?

More screams. "Poppy, I want my mommy! I want my mommy now!" A little girl no more than three years old turned her tear-streaked face to the man who carried her in his arms. "We're gonna find Mommy, Glory Lee, we're gonna find her!" The man promised. He pulled the little girl to his chest and then he broke down in sobs. "God help us, we're gonna find Mommy!"

The bull dozers and end loaders continued with a roar. The National Guard had set up road blocks. No one was allowed in the area that couldn't show a pass that confirmed them to be a resident.

Rose carried her pass in her pocketbook.

All the bridges in the 17 mile stretch of Wolf Laurel Creek were out. Most of them had been demolished as effectively as if they had been bombed. But one of them, completely intact, had been relocated 50 feet further down the hollow.

A Guardsman approached Rose. "Mam. May I see your pass?"

Rose reached into her pocketbook, withdrew her pass, and presented it to the young man for inspection.

"Do you mind if I ask where you're headed?" He asked, returning her pass with raised brows.

"I, uh, I'm going to the grocery store, to, uh, to get something for dinner," Rose stammered. Her emotions were raw, her nerves in shambles.

Despite everything, she was still shaken from the news that Jan was missing in action. Now she was witnessing first hand horrors that were too awful to comprehend.

"Are you a resident?"

"Uh, no, I'm visiting with friends," Rose replied, and then added "With Mustafa."

The soldier snapped his eyes to Rose's eyes.

"Mustafa?"

Rose cringed. Why did she say that she was visiting Mustafa? That name in this region of Appalachia, in the aftermath of the worst flood in Appalachia's history, what was she thinking? People here were seeking comfort. Familiar. Neighborly.

The soldier was not smiling a friendly smile.

Rose explained that Mustafa was a foreign-born doctor who was trying to establish a medical clinic here in Wolf Laurel Creek with Bennett and Suzanne's help and that she was here to help them.

"Doctors huh?" A smile found its way to the guardsman's face.

Rose nodded.

"Well, just be sure you get back home before dark. Someone has looted almost every store that the flood didn't destroy. They broke into the Little Laurel Coal Company store and tried to steal $18,000 from the safe but they didn't get off with it."

The Guardsman's tone had softened. "Everybody around here is desperate and desperate people do desperate things. Just get home before dark, O.K.?"

"Yes, thank you. I will," Rose replied. She felt a wave of relief when the conversation had ended.

She continued on her way past incoming buses from local and out of state churches. The buses had a few people but for the most part were filled with donated clothing, blankets, and various necessities that the flood survivors might need.

An occasional dog, cow, horse or pig wandered through the mud and half frozen puddles, seemingly as lost as the humans who could not find their homes.

Rose resisted the temptation to get in line at one of the many Salvation Army canteens that had been set up to serve food and drink to the survivors and workers in the area.

She was dressed in jeans and a sweater, boots, wool socks, and a wool coat and she could still feel the cold. She would love to have a cup of hot coffee right now.

Rose continued walking for another hour before she found the Island Home Store in Argollite. Hearing that the stores had all been looted had given her doubts but the long lines of people waiting outside the store for food and clothing erased those doubts.

At last she was able to make her purchases and begin the long walk back to Mustafa's house. Her feelings of guilt had returned. How was she going to walk past the survivors of Wolf Laurel Creek with bags of groceries in her arms?

Brighton Baptist Church was a few yards ahead. Rose could see and hear the crowds of cold, wet, coughing people.   They milled about talking quietly before they entered the church.

Brighton Baptist was one of many that had opened its doors to serve as a shelter to the survivors.

Tears returned to her eyes as Rose passed South Morgan Elementary School.   The school was being used as a temporary morgue.   Weeping men, women, and children waited in the damp cold to identify their loved ones. Despite the growing number of victims that had been found, very little positive identification had been made.

Rose was startled to hear in her own voice "If the time comes, will they call me or Klaus or Olga to identify Jan?" She pulled the bags that she carried to her face and wept.

She wanted Jan to be with her, here and now.   She wanted to feel his hand holding hers, wanted to know that he shared this sorrow with her.   Wanted to be reassured that she was not alone.

"Stop it Rose McKinley!"   Rose issued the order to herself between her clinched teeth.   "You ain't got no reason to cry.   These people you see all around you, they got reason to cry!   Get your mind off yourself and on them!   Remember, you're a McKinley and McKinley's don't break!"

Rose raised her head, straightened her shoulders and continued walking. Further along she felt surprised to see so many red *X*'s painted on the few remaining houses. Some of the houses lurched precariously, having been shoved off their foundations by the force of the flood water. Others looked like lean-tos with whole *clap*board fronts or backs or sides missing.

Rose had to detour to the left to avoid one of the condemned houses that sat squarely in her path.

The big red *X* on the side of the house made the white frame structure appear forlorn and angry. The house leaned with its back side on the ground and with its front side jacked up atop a mound of mud and flood debris.

Though hanging at an awkward slant, the front door to the house stood open. With a shudder Rose remarked to herself "It's like that house is wantin' me to come inside."

The National Guard bulldozers roared back and forth between the houses, shoving gobs of mud and debris before them. The houses they bulldozed crackled, snapped, and then fell into heaps of 2' x 4's, white *clap*board slats, roofing tiles, appliances, cabinets, furniture and children's toys.

A guardsman leaned from the seat of his dozer. "I'm sorry Mam, we have to clear this area. Could you please move to the center and keep to the dozer tracks? The ground there's a little drier and you'll be safer. Any one of these marked houses could crumble at any minute."

"Of course," Rose replied. She glanced at the name strip above the Guardsman's left breast pocket and then adjusted her path as Corporal Connor had instructed.

Connor yelled to another Guardsman who operated a front end loader. "I'm gonna take this one down now. Steer clear!" And then he nosed his dozer toward the red *X*'d house that Rose had just passed.

Rose suddenly dropped the bags from her arms. She spun to face the dozer operator. "No! Stop!" She yelled. And for reasons unknown to herself, Rose sprinted to the condemned house.

"Lady, stop! You can't go in there! We have orders!"

Connor yelled to the wind for Rose had disappeared inside the threatened structure. Connor had no choice but to follow. If anything happened to that civilian it would be on his head.

Everybody out here was crazy, crazy with grief, crazy with sorrow, and some, like this woman, were just crazy.

Rose covered her face with a hand and scanned the interior of the house. The stench of the toxic mud and water that she waded into made breathing difficult.

Light filtered through from the back side of the house but the front, the high side, was dark. The kitchen was a mess of overturned appliances and shattered dishes. The bath, empty, with muddy water stains that reached almost to the ceiling.

Navigating through the house was not easy, but there was something, something. Rose did not know what it was that she sought. She knew only that she had to look, had to find *something*.

Connor stormed into the house yelling. "Lady, lady! You have to get out of here. You have to get out of here now!"

Rose peered into the darkness of one bedroom. Nothing. A second bedroom. Nothing. The door to the third bedroom near the front of the house was closed. Rose shoved against it to no avail.

"Lady, did you hear me? You have to get out of here! Now!"

Rose replied with "Help me open this door!"

"What? No! We have to get out of here!"

Rose searched through the dim light, searched for something that would help her open that door. Her eyes fell on a brass lamp that lay mired in mud and debris.

Rose pulled the slick, muddy lamp from the mess and then she swung it at the door with all the strength her determination could muster.

The middle of the door caved inward. Rose's blow had created a hole large enough so that Rose could peer through it and into the bedroom.

Rose stuck her head inside the hole. She blinked for she could not be seeing what her eyes insisted that she saw.

"Oh!" Rose cried. "Oh, little one! Don't be afraid, baby! Please don't be afraid! We're gonna get you out of here!"

"Connor! Knock this door down!"

"Lady, I'm gonna have to haul you out of here if you don't come with me now!"

"Connor! There's a little boy in there and he's alive!"

Connor's anger at Rose's refusal to obey his commands and leave the house vanished in his determination to see for himself what this crazy woman claimed to see.

Without thinking, Connor shoved Rose aside. He peered through the hole in the door. "Oh my God!" Connor straightened himself and then lunged at the door with his shoulder. Anchored waist high in mud and flood debris, the door did not give.

"Uh, hang on!" Connor cried, pointing to Rose. "Don't leave him. I'll get an axe!"

Images and questions fought for attention in Rose's mind. Had this little boy been alone here since the flood? Where were his parents, his family? How had he become trapped in the bedroom? How long had it been since he had eaten? Surely he could not have been here alone, *like this*, for days! Where was Connor? What was keeping him?

Connor returned with the axe. "Tell the little guy not to be afraid, this is going to be noisy."

"Uh, baby, we have to break down the door. Please don't be afraid. It's going to be loud but we're going to get you out of here."

Connor swung the axe and splintered the door. He tore away the pieces, helped Rose step through and then followed.

Connor and Rose kicked at the debris that blocked their path and yanked a curtain and blinds from a window. The little boy shielded his eyes against the sudden bright glare.

After taking a moment to let their eyes adjust to the light Rose and Connor let out horrified gasps in a breath.

The little boy lay on a bed that was mostly submerged in the mud and in the stinking, slimy water. He was filthy and cold and wet and now, in the light, Rose and Connor could see that the little boy held tight the hand of a woman who lay on the bed beside him.

It was evident to Rose and Connor that the woman had been dead for a while. Partially submerged, the woman's body lay between the little boy and the water.

"Oh! Oh, poor baby! Oh, baby, I am so sorry!" Tears gushed from Rose's eyes. She reached for the little boy.

Shrinking from Rose, he pressed his thumb against his chin with four fingers upright.

Rose let out a sob. "He's just a baby but this little boy is signing. This poor baby is deaf!"

Rose looked to Connor. "He hasn't made a sound through all of this so he's probably mute, too. Oh Lord, how do we help this baby?" Rose's heart was breaking for the frightened child. She could not imagine the horrors that this child had endured and neither she nor Connor could guess for how long.

"He's going to hate us," Rose said. "But we have no choice. We have to take him from his mother."

Chapter Five

Suzanne's heart leapt to her throat. "Why is a National Guard Jeep pulling up in the driveway? Has somebody been hurt?" She asked aloud and raced downstairs.

"Rose! Are you all right? What's going on?" Suzanne glanced from the child in Rose's arms to Guardsman Connor. "Is this your little boy? Does he need medical attention?"

Connor pointed to Rose and said with a nod "Maybe she better explain Mam. It's kind of a long story."

Connor sprang from the Jeep intending to help Rose exit with the little boy in her arms but Suzanne raced ahead of him and yanked open the door.

"Where did you find him? Where are his parents? Rose, my God, this little guy's in bad shape! He's dehydrated and," looking stunned, Suzanne demanded "What's that in his mouth?"

"It was a peanut butter and jelly sandwich. He stuffed the whole thing in his mouth as soon as I gave it to him."

"He'll choke! He has to have something to drink!" Suzanne cried. She headed for the door and yelled over her shoulder. "Bring him in out of this cold. I'll get him some milk."

"Suzanne, I need to get these stinking clothes off him. He's soaked in toxic flood water and probably hasn't eaten since before the flood. No wonder the poor baby's dehydrated. It's likely that he hasn't had anything to eat or drink in days."

"Corporal Connor gave him a bottle of water a few minutes ago. This baby drained it in a gulp."

"Corporal who?"

"Oh, Suzanne, I'm sorry!" Rose nodded to Connor and make quick introductions.

"Suzanne, this is Army National Guard Corporal Azle Connor. Corporal Connor, this is my friend, Dr. Suzanne Gardner."

Rose peeled the black gummy pajamas from the little boy and remarked "Poor little guy! No wonder he's starving if he hasn't eaten since Saturday morning."

Suzanne headed for the kitchen. "Oh surely he's eaten since then! Where did you find him? Was he at one of the shelters? I can't imagine that he was just wandering around alone."

"No. He wasn't wandering around alone, Suzanne. We found him lying on a bed that was sunk to the top of the mattress in mud and flood debris holding his dead mother's hand in a house that Corporal Connor was about to plow under with a bulldozer."

Suzanne spun from the kitchen doorway to face Rose. The shocked look on her face defied description. "What! Rose!"

Suzanne stretched her eyes wide and darted them to the little boy. Tears fell on the hand she slapped over her mouth. "This baby has been alone on a bed beside his dead mother in a condemned house SINCE THE FLOOD?"

Rose sniffled and managed a "Yes!"

"Maybe since before the flood, we can't know for sure and we can only guess that the woman beside him was his mother."

"Oh, my God! Oh, my God!" Suzanne cried. She pulled open cabinet doors. "I'll make him some hot soup. Rose, get him in a warm bath. Mr. Connor, there's the coffee pot, cups are over there," she said and pointed to a cabinet above the coffee pot. "Help yourself."

With the little boy in her arms, Rose leaned over the tub to run a warm bath. When she tried to place the child in the water, he fought her in his struggle to be free.

Suzanne returned with a cup of juice that she offered to the child.

He refused it with tears that fell on the little thumb that he pressed to his chin with four fingers upright.

Realizing that the little boy was signing, Suzanne swept her eyes to Rose. She said in dismay "He's signing. Oh Sweet Jesus, Rose, this baby is deaf too?"

Corporal Connor retrieved the bags of groceries from the back of the Jeep, deposited them in the kitchen and then returned to stand in the doorway while Rose bathed the little boy.

"He's saying mother," Connor blurted after a minute.

"What?" As gently as possible Rose tried again to put the little boy in the bath but his protests turned to sobs.

Rose raised desperate eyes to Connor. "How do you know that Mr. Connor?"

"Please Mam, just call me Azle. The Guard don't even call me Mister Connor."

"All right, Azle," Rose said with a smile. "But how do you know what he's saying and why didn't you tell me earlier when we saw that he was deaf?"

"Uh, well, Mam, my wife, Judy, taught the elementary grades at West Virginia School for the Deaf and Blind in Romney. That's where we lived before I got transferred here. She practiced on me a lot," he said and then signed a series of signs to the little boy who nodded when Connor had finished signing.

"If you don't mind Miss Rose," Connor said. He took the juice from Suzanne and gave it to the little boy who quickly gulped it down.

"I asked him if he likes orange juice," Connor said. Then he added "I guess he does."

Rose and Suzanne laughed. "Yes, he likes orange juice all right."

"Can you find out if he likes chicken noodle soup?" Suzanne asked.

Again, Azle signed a series of signs to the child. The little boy responded with a clenched right fist which he moved up and down at the wrist.

"He likes it," Azle said and then signed something else to the boy.

The child executed a number of hand and finger motions in response.

"We're going to be learning sign language, aren't we?" Suzanne said with a laugh to Rose.

"If we want to communicate with this little guy, we are," Rose replied and then turned with interest to Connor. "What are you two saying?"

"I told him our names and I asked him his name. He said his name is Daniel."

Connor folded the fingers of his right hand against his thumb and then stuck his pointer finger upright. "D," he said, and then continued forming each letter with his fingers as he spoke and spelled out the name Daniel.

"At least we know his first name," Rose said.

Connor signed again to the little boy who signed back.

"His last name is Ruddy," Connor said.

"Hmm, Irish maybe?" Suzanne asked. "He does have reddish blonde curls and blue eyes."

Connor shrugged. "Can't answer that one. Got any toys? Anything that a four year old might like?"

"Uh, toys. We don't have any kids so we don't have any toys," Suzanne replied after moment.

Rose raised a hand. "Suzanne, you're married to Bennett Gardner."

A giggle burst from Suzanne's throat. "Of course! Bennett's toys!" She took the empty juice glass to the kitchen and then headed upstairs.

"Daniel might like some toys to play with, maybe make him feel a little more comfortable," Connor said to Rose.

"Poor little guy. How do we tell him? He's so young!" Rose said. "Corporal Connor, sorry, Azle, how will we talk to him after you leave?   All of this is hard enough for a hearing child, but to be in a strange place with no familiar faces and no way to communicate!   My heart just breaks for him."

"Here, will these do?"   Suzanne waved a G.I. Joe doll and a rubber duck at Rose.

Rose chuckled.   "Don't ask me, ask Daniel!"   Rose frowned. "Sorry, I meant…."

"You meant just what you said," Suzanne replied. "Ask Daniel."

Suzanne touched a finger to her lips and bent near the tub.   "Hello Daniel.   I'm Suzanne.   Would you like to play with these toys?"   She held the toys close to the little boy.

Daniel looked past Suzanne to Connor.

Connor signed to Daniel.   "Suzanne and Rose have toys for you.   Do you want to play with them?"

Daniel tapped his chin twice with his thumb while keeping his fingers upright in a five hand.   Then he raised his fists with his thumbs between his pointer and second fingers and then shook both fists.

Rose and Suzanne looked to Connor.

"He said he wants his mother and then he asked for the toys."

Suzanne let out a sigh. She gave the toys to Daniel who quickly submerged them beneath the bubbles in his bath.

Connor rose from his knees with a groan. "I wish I could stay and help with him but duty calls. My sergeant's gonna think I've gone AWOL."

"We wish you didn't have to go too, but we are so grateful. Thank you for bringing me and Daniel home, and for not shooting me for disobeying your orders," Rose said.

"Orders?" Suzanne bounced questioning eyes between Rose and Connor. "What are you talking about?"

"I was about to bulldoze one of the condemned houses when Miss Rose, she walked right past it, and then she turned around, came back, and demanded that I stop. She refused to let me bulldoze that house."

"Excuse my buttin' in Miss Suzanne, Miss Rose, but I'd like to know why." Connor turned a serious face to Rose. "Why did you stop me and then go in that house? Did you know that Daniel was inside?"

Rose squeezed her brows in a frown and twisted strands of her red hair around her fingers. "No, I didn't know that anyone was inside and I certainly had no intention of going into that house."

Rose watched Daniel for a minute before she continued. "My plans were to put as much distance as I could as fast as I could between myself and all that sorrow and get back to Mustafa's house."

"But," she said, hesitating. "There's this little voice inside all of us. Sometimes that voice gives us instructions that we don't understand, sometimes it's instructions that we don't agree with at all. But, if I've learned anything in this lifetime, it's this--*Do not ignore that voice!*"

"Mr. Azle Connor, I heard you yelling at me not to enter that house at the same time as that voice directed me to go inside. You know the rest."

Rose looked at Daniel who splashed and played like any other little boy who didn't have a care in the world. She returned her eyes to Connor. "Where would he be now if I hadn't obeyed that voice?"

The blood drained from Corporal Connor's face in a rush. "Oh my God! He, he would be buried alive under a mountain of smoldering debris that I would have pushed in on him with a bulldozer!"

Rose rested a hand on Connor's forearm. "Sorry I couldn't follow your orders soldier, but in this instance, I had to take my orders from a Higher Command."

Connor splashed water to get Daniel's attention and to Rose he said with a sigh "And he's here because of it!"

Connor smiled at Daniel. He spoke and signed "Miss Rose and Miss Suzanne will take good care of you. I'll see you later little buddy."

To everyone's surprise, Daniel dropped the toys in the water. He signed to Connor whose face broke into a wide smile.

"What did he say?" Rose and Suzanne asked.

"He said "O.K."

Chapter Six

"Something's wrong!" Bennett exclaimed.

Mustafa frowned. "Why you say that? We just get home. I do not see something wrong."

"We should be smelling home cooking, frying chicken, spicy chili or simmering beef stew. I ain't smelling nothing but the stench from this flood and from those piles of burning trash. I don't even smell fresh coffee. Something is definitely wrong!"

"Maybe you have cold. You do not smell so good," Mustafa said in all seriousness.

"Whoa there!" Bennett exclaimed. "Maybe you don't smell so good yourself Moose!"

Mustafa turned to Bennett with questioning eyes.

Bennett gave Moose a playful slap on the shoulder. "Come on Moose my Man, since we both stink let's go have a nice hot shower and some dinner. I know there's some home cooking in there somewhere. We left two women here this morning with nothing to do today but cook us some dinner!"

Bennett and Mustafa scrambled from Bennett's *Ford F150* pick-up. They unloaded medical bags and boxes of medical supplies from the bed of the truck.

"Hmmm, I don't smell any home cooking in here either!" Bennett quipped. He had opened Mustafa's front door but remained outside where he removed his muddy boots and left them on the porch.

"No home cooking. No women. Something's up."

"Bennett is that you?" Suzanne called from upstairs.

Bennett yelled up the stairs. "No, it's my starving identical twin. Mustafa's twin is here too. Where's dinner? We're hungry!"

Bennett walked in his socks to the living room where he placed his medical bag and one of the boxes of supplies on a table that was already stacked high with boxes and cartons.

Mustafa followed in his bare feet as he did not wear socks.

Suzanne skipped down the stairs where she greeted Bennett with a wide smile, a hug and a kiss.

"Don't use those feminine charms on me my love. I'm still hungry and I might add a bit disappointed because there's no dinner cook...."

Bennett stopped midsentence. He pointed to the stairs. "Why is my Kentucky Wildcats sweatshirt walking down the stairs wearing my Kentucky Wildcats socks?"

Suzanne and Rose laughed.

"You've already got two hungry men on your hands and now you've gone and brought home a midget who has obviously been looting my Wildcats stash?" Bennett pretended to pout. "And please tell me that's not MY G.I. Joe in midget's hands!"

"Bennett!" Suzanne tried to control her laughter. "This is not a midget and he hasn't looted anything. He didn't have any clothes and we haven't had time to shop so...."

"So why didn't you give him Mustafa's sweatshirt and socks?"

"Mustafa doesn't have any sweatshirts and socks and Daniel was freezing."

"Oh, so you're babysitting for someone?"

"Uh, no, not exactly."

"You rented him?"

Rose stopped on the stairs behind Daniel who held Bennett's G.I. Joe in one hand and tapped his chin twice with his thumb and four upright fingers.

Bennett's face sobered in an instant. "Suzanne, is he signing?"

"Yes."

"How old is he?"

"We think he's between three and a half and four."

"Parents?"

"We don't know for sure about his father yet but we're fairly certain that his mother is dead."

"Is this story going to break my heart?"

"Probably. It broke mine and Rose's hearts."

"Did ya'll feed him anything today?"

"Bennett Gardner! Yes, we did feed him something today."

"Lucky midget!"

Daniel who had been intently watching Bennett suddenly mouthed the word midget.

"Did you see that?" Suzanne yelped. "He read Bennett's lips and repeated the word midget!"

Bennett turned to Mustafa. "You might want to get some socks. This is going to take a while."

"We have new guest?" Mustafa asked.

Bennett looked from Suzanne to Rose to Daniel. "I think it's safe to say that we have a new guest Moose. Maybe if he asks the girls they'll make us some coffee."

"Oh, you big baby!" Suzanne scolded Bennett. "You and Moose and Rose and Daniel come in the kitchen. I'll make you some coffee and some fried chicken, mashed potatoes and green beans. Rose can tell you the story." Suzanne raised a hand. "But be prepared. It's gonna break your heart."

Bennett pushed his lip out in a pout. I don't even get to be the baby anymore now that he's here."

Mustafa slapped Bennett on the shoulder. "Grow up, Beanie! You are not child anymore!"

Bennett sniffled and looked forlorn. "I know. That's the problem."

Daniel let go Rose's hand. He descended the stairs alone, walked to Bennett, looked up in Bennett's face and with a quivering lip, offered the man the G.I. Joe doll.

Rose and Suzanne pulled hands to their mouths.

Bennett widened his eyes and said with an incredulous look "Oh my God, I'm breaking his heart!"

Swallowing a sob, Bennett grabbed Daniel in his arms. "I'm so sorry little buddy, I am so sorry! I was just playing!"

Bennett hugged Daniel and then looked into the child's face.

Daniel stared back into Bennett's eyes and then he wiped at a tear on Bennett's cheek.

"Midget."   Bennett said.

"Midget."   Daniel mouthed.

Chapter Seven

"There, crybaby.   That ought to make you happy.
Fried eggs, bacon, sausage, homemade biscuits, gravy, hot
coffee and cold orange juice.   You think that will hold you
'til lunch?"   Suzanne dragged a finger through the gravy
on Bennett's plate, wiped it on his lips and then kissed it
off with a loud kiss.

"Careful there, Mama, Midget's watching," Bennett
said with a laugh.   He pulled Daniel's chair closer to the
table and checked to see that the medical books that he and
Mustafa stacked as a booster chair for Daniel hadn't
shifted.

"More coffee anyone before I sit?"   Suzanne asked.   A
quick glance around the table confirmed that all coffee cups
were filled so she seated herself beside Bennett.

Mustafa ladled more gravy onto his biscuits and then
raised his eyes to Bennett.   "So what is plan?"

"Plan?"

"For today. For people in community. Typhoid is become problem. We must immunize people here and over mountain. Flood destroy medical clinics. Where are patients? Pregnant women? Who sees now?"

"Since the flood left 4000 of the 5000 residents of this community homeless, they're scattered everywhere, Moose. The government's setting up mobile homes in four nearby communities. People are supposed to start moving in as soon as the homes are delivered."

"Until then, many are staying with family in other areas, some are with neighbors here and hundreds more are still in the emergency shelters in the local schools and churches."

Rose tore a biscuit into small pieces and placed it on Daniel's plate. She ladled gravy on the biscuit and then watched, smiling, as Daniel wolfed it down. It was his second plate and it appeared that he would have no trouble finishing it.

"And a lot of these people are scattered up on the ridge and in the mountains. They don't trust anything anymore. They're afraid to be inside, afraid the walls will cave in on them and afraid to be outside, afraid that they'll be swept away in another flood."

Bennett took a sip of his coffee and then continued. "Some of the kids are sleeping in layers of clothes so they won't be caught in their underwear or pajamas in the event of another disaster."

"Most of them are having nightmares. Their personalities have changed. They don't want to talk to anybody. They don't want to play. And they want flashlights beside their beds so they can check all night to see if it's raining."

"They're all suffering from disaster syndrome and it isn't going to go away any time soon," Suzanne added.

Rose looked from Suzanne to Bennett. "And what about this little guy? What are we going to do about him?"

Bennett grabbed Daniel's orange juice, pretending that he was going to drink it, thinking that Daniel would laugh.

Daniel tapped his thumb against his chin with his fingers upright.

Bennett shook his head. "Mommy. This little boy wants his mommy and we can't give him his mommy." Bennett's voice broke. "Or his daddy."

"Oh, Bennett! Don't!" Suzanne said, feeling the sorrow that her husband felt for this beautiful little boy. "We'll, we'll find someone. We don't know for sure that his daddy is gone. He may turn up yet. And if he doesn't, Daniel must have a relative somewhere. Maybe an aunt or an uncle, grandparents, someone!"

With concern in his eyes Bennett looked at Daniel. "And if he doesn't? What if we can't find any relatives?"

Suzanne knew what was coming next. Bennett had been orphaned at an early age and, despite all his efforts to exorcise them, the memories still haunted him.

"He's not going to be an orphan, Bennett! Daniel will never be an orphan! If we can't find someone, can't find his father or a relative, then, then… she met Bennett's eyes. "Then if you agree, we'll take him! We'll raise him!"

Bennett looked stunned. "You would do that? You would take this little guy, knowing that he's deaf, and you would raise him? With me?"

"Of course I would if that's what you want!"

Bennett scraped back his chair. He walked to Suzanne and grabbed her in his arms. "God, I love you so much! How did I ever get so lucky?"

Bennett Gardner kissed his wife, Suzanne Gardner, with all the fire and passion that had previously defined their courtship and that now defined their marriage.

"You two aren't going to make this easy, are you?" Rose asked. She picked Daniel up and wiped gravy and orange juice from his face.

Daniel leaned from Rose's arms to Bennett who instantly melted and took Daniel in his arms. "Come here, Midget. Let's go find that G.I. Joe."

Rose scraped and stacked plates. Then, as she filled a sink with hot, soapy water, she said to Suzanne. "Now I'm going to feel guilty if we do find his father or another relative. Bennett's getting attached to Daniel awfully fast. Too fast, maybe. I don't want to see either one of them hurt."

Suzanne wiped the table and then returned the dish cloth to the sink. "Rose, Sweetie, you don't have to worry about Bennett. He's a big boy. He can handle it if we find Daniel's father or another relative. We all want the same thing and that's for this little boy to be happy."

"Suzanne, I saw that look in Bennett's eyes. I know that look."

Suzanne squeezed Rose's shoulders. "Don't you start worrying about this Rose McKinley! You just worry about Jan...."

The wounded look on Rose's face struck Suzanne like a blow to the heart. "Oh, Rose, I am so sorry! I didn't mean that the way it sounded! You know I didn't!"

With her hands full of dishes Rose lifted a shoulder to wipe her tears. "I know you didn't mean anything by it, Suzanne. It's just that, that, I'm afraid that I'll never see him again!"

"I can see his eyes. I can smell the leather of his coat. I can even hear his laugh. I memorized them all the day that I woke up in the hospital and saw his face for the first time."

"It was the day after he found me in the snow and rescued me. He didn't have to come to the hospital. He didn't have to sleep all wadded up on the sofa beside Stump. But he did. He stayed there all night. For me."

"All those debutantes with their fine horses, luxury cars, sparkling jewels and designer clothes, they all wanted him. I'm sure they still do. One of them at least."

"Margaret?" Suzanne asked with a scowl.

Rose nodded. "Margaret isn't going to give up. She's determined to have him. She may be in Vietnam right now looking for him!" Rose said, and then laughed with Suzanne.

"Well, the good news is that despite everything, we still have a sense of humor!   And why shouldn't we? Everything's going to be all right, I'm sure of it."   Suzanne said to Rose with a wink.

She reached for a dish towel and dried the dishes that Rose had washed.   Suzanne had seen that look on Bennett's face too and there was no question.   Bennett would be devastated if Rose found a relative that would take Daniel.

"So in the meantime, what do we do?   Where do we begin?   We have to let someone know that Daniel's here with us," Rose said.

"Daniel is a special needs child and none of us are qualified to help him.   We can't communicate with him on the most primary level and that's not fair to him.   He deserves to be in an environment where all his needs are met quickly and completely."

"I thought about it all night, Suzanne. We can check with the postman, the local clergy, neighbors.   It sounds so simple, but what if we can't find the postman, the local clergy or the neighbors?"

"You and Bennett and I didn't know any of the people who lived here to begin with and now they're all gone. Mustafa didn't spend his time socializing so he didn't know anybody either. Where do we begin? I really don't want to go the authorities because, because," Rose raised troubled eyes to Suzanne.

"Because they might take Daniel?"

Bennett's question startled both women. He entered the kitchen carrying Daniel on his shoulders.

The little boy's face was all smiles.

Bennett kissed Suzanne on the top of her head. "Suz, breakfast was great, I loved it but it didn't love me. Have you seen any Rolaids or something similar?"

"Why do you need Rolaids?" Rose asked.

Bennett rubbed his chest. "Indigestion. It happens with sausage and bacon and good stuff like that."

Rose stepped to a cabinet and took down a bottle of apple cider vinegar. She gave the bottle to Bennett. "Here, try one teaspoon. Instant relief. No side effects."

Bennett cast a quizzical glance at their tall, slender, red haired friend. "Are you prescribing vinegar for my indigestion Dr. McKinley?"

"I am. Try it. It works."

Bennett mumbled. "I'm supposed to be the doctor here." He filled a teaspoon with the vinegar and drank it.

"Wow! Wow! It's gone!" The look of surprise on Bennett's face was grateful and real. "Two minutes ago I thought that both my chest and throat were going to explode. I've never seen anything relieve indigestion so fast! Thanks Rosie. Suz, could you make a note of this in case I forget?"

"Consider it done my love," Suzanne replied. She looked at Bennett with a lopsided grin. "Are we going to have to wean you off Daniel? You can't walk around with him on your shoulder out there," she said, pointing outdoors where a light rain fell.

"Why not? I'll get an umbrella."

"Bennett Gardner, you're hopeless. You and Mustafa better get going. Maybe if enough of the locals get typhoid shots we can prevent a major outbreak. Didn't the Laurel County Clinic have regular immunizations scheduled for today, too?"

"Yeah, ten to noon at the Olive Branch Church of God, diphtheria, tetanus, whooping cough combo, polio, measles, and small pox. I hope the people show up."

Bennett opened cabinets and rummaged through them. "It's going to be slow going, Suz. These people are so shell-shocked they don't trust anybody or anything. They need these immunizations but we can't force them to get them."

"What are you looking for my love?" Suzanne asked.

"Daniel wants a cookie. A homemade chocolate chip cookie with raisins."

Suzanne giggled. "It sounds to me like Bennett wants a cookie."

Bennett smacked Suzanne on the lips with a loud kiss. "He does. What are you going to do about it?"

Suzanne leaned against the kitchen counter. With one arm behind her she pulled the cookie jar to the counter's edge. "Try looking in the cookie jar."

Mustafa walked into the kitchen barefoot and carrying an empty coffee cup. He filled the cup and in his all-business all the time manner, said "The new mothers and their babies need exam."

"The new babies that no nurse need supplements and vitamins they will no get if mothers do not bring to clinic." Mustafa set his coffee on the counter, pulled the cookie jar to him, and took two cookies.

"How come Moose knows where to find the cookies and I don't?" Bennett asked with a pout.

"Because Beanie is boron," Moose said with a laugh.

Bennett reached above his head to give Daniel another bite of his cookie and then replied to Moose. "You just keep telling yourself that, Moose. *Bennett is a boron*...."

"We aren't miracle workers and this clinic isn't going to be established overnight. It's going to take some time and that's the one thing we have plenty of," Bennett said.

"Nobody in all of God's creation should have to suffer through what these people have suffered through."

"Most of them feel guilty because they're alive when so many of their family members, neighbors and friends died in the flood."

"We're looking at an uphill climb that is going to take lots and lots of long hours and hard work but that's not going to stop us. We will get this clinic established and we'll see that Mustafa is on his way to becoming a very trusted and well-respected doctor right here in Wolf Laurel Creek before we go home to Ashford and before Rose returns to Widows Hollow."

Bennett stretched Daniels's arms and spun like a helicopter blade. Then he glanced at Mustafa. "Right Moose?"

Mustafa nodded.

Suzanne slapped her hands on her hips. She pointed to Daniel who, happy and laughing, remained on Bennett's shoulders.

"And, Bennett Gardner, if Daniel's going to have the clothes that he needs you're going to have to leave him here with us so that Rose can take him shopping. Maybe somebody will recognize him and we'll learn something about his family."

"I have to stay put in case the delivery truck shows up with our medical supplies. A few of the trucks are getting through and I don't want to take a chance on missing …."

"*Bam*! *Bam*! *Bam*!"

All four adults turned to the loud and urgent pounding on the front door. Mustafa hurried from the kitchen to answer.

Bennett swung Daniel from his shoulders to Rose and then he followed Mustafa.

A breathless young National Guardsman stood on the porch laden with a stack of books and cardboard tubes.

"Uh, hello, I'm sorry to bother you, Sir, but I'm Corporal Azle Connor with the Army National Guard. I drove Miss Rose and the little boy home yesterday and I remembered that she said there were doctors here."

"There's an emergency up in Red Bone Hollow. A young girl is about to have a baby and she's in trouble. She needs a doctor bad. Can the doctors come with me and help her?"

Mustafa opened the door to Connor. "Come in, please. One moment. We come with you. I am Dr. Mustafa Dhingra, and this is Dr. Bennett Gardner," Mustafa replied.

After he pointed Connor to the kitchen, the two women, and Daniel, Mustafa joined Bennett who took the stairs by twos to get his medical bag and emergency equipment.

"Oh, these are for you, Miss Rose," Connor said upon entering the kitchen. He gave the books and the tubes to Rose. "My wife said these are *American Sign Language* books and charts for beginners who want to learn sign language. We hope they'll come in handy for you and Daniel."

"Thank you, Azle," Rose said. She took the sign language learning aids from Connor and then added pleasantly "And please thank your wife for us. We hope to meet her soon. You better hurry now." Rose gave the young man a gentle push toward the door where he fell in behind Bennett and Mustafa.

Chapter Eight

Daniel started after Bennett but Rose intercepted the little boy. She scooped him up with "Come on little guy, Aunt Rose is going to have to find something to put on you so we can go find something to put on you."

Suzanne looked up from skimming through one of the books that Connor had left. She met Rose's eyes with a grin. "*Aunt Rose,* huh?"

"Right, *Aunt Suzanne*, what's he supposed to call us?"

Rose tried with toys to coax a smile from Daniel but the little boy watched the living room with anxious eyes, obviously wanting Bennett.

"I don't know but I have to believe that Daniel would be happier if we could communicate with him. He must feel so frightened and confused."

"Poor little guy, we don't know anything about him. We're not even sure how old he is. But all things considered, this little boy is handling it very well," Suzanne said. She rearranged items in the freezer while at the same time looking for something to thaw for dinner.

She glanced to Rose. "Tell me if anything sounds good. Steak. Roast. Hamburger. Hamburger. Hamburger."

Rose said with a laugh "How about hamburger?"

"That's a start," Suzanne replied. "Hamburger what?"

"Surprise us," Rose suggested.

"Ha! According to my loving husband that could be dangerous."

Rose said with a giggle "And who pays attention to your loving husband?"

"Good point," Suzanne replied.

Rose turned serious. "Whatever you decide is fine with me, Suzanne. I grew up on pole beans and potatoes, remember?"

Rose looked to Daniel and shook her head. "I guess I'll be taking him shopping in Bennett's sweatshirt and socks. I saw some kids' clothes in that Island Home store. Maybe I can find something in there for Daniel."

Rose reached for the child. "Come here, little guy. You want to go shopping with Aunt Rose?" Daniel looked at Rose with trusting but curious eyes.

Rose carried him to the bathroom and sat him beside the sink where she washed him and brushed his teeth with a spare toothbrush that Mustafa had provided.

Speaking loud enough for Suzanne to hear her in the kitchen, Rose said "Since I don't know my way around I don't want to drive very far.   There are some who accuse me of being navigationally challenged."

"If I had to guess I would say that was Bennett.   That sounds like something he would say," Suzanne remarked with a laugh.

"Rose, if you can't find anything at Island Home, the *Laurel Banner* said this morning that the Red Cross, Salvation Army and the National Guard are asking that people send no more clothing into the area."

"These and other emergency relief groups are overwhelmed with the tons of clothing, quilts, blankets, and household items that people from all over the nation have donated.   Chances are good that if you stop by any of the shelters you'll find something for Daniel."

"The paper said that if people want to help, the survivors need cash for the basics. I'll write a check before I forget and if you don't mind, I'll send it with you."

"Good, I'll write one too," Rose said with a nod.

"You want to sit up here and watch Aunt Rose write a check?" Rose asked Daniel. She lifted the child and sat him on the kitchen counter.

Attracted by water dripping from the faucet, Daniel wanted to play by filling and emptying a cup.

"It can't hurt anything," Rose remarked. She scooted Daniel closer to the faucet and turned on warm water.

Daniel laughed and played while Rose made out a check and then put it in her pocketbook with Suzanne's check.

"I wonder," Rose said, and picked up one of the books that Corporal Connor had left. She opened the book and scanned the index. "Hmm, store. There's a sign in here for store."

Rose flipped to the page and read how to sign the word *store*. She tapped Daniel on his knee, pointed both of her hands downward with her thumbs touching her fingers, and swung her fingertips forward and back twice.

Daniel's face lit up with a smile. He signed yes.

"Suzanne, did you see that? He knows the sign for store, he knows what I said!" Rose exclaimed in her excitement.

"Hey, that's great, Rose!" Suzanne agreed. She patted Daniel's knee and said to him, "And that's great for you too, Daniel."

"These books and charts are a blessing. I can't wait to learn enough so that I can communicate with Daniel on everything. You think the guys will want to learn to sign?"

Suzanne placed a cellophane-wrapped package of hamburger in a bowl and allowed Daniel to fill the bowl with water. "I know one of the guys will want to learn to sign for sure! Bennett's so taken with this child he'd learn Swahili and Mandarin Chinese if he needed to for Daniel."

Bennett whistled a long, low, sustained whistle. "I've seen a lot of poverty lately, but nothing like this."

The ride up the mountain from Wolf Laurel Creek to Red Bone Hollow with Corporal Azle Connor in the National Guard Jeep had been a jarring ordeal of potholes, ruts, ridges and washboard switchbacks.

"I didn't think anything could surprise me after what we've seen, but I was wrong. This is destitution taken to the limit."

Bennett's observation of the unimaginable squalor that lay before them was almost an understatement.

What he had come to know as a classic dogtrot cabin lay ahead more or less centered on hard scrabble earth that offered up nothing but boulders and apparent misery.

The cabin was built of weathered logs with an open breezeway in the middle. Separate sections of the house opened onto the breezeway which served as a cooling mechanism.

The opposite ends of the house had front windows and doors with door screens that hung on by a thread. Chimneys lurched on each side of the house above a patchwork of rusted tin, tarpaper and a hodgepodge of mismatched shingles.

Stacked rocks supported the structure and left a visible opening under the house that ran the length of it. Rusted chains that were staked to the ground disappeared into the opening and lay beside overturned dog bowls and piles of debris, plastic jugs, cola cans, and discarded soda bottles.

The sagging roof extended over a sagging porch that suggested it had once boasted steps that had lead from the ground to the porch.

To the right and beyond the porch a moss-covered Frigidaire refrigerator supported a half-burned mattress and box springs that had been tossed against it. Rusted bicycle parts, a *Howdy Doody* doll head, a blue fifty gallon plastic drum, mounds of bulging trash bags and clothing, and various pieces of broken furniture sprawled in every direction.

Chain link dog pens and chicken coops lay beyond the house. The rusted tin roofs and rotting tarps that covered them were all but lost in the piles of litter and discards.

A gutted and skinned hog hung from three wooden poles that were tied together teepee-style at the top. The hog's head lay in a galvanized tub to the right of the poles and laundry in green, rancid water lay in another galvanized tub on a chair to the left.

A young girl who appeared to be no more than twelve, dressed in a ragged and unwashed dress and a tattered barn coat that was sizes too large for her sat in a squat against a barren tree smoking a hand rolled cigarette.

An older man dressed in overalls and a flannel shirt who looked to be in his late twenties sat on a log beside her stroking the yapping Chihuahua that he held in his arms.

Loud screams from inside the cabin snapped Bennett's attention to the task at hand.

The front door on the right end of the cabin suddenly slammed open. "She's in here!" The large man making the announcement loomed in the doorway dressed in jeans and a flannel shirt with suspenders and a white beard that cascaded to his waist.

He looked over his shoulder in the direction of the screams and then exited the cabin with neither a glance nor a word to Connor and the arriving doctors.

Bennett grabbed his bag and led the way into the cabin. "Oh my God!" He cried upon entering. The cabin's interior reeked of odors that Bennett didn't even want to identify. What appeared to be a kitchen was almost hidden in the piles and mounds and stacks of unwashed kitchen utensils, plastic containers, bulging trash bags, dirty laundry and God only knew what else that might be hidden from view.

Mustafa and Connor cringed at the filth and clutter and tried to follow Bennett without coming in contact with anything.

"Mustafa, we're going to have to have some boiled water at the very least," Bennett said with a frown. "And it doesn't look like we'll be getting it from that faucet." Bennett nodded to the kitchen sink that was piled high with the same type of clutter as the rest of the room they had entered. "Maybe there's a faucet outside that you can use. Do you see a stove anywhere?"

The seemingly twelve year old girl stood in the doorway. "They's a stove all right, but hit's outside by the coops. I'll yell at SnappinClap, he kin git ya some water," she said with a look that was void of any hint of human emotion.

"SnappinClap?" Bennett repeated. "Is that somebody's name?"

"His name's Lenny but nobody calls 'im that. Everbody calls 'im SnappinClap." The girl laughed a derisive laugh and then she added "You'll see."

"I have some water in my canteens," Connor offered. "You can use it. I'll get them."

"Thanks Connor and if you don't mind see if you can find a way to boil some water. We're going to need it."

"I, I, I…" *Snap*! The man dressed in overalls and flannel snapped his fingers. He continued. "Make fire for, for, for…." *Clap!* He skidded one palm against the other making a loud clapping sound and then blurted "Water."

Bennett turned to the man, Lenny, who spoke with a pronounced stutter and who apparently had cultivated the habit of snapping his fingers and clapping his hands as an aid in speaking.

"Thank you Lenny, we would really appreciate it," Bennett said with a nod. "I'm Dr. Bennett Gardner, this is Dr. Mustafa Dhingra, and that's Corporal Connor bringing in the canteens. Now, if you all will excuse me, this young lady needs some privacy."

With his words Bennett dismissed everyone but Mustafa and then searched for a couple of square inches of uncluttered space where he could place his medical bag.

Finding no such place in the unbelievably cluttered bedroom, Bennett frowned. There was barely room for him to squeeze between the teetering piles of stuff and the moaning young girl.

In exasperation Bennett cleared a spot on the bed by using his elbow to push a pile of something to the floor. The young woman's screams had subsided for the moment but she was wet with sweat and was clearly exhausted from her prolonged labor.

Bennett checked her vital signs and temperature. They were stable and by no means life threatening. This looked like a normal delivery to him so what had Connor meant when he said that the girl was in trouble?

Bennett answered that question for himself. He lifted the sheet from the girl preparing to further examine her. "Oh my God!"

Bennett snatched his bag, sanitized his hands, pulled on a pair of latex gloves and whispered a silent prayer. "Lord help me turn him and I hope it's not too late."

The baby's feet were clearly visible and Bennett knew there was no time for if the baby's umbilical cord was wrapped around the baby's neck, he might already have suffocated and if not, seconds counted.

Bennett had to deliver the baby right now.

Not wanting to frighten the young mother, Bennett instructed "Push! Push now, push hard!"

The girl screamed and pushed.

"Again! Do it again!"

The baby's feet were pink, his legs were pink. Bennett's hopes grew.

"Push again, push as hard as you can! He's almost here!"

The girl screamed and cried and pushed.

"One more time, do it just one more time!"

The girl screamed and pushed.

"I need that water!" Bennett yelled. He drew the baby into his hands and pulled the umbilical cord from beneath the newborn's tiny arm.   The cord had wrapped around the baby's chest and under his arm.

Bennett grinned and whispered "Thank you Lord, he's a beauty," and then laughed at the newborn's loud and healthy screams.

Chapter Nine

Bennett handed the baby over to Mustafa who examined him and put drops of silver nitrate in the newborn's eyes. Mustafa weighed and measured the newborn and then wrapped him in a sterile blanket that he had packed for this purpose.

Mustafa tried to return the baby to Bennett. "Ah, Dr. Dhingra, why don't you present this beautiful little newborn to his mother and tell her a little something about her boy."

Mustafa stared at Bennett like he had no idea what Bennett was saying.

Bennett caught Mustafa's eye and led his friend. "Is that a fine boy we just delivered?"

"Oh, yes, very fine boy, beautiful boy!"

"And how much does he weigh?"

"This fine, beautiful boy weighs six pounds and seven ounces."

"Why don't you tell the new mother how long her baby boy is?"

"Oh, oh yes, of course!   Young woman, your fine, beautiful baby boy weighs six pounds and seven…"

Bennett said in a very gentle voice "Dr. Dhingra, it might be good if you look at the baby's mother when you speak to her."

"Oh, oh, yes, of course.   Young woman, your fine, beautiful baby boy weighs six pounds and seven ounces. He is nineteen inches long."

Mustafa, feeling somewhat elated with this accomplishment, turned to Bennett with the baby in Mustafa's arms.

Again Bennett suggested "It might be good if you give Mama her baby now."

"Oh, oh yes, of course!"   Mustafa bowed to the young mother and put the baby in her arms.

Bennett laughed.   "Dr. Dhingra, it's really not necessary to bow to our new mothers.   Bowing might confuse some of the folks around here.   So let's not bow, let's call the patient by name, and let's carry on a friendly conversation with the patient.   It helps put them and you at ease."

Mustafa addressed the young woman with raised brows. "Do you know what I say?"

"Do I know what you say… what?"

Bennett laughed. "Young lady, some of your neighbors and the folks down the mountain complain that they can't understand Dr. Dhingra. He was asking if you can understand him."

"Well, yeah!"

Mustafa looked like a kid that just got a star on a wall chart at school. He was delighted.

Bennett slapped Mustafa on the shoulder. "And that's all there is to it, Dr. Dhingra. You're gonna do just fine."

The young mother eagerly accepted her baby. Bennett was struck by her youthful looks. "If you don't mind my asking, how old are you?"

"Fourteen," The young woman replied

Bennett shook his head. "Fourteen. Are you ready for this little guy?"

The girl answered without raising her eyes to Bennett. "Don't matter if I'm ready or not, he's here, ain't he?"

"He's here all right," Bennett agreed. He called to the woman's family and Corporal Connor. "You can come in now."

Bennett could not imagine being fourteen years old and living in this squalor with a new baby. He wondered about the baby's father too. "Is Lenny your baby's father?"

"SnappinClap my young'uns' pa? Hell no he ain't! SnappinClap's my brother! And the girl out there's my sister, Florette. The old man's my Pa, Micah. Leonard Micah Walker. All our kin name their boy young'uns after their pa's and their grandpa's."

"So what is your name?"

"I'm Melinda."

"Well Melinda, it appears that you have a fine strong son. But that's not something that Dr. Dhingra and I can guarantee without doing a thorough exam and we can't do that here. If you like, we can take you and the baby to the hospital in town where we can do a complete examination."

"No!" The girl met Bennett's eyes. "Ain't no Walker ever been born in a hospital and ain't none of 'em gone to no hospitals fer examinations neither. And Daniel Micah Walker ain't gonna be no different."

Bennett felt something like an electrical jolt at the girl's mention of the name Daniel.

"Daniel. Who is Daniel?" Bennett asked.

"This here youngun, he's Daniel, after his pa and Walker after my pa since I ain't had me no wedding and it ain't likely that I'll ever."

"Your baby's father is named Daniel?" Bennett's mouth felt dry.

"Sorry lyin', connivin', snake son of Satan! Daniel Ruddy! He come up here with his pretty words and promises a'tellin' me how he loved me and wanted to marry me. He never told that he had a wife and a little boy down the mountain, but SnappinClap follered him home one day."

"Folks think that SnappinClap's slow-turned, that he ain't in his right thinkin' mind, and that he ain't nobody to study on. But they's wrong."

"SnappinClap's stronger'n a pair of Bluegrass mules and ain't nothin' wrong with his mind."

"He's got the gift and can't nobody put nothin' over on 'im. Mr. Daniel Ruddy may have bit me like a barnyard dog, but he ain't put nothin' over on SnappinClap"

"SnappinClap met Mr. Daniel's wife, Mary, and he told her what that low-down varmint was up to. SnappinClap met the little boy, too and he's right fond of him. Little Daniel laughs and laughs when his Momma brings him up here to see SnappinClap."

"Daniel's mother brought Daniel up here to visit your brother?" Bennett was having a hard time hearing this. He couldn't imagine Daniel in this environment, in this filth and stench.

"She sure did. And Daniel likes playing with Festus."

"Festus?"

"That little pup what SnappinClap brung home. Somebody throwed him away in a trash bag but SnappinClap heard him and tore up that bag getting' to 'im. He bottle fed him fer the longest and stayed up all night just seein' to that little pup."

"Kin we see the baby now?" Florette asked from the doorway. Keeping her eyes fixed on the ground, she stood with her hands behind her back and with one foot resting on the other.

"It's all right with me if it's all right with the baby's Mama," Bennett said.

"Wa, wa, wa…" *Snap*! "Wash yer hands fir, fir…." *Clap* "First." SnappinClap insisted.

"Melinda, did any of you notice anything different about the little boy Daniel?"

Bennett felt a slight tap on his shoulder. He turned in surprise to SnappinClap who rapidly signed a string of words.

Melinda said with a knowing grin "SnappinClap says that we know Daniel's deaf, maybe he can't talk neither, we don't know fer sure yet."

"You know sign language?" Bennett asked, stunned. "You and your brother?"

"Me and SnappinClap and Florette and Pa, we all learned. Mary, Daniel's mother, taught us. We love Little Daniel. He feels like he's in a world by hisself if nobody can't talk to him."

"Mary will come again soon's the weather warms up. She said she'll teach us some more when she comes."

Bennett knit his brows. "Can you tell me what Mary looks like?" He squeezed himself against a leaking trash bag to allow Florette closer to the bed and the baby.

Florette carefully lifted the baby from Melinda's arms and smiled at him with a bright smile.

Melinda's description of the woman that Rose had found on the bed beside Daniel matched Rose's description of the woman.

Bennett busied himself repacking his medical bag. "Uh, Melinda, you and your family know about the flood?"

"We ain't ignorant as mud hens, Dr. Bennett. Of course we know about the flood! Some of our kin was kilt in it and some of 'em ain't never been found yet."

"I'm sorry to have to tell you this Melinda, but Daniel's mother, you say her name is Mary, is dead. She died in the flood. We don't know about Daniel's father. If he died in the flood he hasn't been identified yet."

SnappinClap's eyes filled with tears. He said in his halting way that Mary had been his friend and that he would miss her and that Daniel would be sad without his mother.

"We's all gonna miss Mary. She was our friend and close as kin, but that no-count husband of hers ain't nobody gonna miss! And he ain't dead, that's fer sure!" Melinda exclaimed.

"How do you know?" Bennett raised curious eyes to meet Melinda's eyes.

"'Cause he's in jail! He's been there fer a while. He was on probation after he did time for robbing a grocery store over in Boyd County, Kentucky."

"He ain't supposed to be a gettin' soused and he ain't supposed to be carryin no gun. He was doin' both when the cops stopped him fer speedin'. Them boys in Boyd County didn't waste no time invitin' Mr. Daniel Ruddy to be their guest for a spell! They put him in the slammer fer violatin' his probation."

"So Ruddy is Daniel's last name?"

Melinda nodded. "Sounds like muddy. That's it."

"Do you know of any other relatives that Daniel has in the area? Does he have any aunts or uncles or grandparents?"

"He ain't got no other relatives in the area or nowhere else. Mary said there ain't nobody but her and Daniel's pa."

"Do you know how old he is?"

"He turned four on January sixth. We know 'cause Mary brung him up here when his pa was drunk and was bedevilin' Daniel."

Mary said his pa was mean to Daniel, called him names and poked fun at him 'cause Daniel's deaf. Mary knowed we wouldn't be mean to Daniel or to Mary. She come here 'cause it was safe to come here. Mary and Daniel is kin as fer as we's concerned."

"He is ki, ki, kin!" Lenny insisted. "This here's Dan, Dan, Daniel's baby brother, Daniel!"

Lenny got through the sentence with no slapping and no *clap*ping.

Thunderstruck, Bennett realized that the big man who had a speech problem and who now cradled baby Daniel so gently in his arms was right.

Chapter Ten

"There you go little guy. I bet you're a lot happier in a shirt, jeans and shoes that fit you," Rose said and then she made a face. She had to remind herself over and over that Daniel could not hear.

Since she could not sign yet, she did the next best thing. She stood Daniel on the sales counter of the Island Home Store, raised both her palms above his head on each side, drew her palms down to his feet, smiled a great smile and then *clap*ped her hands.

"I hope you understand what I'm trying to say little guy, but I'm sure that you don't," she said as she gave him a hug.

She signed *toys* and then laughed when Daniel's face lit up. She lifted him from the counter and held his hand while they made their way to the toy section of the store. She watched as the little boy contemplated the selections and then felt surprised that he made his choices so quickly.

Daniel chose a *Hot Wheels Mongoose Track* with four cars and a can of *Silly Putty*. That didn't seem like a lot of toys to Rose so she tried in her own way to ask him if he wanted more. She pointed to the toy displays, raised her flattened palms to her shoulders and shook her head.

Daniel wasn't interested in Rose's improvised signing. He made it plain that he was interested in opening the Mongoose Track and playing with the cars.

"Uh, excuse me and I apologize if I'm out of line here, but is that child deaf?"

Rose turned to a pretty brunette woman who looked like she had been shopping for a while as her arms were loaded with shopping bags.

"Yes, he is," Rose answered with questioning eyes.

"He must be the little boy that my husband told me about. I'm Corporal Azle Connor's wife, Judy. Are you Rose?" The woman asked.

"Yes, Rose McKinley," Rose said, returning the woman's smile. "And this is Daniel."

"I'd be happy to shake your hand Rose, but it appears that our hands are full."

Rose liked the friendly woman in an instant. "Oh, by the way Mrs. Connor, thank you so much for the books and charts on signing. We haven't really had time to use them yet but we plan to get started tonight."

"He's a beautiful little boy," the woman said. She raised her eyes to Rose. "First, please call me Judy. I wanted to come by and meet you after Azle told me how you found this little one. It's quite a story."

Rose replied with a nod. "Yes it is and I'm so thankful that we found him. I just wish that we could communicate with him. He must feel so lost, especially after losing his mother and maybe his father."

Rose sat aside her packages to open the Mongoose track for Daniel who took a car in each hand and then returned the package to Rose.

"We think that it was his mother in the house with him but we can't know for sure. We know only that when we found him the woman beside him was dead."

Judy responded with a gasp. She glanced to Daniel. "Oh, my Lord! How horrible for him!"

Nodding in agreement, Rose said "Learning more about his family is one of the things that I hope to accomplish this afternoon. I don't know what else to do but ask the local pastors, maybe a postman if I can find one, and anybody else we can think of who might have known Daniel and his parents."

"Nobody knows the whereabouts of this little boy or that he's with me and my friends. Somebody might be looking for him," Rose said.

She looked from Daniel who ran the cars along one of the lower shelves in the store aisle, to Judy.

"Little boys don't really care for shopping, do they?" She remarked.

"From what I know of little boys," Judy replied, "They much prefer to stay home and play. They like getting new toys, of course, but they're more comfortable where they're free to run and play and make noise."

"Which reminds me," Judy's expression changed to the one that women get when, out of the blue, they are struck with a great idea.

Recognizing the expression, Rose asked with sudden interest "What?"

"I have this wonderful friend and neighbor. She's an inspiration to everyone who knows her and there weren't many in Wolf Laurel Creek who didn't know her. Daniel wants to play and I'm pretty sure he can play at her house. She has two little boys and a grown daughter."

Judy shifted the bags in her arms. "If you like you can follow me. And if you're wondering what this could possibly have to do with learning more about Daniel's family, my answer is *everything!*"

Rose followed Judy in her pickup a short distance down the middle of the road (keeping to the Caterpillar tracks) to what had been the Village of Argollite.

The little community was located about a quarter of the way down the seventeen mile stretch of narrow valley that was known as Wolf Laurel Creek.

Before the flood, Argollite had boasted its own post office, three churches, a new school, a hardware store, a grocery store, hair salon, movie theater, and skating rink.

The homes in Argollite had been transformed over the years from stark, identical coal shanties into modern well-kept homes with manicured lawns and picket fences.

Now there were no fences, no stores, no school, no movie theater and no hair salon. The flood had washed them all away with two of the churches. The north side of the village had been erased. Nothing remained but scarred ground.

A single row of neat, tidy houses, the post office and the large red brick Argollite Baptist Church were all that remained on the south side, these sandwiched between great ugly, steaming piles of twisted flood rubble.

Bull dozers, Caterpillars and cranes filled the air with the noises of industry. Somber-faced people talking in hushed tones waited in lines outside the National Guard mobile laundry and shower units.

Stray dogs and stray people wandered about like extras in a horror film.

Rose hoped they would arrive at Judy's friend's home soon. Hearing about the tragic Wolf Laurel Creek Flood pierced the hardest of hearts, but seeing it again and again scarred the softest.

Judy pulled into the driveway of one of the homes. It was a two-story with a covered front porch that ran the length of the house. The neat home was painted a pale yellow with white shutters.

A white picket fence bordered the yard in front and back. Boxes and bags and plastic containers were stacked in neat parallel rows across the porch on each side of the front door.

Rose unbuckled Daniel's seat belt and then lifted him from the pickup.

Daniel signed *toys* and waited impatiently for Rose to get them for him.

"Here you go, Sweetie, you can bring them with you," she said. Rose scowled and shook her head, reminding herself once again that Daniel could not hear her.

Rose and Daniel met Judy at the gate that opened between the driveway and the front of the house. Judy signed to Daniel "Want to play with children?"

What Daniel signed in response was not an answer to Judy's question. His face, all smiles, became animated. He eagerly pushed against the gate and holding up two fingers like a peace sign he rapidly spelled something to Judy.

"*V-E-N-A!*" Daniel spelled Vena. He knows her!" Judy exclaimed.

Feeling lost and very much out of this loop, Rose responded. "Um, okay. Who is Vena?"

"That's my Daniel and he's spellin' Vena Mae, that's me!" Like a whirlwind of energy, a tall, slender black woman burst through the front door, down the steps and across the yard of the pale yellow house.

She threw open the gate and scooped Daniel into her arms. "Oh, baby, my sweet baby, I been so worried about you! Bless God, you are all right. I prayed over you little Daniel, you and your sweet Mama Mary. I prayed for your sorry daddy, too. Where is your mama, Daniel?"

Opening her arms to the woman, Judy squeezed Vena with affection.

"Miss Judy, you bring me some company? That pretty little Irish girl with all them red curls and freckles ain't from around here or I would'a knowed her 'fore she got out of that pickup."

"Come here, Sweet Thing!" Vena invited. "Give Ole Vena a hug and come in my house!" With a glance at the sky Vena waved a hand.

"It ain't mine, not really. It's the Lord's house. He's just letting me borrow it until He calls me to my real home!"

Vena Mae hugged Rose and then she hugged Daniel again. She released the boy and folded herself so that she could be eye to eye with him. "And Mister Daniel, I 'spect you'll be a wantin' to play with the kids. Marty and Augustus are upstairs with Tansy. You take your toys and go on up."

Vena opened the door and laughed at Daniel who scooted through it and up the stairs.

"You ladies think I done forgot that Mister Daniel can't hear but Ole Vena don't forget nothing 'bout her children. Ain't no need fer me to learn that sign language 'cause me and Mister Daniel, we got us an understanding. Yes sir, me and that boy there, we fine just as we be."

"Vena Mae Thompson, this is Rose McKinley, she's visiting friends up the valley in Coleta. Rose, this is my friend and neighbor, Vena Mae Thompson."

Rose smiled at the woman but she did not see the tall, elegant, reed-thin Vena Mae Thompson.

Rose saw a shorter woman with a much greater bulk, a warm, loving woman with ebony skin and graying hair with curls that poked out from beneath the kerchief that she wore, a woman that Rose and her brothers and sister had known and loved all their lives.

She was a neighbor and she was back in Widows Hollow. And Rose suddenly missed her beloved friend, Mama John. She missed her hugs and her smiles and her ever-present wise counsel and goodness.

She missed her like she missed her own mother, Isabel, who had died when Rose was sixteen.

"Would you ladies care for a glass of tea or a cup of coffee? I made some brownies this morning. Brownies go mighty fine with hot coffee."

Judy waved a hand. "None for me. Thanks Vena."

Rose added "No thank you Miss Thompson."

"Ain't no Miss Thompson here, Sweet Child. You call me Vena Mae and you ladies have a seat. Tansy, my eighteen year old daughter is upstairs with the boys. Marty, age six, and Augustus, age four, love little Daniel. They play together just fine."

Rose and Judy seated themselves on a blue and green floral sofa. Across from them Vena Mae took a seat in one of a pair of antique armchairs that were upholstered in blue velvet. She placed her teacup on a polished round table that stood between the chairs.

"Now, what can I do for you ladies? And if you don't mind my asking, why isn't Mary with Daniel?"

With a glance at Rose Judy dropped her head and clasped her hands in her lap.

"Vena, I'm sorry to have to tell you this but Daniel has lost his mother. We believe that Mary died in the flood."

"Oh, sweet Jesus, no!" Vena Mae wailed. She shook her head and drew a hand to her mouth as her tears fell. Who identified my Mary? Did you or did Daniel's daddy?"

Vena Mae pulled open a drawer in the round table and withdrew a box of tissue. She wiped her eyes and shook with sobs.

"Rose, you want to tell her how you found Daniel and Mary?" Judy asked.

Rose shook her head. "No. Please, you go ahead if you don't mind."

Judy told the story of how Rose had found Daniel holding his mother's hand in the house that was about to be bulldozed.

Vena Mae gasped. "Oh my Lord! Sweet Jesus done sent an angel to rescue our baby Daniel! She lifted her eyes to the ceiling and waved a hand. "God, you are so good! I praise you Lord! Thank you Lord!"

"God is good," Judy said, nodding in agreement. She leaned forward from the sofa. "Vena, you asked why we came this afternoon. Since Rose has never seen Mary, we all supposed that the woman with Daniel was Mary."

"Rose had planned to go this afternoon and visit pastors and maybe find a postman who might be able to identify Daniel and his family."

"We don't know anything about Daniel's family. We have no idea what his parents looked like." Judy darted her eyes from Rose to Vena. "But I remembered your hobby and your incredible collection and thought that perhaps you could help us out here."

Vena Mae patted her eyes with the tissue. Her mouth stretched into a smile. "Honey, there ain't no doubt Ole Vena can help you out! You ladies just come on in here with me."

Chapter Eleven

The two women followed Vena Mae.

Judy nudged Rose and said with a look of mystery "Get ready.   You're not gonna believe this!"

Vena led them through the living room to white enamel pocket doors that she slid open into a dining room.

A long rectangular oak dining table with four chairs on each side and chairs at both ends dominated the center of the surprisingly large room.

Newspapers lay strewn on top of the table.   Some of them were folded in neat stacks.   Beside these lay scissors and articles that appeared to have been cut from the papers. Bottles, tubes and sticks of glue were scattered among colored and permanent markers and photo albums.

Some of the albums were oversized black albums with black pages and beige corner pockets that held photos in place.

Others boasted laminated covers of solid colors, nature scenes, holiday themes and international tourist destinations.

Rose glanced from the table to the book cases that lined the walls on each side of the dining table. The book cases ran corner to corner along the wall and rose from the floor to the ceiling. The ten shelves in each bookcase were tightly packed with albums, albums too numerous to count, albums of a dizzying variety, albums in every size, shape and color.

Rose read aloud the words that were neatly printed on the albums' spines. *"Earthquakes, Hurricanes, Floods, Tornadoes, Blizzards, Train Wrecks, Lightning Strikes, Dog Attacks, Korean War Aug 8, 1945 thru Nov 14, 1947, Korean War Nov 14, 1947 thru Sept 9, 1948, and Vietnam War Aug 10, 1950 thru Feb 15, 1951."*

"Wow!" Rose exclaimed. "This is incredible!" Wide-eyed, she turned to Vena. "All of these scrapbooks and albums are made from articles that you cut out of the newspapers?"

"Yes Mam!" Vena Mae said with a laugh. "I got every day of the Korean War, the Vietnam War through last week, I got to catch up but the papers are on the table there," Vena said with a nod to the stacks of newspaper articles.

"I got every day of the life of John F. Kennedy from the time he was a Senator to the day he was murdered in 1963. Of course I got Dr. King and Bobbie Kennedy, too. And I got every day of the Civil War from 1860 through 1865."

"Your scrapbook collection is amazing!" Rose gushed. "I've never seen anything like it! The idea is so unique! I don't know of anyone who has a collection like this."

"How did you get started?" She asked, turning to Vena Mae with a sincere look of appreciation for the woman's dedication to keeping her own personal record of history in newspaper clippings.

"First off," Vena Mae pulled out a chair and seated herself. She motioned with a wave of her hand for Rose and Judy to take seats.

"I didn't start it. There's scrapbooks in here that my great-great-great grandmother put together. She was a slave when she was a young girl and slaves weren't allowed to learn to read or cipher. But my great-great-great grandmother Hattie Louise Johnson was lucky."

"With the help of some friends she escaped the bosses' plantation and found her way in 1863 to Mr. Thomas

Garrett who was a Quaker and who did not believe in slavery."

"Mr. Garrett's home in Northern Pennsylvania was the last station on the Underground Railroad that helped runaway slaves escape from the Southern states to freedom."

"While Hattie waited with other runaways for her passage to freedom Mr. Thomas' wife, Rachel, read the newspapers to Hattie and to the other runaways. She taught them to read and told them it would be important that they be able to read if they wanted to be successful."

"Hattie never forgot Miss Rachel's reading the newspapers to a group of runaway slaves who might make it to freedom and who might not."

"She learned to read and to cipher and she went on to become a teacher. It was her habit every day of her life to read the newspaper to her children."

"When the Civil War started, she cut out the articles and pasted them in a scrapbook because she wanted her children and her grandchildren to know that there were lots of white men like Mr. Thomas and that a lot of young white men died fighting to free the slaves."

Vena Mae rose and walked around the dining room table. From the top shelf of the bookcase to the right of the table she retrieved a scrapbook. It was a large, square black book with heavy black pages that were bound with string.

She ran her hand lovingly over the cardboard cover of the book. "This is the first scrapbook. This was Hattie's scrapbook."

Rose and Judy were impressed with the age and condition of the book. It was obvious to them that it had been well cared for as it was passed down from generation to generation.

The articles and photos from the *Daily Patriot and Union* and from the *Pennsylvania Daily Telegraph* of the 1860s were clear and well preserved.

"What a treasure this must be to you!" Rose exclaimed.

"It's been a treasure to five generations and my Tansy will carry it on. She's started her own collection, too."

While Rose and Judy carefully turned the pages of history Vena Mae scanned her scrapbook collection for another book.

She took the yellow vinyl book that was labeled *1970s Weddings and Baptisms* from a shelf, seated herself and flipped through a few pages. Finding the page that she wanted, she tapped a photo and then raised her eyes to meet Rose and Judy's eyes.

"This should answer your questions. Daniel's mother, Mary, was Catholic. She and young Daniel attended St. Matthew's Catholic Church of Fremont every Sunday. In a rural community like Wolf Laurel Creek, any event is a big event and worthy of newspaper coverage. When Mary had Daniel baptized, the *Laurel Banner* printed it."

Vena Mae turned the book so that Rose and Judy could see the page. Vena Mae pointed to a photo. "That's Mary. That's her husband Daniel, and that sweet baby is our Daniel."

Rose looked at the photo. The woman pictured was of medium height, slender and with brunette hair that hung in soft waves to her shoulders.

"That's her! That's the woman we found on the bed beside Daniel. Her body was the only thing between Daniel and the flood water," Rose said the words with sadness. "Now we know for sure that Daniel's mother is dead and if that caption's correct, it confirms that Daniel's last name is Ruddy."

"That's right, it is Ruddy," Vena Mae said. She pointed to the man in the photo. Much taller than the woman, the man had curly red hair with a mustache and beard. He was thin, too thin, with the look of someone who wanted to be anywhere but where he was.

In contrast, Mary's face beamed with an adoring smile for the child that Daniel Senior held in his arms.

"Daniel's daddy is Irish. He's Catholic too but he didn't care much for attending church. But when Miss Mary pushed, he showed up. I reckon she pushed real hard to get him to church for Daniel's baptism."

"Vena, when a child is baptized in a Catholic church, aren't godparents usually named at the ceremony?" Rose asked. "If Daniel has no living relatives other than his father, maybe he has godparents?"

Vena looked at the article and at the photo of Daniel's baptism. "Honey, I don't see nothin' here about godparents so I 'spect Daniel has no godparents.".

"So that leaves his father," Rose said. "And we don't know if his father is alive or not. If he died in the flood, who could identify his body?"

"I reckon I could if there ain't nobody else. When I go to the post office this afternoon I'll stop at my church, Argollite Baptist. I'll ask if anybody knows anything about Daniel's daddy and if I have to," Vena said, shaking her head, "Lord knows I don't want to, I'll see about identifying his body."

"Vena, if you don't want to go alone, I'll go with you. It's the least I can do," Judy offered.

Vena Mae pushed herself from her chair. "I bet I know some little boys and one young lady who would love a brownie and some milk. They've been awful quiet up there and I like to reward children when they've been good. You ladies join us. It won't take but a minute."

Rose and Judy stood to follow Vena Mae. Rose said "Vena, the flood destroyed everything in their home. All the photos and anything else that might have been of sentimental value to little Daniel are gone."

Rose looked back at the album on the table. "Unless you have more photos, this may be the only photo Daniel will ever have of his family. If you don't mind, could I get a copy of it?" Rose smiled, directed her gaze to the shelves that were filled with scrapbooks and then added "I have no doubt that you will keep this one safe for him."

"Honey, it ain't no problem at all. The post office has a copy machine and I'll be going there today. You say you're stayin' with friends up Coleta?"

"Yes Mam, with Dr. Mustafa Dhingra and our friends Bennett and Suzanne Gardner. They're both doctors too."

"I know that Dr. Mustafa," Vena said. "He's been around here helping folks in every way he can. He's shy, don't talk much, but he knows his business."

"It would be such a help to us if you would spread the word to your neighbors!" Rose cried with enthusiasm. "Mustafa was trying to establish a medical clinic before the flood. The people here view him as a foreigner. They say he's hard to understand because of his Indian accent."

Vena waved a hand. "Honey, people around here, they see Mr. Mustafa carryin' water down the mountain in buckets when the folks didn't have none after the flood."

"When folks was asleep, I see Mr. Mustafa. He ain't asleep 'cause he's carin' for these folks. I see him cry when he couldn't get them little babies breathin' again, seen him cry with one after another of them folks. Don't you worry none Miss Rose, word gets around. People know a good man when they see one."

"And they know a good woman, too," Judy added. "Rose, all that stuff that's stacked and piled on Vena's front porch? It comes from people everywhere. They bring it to Vena because they know that she spends a good deal of her time taking it to people in need. She did it long before the flood."

133

"Law, child!   God's been good to me.   I'm blessed and my family is blessed.   We always got just what we need, just in time.   It makes me feel good to help other folks," Vena said and then she sliced into the pan of brownies

Chapter Twelve

Bennett rocked his hands like he was holding a steering wheel and said to Daniel "Car."

With a burst of laughter Daniel pushed another car down the Hot Wheels track. "This isn't bad," Bennett remarked. "The women are in the kitchen cooking up something wonderful for the hard-working, bill-paying men of the house. Moose is busy trying to memorize the whole *American Sign Language* alphabet and charts, and Bennett gets to play cars with Daniel. That's a good deal, huh Daniel?" Bennett said with a laugh.

Mustafa was not laughing.

"What's the matter, Moose, why the scowl?"

"What is sign for word *deal*?"

"I think you have to spell that one Mustafa," Rose called from the kitchen.

Mustafa looked to the American Sign Language alphabet chart that he had hung on the back of the front door. He curled three fingers to make a circle with his thumb while keeping his pinky upright.

"*D*," Rose, Bennett and Suzanne said together. Mustafa formed the letters and they repeated, *E, A*, and *L*."

"Good work, we're learning sign language but Daniel's too busy playing with his cars." Bennett lay on his stomach on a rug in the living room where he played with Daniel. He lifted his face to Daniel and said "Lucky midget!"

Bennett grinned in anticipation, expecting Daniel to mouth the words back to him. Daniel flattened his fingers against his thumb, creating a squished hand, and moved his hand to his mouth.

Bennett laughed and said to Mustafa "Did you see that?"

"Smart boy," Mustafa replied. "He doesn't want to play with Beanie, he wants to eat."

"You women hear that? Daniel says it time to eat," Bennett said over his shoulder in the direction of the kitchen.

Suzanne stood in the kitchen doorway wiping her hands on a towel. "Daniel's right. Come and get it. But you boys wash up first."

"Who is boy? Mustafa is no boy," Mustafa grumbled as he followed Bennett who carried Daniel to the bathroom.

Bennett washed Daniel's face and hands and then turned the boy loose. Daniel ran to the kitchen and Suzanne.

"Moose, we're dealing with women here. Men came from caves and women came from behind the waterfalls. It's nothing like anything else you will ever experience. They are nothing like men, they do not think like men, there is no logic to them and if you say anything they will whack you with a skillet, or pout or disappear for three days."

Mustafa returned a blank stare to Bennett.

"That's best Moose. Never argue with a woman, say something wonderful, grab 'em and hug 'em and kiss 'em and they'll cook for you, do your laundry, make you homemade apple pies, and other, better stuff that Daniel's too young to hear about."

"Daniel can no hear, Beanie!"

"Well, we've save it for later anyway!"

"Uh, could one of you two genius men get Daniel's booster chair? His eyebrows are even with the table top," Suzanne said in a huff.

"Rose, did you get Daniel a booster chair today?"
Bennett asked.

Suzanne shook her head. "Where's the skillet?
Bennett! Get the books we've been using for Daniel since
he doesn't have a booster chair!"

"Oh, uh, right!" Bennett replied.

"I can believe they came from caves, can't you Rose?"
Suzanne asked with a giggle.

Bennett arranged the books, seated Daniel, and then
pulled his chair close to the little boy's chair.

Rose tucked a napkin in the front of Daniel's shirt and
then took a chair across the table from Suzanne.

When everybody was seated Rose asked Bennett "Will
you say grace?"

The friends joined hands with Bennett and Suzanne
holding Daniel's hands.

"Lord, we come to thank you for this day, for the safe
delivery of another one of your children, for good friends,
and for this wonderful meal that we are about to share.
Bless those who are less fortunate and keep us ever mindful
of our great blessings. In Jesus name. Amen."

"Who wants to start?" Bennett asked. "Shall Mustafa
and I tell you about our day or do you ladies want to

enthrall us with exciting tales of delivery truck drama and shopping experiences in Wolf Laurel Creek?"

"You left this morning for Red Bone Hollow to deliver a baby. How did it go? How are the baby and the mother?" Suzanne asked. She ladled brown gravy over pot roast, carrots and potatoes that she had cut up on a plate for Daniel.

"Piece of cake," Bennett quipped at the same time as he stuck a bite in his mouth. The baby was turned. When I saw that the little guy was coming feet first, I sprang into action, put on my cape and mask and delivered him."

Mustafa scrunched his face and held his fork suspended in the air. "You do not put on cape and mask. What are you talking for?" Mustafa asked.

"That's talking *about*, Moose."

Suzanne giggled. "Bennett, stop it! You're driving Mustafa nuts. He takes everything you say seriously."

"But it was a learning experience," Bennett continued. His playfulness vanished. "The mother was fourteen and the place they live in would rival any Chicago inner city dump. I don't know which was worse the poverty or the filth. Maybe they go hand in hand, but this was indescribable."

"I still don't know if the water worked because you couldn't get to the kitchen faucet for the trash and clutter inside the house. I think they said the stove was outside. I know there was a refrigerator outside with mattresses piled on top of it. I know this because we saw them and both refrigerator and mattresses were growing green mold."

"I don't understand how anyone can live like that. Where was the girl's mother?" Rose asked.

"Nobody mentioned the girl's mother but her father, brother and sister were there." Bennett looked from Rose to Suzanne. "Rosie, Suz, what I've just given you is the good news. You might want to brace yourselves for this next part."

"What is it Bennett?" Suzanne picked up a chunk of carrot that fell from Daniel's fork and then raised her eyes to her husband's eyes.

"Tell us," Rose added. She had a sudden and uneasy feeling that Bennett's revelation would concern Daniel. With a glance at the smiling boy she commented "It's about Daniel, isn't it?"

"Well it seems that Daniel's daddy strayed from home a lot, drinks a lot too, and tends to mistreat his wife and child. The baby boy that we delivered this morning has the very same daddy as this little boy right here, and he has the very same first name, too."

"The baby you delivered is, is Daniel's brother? And his name is Daniel too?"

"Yep!" Bennett said with a nod. "He's named Daniel after his daddy, Daniel. He's named Micah after his fourteen year old mother, Melinda's, father and Walker, the girl's maiden name because she and Daddy Daniel couldn't marry because Daddy Daniel already had a wife."

Suzanne raised a hand. "Give me a minute. I have to let this sink in." She shook her head. "So our Daniel has a new baby brother named Daniel?"

"Yep, seems so."

"But our Daniel is not blood related to any of these Walkers, just to the baby through Daniel's father."

"That's the way I understand it, my love." Bennett said and kissed Suzanne on the forehead. "I love the way you say *Our Daniel*," Bennett added with an adoring smile.

"Melinda and her brother SlappinClap didn't take it too well when I told them that Daniel's mother is dead. Daniel's mother's name was Mary and apparently she visited the Walkers from time to time when Daniel's daddy was misbehaving."

"Bennett. Did you say SlappinClap? Is that really somebody's name?"

"Moose, could you tell them this story? I'm gonna mop the muck off Daniel's face. I think there's more gravy on him than in him."

Mustafa laughed. "SlappinClap is no real name, is name family call older brother, Daniel. Daniel has speech problem, pronounced stutter. Daniel *slaps*! Hands. Mustafa demonstrated by skidding one palm against the other in a loud *slap*! To stop stutter, and *claps*! Hands also to stop stutter."

Suzanne and Rose looked at one another. "Is there anything else we should know about Daniel's baby brother's family?" Suzanne asked.

Bennett left the table carrying Daniel about the waist like a sack of potatoes. Bennett searched on top of the refrigerator, inside the antique wooden bread box, and in the upper kitchen cabinets.

"Bennett, what are you looking for?" Suzanne asked with a grin that indicated that she already knew the answer.

"Rose was gone all day with Daniel. Suzanne was at home alone with nothing to do but answer the door. Suzanne knows that Bennett likes dessert and Bennett knows that Suzanne lives to please Bennett." Bennett turned to Suzanne. He lifted Daniel so that they were eye to eye and nodded. "So there's dessert here somewhere, Midget."

Suzanne and Rose laughed.

"Do not can tell which one is child!" Mustafa huffed.

Bennett squeezed his eyes shut and twisted his mouth. "Good thing language can't hear when you slaughter it, Moose!"

"My love," Suzanne said, catching Bennett's eye. "I notice that your waist is getting a little thicker. Since I like my man slim and trim, there's no dessert tonight. And that's only because I have your best interests at heart."

Bennett looked at Suzanne like she had just condemned him to ten years of hard labor. He turtled his head away from Daniel, tapped his chin to get the little boy's attention, and then poked out his bottom lip.

"Pout," Bennett said, emphasizing the word.

Daniel mouthed the word back to Bennett. "Pout."

Bennett stuck out his bottom lip again.

Daniel stuck out his bottom lip.

"That's my boy!" Bennett shouted in delight.

"I don't know if I can handle a Bennett Senior and a Bennett Junior!" Suzanne exclaimed.

Rose laughed at Bennett's antics. "Apparently young Daniel here gets around. We were shopping this morning when we met Connor's wife, Judy. I told her we needed to learn about Daniel's family and she took us to her friend, Vena Mae Thompson's home."

"Vena Mae has a hobby. She collects newspaper articles on just about everything you can imagine, hurricanes, floods, lightning strikes, dog attacks, the Korean War, the Vietnam War, train wrecks, weddings and baptisms, you name it, chances are good that Vena Mae has a scrapbook on it."

"She cuts out all the articles and puts them in scrapbooks. Her dining room has bookcases on two sides that are filled with her scrapbooks. One of them is the daily account of the Civil War, a scrapbook that her great-great-great grandmother put together!"

Bennett whistled. "That must be something to see. I wouldn't mind seeing it myself."

"Vena is so sweet! She and her sons, Augustus and Marty, and her daughter, Tansy, love Daniel too. Vena cried when I told her about Mary." Rose's expression turned somber. "We don't have to wonder anymore if the woman we found beside Daniel is his mother."

Rose took an envelope from the kitchen counter and pulled out the photo that Vena had copied for her. "This is Daniel and his parents at Daniel's baptism." Rose placed the photo on the table for all to see.

"She's beautiful," Suzanne said.

"So that's Daniel Ruddy, Daniel's dad. He has red hair and he definitely looks Irish," Bennett said. He looked at Daniel who played with a blue car and a green car on the floor. "Daniel must get his looks from his mother. His hair's curly but it's not red, it's blonde. And more than likely, as he gets older his blonde hair will turn darker like his mother's hair."

Bennett looked at the alphabet chart that was on the side of the refrigerator and spelled out handsome in sign language.

Suzanne turned serious eyes to Bennett. "So where is Daniel Ruddy Senior?"

"Oh!" Bennett cried. He stooped to capture a blue car and roll it back to Daniel. "Mister Daniel Ruddy Senior is in the Boyd County Jail in Kentucky and Melinda claims that he will be there for a while."

"It seems that Mr. Ruddy was on probation after a jail spell for attempting to rob a convenience store. No guns, no alcohol allowed so when cops stopped Ruddy with both, they invited him to serve some more time in Boyd County for violating his probation. I don't think Mr. Ruddy will be in the neighborhood for a while."

"But we still have to let him know that Daniel's all right and that he's with us." Rose squeezed her brows together. "And we may be the ones who have to let him know that his wife is dead."

"Oh, Rose! You're right! Who else is there?" Suzanne cried.

"This little guy looks like he's ready to go night-night," Bennett said. He tapped Daniel on the shoulder to get his attention. Bennett put both Bennett's palms together beside his face and then tapped his watch, signing bedtime to Daniel.

Daniel held his left palm upright and formed the fingers of his right hand like an umbrella and bounced it against his palm.

"Cookies!" Daniel signs *cookies*," Mustafa cried with a laugh.

"You think like me, don't you Midget?" Bennett said and scooped Daniel into his arms. "Well ladies shall I wash dishes or bathe the rug rat?"

"There no is rats in Mustafa's house Beanie!" Mustafa cried, clearly indignant.

"Whoa there, Moose, no insult intended!" Bennett exclaimed. To Daniel he said "I want cookies too, but Mommy's mean, she won't let us have any dessert. Pout."

Bennett stuck out his bottom lip.

Daniel stuck out his bottom lip.

Rose and Suzanne laughed.

Suzanne opened a bottom kitchen cabinet and withdrew a foil covered cookie sheet. Removing the foil she exclaimed "What do you know! I found some fresh, homemade chocolate chip cookies with raisins!"

Bennett signed to Daniel "Kiss Mommy, good Mommy!"

Daniel signed to Bennett—*cookies.*

Chapter Thirteen

"Suzanne, I can't find the top to my blue plaid pajamas. Got any idea where it might be? You didn't appropriate it for Daniel, did you?"

Bennett searched through the dresser drawer for the missing top. "Wowza, it's cold in here!" He exclaimed and glanced to Suzanne who appeared in the bathroom doorway.

Suzanne leaned against the door facing. Her damp ebony hair hung to her waist and her fresh scrubbed face glowed. She was dressed in fuzzy pink slippers and Bennett's extra-large blue plaid pajama top which fell below her knees. The cuffs of the long sleeves hung inches off her hands.

Bennett whistled. "My top never looked that good on me!"

"I can warm you up," Suzanne purred. She impishly shifted her petite frame into a more provocative position.

"What are you waiting for?" Bennett cried. He yanked back the covers and dived onto the bed with the enthusiasm of a kid on a trampoline. He bounced his eyes to Suzanne and patted the spot beside him.

Suzanne slowly rolled the right sleeve of his pajama top, turning the fabric one cuff width at a time.

"Suz!"

With her eyes fixed on Bennett's eyes Suzanne lifted one corner of her mouth in a slight, barely perceptible smile. She wriggled against the door frame in a manner that Webster's Dictionary describes as *provoking or tending to provoke, as to action, thought, feeling, etc.; stimulating, erotic.*

"Suz!" Bennett cried.

Suzanne rolled the left sleeve of his pajama top more slowly than she had rolled the right sleeve and with a maddening determination that was testing Bennett's good humor.

When at last Suzanne finished rolling the sleeve Bennett patted the bed again and then spread his arms wide as if expecting Suzanne to dive into them.

With her brown eyes burning into his Suzanne slowly shook her head and then turned her eyes to her fuzzy pink slippers.

Bennett slapped his forehead.

Suzanne glanced to Bennett's tortured expression and then again to her slippers. She bent slightly at the waist, placed one of her tiny hands on each side of her damp thighs and slowly, slowly slid her hands down her legs. The further she slid her hands down her legs, the more visible and enticing her petite posterior became.

"Smokin'!" Bennett cried, and then "Suz, if you don't get over here somebody's gonna be callin' 911 'cause either me or that doorframe is gonna burst into flames any minute!"

Suzanne giggled and pressed a finger to her lips. "Sshhh, you'll wake Rose and Mustafa!"

Her smile disappeared as she straightened herself and kicked off her slippers. "Bennett, we have to talk."

"Talk?" Bennett stared with incredulous eyes at Suzanne. "Talk? Now? You're not serious!"

"Oh but I am my love. We have some decisions to make and we're going to be getting busier and busier so we need to make them now. With a father in jail and no other relatives, Daniel needs someone to be legally responsible for him at least until his father gets out of jail. Somebody needs to file a petition for temporary guardianship."

"Rose and I discussed this. Since she discovered Daniel and is likely responsible for saving his life, I felt it was only fair to ask her first if she wants to be Daniel's guardian."

"Rose said that since Jan's missing and can't be here to discuss Daniel with her it might be best if you and I file for temporary guardianship."

Bennett reached for Suzanne's hand and kissed it. "You know I'm in. There's something about that little boy."

Suzanne kissed Bennett's forehead. "I know my love. It was love at first sight between the two of you."

"But Suz, what happens when Daniel's daddy gets out of jail? I can't imagine that he'll just say to us *Take him, he's yours!*"

Suzanne heaved a sigh. "I know. But Daniel can't wait. We can file for guardianship now and cross that Daniel Senior Bridge when we come to it."

"Suzanne, I don't have to think twice but I'm not the one who will have to handle the bulk of the responsibility in caring for a little boy, and this little boy is deaf which requires a little more handling."

"You know how I feel but this is our decision, not my decision. You, my love, are the number one priority of my life. If you agree, we take Daniel for however long we can have him. If you don't, we'll turn him over to the authorities and let them find a home for him."

Suzanne climbed over Bennett in the bed. She turned on her side and pulled a knee across his stomach. "Bennett Gardner, making you happy is my number one priority in life. If having Daniel makes you happy, then having Daniel makes me happy."

"I love the little boy, too. So, it's settled. Tomorrow you and Mustafa clean flood debris from the building that is to become Wolf Laurel Creek Walk-In Medical and I go to the Laurel County Courthouse and file a petition that names us as Daniel's temporary legal guardians."

Bennett pulled Suzanne on top of him. "So, Mrs. Gardner, I get to do the heavy lifting as usual and you get to go and play in town?"

"So it seems, my love."

"That's O.K. by me," Bennett said and then kissed Suzanne with the pent up passion that had simmered for too long. "Let me start by lifting that heavy pajama top off you."

Pink streaks of daylight tinted the sky, lighting Suzanne's way into the kitchen where she was startled to find Rose sitting alone at the table, crying in the semi-darkness.

"Rose, what is it?" Looks of compassion creased Suzanne's face beneath her knit brows. She stood behind Rose's chair and wrapped her arms around her sobbing friend.

Rose sniffled and then wiped her tears with a tissue. "Klaus called," she said. "He had to take Olga to the emergency room last night. She's developed stomach ulcers because she's so worried about Jan. Klaus said she calls the Defense Department every day and every day that Jan continues to be listed as missing in action, Olga slips further into depression."

Rose stood to her feet. "Here, I'll make us some coffee."

Suzanne protested with a firm hand on Rose's shoulder. You just keep your seat. I'll make the coffee. You talk."

Rose pulled her hair over her shoulder and played at braiding it. "Olga has stopped going out. She won't allow friends to visit, and Klaus says she's withdrawn from everything outside their home. He's as worried about Jan as Olga is and now he's getting desperately worried about Olga. She went to sleep with medications so he called."

Suzanne poured water into the coffee maker. "I'm sorry to hear that Olga is in such bad shape. I can't imagine being a mother and hearing that my child is missing in a war zone in a foreign country."

Rose tried to hide the tears that stung her eyes. "I know exactly how she feels! How do we know that he's just missing? How do we know if he's dead or alive? How do we continue on day after day as if everything is fine? We can't talk, we can't plan a future, we can't do anything but cry and watch every soldier that walks up the road, every truck that passes, and jump every time the phone rings or someone knocks on the door!"

"I understand Olga and I don't blame her. I would love to curl up on my bed and shut my eyes until Jan comes home. I don't want to be awake, I don't want to feel or think or guess or hope or…!"

"I can't let myself believe that I will never see him again. I love him too much! Nobody will ever love him as much as I do! I sleep with his picture on my pillow, pretending that he's here with me, fantasizing that I'll wake up and he'll be here and that nothing will ever keep us apart again!" Rose wiped her tears on her forearm and then crumpled in a wailing mass of long red hair.

"Oh, Rose! I wish there was something I could say or something I could do to comfort you! I know how much you miss him, how much it hurts you to wait day after day with no word, no news, nothing! Sweetie, I feel so helpless! And it breaks my heart to see you cry like this!"

"But Rose, you have an uncanny intuition, we've seen you demonstrate it time and again. That intuition must tell you something! Do you feel that Jan is dead? Don't you think that you would know it if Jan was dead?"

Rose sniffled and met Suzanne's eyes. "I know that I would know. My heart would tell me in an instant if Jan was dead. Jan's alive, I can feel him, but he's lost. There's something that keeps him from finding his way home. He may be injured or held against his will, but he's trying to get home, I know he is, I can feel it!"

"Are you going to tell Olga? Don't you think this would lift her spirits, maybe rescue her?" Suzanne's face brightened with a smile.

Rose inhaled a deep breath and scrubbed her hands over her face. "I must look a mess! And yes, I plan to tell Olga this morning. And Suzanne, I would not tell her that Jan is alive unless I felt certain of it!"

Suzanne hugged Rose with Suzanne's characteristic enthusiasm. "How about some coffee and some breakfast? We have a busy day ahead."

Widows Hollow
Kentucky

"Mama, what's got you up so early? You kept me awake all night with your tossin' and turnin'."

"Mule Johnson, you just carry yourself on back to bed! Something's bothering my Rose 'cause she didn't get no sleep last night and she's up early cryin'."

Mule shook his head of snowy curls and said with a grin "I ain't gonna axt how you know that. I am gonna axt what yer a studyin on doin' about it."

"I just fried up some chicken and I'm planning to make some homemade potato salad and some of my own special Kentucky baked beans." She turned from the kitchen counter where she made coffee and lowered her eyes to her husband. "And some fresh apple pies that my sweet baby Rose loves."

Mama John pointed with the metal coffee filter basket in hand. "So since yer up and here in my kitchen botherin' me, you can peel me some apples. They're right there in the pantry."

Mule pushed himself from his chair at the head of a dark oak dining table and dutifully shuffled across the gleaming tile floor to the pantry. Returning to the table with a basket of apples, he stopped to pull a knife from a wooden block on the counter.

He resumed his seat, began peeling an apple but stopped midway. He lifted his eyes to his wife, Early Mae Johnson. "You ain't plannin' no picnic when it's too cold fer bein' outside so what is it yer a plannin' with all this cookin' goin' on when even them danged ole noisy roosters gots the good sense to know it's too early to be a risin'!"

"I'm planning on loading me up a picnic basket of Early Mae's home cookin', putting it in the back of that shiny new black and white Ford Ranger pickup that yer so proud of yonder, and then takin' me a nap while you drive us to Wolf Laurel Creek, West Virginia!"

"Woman, has you done lost yore senses? We can't be traipsin' off to no West Virginia! We gots horses to see to, a farm to run, mares what need close tendin' and young'uns what ain't got a lick of sense without we're here to remind em'!"

"Daddy, you know there's no use in arguing with Mama! And there's no reason for you not to go."

Mama John beamed a smile and wrapped Jimbo, the oldest of her six children, in her arms. This was no easy feat as the twenty-six year old stood 6' 4" and had the broad shoulders and muscular build of both of his NFL heroes, Dallas Cowboys Roger Staubach and Craig Morton.

Jimbo, after asking his family repeatedly to abandon calling him by his childhood name had finally resigned himself to the reality that they would always call him Jimbo.

He had entered the kitchen through the back door and returned now to open it upon hearing a knock.

"Jimmy Joe! I thought you had an early meeting with contractors in Ashford," Jimbo said and landed a friendly punch on Jimmy Joe's shoulder.

Jimmy Joe grinned. "I do but the chickens are still sleeping!" He turned to Mama John and said as he gave her a hug "What are you cooking, Mama? I couldn't sleep for smelling it!"

Mule wagged his head. "She's a wakin' up the whole neighborhood! Can't nobody get no sleep around here. If Early Mae's up, everbody's up."

A rooster crowed from a far pasture fence. "She done gone and waked up them danged roosters!" Mule complained.

"Cheer up, Daddy! You and Mama need to take some time off," Jimbo said and squeezed Mule's thin shoulders with affection. He took cups from the cabinet and poured coffee for himself and for Rose McKinley's oldest brother, Jimmy Joe.

"Daddy, you want some coffee?"

"Might as well, I'm up."

"You sit. I'll get his coffee," Mama John instructed Jimbo.

She poured coffee for herself and for Mule and then placed Mule's coffee before him. "I best make another pot, ain't no telling who's gonna show up here this morning."

"Umm, good idea Mama!" Two voices cried in unison as Lucy and Lottie, Mama John's eighteen-year-old twin daughters banged through the back door.

"It's cold out there!" Lottie exclaimed. "What are you cooking? We smelled it all the way up the hollow!"

"Morning girls! I fried up some chicken to take to Rose and her friends in West Virginia."

"So you told Daddy you're going?" Lucy asked with a laugh and hugged her father.

Mule shot a glance from his identical twin daughters to Jimmy Joe and Jimbo. "That's why all of you is showin' up here this mornin' when the sun ain't even up yet!"

"Mama knew you'd find a hundred excuses not to go so we're here to eliminate them for you," Lucy said. She glanced about the room. "Anybody else hungry? I'm gonna bake some biscuits and fry up some ham and eggs."

"Great! I'll take two over easy," Jimmy Joe said. He stepped to the refrigerator and removed a carton of eggs and left-over ham.

"We might as well make enough for everybody, Lucy. Our little brothers, Buddy, Willie, and Petey, are in the front barn watching their favorite mare, Lady Anne. She could foal any time and they want to stay with her in case there are complications. From all appearances, her foal may be bigger than Lady Anne."

Lottie got out a baking sheet, opened two cans of biscuits and placed them on the sheet. "Me and Lucy will take care of our baby sister, Jasmine, get her off to school and back. She's protesting of course, she thinks that at age sixteen she doesn't need anyone to look after her, but don't you worry, Daddy, we'll look after her anyway, and Jimmy Joe, your baby sister's gonna stay with us, too."

"I don't need anyone to look after me but I do need someone to get out of the way so I can get to the coffee!" Jasmine exclaimed.

Long and lanky with golden chocolate skin, she skipped down the stairs dressed in dark blue Kentucky Wildcat pajamas that had a big cat paw on the front of her shirt.

"Olivia's got basketball practice this afternoon. I'll stay in the gym and then ride home with her. I can do my homework while she's practicing. Lady Anne's not going to foal any sooner than tonight. I want my homework out of the way so I'll be free to concentrate on her."

"What makes you so sure she won't foal until tonight Lil' Sista? Buddy, Willie, and Petey slept in the barn last night, waiting on her," Jimbo said.

Jasmine poured herself a cup of coffee. "I don't know what makes me so sure, I just feel it."

"Come hug your mama, baby girl!" Mama John invited. She opened her arms and embraced her beautiful daughter. "I know this old woman can't explain it, but you have instincts about animals like nobody has ever seen. You're gonna make a right fine veterinarian, Jasmine."

"I hope so, Mama, but I wish I could do it without all this studying. I'd rather be with the horses and mules than at a desk with a book in my face."

"Nothing worth having comes easy, child. You have to work for what you get. But the Good Lord has given you a special gift with animals and if you continue with your grades, you'll have a scholarship to vet school."

"Texas A&M University, Mama, not vet school. I want to be the first black woman to earn a DVM degree from Texas A&M. Two years ago Dr. James Courtney was A&M's first black man to receive a DVM degree and I plan to be the first black woman!"

"Well in the meantime, Madame Veterinarian, how about getting the biscuits out of the oven? The gravy's almost done and somebody needs to yell for Peach, Olivia and the boys," Jimmy Joe said to Jasmine at the same time as he tossed her an oven mitt.

Jimbo pulled open the back door to a blast of cold air. He stuck his head out the door and yelled. "Buddy, Willie, Petey, Olivia! Breakfast is ready, come and get it!"

He quickly crossed the kitchen in his long strides and then yelled from the foot of the stairs "Peach, if you want some breakfast you better get down here now!"

"If there was one soul still a sleepin' in this holler, they awake now!" Mule grumbled. "Pass me a biscuit 'fore them wild young'uns gets in here."

When the remaining members of the Johnson and McKinley families had washed up and seated themselves around Mama John's table they bowed their heads with their older siblings and with Mule and Mama John and joined hands.

"Lord, we thank you for this day, for our family and our neighbors and for this food. Remind us, Lord, that we are blessed. Watch over Rose while she's away from us and return her safely home. Help us to care and to share with all those we meet. In Jesus' name, Amen."

Mule asked the blessing as he always did as head of the house and then he wasted no time in ticking off a list of chores that he felt needed immediate attention at Rose McKinley's S&S Stables.

"Daddy, you don't need to worry about any of this," Jimbo said. "Buddy, Willie and Petey will help the hands feed the horses. I'll bring the hay up from the North pasture. Jimmy Joe's gonna pick up the feed and the rest of the supplies on the list when he goes into town for his meeting. We'll all help bathe and exercise the horses."

"Lucy and I won't let anybody starve while you're gone, Mama," Lottie said with a glance around the table at the ten adult children of the McKinley and Johnson families.

"We'll feed the girls and these five overgrown human garbage disposals that call themselves boys," she added with a playful poke at Jimmy Joe.

"Who are you calling boys?" He shot back. "Nothing at this table but men, hardworking men!"

"That'll be the day!" Jasmine exclaimed.

Seeing her mother's coffee cup empty, Lottie took the cup to refill it. She replaced the cup in front of her mother and said "Jasmine, Peach, and Olivia will be fine, Mama. We'll lock them in the barn if they get to giggling too loud watching their favorite TV shows, *Mash, Sanford and Son, and The Waltons.*"

Jimbo caught his father's eye. "And Daddy, if we run into a problem, the hands are here. And if it's something they can't handle, we'll call Klaus."

Jimmy Joe swallowed a last bite and then cleared his throat. "This might not be the best time to call Klaus," he said.

He glanced around the table at the white faces of his siblings and at the black faces of the neighbors who were the same as family although they had lived across the road from a time before he, Rose or any of their younger siblings were born.

There was no line to blur, no difference between the two families other than the physical address of their separate homes.

Everyone in the remote Appalachian Mountain community known as Widows Hollow in the far Southeastern corner of the Cumberland Mountains had called Early Mae Johnson Mama John for as far back as Jimmy Joe could remember.

Rose was Jimmy Joe's older sibling by fourteen months. And it was Rose, who, at age sixteen had inherited the task of raising her three younger brothers and one sister.

Mama John had become Mama to the McKinley brood following the death of their mother, Isabel, who had died from the complications of a stroke that had left her paralyzed on one side.

The two families had shared everything. Members of both families bore one another's sorrows. And the news that Jimmy Joe was about to share concerning Olga Vandeventer was another of those sorrows.

Olga was Rose McKinley's fiancé, Jan's, mother.

Rose and Jan's engagement would itself be classified by any astute writer as a miracle. But that's another story.

"I talked to Rose this morning. She said that Klaus has his hands full. Olga has developed stomach ulcers. They're getting really bad because she's so worried about Jan and the news that he's missing in Vietnam."

"The doctors recommend that Olga have surgery but she refuses. She's becoming reclusive and depressed. Klaus says that she's lost interest in anything outside their home."

Jimmy Joe felt the concern around the table for Olga. It showed in the faces of his friends and his family. It showed in the tears in Mama John's eyes.

"Klaus still has a world-class thoroughbred farm to run but he feels that he can't leave Olga's side. So, all things considered, if we have a problem here, we don't want to call Klaus. Not until things get better for him and Olga."

"Jimmy Joe, hearing about that sweet little woman just breaks my heart. God bless her, I wish there was something this ole black woman could do for her," Mama John said, and wiped tears from her eyes.

"There is something Mama and you're good at it. You can pray for her. We can all pray for her. And for Jan."

Chapter Fourteen

"Rose, this is ridiculous!   Why do I feel so nervous?
I haven't felt nerves like this since the day I took my exam
before the Kentucky Medical Review Board."

Rose laughed.

Suzanne made a face.   "How can you laugh?   It isn't
funny."

"It's funny to me," Rose said.   "I don't think I've ever
seen you nervous about anything.   It's not like you're
asking for an audience with the pope.   You're just asking
for temporary guardianship of Daniel."

Rose tried to think of something encouraging to say.
Suzanne looked so unlike Suzanne.   The poor woman was
really upset.

"Honestly, I don't see a problem here!" Rose
exclaimed.   "His father can't take care of him while he's in
jail and there isn't anyone else.   Vena said Daniel doesn't
have any other relatives.   So what are you worried about?"

"I don't know. It's silly isn't it?" Suzanne had a sheepish look on her face.

"Uh oh!"

"Uh oh, what?" Suzanne looked alarmed. She glanced at Rose from the passenger side of Rose's pickup.

"Daniel's shaking a "T" hand at us. He has to go to the bathroom. Good timing, too!" Rose said, spewing a breath. "Here's the courthouse."

"Well, at least it's not as bad as it was," Bennett said, noting the progress that the National Guard and many other organizations had made in cleaning up the stark reminders of the worst flood in West Virginia's history.

"Wonder how they're going to get that church off the railroad tracks?" He asked Mustafa who drove the two of them down the valley to the site of Mustafa's future medical clinic.

Mustafa looked on with interest at the white frame church that sat in the middle of the railroad tracks that bordered the East side of the narrow valley.

"What is that?" He asked, pointing to a large green Army truck that sped toward one corner of the church.

Shouting men who stood near the church seemed to be directing the truck.

"The military call that a Deuce N Half, Moose. Wonder what those guys are yelling?"

Bennett rolled down his window as Mustafa approached the scene.

"Over here, bring that truck over here! There's a woman's body under the corner of this church!"

Mustafa shifted his eyes to Bennett. "You want I stop?"

"No need, Moose. There isn't anything that we can do. We'd just be in the way. There's no way that woman is alive after all this time. She's another victim and from what we've seen, there's no in-between in this disaster. The victims are either dead or they're alive and unscathed."

Mustafa drove a short distance further when Bennett pointed and cried in excitement. "Look at that! That's a 1965 Chevy Impala and it doesn't have a scratch on it."

The red and white Impala was parked in a garage that seemingly hadn't been touched by the flood, yet there were no other structures nearby. The house that had once belonged with the garage and any neighboring structures were gone.

"This is just mind-blowing, Moose! Hundreds of houses are piled up in a heap, washed downriver by the flood while others remain untouched. Some families lost multiple family members, others lost none. It just doesn't make any sense at all," Bennett lamented.

"But it's times like these Moose," Bennett said with a shake of his head "that I'm glad that we're doctors. I'm glad we can contribute, that we can help these poor people in some small way."

Mustafa pulled up in front of a single story sand colored building that was located in the little town of Fremont, about eight miles down the valley from his home. Two–story white framed homes flanked the building, homes that looked to have escaped the flood's ravages altogether.

But across the road things looked different. Railroad track lay twisted like pretzels on top of houses that had been smashed together by the flood.

A bass boat sat on its trailer beside the gnarled track as though waiting for transport to any one of West Virginia's lakes.

Uprooted trees lay on their sides among twisted bicycles, overturned rail cars, furniture and household items that sank into the wet, knee-deep, stinking mud.

"Face masks might have been a good idea today. The stench from the flood waters is unbearable," Bennett said, making a face.

Having arrived at the site of what was to be Mustafa's clinic, Bennett scrambled from the truck. He pulled on leather gloves and began unloading window glass from the back of Mustafa's truck while Mustafa unlocked the building.

The approximately 4000 square foot stucco building which had in the past served the townspeople as a drugstore and delicatessen combination had chain link fencing stretched across the front windows and the glass door of the building.

"Interesting touch," Bennett remarked.

"Realtor tells me young people looking for heroin and cocaine break windows so owner use fence," Mustafa replied.

"That's not good," Bennett replied. "You don't want to be replacing windows and that fencing doesn't look like a warm welcome to a clinic. It looks kind of scary, actually."

"Nobody break Mustafa's windows!" Mustafa exclaimed and then returned to the truck to help Bennett unload the glass.

"Ugh!" Bennett grunted. "I believe you! What is this glass, bullet proof?"

"Nobody break," Mustafa repeated.

They carried the glass inside and then stopped to catch their breath. "So, Dr. Dhingra, where do we begin? Have you had someone inspect the roof? Is it sound or does it need replacing or repair? There's no point in starting on the interior unless the roof is sound," Bennett said.

He walked from room to room looking for water marks on the ceiling or puddles on the floor. "It appears that your roof may have escaped any flood damage."

"I get ladder. We check roof one time again," Mustafa said.

"I knew you were gonna say that," Bennett quipped but dutifully followed Mustafa back to the truck.

"Well that was a brief but thorough education on how to file a petition for temporary guardianship in Laurel County, West Virginia." Suzanne said with a laugh. "The Circuit Court Clerk really knows her stuff. What made me think that I could do this without an attorney?"

"This list of eligibility factors that she gave me says that any adult may qualify for a West Virginia guardianship or conservatorship. Mine and Bennett's backgrounds will be investigated, criminal, financial, and any relationship that we may have had with Daniel as well as our overall character."

Suzanne read from the list: "The court will always hear testimony from the ward."

"Probably not in this case," she remarked.

"Bennett and I will have to complete an educational class and training as required by the court within 30 days of being approved, then we must submit an affidavit to the court, and then take an oath to fulfill all the duties required in West Virginia guardianships."

"Copies must be sent to Daniel," Suzanne said with a giggle. "A lot of good that will do since Daniel doesn't do a lot of reading."

"And to all people who received a copy of the petition within fourteen days of the appointment. After that we will need to file annual reports with the court."

"That sounds easy enough," Rose said in an encouraging tone.

"Yes, but then there's this little section that says that "West Virginia guardianships also give the respondent certain rights after the petition has been filed. The respondent," Suzanne said with a glance at Rose, "being Daniel's father who we believe to this point to be of questionable character with violent tendencies."

"He has to be notified of the time and place of the hearing, has to be represented by legal counsel, and has to be present at all proceedings unless he's medically exempt. And he also has a right to trial by jury and can even cross examine witnesses!"

Rose winced and bit her lip. "Ooh, that could get sticky."

Suzanne nodded. "But if what Vena Mae and that young girl, Melinda, said about Daniel's father not really wanting Daniel, he may not be a problem at all."

Having no idea just how wrong she was, Suzanne glanced at Daniel and smiled.

Chapter Fifteen

Daniel squashed his hand and brought it to his mouth.

"Our boy's hungry. Let's stop by the house and make the guys some lunch. We can check on them and see if they need anything. After that maybe I'll find an attorney who can file the guardianship petition for us."

"Suzanne, there's someone in Mustafa's driveway. Do you recognize that truck?"

"No, but it has Kentucky plates."

Rose pulled into the driveway beside the truck and then squealed in delight. "It's Mama John and Mule!"

She shoved open her door and then yanked open the passenger door of Mule's truck. "Mama John!" She cried and hugged the woman with a fierce hug. "I'm so glad to see you! What brings you to West Virginia? Is everything all right at home? I just talked to Jimmy Joe yesterday."

Suzanne joined them with Daniel in her arms.

Mama John hugged Suzanne. "Miss Suzanne, you're lookin' pretty as ever! And who is this young fella? He's a mighty handsome child."

Mule completed the circle and hugged Rose and Suzanne. "Hit shore is good to see you ladies agin, but I ain't never seen nothin' like that mess back there!"

Mule removed his UK Wildcats ball cap and shook his head. "I didn't reckon there was no power on this earth what could twist a steel railroad tie like hit was nothin'!"

Mule wagged his head. "Hearin' 'bout this flood was one thing, seein' all these torn up houses and church houses piled on top of one another and hearin' all this noise and commotion with the National Guard and all them other military outfits tryin' to sort it all out is another!"

"Uh Um!" He repeated. "I ain't never seen nothin' like it!"

"Mama John, Mule, this is Daniel," Suzanne said. Pointing first to Mama John, and then to Mule, she spelled their names with her fingers for Daniel.

"This child can't hear?" Mama John cried. She reached for Daniel and hugged the little guy. "Bless your heart, baby, bless your little heart!"

"Well, what are we standing out here for? Mama John, you and Mule come on in. We just stopped by here to make some lunch for Bennett and Mustafa. They're down at Mustafa's building, trying to turn it into a clinic."

Mama John waved a hand in the air. "Don't you worry none about makin' lunch fer Mr. Bennett and Mr. Mustafa. I done brought along some fried chicken with all the trimmings and a couple of apple pies that I baked just this morning!"

"There's some soda pop in that cooler, plates and everything else we need for a picnic right here in these bags. You just lead the way, Rose Baby, and we'll go feed Mr. Bennett and Mr. Mustafa."

Rose's eyes sparkled. "Did you hear that, Suzanne, Mama John's fried chicken and apple pies? I can't wait! Let's go!"

She said to Daniel "Fried chicken and apple pies, you're gonna love it!"

"Love it!" Daniel formed the words with his lips.

Suzanne pulled him close and hugged him. "This child is incredible! He's teaching himself to read lips!"

The four adults and Daniel piled back into their pickups for the short drive down the valley to Mustafa's new site.

Bennett had just replaced the ladder in the back of the truck when Suzanne and friends arrived.

"Hey there Mama John, Mule!"

He said with a grin to Suzanne "You went all the way to Kentucky to recruit help?"

"Yep! And help has arrived. They brought with them Mama John's fried chicken and homemade apple pies!"

Bennett hugged the old black woman who beamed at him with "You been missing my cookin', Mister Bennett?"

"I can't tell you how badly I've been missing it, Mama! How is everyone? All the kids?"

Are they getting the hang of thoroughbred ranching?"

"They're working at it," Mule answered. Getting better little by little. They love them horses like they's children."

Bennett stuck out his hand to Mule, shook Mule's heartily, and then grabbed the man in a bear hug. "How's that wild bunch in Kentucky treating you Mule? You and Mama come inside and meet our friend, Mustafa."

"Mustafa, our friends Mule and Mama John Johnson."

Mustafa nodded a polite nod to Mama John. He shook hands with Mule and invited him to come with Bennett and look around.

The women set out a picnic on the counter of what had formerly been the town's drugstore-delicatessen. The chrome counter stools with their red and white plastic checkerboard seats remained lined up in front of the counter.

Suzanne pulled pieces of chicken from a leg for Daniel and then scooped potato salad and baked beans on his plate. She signed to him, *eat now*, and then lifted him onto a stool but Daniel protested.

Before Suzanne could stop him, Daniel flipped onto his stomach, squirmed off the stool and ran after Bennett as fast as his little legs could move.

"Bennett!" Suzanne yelled.

Bennett turned just in time to prevent Daniel from colliding with him and then he caught the child up in his arms.

Bennett looked to Suzanne for instructions.

"We won't push it this time, Bennett. Daniel has enough to deal with. We won't make an issue of his refusing to eat because he prefers to be with you."

Suzanne smiled one of those smiles that melted Bennett's heart. "I certainly don't blame him. I prefer to be with you too."

With Daniel in his arms, Bennett walked back to Suzanne and kissed her.

Suzanne spelled *kiss* with her fingers for Daniel.

Bennett smiled. "Like this," he said, and kissed Suzanne again.

Daniel leaned from Bennett's arms and kissed Suzanne in the same way that Bennett had just kissed her. "Like this," he mouthed.

"That's my boy!" Bennett whooped.

Rose and Suzanne and Mama John did some catching up while the men decided how and in what steps they would remodel Mustafa's building.

Securing the outside of the building would have to come first in case any nearby residents suffered from the same drug addictions that had made it necessary to cover the existing windows with fencing.

"It's a good thing you showed up today Mule. Mustafa and I together can't lift those windows. Those suckers are heavy and because of their weight we're going to have to reinforce the window frames, too."

"You guys come and get it!" Rose called out. She stopped to squeeze Mama John's shoulders in passing. "This is such an unexpected treat, Mama, I'm so glad you and Mule are here."

The men wasted no time climbing onto stools and making their plates. Bennett seated Daniel on a stool between himself and Suzanne.

Suzanne placed Daniel's plate before him, pointed to the food on his plate, and spelled the words with her fingers.

Daniel replied by signing *Eat now*.

"Oh, Lord," Suzanne said. "You're already acting like Bennett!"

Bennett could not respond as his mouth was full of Mama John's chicken. "Heavenly!" He cried and waved what remained of a chicken leg at Mule. "Mule, I will never understand how you can be rail thin and be married to this woman! Don't you eat?"

Mule chuckled and said "I shore do, I eat Mama's cooking at least three times a day, but I don't sit much. I like to be outside, messing with the horses, and taking care of the pastures on my tractor. There's always plenty to do and when I think I might catch up, something else comes along that I didn't reckon on havin' to do."

"I know what you mean, Mule. Nobody around here figured on having their lives destroyed or rearranged by this flood. This valley was home to 5000 before the flood and now 4000 of those people are homeless."

"Mustafa's one of the lucky ones. The flood didn't touch his home or this building. That's the good news. The bad news is that the people of Wolf Laurel Creek have ingrained mountain ways. They tend to be suspicious of outsiders or anyone else that is not neighbor or kin."

"That sort of clannish thinking wasn't so bad here in the communities where socializing was part of everyone's routine, but higher up in the mountains and in the more remote hollows and ridges, things are different."

"Those folks were distrusting to begin with but little by little they ventured further and further away from their homes and grew more confident in a larger community. Now this flood has set them back in a way that can't be determined for who knows how long?"

"Can I get anybody anything from the cooler?" Suzanne asked. "Daniel wants more pop." She snapped the lid off a can and poured soda into Daniel's cup.

"Mustafa told us that it took the people in the outlying areas a while but they finally came to trust the mining company that operated at the top of this valley."

"They believed the officials who assured them repeatedly that the dams were safe. And now they've learned in the most horrific way that those responsible for the mines betrayed their trust."

"We saw that ourselves in Widows Hollow," Rose commented. "Government people came around wanting to buy trees, then the mineral rights. They made it sound like they were offering us a great deal but in fact had we accepted their offers, they would have been robbing us outright. Most everyone in the hollow, including me, fell for their lies. But we had a friend who didn't."

Mule wagged his head. "And that would be Stump. I ain't never gonna stop missin' my dear old friend and fishin' buddy! There wasn't much that Stump didn't know. And before the Good Lord taked him, Mister Stump seen to it that ever one of his friends and neighbors in Widows Hollow would be seen to."

"Stump never had no schoolin' but what he did know was enough to save our homes from bein' mowed down and turned into a high-falutin' country club fer the rich folk."

"God bless his soul! May that good man rest in peace!" Mama John added.

"When Mustafa come here, mountain people come to town to clinics. They bring children and babies. Since flood, Mustafa see no one from mountains. But sickness does no stop because of flood. Mountain people need doctor but do not come for afraid."

"Somebody's sleepy," Bennett said. His words drew everyone's attention to Daniel's heavy eyes.

"Let me rock that baby to sleep," Mama John offered. "It's been way too long since this ole woman rocked a sweet baby."

Suzanne looked to Bennett with doubtful eyes. "Um, Mama John, Daniel's kind of skittish around strangers. He seems to be most comfortable with Bennett."

Mama John lifted the little boy from the stool and cradled him against her shoulder.

Daniel did not resist, but wrapped his arms about Mama John's neck and lay limp and still in her arms.

Mama John cradled Daniel. She rocked her body back and forth and softly sang one of her favorite hymns, "His Eye is on the Sparrow".

"Early Mae done always had a way with kids," Mule said. "I ain't never seen one what wouldn't take to 'er immediate like."

"Mama John, Daniel's heavy. Let's take him to the house so you can sit in a rocking chair and be comfort...."

"Doc, Doc.... *Slap*! "Doctor. Neigh, neigh...." *Clap!* "Neighbor needs doctor!"

Lenny Walker burst through the door and attempted to communicate to Bennett and Mustafa a medical emergency in the only way he knew.

The man was dressed in the same flannel shirt and overalls that he wore when the two doctors first met him.

"Is it your sister or the baby?" Bennett asked, assuming that it would be one or the other.

Lenny's stutter seemed to get worse when the man was excited or agitated. Despite his stutter, he slapped and clapped until he got his message delivered. "No, Frank Perkins. Ellie says Frank dying."

Bennett wiped his hands as he spoke. "Where is he?"

"In…, in…." *Slap*! "Frank's…, Frank's …." *Clap!* "Truck."

Satisfied that he had delivered his message to the doctors, Lenny clasped his hands behind his back and hurried to get close to Mama John so that he could see Daniel's face.

Lenny kissed Daniel on top of his head and then gently patted the boy on his back.

With Mustafa and Mule following close behind, Bennett rushed outside to the parking lot and to a beat up pickup truck. The dust and dirt on the truck was so thick that seeing inside the vehicle was impossible except through the windshield.

Bennett yanked open the passenger door and with a gasp, caught the corpse-like man that fell from the seat and into Bennett's arms.

The man appeared to be in his mid to late sixties with skin as wrinkled and dry as parchment.

He had a dirty gray beard and a patch of gray hair on the back of his head. His eyes were sunken and hollow with blood red rims. The near-skeletal figure was skin and bones with a stomach that was distended and engorged.

Bennett had no trouble carrying the weightless man but walked quickly as the man retched continually.

Bennett lay the man on the counter and began to examine him. "What's going on here? How long has he been like this?" Bennett addressed his question to a small, stooped woman who was dressed in a plaid housedress with a white sweater and worn sneakers.

The woman did not answer. She looked terrified, so terrified that Rose feared the fragile creature might faint any minute.

Rose lay a hand on the woman's shoulder and chose to talk to her in the same way that Rose has talked as a child in Widows Hollow.

"Ain't no reason fer you to be afeared. Ain't nobody gonna hurt you or your man. My name's Rose McKinley,

I'm from Widows Hollow, Kentucky where I grew up in them mountains."

"This here's Doctor Bennett Gardner and this is Dr. Mustafa Dhingra. These ladies here are my friends, Suzanne," Rose said, and pointed to the women as she introduced them, "and Mama John." She pointed to Mule. "And this is Mama John's husband, Mule, and this little baby here is Daniel."

Lenny jabbed a finger at the woman. "And.... And...." *Slap!* "This is…, is…," *Clap!* "Ellie Perkins."

Rose lay a gentle hand on the woman's shoulder and guided her to one of the counter stools. "Please sit Miss Ellie. Could I get you some pop or a glass of water?"

With her eyes fixed on her husband, the woman shook her head rapidly. "No, child, thank you." She clasped her hands in her lap and rolled her handkerchief with her thumbs.

"He ain't et nothin' in a week or more. He looks to be gainin' weight and gettin' on better fer a spell, then he lapses back to this where he ain't eatin' and is a wantin' to throw up all the time."

Mustafa and Bennett examined the man and quickly came to the same conclusion.

Mustafa glanced to Rose and then followed her lead in talking to the woman. "Miss Ellie, your husband is very ill. He needs some tests for to know what is wrong. We can no do tests here, he must go to hospital. We will drive if you like."

Ellie clutched a hand to her heart. A look of sheer panic twisted her face. "Oh, law, no! My Frank don't cotton to no hospitals! He ain't never been to no hospital and he ain't never gonna go to no hospital! Hit ain't our way!" Her eyes grew wide and filled with tears.

"Miss Ellie, your husband is gravely ill. If he gets any weaker, his heart will stop. There's no way for us to know what's wrong with him without running some tests. We can't run them here because we don't have our equipment yet," Bennett said in a firm voice in an attempt to reason with the woman.

"I can't take Frank to no hospital! He won't hear of it!" Ellie sobbed.

Suzanne pulled a hand to her mouth. Her heart went out to the frightened, weeping woman.

Mama John prayed and continued to rock Daniel.

Rose looked from the dying man to the boxes and bags of picnic items that she and Suzanne had packed away.

She began searching through bags and containers until she found jars of sugar and honey and a plastic spoon.

With items in hand she walked past Bennett and Mustafa who looked on with questioning eyes, and on to the sick man who no longer retched, but lay still and quiet.

"He's so weak he can't even try to throw up no more," Rose said. She filled the plastic spoon with sugar and forced it into the man's mouth. After a minute she filled the spoon with honey and forced it into the man's mouth.

"What are you…?" Bennett began.

Rose cut him off with "I need you to go get me some molasses. Mustafa has some on the bottom shelf nearest the refrigerator. Mr. Perkins ain't got long so you need to hurry."

Bennett met his wife's eyes. "Come on, I'll go with you. I can find the molasses faster," Suzanne said.

"Mustafa, can you and Lenny build a fire? It doesn't need to be a big one, just a fire." Rose asked.

"Sure, we build fire. No problem," Mustafa replied. "But Mustafa no understand."

"Let me give you a hand with that fire," Mule said, and followed the two men outside.

Ellie patted her eyes with her handkerchief and then looked to Rose. "I thought you was from the mountains like me and Frank fer yer speakin' like our kind. But then yer speakin' changed and now I ain't got no notion 'bout you."

A softness entered Rose's eyes with her smile. "Miss Ellie, I'm from Widows Hollow, high up in the Cumberland Highlands of the Appalachian Mountains of Kentucky. I was raised speakin' like you and my brothers and sister and all my neighbors were raised speakin' like you."

"When I was sixteen my life changed and I got opportunities that I never had before. I was fortunate enough to be able to go to school and to learn some fine things."

"There's a time fer speakin' like I was raised and a time for speaking like I learned in school. You was too afeared of all of us strangers and I didn't want you to be afraid of us so I talked like I was raised so that you wouldn't be afraid."

"And you ain't afeared now, are you?" Rose's smiled widened.

"No 'em, I reckon I ain't, but I still can't be takin' my Frank to no hospital. Hit would rile him somethin' awful."

Rose winked at the woman. "Well now Miss Ellie, we don't want to be a rilin' yer Frank, so how about we make him better so he kin go home and enjoy hisself?"

Ellie burst into tears.

Rose hurried to her. "What is it? What is it, Ellie?"

The woman wagged her head. "He's been sick fer such a long time. I can't recollect when he wasn't sick. Kin you make 'im better? Kin you make my Frank well?"

The pleading in the woman's eyes tore at Rose's heart. She squeezed the woman against her and said "Miss Ellie, I can't do nothin' but I got a friend and there ain't nothin' He can't do."

"We make fire," Mustafa announced upon his return with Mule and Lenny.

"Molasses as requested!" Bennett exclaimed as he and Suzanne hurried through the door.

Bennett placed the jar of molasses on the counter and then lay his hand on Frank Perkins' heart. "This man needs to be in the hospital," Bennett said unhappily.

Rose grabbed the molasses and to his surprise, she grabbed Mustafa's hand. Rose pulled the man along with her and away from the others. She whispered something to him in a hurried, urgent manner.

Rose ended the conversation with a nod and then released Mustafa's hand. She returned to Ellie's side and seated herself on a stool.

Mama John caught Rose's eye with an expression that Rose alone could interpret. Mama John began to hum *What a Friend we have in Jesus.*

Mustafa stepped to the counter beside the sick man. He straightened his shoulders and stood tall.

Bennett shot a glance to Rose who nodded and then turned her attention again to Mustafa who gently turned Frank Perkins on his side so that the desperately ill man faced the front of the counter.

Mustafa opened the jar of molasses and placed the open jar next to Frank's mouth.

Bennett scowled. "Suzanne, I don't know if I can sit here and watch this. What the heck is Mustafa doing? That man's heart is so weak I don't expect him to live another thirty minutes! Wasting time like this isn't going to help him."

Suzanne took Bennett's hands in her own. "I understand your concerns my love. But I also remember a young girl named Pick. And a friend that was to have his leg amputated. And a dying baby."

Bennett squeezed Suzanne's hands and then he kissed her. "You're right. Her name has changed but she hasn't."

"Mustafa's performing the procedure but Rosemillion is the coach."

Bennett snapped his fingers. "That's what she was whispering to him about! She wants Mustafa to get the credit if Frank pulls through!"

Suzanne's eyes sparkled. "If?"

Bennett looked again to Rose.

The woman held Ellie's hand. Bennett could not see Rose's eyes because Rose had her head bowed and she moved her lips in silence.

Hearing an alarming and sudden noise, Bennett turned in horror to Frank Perkins.

The man wheezed a violent, rattling breath. His eyes flew open. His chest rose and fell with his struggle.

Mama John's face convulsed. "Oh, my good Lord in Heaven!" She cried. "Mule, get in front of me! I don't want to see no more of this!"

Bennett looked stricken. "Oh, my God!" He cried. "Is that what I think it is?"

Wide-eyed and with an otherwise blank expression, Mustafa turned to Bennett who sprang from his seat. He grabbed plastic bags off the picnic items and pulled them over his hands.

Frank choked and heaved and retched as Bennett pulled the monstrous tape worm that had come close to stealing Frank's life from Frank's throat.

Susanne grabbed her stomach and ran out the door.

Rose squeezed Ellie's hand. "Yer Frank's gonna be all better now!" She said. "He's likely been sharing his supper with that worm for quite a while, feeding him until the worm got too big and Frank got too weak to feed the both of them."

Ellie's lips trembled. Tears fell from her eyes. Without a word she clutched Rose to her and wept on her shoulder.

"Unbelievable! Look at that monster!" Bennett pointed to the slimy heap that was the worm. "That thing has to be at least twelve feet long!" Bennett exclaimed.

"Mule Johnson, I done told you I didn't want to see that thing!" Mama John cried.

"Woman, I done stood in front of you like you axt! If you ain't a' wantin' to see that nasty worm what was killing Mister Frank, close yer eyes!"

"Throw in fire!" Mustafa instructed.

"Gladly, Moose!" Bennett said, feeling only too glad to dispose of the horrible thing.

Within the hour Frank Perkins sat upright and complained that he was starving. His stomach had shrunk back to its normal size.

Ellie Perkins could not hug the doctors and their friends often enough. "Thank you!" She repeated with every hug.

Hugging Rose for the third or fourth time she said "If there's anything yer a'needin' or anything we can do fer you, you just come on up to Low Gap Hollow and let us know! We'll be tellin' everbody on the mountain about how you saved my Frank's life."

"Wait, Ellie," Rose said in dismay. "I didn't do anything. It was Dr. Dhingra, Dr. Mustafa Dhingra. He's the one that saved your Frank. Dr. Dhingra is a wonderful doctor and you can help us by telling your neighbors."

"Your neighbors and all the people in this valley need Dr. Dhingra. He needs for them to trust him and to depend on him." Rose changed her expression to one of hopeful expectation. "So will you spread the word for us?"

"We shore will!" Frank cried. "You kin count on it Miss Rose! And Miss Mama John, this here's the best fried chicken I ever et!"

Chapter Sixteen

"So what are you and this young man going to do today while I see the attorney?" Suzanne asked. She poured coffee for herself and Rose and then made a bowl of cereal for Daniel.

Rose added the milk and sugar to Daniel's cereal and then replied with a laugh. "I know its early March but I'm craving ice cream. Real ice cream that has to be scooped from the container and piled into a cone.

"Ice cream doesn't sound bad to me, either," Suzanne said. "It's been a while."

"I think it'll be fun to take Daniel to an ice cream parlor. I've practiced signing ice cream."

"Show me," Suzanne said.

Rose formed her right hand like she was holding an ice cream cone. She raised her hand to her mouth and imitated someone licking an ice cream cone.

"That's easy enough!" Suzanne said. "I bet Daniel will like learning this one."

"Yeah, and showing him the real thing will make it that much easier," Rose replied.

Suzanne waited for Daniel's attention and then held up her pointer finger. With her second hand she imitated someone peeling a banana.

Daniel nodded.

As she peeled and cut up the banana, Suzanne leaned close to Daniel and said the word *banana*.

The little boy happily took his spoon and beat the slices of banana into his cereal.

Suzanne poured herself a bowl and then ate a spoonful. "You know it is a little scary."

"What's scary?" Rose asked. She turned from the toast that she had removed from the toaster and smeared with butter.

"Him," Suzanne said with a nod to Daniel. "We don't know if he has any allergies. We don't know his family's medical history. We don't even know his blood type!"

"I mean, it's possible, isn't it, that he could be allergic to shell fish or peanuts or anything else for that matter. And it's not like we have a fully equipped ER right around the corner out here."

Rose squeezed her brows together. "You're not having second thoughts about asking for temporary guardianship, are you Suzanne?"

Suzanne looked surprised. "No. Are you kidding? Bennett Gardner thinks this little boy hung the moon and I think that Bennett Gardner hung the moon. If Daniel makes Bennett happy, Daniel makes Suzanne happy."

"But that's not fair," Rose said in protest. "Let's take Bennett out of the picture. Now, there's only you and Daniel. Do you still want Daniel?"

Suzanne watched Daniel play with his cereal and bananas for a minute. She looked at his curly hair, his long, dark eyelashes, and his small hands. He kicked his feet in enjoyment and banged the banana slices with his spoon. He banged one of them with gusto and splashed milk in his face.

He caught his breath in surprise at the unexpected drenching. He sat still for a minute, looked from Suzanne to Rose, and then shook his head and banged the bananas again with renewed vigor.

"Yes!" Suzanne exclaimed. "Yes!" She repeated with a sniffle. "I would want this little boy, Bennett or no Bennett."

"So I am correct in saying that Suzanne thinks that Bennett and Daniel hung the moon?"

"Yes, Rosemillion McKinley, you are!"

"Wow!"

"Wow what?"

"Wow, hearing that name startled me. I don't think anybody has ever called me that. At least no one has called me that since the day at the courthouse when Mama John called me *Rosemillion*. For the first time."

Suzanne's face broke into a great smile. "That was a good day at the court house, wasn't it?"

"It was a day that I'll never forget."

More smiles creased Suzanne's face. "And I feel fairly certain that it was a day that Jan will never forget."

Rose smiled. "He was pretty surprised."

"That's an understatement!" Suzanne exclaimed. "Here's a young man that could easily be called the most eligible bachelor in Ashford, Kentucky. His family is rich and famous for the world class thoroughbreds they breed and train. The debutantes are panting after him everywhere he goes, but he wants none of them."

"No, he wants the one woman in all of the world who feels certain that she's not good enough for him, and who refuses him outright because of her feelings."

Suzanne wiped the milk from Daniel's face and freed him from his new high chair. "Jan Vandeventer looked like he had risen from the dead when he saw his ring on that chain around your neck."

"I'm still not good enough for him," Rose said.

"You know better than that, Rose McKinley. I don't want to hear that! And by the way, you seem happier this morning, or maybe more optimistic. What's up?"

Rose poured herself another cup of coffee and then she refilled Suzanne's cup. "I dreamed about Jan again last night."

Suzanne met Rose's eyes. "And…."

"And he was climbing a fence. Some people dressed in clothes like I've never seen helped him but they didn't go over the fence with him."

Suzanne locked eyes with Rose. "What do you think it means?"

"I don't know, but I still believe that Jan's on his way home."

"Oh, Rose! That would be so great! Do you feel it? Do you feel like he's coming home?"

A smile animated Rose's face. "I do. The hopelessness that I felt before is gone."

"I think we should celebrate!   With ice cream!" Suzanne declared.

She and Rose burst into giggles.

"But until we can do that, I have a little boy to dress and an attorney to meet."

"I'll clean up the kitchen," Rose offered.   "You scoot and get Daniel dressed, then he and I will be off on our adventure."

Vandeventer Farms
Ashford, Kentucky

"Klaus Vandeventer, don't you dare close this door and do not bother to tell me that Olga is not in!   I know full well that she is and I intend to see her!"   Katharine Olliphant stormed.

The woman was dressed in white leather knee boots, a white wool coat and hat that were trimmed in tiger skin and black leather gloves.   She peeled one of the gloves from her hand and then, with an angry glare, fixed her eyes on Klaus.

"I've phoned at least ten times this week and every time I've been put off.   I wasn't born yesterday.   I know when something is wrong with my best friend.   Now are you going to behave like a gentleman and invite me and

Margaret in or am I going to have to shove past you and go searching for Olga myself?"

Klaus sighed a deep sigh.

Katharine, at five foot ten, towered above Klaus who stood five foot five with salt and pepper hair. His mustache and beard had only recently turned snow white.

Despite Klaus's status in Ashford as a world renowned horse breeder and trainer, one who was well respected among his peers, the man's kindly demeanor consistently tempered his behavior.

Klaus demonstrated this now. He did not want to allow Katharine and her daughter, Margaret, entrance, but he did so.

"Come Katharine, I led you and Margaret see Mama for a minute. Mama has been bery sick so you must not stay long."

Klaus led his guests through the living room and study and into the sitting room that overlooked the stables and pastures from the back of the Vandeventer home.

In a cloud of pink pillows Olga reclined on a custom crafted sectional sofa.

Formed in an *L* shape, the sofa was upholstered in the same dark lavender glove leather as the wall behind it. Oversized photos of the ranches' top money makers hung in gilt frames above the sofa. The opposing wall and the adjacent wall to the right featured white oak book cases that soared twelve vertical feet from the floor to the expansive white oak cathedral ceiling.

Vandeventer family photos and trophies decorated the shelves of the wall to the right. On the wall opposite the sofa, shelves of books on horse breeding, championship bloodlines, veterinarian practices and thoroughbred racing framed a large black Sony Trinitron television set that flashed scenes from the hit television series Bonanza.

To the left of the sitting area two dogs lay stretched out on a scatter rug before a massive river stone fireplace.

One of the dogs, Olga's pet, was a medium sized Australian Shepherd named Annie. The other was a larger Collie named Maverick. Both dogs barked at the arriving visitors in a way that indicated that they were no happier to see Katharine and Margaret than was their owner, Olga.

Klaus's attempt to quiet the dogs was challenged by Olga's distressed cries which served to further excite the animals.

"Klaus! I tell you that I vant to see no one! I am not dressed, I, I...."

Katharine removed her coat. She tossed it on the short end of the sofa away from Olga. "Olga! Don't blame

Klaus. He tried to send us off but I refused to leave without seeing you!"

"And it's a good thing, too. You look awful, honey. Why, you're skin and bones! What's going on with you? Why have you shut us all out? Our friends are calling to ask about you and it's embarrassing!"

"I'm supposed to be your best friend, yet I can tell them nothing because I know nothing!" The volume and tone of Katharine's voice set the dogs off again.

Olga squeezed her eyes closed and sank deeper into her pillows.

"Annie! Maverick!" Klaus yelled to the dogs.

"Mommy, everyone says Olga is sick because she hasn't heard from Jan. He's rumored to be missing in Vietnam. But of course that can't be true," Margaret remarked. She entertained herself at the book case where she lingered over photos of Jan.

Dressed in denim bell bottoms, a beige poet's shirt, fringed brown leather vest, and white boots, Margaret looked the part of a fashion-savvy, spoiled, over-indulged daughter of one of Ashford's wealthiest, most elite families.

She studied a photo that she took from the book case. It was a picture of Jan in uniform kneeling in the deep grass of the Quang Tri Province of Vietnam.

Despite the hard hat, jungle camouflage uniform and ammunition belt that he wore, it was the same incredibly handsome Jan Vandeventer that Margaret remembered. And the same Jan Vandeventer that she secretly hoped to date upon his return from Vietnam.

Margaret shifted her gaze to Olga. "It's nothing more than a hateful rumor, isn't it Olga? Jan will be home soon, won't he?"

Klaus darted his eyes from Margaret to Olga. His expression turned from one of interest to one of horror.

Tears filled Olga's eyes. She tossed off her covers and clapped a hand over her mouth. She tried to push herself from the sofa but could not find the strength.

Klaus rushed to his wife who wept openly now.

With her husband's help, Olga stood, teetered in a precarious manner, and then collapsed in Klaus's arms. The retching woman convulsed repeatedly as Klaus carried her from the room with both dogs close on his heels.

"I don't understand why Olga isn't in the hospital!" Katharine exclaimed. "I'm no doctor but it doesn't take a medical expert to know that Olga is far too ill to be here, home alone with Klaus."

Margaret's attention remained fixed on the photo in her hands. "He's still just as handsome as ever! And I for one don't believe the rumors. Jan will be home soon. He can't be missing in Vietnam!"

Klaus returned to the room with a storm in his eyes. "Margaret! I tell you before that my vife is bery ill! And she is ill because Jan IS missing in Vietnam. Ve hab heard nothing and my Olga fears that our Jan is dead!"

"What? That can't be true! Jan? Missing in Vietnam? It's impossible!"

Klaus reached to the sofa table for a prescription bottle. "It is true and it is killing my Olga! But vy do you concern yourself, Margaret? You are married for long time."

"Not any more, Klaus," Katharine spoke. "Margaret's divorce is final." The woman avoided Klaus's eyes. She busied herself straightening stacks of magazines and tossing wads of tissue into the waste basket.

With the medicine bottle in hand Klaus paused to look at Margaret. "I am sorry to hear," he said.

"Army tell us dat Jan is with patrol in jungle. Dey come under fire. No American die, but Jan and two other American soldiers gone missing."

"Mama believes that she vill never see our Jan again. She has ulcers. Ulcers bleed. Doctors vant Mama have surgery. She vill nod. She vill nod leave house. Army might call. Jan might come home."

The sorrow in Klaus's eyes was hopeless. "I vill lose my Mama if ve don't hear soon from our Jan. Mama believes he ees lost already. She believes he vill never come home."

Katharine pulled a manicured hand to her face. "Oh, Klaus! How dreadful! I had no idea that it was this bad. Poor Olga is in worse shape than any of us imagined."

"Let us help! I insist!" She trumpeted. "Margaret and I can cook and clean. Having friends around will only lift Olga's spirits. It's the least we can do Klaus!"

Klaus shook his head. "I appreciate offer, Katharine, but Mama vants no one. She need dis medicine now. I take it to her. If you do not mind, I stay vid Mama. You and Margaret see yourselves out."

Klaus started from the room but turned again from the study doorway. "Oh, I am sorry. I nearly forged, but thank you for coming. You are good friends."

Katharine retrieved her coat and had one arm in it when Margaret blurted "I wish I could take this photo. He's just as handsome as ever!"

"But of course you won't!" Katharine spluttered. "I can't imagine that you could suggest such a thing!"

Margaret replaced the photo. "Of course not, Mommy, but don't you find it odd?"

Katharine buttoned her coat. "Find what odd, Margaret?" "Klaus never mentioned her."

Katharine met her daughter's eyes with a look of confusion. "Her? Margaret, what are you talking about?"

"Jan's supposed fiancée, that little hillbilly, that Peck, or Pick, or whatever god-awful name she had! You remember her, that heathen that nearly destroyed the Stalworths?"

Katharine leveled a glare at her daughter. "Margaret, you know as well as I do that they call her Rose now. She's still engaged to Jan. There's nothing you can do about it so I suggest that you leave it alone," Katharine insisted.

She pulled on her gloves and then took Margaret by the arm. "Let's get out of here. I'm hungry and I find this whole missing in action thing depressing!"

The telephone on the sofa table rang. When it became apparent that neither Klaus nor Olga would answer, Margaret snatched up the receiver.

"Vandeventers!" She barked.

"Uh, um, who is this please?" The caller asked.

"This is Margaret Olliphant-Beckworth, uh, Margaret Olliphant! Who's calling, please?"

The caller fell silent for a moment. "Could I speak with Klaus or Olga?"

Recognizing the caller to be none other than Rose McKinley, Margaret replied "They're out. Could I take a message?"

"Um, uh, no. Thank you. I'll try again later."

Not thirty minutes after Katharine and Margaret had gone, Klaus turned down the volume of the television set in the master bedroom.

"Vat is dat sound?" He asked of his sleeping wife. His words, however, failed to waken her from her medicated slumber.

The pounding on the front door increased in volume and in intensity. With a worried glance at Olga, Klaus hurried down the stairs to answer.

Chapter Seventeen

Holding the paint bucket in one hand and the dripping paint brush in the other, Rose scratched her nose with her wrist.

"What do you think, Mustafa? Are you happy that Bennett talked you out of painting the walls yellow?"

"I am maybe happy," Mustafa replied. "You do good job. Mustafa good with roller, not so much with brush."

"I like the white enamel on the doors and base boards with the beige semi-gloss on the walls. The white looks so clean and the semi-gloss on the walls will be easier to maintain. "

Rose paused a minute to admire the newly painted walls and doors. "Flat paint doesn't hold up well where there's a lot of traffic, especially if a good deal of that traffic is children. They like to touch and feel things and that includes walls."

She pointed to Daniel. "See what I mean?"

Daniel had dragged a chair across the floor and placed it close to the table that Mustafa and Bennett had made with saw horses and a sheet of plywood.

Mustafa's pride and joy, a Grundig Radio TK2400 FM, sat on the table belting out in medium volume Redbone's "The Witch Queen of New Orleans". The song was one of many that Mustafa had recorded so that he could play it back on the radio's reel to reel function.

Daniel had both Rose's and Mustafa's attention now. Oblivious to the two adults, Daniel reached for the radio and twisted the volume knob to loud. A big smile swept across the little boy's face. He climbed off the chair and, standing near the radio, began to dance.

Rose's jaw dropped. Daniel was dancing with the rhythm of the music.

"Mustafa, look at him! He can't hear that music but he's dancing to it like he can!"

Mustafa laughed and folded his arms across his chest. Clearly enjoying Daniel's antics, he said "Daniel can no hear music but feels vibration."

"Yeah," Rose said with a laugh. "He feels the vibrations really well." She knit her brows and looked to Mustafa. "I can understand him feeling the vibrations when the volume is up, but apparently, he felt them when the volume was down.   How does that happen?"

Mustafa shrugged.   "Ask Beanie.   Beanie know everything!"

Rose laughed and shook her head.   "You and Bennett act more like children than Daniel!"

At that same moment, Daniel glanced from the radio that had so entranced him to Rose.   He squished his right hand and brought it to his mouth.

Rose glanced at her watch.   "No wonder you're hungry little guy.   It's almost 1:00 o'clock."

She picked up the paint bucket and brush.   After replacing the lid on the paint bucket, she brushed a few strokes on a newspaper to remove excess paint from the brush, then she rinsed the brush in warm soapy water and finally stuck it in a jar of turpentine.

Having no mirror she said to Mustafa with a laugh "I don't have any paint on my face, do I?"

"Maybe you do.   Maybe Mustafa no tell you."

Rose stretched her eyes wide at Mustafa's remark. "Hey, wait a minute Moose! You're confusing me with Bennett!"

Rose and Mustafa laughed.   Rose nodded to Daniel, squished her right hand and brought it to her mouth.

Daniel ran to Rose who wiped his face and hands and then signed *toys* to him.

Daniel hurried to the wicker basket that Suzanne and Bennett had designated for his playthings. He selected plastic figures of Big Bird and Cookie Monster, a couple of his favorite Hot Wheels cars, and then he wrapped something black around his wrist.

"What's that?" Rose asked, pointing to the black something.

"That's Beanie's Snidely Whiplash doll," Mustafa said with a laugh. Looks like Beanie, huh?"

"Wow! Mustafa, I'm impressed! You're sounding more like Bennett every minute!"

"Mustafa practice."

Rose burst out laughing. "No kidding!"

"Well I'm gonna take Midget and get him some lunch. I don't know when Suzanne and Bennett will be back. They went together to meet with the attorney who is going to file the temporary guardianship papers for them. You want to come with us?"

"No, thank you Rose, I stay and hang doors. You bring hamburger maybe?"

"Sure. Double meat, no onions, lettuce, tomato and mustard?"

"Yes, thank you. We have drink here."

"You want fries?"

"Yes, please."

"Ice cream?"

"Ice cream?" Mustafa raised his brows in surprise.

"Yes. This glorious sunshine and warm weather must be celebrated. With ice cream. Daniel and I were going to get one earlier but we got sidetracked with buckets and brushes and paint."

Rose signed to Daniel that it was time to go eat. She pulled the shoulder strap of her pocketbook over her shoulder and then took Daniel by the hand and left.

Daniel played with Snidely through lunch. He wrapped the bendable rubber doll around his drink cup, around his French fries, around the salt and pepper shakers and around the shoulder strap of Rose's pocketbook.

Daniel's eyes grew heavy and Rose did not want him to fall asleep in the restaurant. Signing *ice cream* did the trick. Daniel was wide awake.

Rose pulled her pickup into a parking space at Austin's Burgers and Cones. She could not help but notice the close proximity of Austin's back door to the railroad tracks. There couldn't be more than a hundred feet between them.

Rose lifted Daniel above the counter so that he could see the various flavors of ice cream. He seemed to like the pastel orange and green colors of the sherbets. He stuck the tip of his pointer finger in his mouth and lingered over the strawberry, and then over the vanilla, and then back to the sherbets.

While she waited for Daniel to decide, Rose ordered a double dip of chocolate. She took the cone from the clerk, raised it to her mouth, and then froze.

"Hello."

Rose became acutely aware that her heart continued to beat and that the beat was incredibly loud.

"He…. Hello," she managed.

The stranger smiled at her. He towered above her. At least six foot six she estimated. *Handsome.* The word inserted itself in her mind in such a way as to blank out any other.

"Excuse me, am I making you nervous?" Handsome spoke.

His eyes were so blue, so blue that…. The thought was lost. Or was that a thought? His face was rugged, like it was carved, carved of something that Rose could not define.

If she held that face in her hands. Maybe…. *What are you thinking! Stop it! You've seen handsome men before!*

This one, this one with his thick, longish, grayish, salt-and-pepperish hair that was shot through with glints of sunlight and parted in the middle so that it framed his mesmerizing smiling eyes—it was perfect.

Perfect like his mouth, his dark mustache and his salt-and-pepperish beard. *Where's my heart beat? I can't feel it!*

Handsome smiled at her. What was he waiting for? *Oh, his question….*

"No, no," Rose stammered. She managed a smile. "You're not making me nervous."

Handsome nodded to her pocketbook. "Then perhaps you meant to put your ice cream cone in there?"

Rose gasped. She held Daniel by his waist like a sack of potatoes. She put him down and pulled the strap of her pocketbook off her shoulder. She opened the bag wide and pulled out the cone, followed by the two mushy scoops of chocolate ice cream.

Handsome pulled napkins from a dispenser on the counter. He took the mushed chocolate and cone from Rose and then he wiped her hand. He tossed the napkins in the waste receptacle and then said to the clerk "Could I have two double scoop and one single scoop chocolate cones please?"

The young, pony-tailed clerk smiled a dazzling smile at Handsome before she found her tongue and replied "Certainly. Right away!"

Handsome nodded to Daniel and then met Rose's eyes. "He wants chocolate."

"I, how…?" Rose felt aggravated. Could it be possible that she had forgotten how to speak in complete sentences?

Handsome smiled. His teeth were sparkling white. Of course.

Could perfect get perfect-er?

"Let's start at the beginning. Hello. My name is Quayle Johnson. I'm the engineer on that train out there and have been for the past twenty years."

"Engineers on the *CSX* see a lot. I've seen enough to know that your little boy signed the word chocolate to you. Twice."

"I feel my face turning red!" Rose blurted. "Oh, my Lord! I didn't say that out loud did I?" *If I could click my heels together and vanish, I would.*

Quayle took the single dip cone and gave it to Daniel. He took one of the double dips for himself and gave one to Rose. "Care to sit?"

Not waiting for this intriguing, ginger-haired, porcelain-skinned creature to answer, Quayle led the way to a corner booth.

He did not hesitate to pick up Daniel, place him in a seat and then seat himself on the opposite side of the table.

Rose seated herself. She pulled napkins from the dispenser and wiped drips from Daniel's cone.

With Daniel happily eating his ice cream and smearing his face with the chocolaty stuff, Rose licked at the chocolate on her cone. After a moment she allowed herself to glance up and into Quayle Johnson's eyes.

"And your name is?" He asked. His smile was unlike any smile that Rose had ever seen.

"Uh, it's Rose. Rose McKinley," she said and for reasons unknown even to herself, she thrust her hand across the table and waved it in the man's face. "And I'm engaged to Jan Vandeventer."

"So that explains the rock on your finger," Quayle said with a nod at Rose's two carat diamond engagement ring.

"Rock?" Rose repeated with narrowed eyes and knit brows.

"Diamond. Sorry," Quayle said, knitting his brows. "Slang becomes a habit I guess, in my line of work anyway. But I'll make no excuses. That was rather boorish of me. I should have said diamond and in this case, big diamond."

Rose relaxed. All the tension that had riddled her being from the moment that she first laid eyes on this man left her body as easily as a breath too long held and then quickly expelled.

"I apologize for being so clumsy, but I came in here to get ice cream for Daniel and me. I didn't expect to meet anyone and I sure didn't expect to meet anyone as handsome as you."

Rose made a face. "I guess you could say that you took my breath away. Jan's handsome but I got used to seeing his face so he doesn't startle me or take my breath away like you did."

"That is…." A look of dismay clouded Rose's face. "But I haven't seen him in a long time," she confessed in a breaking voice.

"He's in Vietnam." Rose reached for more napkins from the dispenser as much to distract herself from the intensity of Quayle's eyes as for any other reason that came to mind.

She wiped at the chocolate that had made its way from the cone to Daniel's face and on to his shirt and hands.

Keeping her eyes on Daniel, Rose continued. "The Army tells us that he's missing in action. I'm sorry, but I wish he was here. You would like him. He would like you and he would ask you if he could walk all around and inside your train."

Quayle found himself fighting the urge to reach for her hand and hold it. That was probably not a good idea, he knew, so he remained still and silent.

"He and his folks raise horses, fine thoroughbreds," Rose stated in a matter of fact voice.

Quayle finished his ice cream and wiped his mouth. He was going to look into her eyes no matter how hard she tried to prevent it. Just my luck. She would have to be engaged.

"I know of the Vandeventers, Klaus and Olga, but I've never had the privilege of meeting them." His blue eyes sparkled. He had dimples on both sides of his face, dimples that only made him appear more handsome.

A smile played around his lips. "And before you ask, no, I've not had the privilege of meeting their only son, Jan, either."

Daniel shoved his dripping cone at Rose, signaling that he was finished with his ice cream. Rose laughed. "It looks to me like maybe the ice cream is finished with you. I don't think you could possibly have gotten more on you," she said and kissed Daniel's chocolate face. She took the cone and looked for a place to dispose of it so that she could clean up the little boy.

"Let me have it," Quayle said. He took the cone. "Do you want to finish this when you're done there?"

"No," Rose said with a laugh that, without warning, turned to a sob. "It ain't right! I got no business here eating ice cream with you when Jan's lost, lost somewhere in the jungles of Vietnam! I don't want him lost in Vietnam! I want him home, home in Kentucky with me!"

Rose stood and stretched her arms to Daniel. She lifted him and then swung him onto her hip. She glanced from Quayle to the table, picked up her pocketbook, and placed the strap over her shoulder.

"Miss Rose!"

"Miss Rose! We seen yer truck out there and we come to ask fer yer help. Mary Nell Fuquay is havin' a young'un and she won't come down off the mountain to see no doctor. Her family won't let no one come up the mountain what they gotta know a Fuquay."

"Them Fuquays will shoot you deader'n a stump what you come messin' around up there and ain't got no invite."

Rose offered a hand to Frank Perkins. "Take a minute to catch your breath, Frank. Now tell me what this lady needs."

Frank glanced about uneasily like he kept a powerful secret that could not be told out loud.

Proof came quickly. "Miss Rose, I can't say hit out loud. Kin I get close and whisper?"

Rose darted her eyes from Frank to Quayle who was not about to leave now, at least not before he satisfied his curiosity.

"It's all right, Frank," Rose motioned with her hand. "Come close and whisper."

In his slow way Frank shuffled closer to Rose on the side furthest from Daniel. He cupped his hands to his mouth and whispered in Rose's ear.

"What?" Anger trumped the doubt that blazed in Rose's eyes. "Frank, that's impossible! I've never heard of anything like that!" She shook her head. "Are you sure?"

"Yes, Mam, Miss Rose! Cross my heart! Others what didn't believe it neither and tried to sneak up on the mountain to get a look-see got theirselves a belly or a backside full of buckshot!"

"Frank, we can't go up there without a doctor. If what you are telling me is true, we need the best we can find. Will this family, you say their name is Fuquay, will they allow a doctor up there?"

"I told 'em about yer doctor friend. Since yer from the mountains yerself, yer doctor friend can come but not by hisself, he has to come with us."

"I understand Frank. Let's go. We'll stop for Dr. Dhingra on the way."

Quayle looked at his watch. "I really want to come with you to see that you and your friends are safe but the *CSX* runs on a tight schedule."

"I don't want to, but I have to go," he said, and held Rose's eyes with a magnetism that she could not fight.

Quayle tore his eyes at last from Rose to glance to his waiting train, a glance that one moment sooner would have caught the silent figure that sneaked into the back of Rose's truck and hid beneath the paint tarps.

Quayle started for the door beside Rose when she turned abruptly. "What about Daniel? Suzanne and Bennett are away and there's no one else to care for him. I won't take Daniel up there if he might be in danger!"

"Don't you worry none about Daniel, Miss Rose. This young'un will be safe with us," Frank assured her.

"Good bye, Rose. Meeting you has been a most unexpected pleasure," Quayle said, taking Rose's hands in his own. It was with a stinging reluctance that he let her go to pat Daniel on the head.

Daniel looked up and flashed a smile at Quayle.

"Bye Sprout, see you later," Quayle said and ruffled Daniel's curls with his hand.

"Rose, please be safe up in those mountains." *Good God! I just met the woman. Why do I feel like something is being torn from me?*

"I hate to see you going up there alone if it's as dangerous as your friend says it might be."

"I'm never alone, Mr. Johnson," Rose said with her eyes fixed on Quayle's eyes. "God is always with me. I'm not afraid of the mountains or of anyone from the mountains."

"No, I suppose you're not," Quayle said. *When will I see you again? I can go now if I can be certain that I will see you again.*

The look of reluctance returned to Quayle's eyes. "If you see the *CSX* sitting out there about this time of day, I'll be inside here or close by," he said. "Please, if you need me or just need someone to talk to, promise me that you'll find me."

"Thank you, Mr. Johnson, that's kind of you," Rose said. Without a backward glance she took Daniel by the hand and followed Frank out the door.

The ruts and ridges of Widows Hollow had been bad, the roads almost impassable, but in Rose's opinion, this so-called road was worse.

She shared Frank's secret with Mustafa in bursts of sharply exhaled words and broken sentences. She complained "I don't know what folks call this area, but I would call it Nightmare, West Virginia! This road could rattle the teeth out of a rattler!" She exclaimed.

She shifted her pickup in reverse behind Frank who was in his truck ahead of her. Frank had reversed his direction to get them out of a turn that proved impossible to navigate in any vehicle.

Mustafa had never seen such sights. Although he had been in this area for a few years, he hadn't ventured too far into the mountains from the valley of Wolf Laurel Creek.

He pointed to several blackened patches that looked like someone had built campfires in the middle of the pitted, sandy road. The terrain on each side of the road was too rocky and treacherous for anything other than a horse or mule to pass.

"Why people build fire in road?" With narrowed eyes and knitted brows, Mustafa questioned Rose.

Rose answered with a laugh. "It's an old mountain trick. When strangers get lickered up and lose their way in the mountains and the hollows, the local boys build a fire in the road. The strangers can't drive through the fire, they can't go around it so they're forced to stop."

"The local boys threaten and shout, scare the daylights out of the strangers who are more than likely city folk, but all that the local boys really want is whatever beer, whisky, or white lightening the strangers may have."

Rose laughed again. "It's a game. The fire stops the strangers. The local boys take their liquor and then they put out the fire. The strangers go on their way. Everybody's happy."

"Mustafa is not happy." Mustafa scowled and wagged his head. "I never see so bad sights. These people in mountain are very poor." He gaped at the shacks and shanties, rubbish piles, and at the large boulders that loomed around every pothole- infested switchback and turn.

Rose noticed that the hand printed Keep-Out and No Trespassing signs showed up with greater frequency now.

The boulders were getting bigger and it was anybody's guess what might be hidden behind the next one.

Rusted out school buses that served as home and shelter dotted the landscape. These were interspersed with rotted cabins boasting porches that had fallen away from the main structure leaving a gap between porch and house.

Clothing hung from tree limbs, porch rails, ropes and wires that were stretched from rickety barns to equally rickety dwellings.

Rose suddenly hit her brakes hard.

Ahead of her Frank had stopped without warning and now his horn emitted a series of loud bleeps. He quickly climbed from his truck and hurried to the driver's door of Rose's truck.

"I'm sorry Miss Rose, but we have to walk in. The Fuquays ain't gonna allow no cars nor trucks up in here. So if you and Doctor, Doctor…. "

"Dr. Dhingra," Rose said.

"Yes Mam, Dr. Dhingra," Frank repeated with a nod to Mustafa. "If you folks will follow me and don't be scart. The Fuquay boys is up there. They got their guns on they shoulders, but don't be scart. Hit's their way, so just walk slow and friendly like and they ain't gonna hurt nobody."

Rose had been walking hand in hand with Daniel beside
Mustafa who carried his medical bag she suddenly snatched
Daniel from the ground and swung him to her hip.

"Frank! Are you sure that Daniel is in no danger?"

"This fine little boy ain't in no danger Miss Rose. The
Fuquays, well, they may be a little different, but they's
right fond of little uns'. The little un's don't pay 'em no
mind and they get along just fine."

Frank led the way past more boulders through a
wilderness of undergrowth and waist high weeds. A maze
of overgrown hawthorn hedges and scrub pines obscured
from view what appeared to be a house in a clearing.

Frank, Mustafa, Rose and Daniel stepped into the
clearing.

"Stop right there!" A man with a gravelly voice and a
shotgun on his shoulder barked. "What's that yer a
carryin'?" He demanded, lowering his double barrel
shotgun at Mustafa's medical bag.

Rose looked to Mustafa, anticipating the man's reply.

Mustafa did not and would not reply. He stood staring
at the spectacle before him with an expression that Rose
could not define.

These people were blue. They had all the characteristics of regular, normal *Homo sapiens*, but they were blue. Blue!

Mustafa had heard of blue people in medical school but hearing of them and seeing them were two different matters.

"It's a medical bag," Rose said to the man.

The man's face, what showed of his head inside his halo of white hair, his arms and his hands were unmistakably blue. Not blue-black, or tanned or tinted to appear blue. They were *blue*.

Rose continued in a steady voice. "It's the supplies that the doctor needs to help the lady who is having the baby."

"Toss it over here," the blue man ordered, motioning with his shotgun.

Mustafa hesitated with a glance at Rose.

She nodded.

Mustafa took a few steps forward, placed his bag on the ground and opened it so that the man could see inside the bag.

Daniel squirmed to be free from Rose's arms. He gave Rose no choice but to put him down. Once freed, the little boy ran to the blue man. The man lowered his shotgun and squatted before Daniel.

Daniel ran his hand over the man's arms, then he reached to touch the man's face. Daniel smiled at the man and with his fingers spelled the word *blue.*

"His name is Daniel," Rose said. "He can't hear or speak and he just spelled blue with his fingers."

"Elizabeth!" The man barked.

A little girl dressed in a long gingham skirt, white blouse and tennis shoes materialized from behind a boulder. Shy and silent, she ran to the blue man and stood behind him, peering at Daniel.

The little girl was blue, a darker blue than the man and she wore her long blonde hair in a braid down her back.

"Take Daniel over to your playhouse for a little while. He can't talk or hear but he knows how to play like you do."

"Frank!" Rose cried.

"Don't be feared fer him, Miss. He'll be all right with Elizabeth," the blue man said to Rose without so much as a glance.

Remaining in a squat, he opened Mustafa's medical bag and looked over the contents.

"I guess it's all right. Ain't no camera in here! You'uns follow me." The blue man stood and started for the house and then turned to Rose and Mustafa and Frank.

"My name's Silas." He chucked his head to where they had parked their trucks. "Ain't nobody follered you or is a hidin' behind you?"

Rose shook her head and to her knowledge, answered in all honesty. "No, there's nobody but us."

Rose had no way of knowing that she was wrong. She equally had no way of knowing what a disastrous chain of events her hidden stowaway, Lenny Walker, would set off in the immediate future.

Vandeventer Farms
Ashford, Kentucky

Klaus pulled open the door to a breathless Early Mae Johnson.

"Mama John, vot is the matter? Is something wrong?" Klaus asked, his brows knotted with concern.

"Something surely is wrong, Mister Klaus, and it's with Miss Olga! I come to see her."

Klaus's eyes softened. "I am sorry Mama, but my Olga vill see nobody. She is bery ill and she is sleeping now. Can you maybe come back another time?"

Mama John shifted the basket that she carried by its wicker handle. "I can come back another time but I ain't goin' to. I intend to see Miss Olga now and I'll wait right here on the porch if you don't mind."

"Mama! You cannot stay out on the porch! You must come in, but I do nod know when my Olga vill vake."

Klaus opened the door to Mama John who stormed into the foyer with a less-than-friendly determination.

"Klaus? Klaus? Where are you?" Olga called in a weak voice from upstairs.

"Coming, Mama! I be right dere!" Klaus cast a worried glance up the stairs. "My Olga vill nod like it if I bring somebody up the stairs. She vants no company," Klaus said with pleading eyes that he hoped would convince Mama John to leave.

"Mister Klaus, you don't have to bring me up the stairs, I can find my way just fine. Why don't you wait down here?"

Mama John started up the stairs despite Klaus's objections. She looked over her shoulder at him, waiting for Klaus to point out which door to open. He indicated a set of golden oak double doors. Mama John breezed through the doors as if she were in her own home.

"Here now, Miss Olga, what's all this? You ain't seein' nobody and you gots ulcers what's eatin' away your stomach. Good thing somethin's eatin' 'cause you sho ain't!"

Mama John placed her basket on a satin-covered bench at the foot of Olga's bed. She marched into the opulent bathroom, took a wash cloth from a towel rack, soaked it in warm water and soap and returned to Olga's bedside.

"Come on, Honey, sit up for Mama John," Mama John said and gently lifted Olga into a sitting position. Mama John piled pillows behind Olga and then smoothed the covers over her.

"You probably can't remember when you ate last so I ain't gonna bother asking," Mama John said. She gently patted Olga's face with the warm cloth, then pushed up the sleeves of her dressing gown and washed her arms and hands.

"There, don't that feel better, Baby?" Mama John returned to the bathroom, washed out the wash cloth and replaced it on the towel rack. She removed an oversized plush towel from the rack and carried it back to Olga.

Mama John placed the towel beneath Olga's chin and spread it across Olga's body. She then opened the wicker basket and removed a covered bowl. She took the plastic cover from the bowl and placed the bowl on a plate. She opened another container and spilled out crackers. She replaced the container, picked up a spoon and returned to Olga.

"Here, Baby, you take a bite. This is Mama John's homemade chicken soup and it'll do you good."

"Mama, I can nod eat, please take it away," Olga moaned.

"Miss Olga, I got some news about Mister Jan! If you want to hear it, you're gonna hafta eat a little bit of this soup!" Mama John argued.

Olga opened her eyes wide. "You have news about my Zhan?"

Mama John nodded. "I do! You take a bite and I'll tell you." Mama John filled the spoon with soup and brought it to Olga's mouth.

Olga ate first one spoonful, then another, then another.

"Now have some crackers, Baby, they'll help keep your stomach settled."

Dutifully, Olga accepted the crackers and bit into one of them.

Klaus clasped his hands. "Mama, you eat at last!"

He said to Mama John "Thank you!   I don't know how you do it, she vill nod eat for me, for nobody, she been so sick for so long."

"I reckon good news about Mister Jan is just what Miss Olga needs," Mama John said brightly.   She placed a gentle hand on Olga's arm.

"Miss Olga, Rose done dreamed that Mister Jan is on his way home.   He's still in the jungle in Vietnam, but he's free now to make his way home.   He ain't dead, Honey, Rose is certain that he's all right."

"Maybe someone was holding him against his will or maybe he's been sick and someone's been seeing to him, but no matter, Olga Honey, you can stop this worryin' now! Rose said your boy is on his way home."

Olga burst into tears and grabbed Mama John in a fierce hug.

Klaus fought tears as he took Olga's hand and squeezed it.   "Thank you, Mama John, it been so long since I see my Olga smile!"

Chapter Eighteen

Boyd County Jail
Ashford, Kentucky

"Ruddy! Ruddy! Wake up! The boss man called your name."

"What for? Are they gonna turn me loose for good behavior and because the women are missing me so bad?"

"No stupid, you gotta be in court this morning! Don't you remember anything? And if I were you I'd put on some clothes. His Honor ain't likely to be impressed by yer showin' up in yer skivvies!"

"Ruddy! You got three minutes to be standing at this cell door ready to go! You got that? And you'd best remember that I don't like to be kept waiting!"

"Be right there, Deputy!" Ruddy growled and made an obscene gesture toward the cell door.

Daniel Ruddy rolled out of his bottom bunk and pulled on his black and white striped prison jumpsuit.

He walked the two feet to a stainless steel sink and splashed water on his face and head. He ran a comb through his red hair and then said with a grin "No wonder the women love me. I'm the best looking thing they'll ever meet!"

"Ruddy! We got thousands of miles of roads to build and I'm thinking you'd rather be out there on a chain gang than in the courthouse! Get your skinny backside to this door right now!" The deputy barked.

Ruddy punched his open palm with a fist. "Just once I'd like to shut that fat sucker's mouth for him!"

"Seems to me yer in enough trouble already! Don't you want to get outta here and see yer little boy?" Ruddy's cell mate, Solomon "Spider" Swartz asked.

Ruddy plopped on his bunk to put on his boots. "Hell no!" He replied. "There ain't no way of knowing if that's my kid or not! It could be anybody's," he said, knowing that he was lying.

"The little freak can't hear or talk. He just makes googly signs with his fingers and whines for his mama."

"Ruddy, they told you that she's dead. I don't care how you feel, you should respect the dead no matter what!" Spider said. He crossed himself and then glanced heavenward.

Ruddy stood. "Don't you go and turn preacher on me, Cujo! You mind your business and keep yer ugly mug out of mine!"

A loud, metallic banging sound blasted from the cell door. Deputy Robert Triplett played the cell bars like a xylophone, banging back and forth across them with his night stick.

With his face fixed in a surly frown, Ruddy strode to the cell door.

Deputy Triplett, a sweaty, doughy, self-indulging slacker who hated his job and who was overly fond of doughnuts unlocked the heavy door and then propelled his massive frame into the doorway.

"Turn around and spread 'em!" He ordered.

Ruddy turned around so that he faced away from the deputy.

"Come on, Ruddy! You know how to play this game! Put ém behind you!"

Ruddy put his arms behind his back and crossed them at the wrists.

The deputy *clap*ped on a pair of handcuffs and then with his night stick smacked one of Ruddy's legs below the knee.

Ruddy spread his feet further apart.

The deputy patted him down and then snapped on leg irons.

"Now we're all dressed up and ready to go impress the ladies, aren't we Ruddy?" Triplett asked in a mocking tone.

Escorting prisoners on field trips to outlying court houses ranked near the top of the deputy's list of least favorite things to do. Reminding himself of this fact, Triplett smacked Ruddy's head with the back of his hand.

"All rise!" Court Clerk Mike Renna instructed those seated in West Virginia's Laurel County courtroom.

With a rolled newspaper in one hand and a gavel in the other The Honorable George C. Thompson, Jr., entered and took his seat before a large framed image of the seal of the great state of West Virginia.

The impressive seal graced the wall behind him and bore the legend, State of West Virginia, together with the motto *Montani Semper Liberi* (Mountaineers Are Always Free).

A farmer stands to the right and a miner to the left of a large rock that is engraved with the date of West Virginia's admission to the Union, June 20, 1863.

Two hunters' rifles lie before the rock with a Cap of Liberty resting at the cross of the rifles.

Court Clerk Renna called the court to order and together with Judge Thompson moved swiftly through the docket.

Bennett Gardner's wrinkled forehead and his tightly squeezed brows painted a picture of concern. "Suzanne, calm down. I can feel your heart racing from over here!"

"Hold my hand," Suzanne whispered. She curled her small hand inside Bennett's massive hand and then looked to the front row on the opposite side of the courtroom where a Boyd County Sheriff marched a handcuffed and shackled prisoner before him.

The prisoner was tall and thin with red hair that needed combing and a stubbled face that needed shaving.

He laughed loudly at something at the same time as the deputy shoved him onto the front bench beside other inmates in similar restraints who were also dressed in black and white prison stripes.

Suzanne watched, certain that Ruddy would turn and scan the courtroom looking for his son Daniel.

Ruddy did not turn around. He did not glance from side to side or across the courtroom. He bent over and appeared to be shaking the chain that linked the leg irons that the deputy had locked about his ankles.

"Bennett and Carolyn Suzanne Gardner!" The judge read from the docket.

Attorney Tom Drake quickly stood to his feet. "My clients are present your honor."

"Daniel Ruddy!" The judge called out. "Ruddy!" He repeated in a tone that was less than amiable. The judge peered over his reading glasses to the front row of inmates. "Deputy! Is Ruddy present or isn't he?"

The deputy jumped to his feet and kicked at Ruddy who sat slouched over playing with the leg iron chains.

"Stand up when the judge calls your name!" The deputy barked between clenched teeth.

A sullen Ruddy shot the deputy an angry glare and staggered to his feet.

"In the matter of Bennett and Carolyn Suzanne Gardner vs. Daniel Ruddy it appears to this court that Mr. and Mrs. Gardner seek to be appointed temporary guardians of the minor child, Daniel Ruddy."

The judge fixed his eyes on Ruddy. "Do you understand these proceedings Mr. Ruddy?"

"Yeah, sure I get it. These fine upstanding do-gooders want the kid."

Judge Thompson scowled. "Mr. Ruddy, do you have counsel?"

"Counsel?" Ruddy repeated with a snicker. "What's counsel?"

"An attorney, Mr. Ruddy. Do you have an attorney? If you wish to have an attorney and cannot afford one, this court will appoint...."

"Naw! I ain't got no attorney and I don't need no attorney. If they want the kid, they got the kid. He most likely ain't mine nohow."

"And I don't see no reason to make it temporary. If they want the little googly fingered freak they can have him! From now on!" Ruddy turned to Bennett and Suzanne with a self-satisfied sneer.

"Mr. Drake you may need to restrain me! I want to punch that low-life's face so bad!" Bennett hissed under his breath and then turned to Suzanne.

"Suzanne! What's the matter? Don't.... Don't....!"

Suzanne looked green. Heaving dry heaves, she lurched to her feet, clutched her stomach, and darted from the courtroom with a hand over her mouth.

Bennett jumped to his feet, caught his wife in his arms and hurried with her down the aisle and out into the corridor.

Drake stood and with anxious eyes followed his clients in their hurried exit.

He respectfully addressed Judge Thompson. "Uh, your honor, we're going to need a few minutes. It seems that my client has taken ill."

The judge glanced at his watch. "This court will recess for thirty minutes!" He ordered.

"Suzanne?" Bennett began, his face etched with worry.

"How could he do that? How could he do that?" Suzanne shrieked. She stood with her face level to Bennett's chest and wrapped her fists in his shirt.

"That man never once looked to see if Daniel was in the courtroom. He never turned around at all! Bennett, he threw that precious little boy away like Daniel is nothing more than a squashed toad or last week's news!"

Tears spilled from Suzanne's eyes. "I don't understand! How can a parent throw away a child? Daniel must have trusted his parents. He must have felt that he could depend on them, must have believed that they would be there for him! He's only four! And maybe he's not even that! He can't help that his mother died. But his father, his father!"

"Oh, Bennett! I'm so glad that Daniel wasn't here! I am so thankful that that little boy will never have in his memory the moment that his father threw him away!"

Dissolving in tears, Suzanne grabbed her stomach and ran for the ladies' room.

With his heels clicking loudly on the corridor's marble tile, Attorney Tom Drake approached Bennett. He shifted his briefcase from his left to his right hand and then asked "Is she going to be all right?"

Bennett ran a hand through his hair. He said on an exhaled breath "Yes sir, I think she'll be all right. My girl is a little hyper-sensitive but we've learned how to deal with it. She was prepared to do battle with Daniel's daddy for the boy today."

Bennett glanced behind Drake, watching for Suzanne. "She was not prepared for that heartless son of a snake to let Daniel go with a *good-riddance* smirk. It made her sick to her stomach. Suzanne doesn't deal well with heartless. It's foreign to her nature."

Bennett could see Suzanne exit the ladies' room down the hallway. He waited for her and felt heartened when she returned his smile.

"That's my girl!" Bennett said, taking Suzanne's hand when she returned to his side. "All better now?" He asked.

Suzanne nodded and then again burst into tears. She waved a hand at Bennett. "Don't pay me any mind. I'll be all right in a minute."

Bennett wiped tears from Suzanne's cheeks with his fingers. "Suz, all that matters now is that in just a few minutes that incredible four year old, Daniel Ruddy, who already has us both, hook, line, and sinker, will be our little boy, not temporarily, but for good. Think about that Sweetie and then we'll go home and celebrate."

"Um, Mr. Drake, since Ruddy isn't going to put up a fight, all we need to do now is sign some papers. Am I understanding this correctly?"

Drake shook his head in the affirmative. "That's how it works. If a minor child's mother is deceased and his father wants to assign his parental rights to you, it becomes a matter of signing papers, having the signatures notarized, and then having the judge sign the order."

Drake glanced at his watch and then continued. "Of course the court will require reasonable proof that you and Mrs. Gardner are worthy candidates to become Daniel's parents. There will be the obligatory background checks and financial inquiries. They will want to be certain that you can provide food and shelter, clothing, the basics."

He assessed the Gardners and then said with the rehearsed look of confidence that comes from graduating law school in the top of your class and from scoring consistent wins in weekly contests of eighteen-hole golf "From what I can see, you folks have nothing to worry about."

Drake's words should have been a comfort to Suzanne but Suzanne did not feel comforted. Her stomach rolled and churned acid. Something wasn't right. Tears splashed her cheeks.

"Hold my hand, Bennett. Hold it tight."

Bennett took Suzanne's hand in his and squeezed his fingers around it.

Suzanne sniffled and fought her tears. Getting permanent custody of Daniel shouldn't be this easy. Couldn't be this easy.

Women's intuition is talked about in social circles. It's mentioned in mind science classes. Studies and experiments have been conducted, data recorded and analyzed, but the mysteries remain.

How does it work? Is it infallible? Do all women have an inborn sense that registers danger or hardship or turmoil in the distance?   The question on the human scale is yet to be answered.

But Carolyn Suzanne Gardners' intuition on this day was deadly accurate. Getting permanent custody of young Daniel Ruddy could not and would not be this easy.

Despite the tears that leaked anew from her eyes, despite the sudden illness that beset her, and despite the alarms of her intuition registering red and critical, Suzanne Gardner had no way of knowing that the battle for little four-year old Daniel Ruddy had just begun or that the battle would prove to be both horrible and tragic.

Chapter Nineteen

Suzanne and Bennett knelt nose to nose on their all fours.   They installed a new ceramic tile floor in one of the clinic's bathrooms.

Without looking Suzanne stuck her roller into the bucket of adhesive.   Hearing an unexpected *clunk*! She looked into the bucket and with a laugh pulled one of Daniel's Matchbox cars from the muck.

"You boys and your toys!" She blurted to Bennett with a mischievous glint in her eyes.

"Yeah," Bennett replied "Daniel likes cars but Bennett likes girls.   He bounced his brows and said in a suggestive tone "Suz, if we close the door, do you think we could…."

"Bennett Gardner!   You better get your mind on your business and off," she said with a glance at Bennett's waistline, "your business."

Bennett kissed Suzanne on her nose.   "You are my business my love."

Suzanne looked into the adjoining room where Daniel sat on an upturned paint bucket playing at the table that Bennett and Mustafa had built for him.

He zoomed his cars across a racetrack and then laughed when they fell off the table and into his toy basket.

Suzanne met Bennett's eyes. "I love to hear that little boy laugh but I want to hear him talk too. Bennett, we need to enroll him in West Virginia's School for the Deaf and Blind in Romney."

"Suz, he's just a baby. I don't want to send him off alone among strangers. It can wait until he's a little older."

"But it can't wait my love," Suzanne said and trapped Bennett's eyes with her beautiful, soft and imploring eyes.

Bennett was had and he knew it. He felt grateful that he didn't melt into a puddle.

Summoning her sweetest smile, Suzanne continued. "I've talked with their administrator. He convinced me that the younger the student, the more quickly he learns to read lips and to speak."

"I've given this a lot of thought my love. I agree that he's too young to send off by himself so I've done some checking. I could work at one of the local clinics in Romney and be with Daniel when he's not in classes."

"What?" Bennett raised his voice. "Daniel is off to Romney for months to be in school and Suzanne is off to Romney for months to be with Daniel and Bennett is left home alone in West Virginia or Kentucky? It ain't gonna happen, Suzanne!" Bennett exclaimed in anger.

"We didn't sign on as partners in a business venture. We signed on as man and wife. Where Bennett goes, Suzanne goes! Where Suzanne goes, Bennett goes!"

"If Suzanne goes to Kenya, Africa, Bennett goes to Kenya, Africa. If Bennett goes mountain climbing in the Himalayas, Suzanne goes mountain climbing in the Himalayas."

"No room here for compromise Suzanne! This is the compromise!" Bennett exclaimed.

Suzanne felt stunned. She had never, ever seen Bennett angry at her. He had never raised his voice to her. His face was stormy, his tone belligerent, his words loud and yet he looked like he could cry.

Daniel burst into the bathroom and flew into Bennett's arms. With his lip quivering the little boy bounced his eyes from Bennett's eyes to Suzanne's eyes.

He wrapped an arm around Bennett's neck and with the other reached to pull Suzanne closer.

Tears spilled from Suzanne's eyes. "Oh Bennett! He felt the tension, the anger."

Bennett kissed Suzanne and Daniel.

Suzanne returned Bennett's kiss, kissed Daniel and hugged the little boy. "Oh, baby! We're so sorry! We didn't mean to, to…."

Bennett held Daniel away from him and repeated to the little boy as he signed "*Mommy. Daddy. Daniel. School.*" And then he said to Daniel's eyes "It's okay little guy. Mommy and Daddy are going to school with Daniel."

"Oh, dang it!" Rose swore.

She stood on top of a scaffold in the clinic's dual purpose reception -waiting room with her arms stretched above her head trying to apply a wallpaper border just below the ceiling.

The dark green roll of wallpaper with its bright alphabet letters of orange and yellow was too heavy. When Rose let go the roll to smooth a section of border in place the heavy roll fell and pulled the newly placed section with it.

"Help!" She yelled.

Determined to finish the border, Rose smoothed a strip with the straight edge of a trowel while holding the roll tucked under her chin.

It was awkward, but it was at times like these that her father, Joseph McKinley's, words rang in her ears. "We ain't no hillbillies, Pick. We's survivors!"

"Maybe I can help?"

Startled by the unexpected voice, Rose turned too quickly. She teetered on the scaffold.

"Whoa there!" Quayle Johnson commanded. He reached a hand to steady Rose.

Rose's heart somersaulted in her chest. Quayle Johnson was the last person she expected to see this morning.

He was dressed in a gray chambray shirt, denim jacket and jeans. He smiled up at her with those incredible blue eyes while his dimples sank deep in his cheeks.

"Uh, hello," Rose managed. She darted her eyes to the wallpaper paste that clung to her hands and nails. Dried bits of it splotched her arms and most probably her face. She couldn't know for sure without a mirror but she would feel embarrassed just in case.

Her hair was tied up in one of the bandanas that Jan had worn around his neck when he worked horses on his parents' farm.

"I'm sorry if I startled you," Quayle apologized. "But this new clinic has the locals talking. It's noon so I thought I'd stop in and see for myself what they're talking about and ask if you might join me for lunch?" Quayle tilted his face and lifted his brows to Rose.

"Um, maybe," Rose replied with her eyes on the wallpaper roll. After a moment she allowed her eyes to wander to Quayle's face. "And what are the locals talking about?" She asked.

Quayle chuckled on an exhaled breath. "Maybe?"

"Yes, maybe," Rose repeated with a scowl. "This wallpaper border has me swearing. Every time I get a strip in place and let go the roll, it falls and pulls the strip down with it. I've been doing the one step forward, two steps back thing all morning."

Not waiting for Rose to invite him, Quayle climbed up beside her on the scaffold. "How about you hold the roll. I'll paste the border?"

"Gladly!" Rose replied and slapped the trowel that she had been using in his hand. Standing beside Quayle, Rose suddenly felt small. Her body shifted into auto pilot. She inhaled deeply his masculine scent and an after shave that she could not identify. *Umm. He smells so good.*

Quayle reached over Rose's head to smooth a strip of paper to the corner of the wall. Standing just behind her, he accidentally brushed against her and felt a jolt that caught him by surprise. *The mere touch of her electrifies me. It would be so easy. If I just dropped my arms they would fall around her.*

Quayle glanced to her face and swore to himself. She's engaged, damn it! She's engaged! He followed across the paper with the straight edge of the trowel.

Rose was amazed at the amount of paste that oozed from the bottom edges of the paper. Quayle's strength was obviously much greater than her strength.

Musky. He smells musky. Rose suddenly became aware of her thoughts and of her feelings. She didn't like them.

"That should do it!" Quayle announced. He reached into a pocket of his jeans for a pocketknife and with the knife neatly trimmed the edge of the border, freeing the roll.

He climbed off the scaffold and then reached a hand to Rose. "How about that lunch?"

"I couldn't, really," Rose protested. *His hands are huge. Wonder what they would feel like if....* She snapped her eyes to Quayle's eyes and her attention to his question. "I'm a mess. I didn't dress for entertaining visitors this morning."

"You're making excuses," Quayle challenged. "That wallpaper paste will wash off, you can take that bandana from your head and you'll be as beautiful as ever."

Rose blushed. *You can't call me beautiful. I'm engaged to….*

"I know," Quayle said as if he had read her mind. "I shouldn't say things like that. You're engaged to Jan Vandeventer, only son and sole heir to the Vandeventer estate of Ashford, Kentucky. Enjoys worldwide renown, an impeccable reputation, is fabulously wealthy and is also missing in action in Vietnam."

"That's, that's right!" Rose exclaimed, her tone loud and angry.

"And he isn't here. And you're hungry and I'm hungry and I don't think he would mind one bit if I take you to lunch," Quayle said evenly with a grin that started small and grew bigger.

Unhappy with her own frustration, Rose pulled the bandana from her hair and shook her heavy copper tendrils loose. She scowled at Quayle who held up a hand.

"Wait a minute. Let's start over."

"First, I respect that you're engaged and that your fiancé would be here if he could be here. And if the tables were turned and I was missing in Vietnam I would not mind if a well-meaning gentleman took my fiancée to lunch. As a matter of fact I would appreciate it." Quayle's eyes bore into Rose's eyes with such intensity that she could not have looked away if she wanted.

"Miss McKinley," his voice sounded deeper if that were possible. "I have no intention of encroaching on your engagement. I have too much respect for myself, for you and certainly for your fiancé."

"So how about let's be friends? I'll be here for you if you need me." His tone and his face changed. "Perhaps we can share drippy ice cream cones once in a while or maybe a burger and fries. Like now, for instance. What do you say?"

His smile could melt a glacier. Why does he have to be so handsome?

Rose snapped the lid on the bucket of wallpaper paste, placed the roller and the brush in a cleaning solvent and then wiped the paste from her hands and face.

"Oh, ho!" Bennett cried. "Fresh meat!" He charged into the clinic-in-progress carrying Daniel slung across his shoulder.

Suzanne followed on Bennett's heels.

Quayle darted his look of confusion from Bennett to Rose. "Fresh meat?"

Rose laughed. "Quayle Johnson, this is Dr. Bennett Gardner, his wife, Dr. Suzanne Gardner, and their son, Daniel."

"Suzanne, Bennett, this is Quayle Johnson. He's the engineer of the *CSX* Railroad Train that sits behind Austin's about this time every day."

Quayle stuck out a hand to Bennett and to Suzanne. "Pleased to meet you folks at last, doctors. I've heard a lot about you and your partner and your new clinic. The locals are intrigued."

Quayle smiled at Daniel. "And I recently made this fine lad's acquaintance over some mushed ice cream cones." Amused, Quayle noted the crimson blush that crept into Rose's cheeks.

"Intrigued?" Bennett repeated. "That's one we haven't heard, huh, Suz?"

Quayle lifted his brows. "And I must admit, Dr. Gardner, that I find your "Fresh meat!" To be equally curious.

"Quayle, Bennett calls anyone who walks in when we could use an extra hand around here "Fresh meat"." Rose said with a laugh.

Quayle's smile stretched across his face to reveal perfectly aligned, sparkling white toothpaste-commercial teeth.

"At your service, sir!" Quayle quipped and snapped his heels together.

"But you're only here on your lunch break," Rose protested.

"Most days, Miss McKinley, that is the case, but every once in a while I do escape the close quarters of the *CSX*."

Bennett grinned. "So, Rosie, your friend here has some time on his hands?"

"I guess he does," Rose replied.

Bennett bounced his brows and crooked a finger in Quayle's direction. "Come with me, friend."

"Bennett! Are you going to keep Daniel on your shoulder all afternoon?" Suzanne asked, making a face.

"Maybe," Bennett replied with a shrug. He twisted his head to see Daniel's face. "He doesn't seem to mind," Bennett said and, with Quayle at his side and with Daniel hanging over his shoulder, he left the room.

"Well that was weird!" Suzanne exclaimed.

"Not weird for Bennett!" Rose replied. "Wonder what he's got in mind for Quayle?"

"That is anybody's guess," Suzanne remarked. "By the way Miss McKinley, why haven't I heard about this Quayle Johnson before now? You've met before, I take it?"

"Uh, yeah. At Austin's the day I took Daniel for ice cream," Rose replied. The red blush had returned to her cheeks.

Grinning the conspiratorial girl grin that is common worldwide among women who are about to share secrets, Suzanne uttered the single word "And...."

Chapter Twenty

Boyd County Jail
Boyd County, Kentucky

"Ruddy! Ruddy! Wake up. You have a visitor," Ruddy's cell mate, Spider, yelled from the farthest distance allowed by the tiny six foot by ten foot cell.

Spider, who was missing his four front teeth, had learned the hard way that you don't wake an inmate by touch, not if you wanted to keep your teeth and to continue to breathe.

"I'm gonna kill you, Spider! I ain't got no visitors, ain't nobody knows that I'm a guest of this county but the cops and the court!" Ruddy snarled.

Deputy Triplett materialized at the cell door. "Ruddy, you makin' a habit of keepin' me waitin', aren't cha? Get the lead out of your lazy butt and get to this door right now or I'm gonna have you beautifyin' this county from sunup to sunset, you hear me?" Triplett wheezed, wiped sweat from his face and emphasized his words with his night stick on the cell bars.

Ruddy didn't bother to splash water on his face or to comb his hair. He wasn't going any farther than fifty feet down the hall to another square that was divided into smaller squares by cinder block half walls on both sides of a cinderblock and glass wall.

Telephone receivers were anchored in the cinder block walls in each of the smaller squares on both the inmates' and the visitors' side of the glass wall.

On the inmates' side there were metal stools anchored in the concrete floor.

On the visitors' side there was a mix of plastic lawn chairs and metal stools that were anchored in the concrete floor.

Sullen as always, Ruddy threw off the stained blanket and climbed from the top bunk. He jabbed at Spider in passing as Ruddy strode to the cell door.

"You two make a right nice couple!" Triplett said, leering at Ruddy and Spider. Triplett pulled a noisy ring of keys from a snap-lock at his waist. He unlocked the door and stepped aside to allow the two inmates to go before him.

"Spider, number one! Ruddy, number two!" Triplett barked, indicating which cubicle the two men were to occupy.

"This is right cozy, ain't it?" Spider said as he and Ruddy took their places side by side in the cinderblock squares.

"What in thunder's she doing here?" Ruddy said and twisted his head in Spider's direction.

"She misses ya, handsome!" Spider goaded and batted his eyelashes.

Ruddy picked up the receiver.

"Hello Daniel," Melinda said. She held the receiver in one hand and held a baby that was wrapped in a blue blanket in the other.

"What are you doin' here? I don't recollect askin' for no visitors!" Ruddy snarled.

Melinda held the baby close to the window. "I come to introduce your son here, Daniel Micah Walker, to his daddy. Ain't he purty?" She said with a smile and then added "He looks just like you."

"You're wastin' your time. That kid could be anybody's and he don't look a damn thing like me," Ruddy growled.

"He does too!" Melinda exclaimed. "He looks just like you and his older brother, Daniel."

"He ain't got no older brother Daniel. I done signed him off to a couple of do-gooders what was pinin' fer a little googly- fingered freak!"

Spider banged his receiver on the cinder block half wall that separated him from Ruddy. "You give up yer kid? That one what couldn't speak nor hear?"

"Shore did!" Ruddy said proudly.

"Yer a confound, damned idiot Ruddy! Didn't your attorney tell you not to do that? Didn't he tell you yer fatherly rights?"

"I didn't have no attorney and I didn't need no attorney! I got rid of that whiney little Mama's boy all by myself!" Ruddy crowed proudly.

"That ain't all you got rid of you ignerant idiot!" Spider goaded. He banged the receiver on the wall and laughed an uproarious laugh.

"You also got rid of the five hunerd simoleans that the great Bluegrass State of Kentucky would have paid your sorry hide ever month just fer havin' a kid with what they call disabilities!"

"You didn't need no attorney, all right!" Spider said with a sneer. "You done give away enough money to buy all the smokes and beer you could need in any one month!"

Ruddy grabbed the receiver to his ear. "Melinda! Is that true? We could have had us five hunerd a month just fer havin' the little freak?"

Melinda nodded. "That's right. We could have fixed up our place and had a fine, decent home for us and both your boys."

"Damn! Damn!" Ruddy swore. The hard lines that had defined his face earlier had vanished. His eyes softened. His voice softened.

"Melinda, Honey, we got to undo this! There's gotta be a way to undo this! I didn't want to give up my little boy. I wasn't in my right mind! Bein' in a cell all day and all night gets to a body, won't let 'em think straight!"

Spider banged the receiver on the wall and then imitated someone playing a violin. Howling with laughter he banged the receiver again.

"Ruddy grabbed Spider by the wrist. "You bang that danged receiver one more time and I'm gonna cram it down yer throat? You got that? You better hope I can undo this mess because if I can't, it's gonna get real unpleasant in that cell! Real unpleasant, real fast, you hear me Spider?"

264

"Daniel, Honey, it might not matter no how if you can't undo this because we got us a Plan B and if Plan B works, we ain't gonna need no money from the great Bluegrass State! We'll have us all the money we could ever need."

Ruddy was in no mood for further conversation. He wanted to get back to his cell and see how fast he could rescind his actions in relinquishing his parental rights to Bennett and Suzanne.

But Melinda was talking about money. Albeit grudgingly, Ruddy felt obliged to listen.

The story that Melinda told Ruddy was so strange, so far-fetched and so downright unbelievable that Ruddy swore in a temper.

"Damn it, Melinda! Why'd you go and make me think we had us a Plan B? The only plan we got is Plan A and that's to get my little boy back home where he belongs!"

"Daniel, I ain't lyin'!" Melinda insisted and pressed a hand against the glass window. "SnappinClap sneaked up there under the tarps in the lady's truck. He done saw 'em with his own eyes! Cross my heart and hope to die!" Melinda said with a solemn face. And to prove her sincerity she crossed her heart with her hand.

She pressed her face to the glass window and whispered into the receiver *The National Enquirer* will pay us hunderds fer pictures of them folks!"

Ruddy glanced about as if he had been handed some great treasure to safeguard. He pressed the receiver closer to his mouth. "And you swear that SnappinClap done seen ém with his own eyes!"

"I swear it on this here young'un!" Melinda exclaimed. She lifted the baby to the window.

Ruddy cupped a hand around his mouth and spoke in hushed tones into the receiver. "Then all's we need is to get us a camera, a good camera. I'll be out of this joint soon and then we's gonna take up a little trip!"

"Don't you worry none, Honey," Melinda cooed. "I'll get us a camera!"

"Melinda! You be dang sure you don't go tellin' nobody else about this! You clap yer trap, you hear me?" Ruddy demanded and jabbed a finger at the window.

"I won't tell nobody, Honey!" Melinda promised.

Chapter Twenty-One

Quang Tri Province
Northern Central Vietnam

The tiny woman with brown skin, her face hidden beneath the wide brimmed *non la* she wore walked at a rapid pace moving quietly as a cat, careful to avoid snapping twigs or any other misstep that could be heard and possibly alert the Viet Cong to her presence and perhaps result in her death.

With the help of Soviet Tanks, Vo Nguyen Giap's troops had invaded her quiet village and the surrounding jungle earlier this month.

Giap had launched a massive attack across the DMZ into the Quang Tri Province in what the newspapers called the Easter Offensive.

Despite the war and the unwelcome invaders, the woman had a reverence for the countryside. It was pretty, fresh, alive and green.   Rice fields flourished in the wet foreground.

Dressed in the traditional *aobàba,* Vietnamese silk pajamas, the woman was intent on getting two hay bales home to her water buffalo. She easily carried the heavy bales suspended from opposite ends of a stout rod that lay across her shoulders.

Beneath bright blue skies the woman hurried past a sloping clearing and on to a wooded copse over a thick carpet of pine needles.

The woman lost her footing and fell on the slippery needles. She retrieved the rod, replaced it on her shoulders, adjusted the weight of the bales to a balance and then screamed.

The decaying body of an American soldier with a U.S. Army Colt M-7 bayonet protruding from his chest lay within inches.

This soldier was a friend, an ally. He and thousands of others like him had come to her village, to her world, to rescue her and to fight off the Viet Cong that murdered, ransacked, raped and pillaged, threatening her and her countrymen's way of life.

The woman lay aside her burden. Carefully and with great reverence she removed the dog tags that identified the soldier as E-4, PFC Randall James Fitzpatrick with his Army identification number following.

She wrapped her hands around the end of the bayonet and yanked. The knife pulled free.

The woman sat on the ground beside the soldier. Tears fell from her eyes as she prayed over the fallen warrior. She vowed to alert the Americans that she knew would inform his family, retrieve his body, and return him home to American soil.

The woman flattened a palm on the pine needle carpet to push herself from the ground when her hand fell on a metallic object.

She brushed away pine needles and picked up a second set of dog tags. These identified a soldier as E-6 Klaus Janssen Vandeventer, Jr...

The woman knelt and dug beneath the pine needles with her hands. She struck the ground with the bayonet, digging, searching, to no avail.

If there had been a second body here, forces from either side could have removed it. Wildlife could have dragged it away, or could have so completely devoured the remains that nothing would be left to recover.

Again, the woman offered a prayer for the second fallen hero. She carefully placed the two sets of dog tags in the pocket of her *aobàba* and then plunged the bayonet deep into one of her hay bales for safe keeping.

She stood, retrieved her burden and then set off for home.

"Look at them," Rose said. She drove slowly through the community of Wolf Laurel Creek with Suzanne and Daniel. The women had passed the morning purchasing additional building supplies for Mustafa's clinic.

Wolf Laurel Creek returned slowly to some semblance of normal. The Army National Guard had completed its search and rescue mission. The remaining Guardsmen busied themselves with the final stages of clean-up.

Houses that had been deemed too damaged to occupy had been bulldozed and removed.

Those homes that could be salvaged and restored looked like beehives with scaffolds, carpenters, electricians and other tradesmen coming and going and plying their trades.

A number of citizens had gathered this week in Loganville to discuss building a memorial to the deceased flood victims.

The Federal Department of Housing and Urban Development had delivered several small, identical, white clapboard mobile homes in an attempt to create communities for the homeless.

The walls of the units were paper thin. There was no front porch and no back porch. The displaced citizens complained that the flimsy structures afforded no privacy.

"If you flush the toilet everybody in the community hears it," Lindsey Watson, one of the flood's many teen survivors, had complained to Rose. "There ain't nothing to do no more. We all used to get together and have cook-outs. We played volleyball and baseball and went to the picture shows together."

"We visited our neighbors and they visited us. Nobody worried for their young'uns 'cause there wasn't no strangers nowhere. Everbody knew everbody. Now I don't know who's flushing the toilet next door but I can hear 'em!"

Lindsey was also one of the communities' many pregnant teens. Widespread teen pregnancy was a new phenomenon in Wolf Laurel Creek.

Before the flood, families had enjoyed close bonds. They had attended church together. Two-parent families had been the rule rather than the exception but the flood had changed all that.

"You can't help but feel sorry for them," Suzanne said of a gang of teens that milled about under a tree. Some sat on the cold ground, others stood or wrestled or smoked cigarettes. They all talked and laughed in loud voices.

"One, two, three, four," she counted aloud. "I met those girls this week and they're all pregnant. None of them are married and none of them have the means to support a child."

"These people lost a lot more than family members, neighbors, and homes. They lost a way of life. Any sense of community that these kids or their families previously enjoyed is gone, swept away in flood waters."

Rose nodded in agreement. "Mustafa's going to have his hands full. All of these girls will need a pediatrician and some crash courses on how to care for and raise a baby. In the meantime, they need nutritional information for themselves so they can be as healthy as possible during their pregnancies."

"Are you getting hungry?" Rose asked. She glanced over Daniel to Suzanne on the passenger side of Rose's pickup.

"As a matter of fact I am," Suzanne replied. "That bowl of shredded wheat that I had for breakfast wore off a while ago.   She asked Daniel in sign language if he was hungry and then laughed as he signed *Yes. Ice cream.*

Rose pulled into the parking lot where the renovations of the building that had been a former drugstore and deli were taking shape.   The building was beginning to look like a medical facility.

"Don't you think that maybe ice cream and cake are in order?   It's time we had a celebration!   I think we should celebrate Daniel's new parents and Mustafa's new clinic. It's almost done."

Rose looked to Suzanne.   "What do you say, Mommy?"

"I'm all for it!" Suzanne agreed.   "We'll make lunch a mini-celebration with burgers and ice cream.   And since we are getting so close to finishing the clinic, maybe we can have a combined celebration later."

"We'll celebrate the little boy who has made our family complete and the opening of Mustafa's clinic at one time. That'll give us an opportunity to meet some more neighbors and to introduce Mustafa.   He's still worried that the locals won't accept him."

Recognizing the familiar site, Daniel squirmed to be free of his seat restraints.   Suzanne pressed the release on his booster seat as Rose climbed out of the truck.

Rose opened the passenger door and lifted Daniel from Suzanne. She placed the child on the ground. "There you go, Daniel," she said.

The child wasted no time running into the building looking for Bennett.

Suzanne and Rose unloaded tile squares and cabinet hardware from the bed of the pickup. "That little boy loves Bennett just as much as Bennett loves him," Suzanne commented.

"From what I see he's pretty fond of his mother too," Rose said.

"You know Rose, in my wildest dreams I never thought that Bennett and I would come to West Virginia to help Mustafa and then return to Kentucky with a little boy of our own. How did it happen?"

"I don't know," Rose replied. "But I'm glad it did. You and Bennett have always had a wonderful, close relationship, but I think that Daniel has added something even more special and wonderful to it."

"Hey, didn't you girls feed this boy? He's telling Daddy that he's hungry," Bennett said with the widest of grins.

"Daddy, huh?" Suzanne repeated. She kissed the back of Bennett's hand as Bennett held Daniel in his arms.

"Actually, we girls thought that you boys might like to join us for burgers and ice cream at Austin's. Daniel told Mommy that he wanted ice cream.

"Come here, you!" Bennett's eyes sparkled with a love for Suzanne that he felt certain nothing would ever diminish.

Suzanne gladly returned to Bennett, put her arms around him and Daniel and hugged them both.

"Moose, are you up for burgers and ice cream?" Bennett called to Mustafa.

"Why Mustafa must be up for burgers and ice cream? They serve in elevator now?"

"Wow! Way to go Moose!" Suzanne said and clapped her hands.

"He's learning, he is!" Bennett added.

Rose shook her head. "Poor Daniel! He's going to have to get the hang of all this and fast!"

"Don't you worry about my boy Rosie! He'll get the hang of it in no time. Me, Mommy, Uncle Moose and Aunt Rosie will see to it!"

"Who's driving what?" Rose asked.

"We'll take the minivan so we can all fit," Bennett replied. He added "I think we got it unloaded yesterday."

"Suz, you girls grab that booth over there. We'll order for you."

"Want me to take Daniel?"

"Nah, it'll be fun watching him order in sign language."

Suzanne smacked Bennett's shoulder. "Bennett Gardner, that was awful!"

"No it wasn't. It was funny!"

Mustafa made no reply distracted as he was, watching diners at a corner table.

"Help him! Somebody help him!" A woman cried. She stood and frantically waved her arms.

The man beside her clutched his throat and made loud choking sounds. The color had drained from his face.

Mustafa sprinted across the diner. He shoved the table out of the way so that he could get to the distressed man. In a lightning stroke Mustafa yanked the man to his feet and then stepped behind him. With the heel of his hand, Mustafa struck the man high on his back, between the man's shoulder blades.

The man continued to fight for air.

Mustafa centered himself behind the man, and then, reaching from behind, felt for the man's rib cage. Mustafa covered his left hand with his right hand, thumbs in, and then he pulled his hands inward and upward with quick upward thrusts while pressing into the man's abdomen.

Mustafa repeated the maneuver.

The man coughed until he expelled the French fry that had lodged in his throat and cut off his breathing.

The man's wife who had watched in fearful silence grabbed Mustafa in a bear hug. She squeezed the surprised doctor and gushed "Thank you Mister! I don't know what we would have done if you hadn't been here. God bless you Sir."

Calming a little, the woman continued "I'm sorry, I can't place you. You must be new around here or visiting, maybe." She glanced to her husband. "There aren't too many people in this valley that we don't know."

"Janice, Honey, this is Dr. Mustafa Dhingra, the doctor I was telling you about. He's opening the new clinic up the road in Argollite."

"These are his friends, Dr. Suzanne Gardner, Dr. Bennett Gardner, and Rose McKinley. The Gardners are the folks that are seeing to our little Daniel here," Vena Mae Thompson said.

Having entered the restaurant moments earlier, in time to observe Dr. Dhingra performing the Heimlich maneuver on her pastor, she shifted her pocketbook to the opposite shoulder, held out her arms to Daniel and laughed as the smiling child ran into her arms.

Rose and Suzanne hugged their friend in turn. "Vena! It's so good to see you! Please join us, we're having a mini celebration because the court granted us custody of Daniel and because Daniel wanted ice cream for lunch!"

"Well bless God!" Vena cried. "He's still in the business of answering prayer!"

Vena winked at Mustafa. "Not a bad start in this community, Doctor. My friend here that you just saved from choking is Reverend Dr. Darryl Hobson, and this is his wife, Janice."

"Dr. Hobson's the pastor of that great big white stone church up on the hill, Argollite Baptist Church."

"I am that," Hobson said. "And I would first like to thank you Dr. Dhingra for coming to my rescue. For a moment there I envisioned meeting Our Lord today. While I do look so forward to that glorious day, I feel that there is still much work to do before I go."

"Thank you, Sir. And I would like to invite all of you to be our special guests this Sunday. We provide children's church for the little ones and Daniel here will find plenty of friends."

"Thank you Dr. Hobson," Mustafa said. He shook the man's hand and said with a polite nod to Hobson's wife "Mrs. Hobson."

"We better feed this boy before his cheeseburger gets cold!" Bennett announced. He took a tray loaded with burgers and fries from the counter and said to the Hobsons and Vena "Vena, Dr. Hobson, Mrs. Hobson, you folks are welcome to join…."

The door to Austin's Burgers and Cones slammed open with a reverberating bang!

"Rose! I saw your truck out there. Where are your doctor friends? This little girl needs a doctor! Her daddy said she ate some peanuts and then she passed out. She's not breathing. He tried in the parking lot to give her *CPR* but she's still not breathing!" Quayle Johnson yelled.

Breathless, he crossed the diner quickly with his long strides. The young girl in his arms was still and pale. Her lips had turned blue.

"She's all I got! She's all I got!" Her father wailed.

A wiry little man in overalls and a dark tee-shirt, he followed Quayle into the restaurant bellowing. "The flood took her mama and her brother! Jenny's all I got. Lord help me, don't take my Jenny! Jenny's all I got!"

Reverend and Mrs. Hobson quickly made their way to the man.

Rose and Suzanne cleared a padded bench in a corner of the restaurant where Quayle placed the girl.

Suzanne bent over the child and administered *CPR* while Vena and Rose assured Daniel that the little girl would be fine, no need for worry.

Bennett and Mustafa raced to the parking lot and to Bennett's minivan. "You got any epinephrine in your bag, Moose?"

"Yes!"

"Hypodermics?   Alcohol?"

"Mustafa have all in bag."

"Grab it, let's go!   I'll sterilize, you give her the injection."

Bennett and Mustafa worked together quickly and efficiently.

Bennett sterilized the point of injection on the little girl's thigh with an alcohol-soaked gauze square.

Mustafa injected the epinephrine.

No one in the diner had remained seated.   Patrons and their children stood watching the little girl and the circle of friends and doctors who had moved swiftly to help her.

When Jenny opened her eyes the patrons applauded, whistled and cheered.

"Isn't that something?   The Lord seen fit to have these doctors here to save that little girl!"

The conversation in the diner focused on Mustafa, the new doctor with the hard –to- pronounce name, an accent that was hard to understand, and a genuine love for helping people.

Reverend Darryl Hobson prayed over the child, thanked the Lord for her recovery and then loudly praised Dr. Mustafa Dhingra.

The patrons would spread the word throughout Wolf Laurel Creek that "Dr. Moose" had saved two lives in less than thirty minutes at Austin's Burgers and Cones.

Chapter Twenty-Two

Widows Hollow
Titus County, Kentucky

"Mama, Mama! What has done got you up a makin'
coffee at three o'clock in the mornin'? You ain't been still
a minute all night and I ain't been still neither 'cause of it!
What is goin' on, Early Mae?"

"I gots to axt but I ain't sure I'm wantin' to hear the
answer 'cause, Lord I done know it ain't good," Mule drug
down one corner of his mouth, his eyes were dark with
foreboding. "Naw, it ain't good a'tall!"

Mule Johnson could perhaps have claimed the prize if a
prize had been offered for husband who best knows his
wife.

Mule, having been married to Early Mae, "Mama John"
Johnson, for over forty years could read her like a book,
predict her moods, and could wordlessly communicate with
her over any distance.

If Mule was hunting three counties away and Mama John needed him, Mule knew it. It was like she sent him mental teletype. "Mule Johnson, get yourself home. I'm needing you."

The signals were never mixed. The message was never wrong. Mule would arrive home to a circumstance that required his hand, his skills, his strength or his emotional support. It had been this way from the beginning.

Now, looking at Mama John's face, Mule knew that it was dark clouds that gathered. He equally knew that this news would not be bad. This news would be devastating.

As if she had read Mule's thoughts, Mama John burst into tears. She wailed loud and pitiful. Her body shook with sobs.

"Them soldier officers, the ones in the nice uniforms with the creases in the pants and the shiny shoes and with they caps on just so, and with quiet words, them soldier officers is coming. They coming this morning!"

Tears slipped from Mule's eyes. He understood. He understood completely.

"There you big baby!" Suzanne huffed. She placed a plate of roast beef, potatoes, carrots, and onions before Bennett.

"There's the home cooking that you've been whining for and you better enjoy it because it may be the last you get for a while."

Bennett planted a kiss on Suzanne's cheek. "Why is that?" He asked. "Are you planning to fire the cook?"

"I'd like to," Suzanne replied. "But we're going to be so busy in the next couple of weeks I doubt that we have time to cook."

"We're planning a little get together to celebrate opening Mustafa's clinic and to celebrate your being new parents," Rose said.

She ladled brown gravy over her potatoes and continued. "Thanks to Pastor Darryl and Janice Hobson, Vena, Quayle, and Austin's Burgers and Cones, I think "Dr. Moose" Dhingra and his new clinic will do just fine here in Wolf Laurel Creek."

"People have dropped off enough plants at the clinic this week to start a nursery," Suzanne said.

She cut up roast beef for Daniel who ate carrots like they were candy.

"I've never seen a child choose vegetables over sweets like Daniel does," she remarked.

"But he likes ice cream," Rose said.

"That he does so we will have ice cream at our get-together," Suzanne replied. "Chocolate ice cream," she added.

"So who are you inviting to this shindig?" Bennett asked.

Seeing that Daniel had finished all the carrots on his plate Bennett signed to Daniel *more carrots*?

Daniel nodded with enthusiasm and banged his fork on his plate.

Bennett spooned carrots onto the little boy's plate. With that proud parent look on his face he quipped to Suzanne "Look Suz, we have us a drummer in the family!"

"Where you going to have shindig, Beanie?" Mustafa asked. He squeezed his brows together as if deep in thought. "And what is shindig?"

Bennett laughed. "It's a party, a celebration, happy gathering, anything along those lines."

"And where we going to have shindig? Mustafa's house or at clinic?" Mustafa asked. He suddenly snapped his head backward and reached a hand to his forehead.

"Daniel, no!" Bennett barked. He shook his head and squashed his first two fingers down on his extended thumb.

Rose and Suzanne had to hide their laughter for Daniel had just fired his last chunk of carrot across the table and it had landed square in the middle of Mustafa's forehead.

The women's laughter was contagious.

Bennett had to gather himself. He realized quickly that wiping a grin off a new father's face was not as simple as one might expect.

Bennett did not want to scold Daniel but throwing vegetables at the table could not be allowed no matter how funny Bennett found Daniel's antics to be.

Mustafa recovered in an instant from the sudden and unexpected impact. He laughed. "This boy all boy," he said.

Mustafa stood, rumpled a hand through Daniel's hair and headed for the sink to rinse his plate. He turned on the faucet when the phone rang.

"Hello. Yes, you hold one minute, please," he said into the receiver. "Rose, is your brother, Jimmy Joe."

Still smiling at Daniel, Rose took the phone. "Hello," she said and then listened in silence for a moment.

"What?" She cried in a tone that drew the immediate attention of her friends. "Was anybody hurt? Did you get the horses out?"

"Jimmy Joe! How could this happen? We've practiced every possible precaution from the beginning to prevent anything like this!"

Rose's expression turned from one of dismay to one of anger. "The dogs didn't sound off?   Where were the hands? We pay them to take care of the horses! All they have to do is take care of the horses! Where were they Jimmy Joe?"

Rose listened again for a few moments and then replied. "I don't know! I hadn't planned on returning anytime soon. We still have a good bit to finish up here."

Rose let out a gasp and then slapped a hand over her mouth. With her eyes stretched wide, she gave her head a violent shake.

"Arson? The fire chief said it was arson? Somebody deliberately set our stables on fire?" Tears welled in Rose's eyes. "I can't imagine! Who would do such a horrible thing?"

Suzanne scraped back her chair. With her unfailing support she hurried to Rose.

"Arson?" Bennett repeated. He shook his head as if to remove the thought and then met Mustafa's eyes. "Somebody deliberately set Rose's stables on fire?"

Bennett wagged his head again, this time with anger. "I can't believe it! I can't think of any single individual in Widows Hollow that is more loved than Rose McKinley!"

"She doesn't have an enemy!" Bennett slammed a fist on the table. "So who in the hell would set her stables on fire?!"

Suzanne glanced from Bennett to Daniel.

Bennett's eyes softened. "Sorry my love. Guess sometimes it's a good thing that Daniel can't hear."

"I don't blame you Sweetie. I can't accept this either and believe me, I feel so angry I could swear too!"

Klaus Vandeventer unbuckled the cinch beneath his horse's belly and then lifted the saddle from his shining ebony thoroughbred, Rogue.

He swung the saddle up and onto the fence that encircled his pasture nearest the front barns.

Dust in the distance down the tree-lined lane that led from Vandeventer Farms to the highway announced an arriving vehicle.

Klaus had planned to bathe and brush Rogue but waited now to identify his visitors.

The tags on the dark green vehicle said U.S. Government.

Two officers in meticulous dress uniforms and an Army Chaplain exited the car. The ranking *NCO* carried an envelope which he gave to Klaus. "I'm sorry sir."

Klaus looked from the envelope to the man and blinked. He didn't understand.

"You are sorry? Sorry for why?"

The officer nodded to the envelope.

Klaus opened the envelope and read the brief paragraph. "Dis cannot be!" He cried. "Dis cannot be!"

The chaplain stepped forward. "Sir, I...."

The ranking *NCO* began "Sir if there is anything the Army can...."

Klaus shook his head. "I am sorry, I have no wish to be rude, but go. Please go. Please!"

Silently the two officers and the chaplain returned to their vehicle and drove away.

Klaus slumped to the ground where he stood. He had lost his son.

Tears splashed on the man's face. Klaus Janssen Vandeventer Senior pulled his knees to his chest, dropped his head to his knees and bawled.

In an insane world where nothing is certain, where in a split second the life you know can vanish forever, Klaus was certain of one thing. After he shared this news with Olga, it would not be long before he would lose his beloved wife too.

Chapter Twenty-Three

"I'm glad the weather's cooperating today. If the weatherman's right, we'll be able to walk around without sweaters. He said the temperature should climb into the seventies this afternoon."

Rose leaned to her right in her pickup to kiss Daniel on his forehead. She unbuckled his car seat and then waited while Suzanne gathered the items that were necessary for a short outing with a four year old.

"Juice, snacks, toys," Suzanne said, naming off the items that she had brought and had packed into a shoulder bag.

She slipped the bag's strap over her shoulder and then lifted Daniel from his safety seat.

"Yeah, I agree, Rose, but I can't help but feel a little guilty. There's still so much to be done before Mustafa can open his clinic. I feel like I should be there helping him and Bennett."

"All work and no play makes Suzanne, Rose and Daniel stir crazy!" Rose remarked with a laugh.

"I don't think I've ever spent so much time indoors in my life. I miss the outdoors, the smell and touch of trees and grass and flowers. I miss my garden. There's something therapeutic about digging in the dirt, planting seeds and sprouts and then watching them pop out of the ground."

"Seeds and plants become a community that includes blue jays, dragonflies, lady bugs, butterflies, bees, wasps, frogs, you name it. I'm convinced that they come to play and to enjoy the beauty just like humans."

Rose locked the pickup. Walking beside Suzanne and Daniel, she continued. "When I get home building a greenhouse will be my top priority. There's no doubt that Olga's greenhouse inspired my love for them even though Olga's is for flowers, trees and shrubs and mine will be primarily for vegetables."

Rose took the shoulder bag from Suzanne's shoulder and placed it on her own. "I can almost taste them now, garden fresh tomatoes, onions, jalapenos, asparagus, and pole beans."

"Sounds to me like someone's getting homesick," Suzanne remarked. She looked to the rows of vendor

stalls, colorful rides and big tents. "This flea market looks
like it goes on and on. Daniel's ready to run and play and
explore. Where shall we begin?"

"Whoa!" Suzanne yelled with a laugh. She grabbed
for Daniel who sprinted off to investigate the toys that
beckoned from tables that were just the right height for a
curious little boy.

"You're gonna have to get faster!" Rose exclaimed.
Together with Suzanne she raced after Daniel.

"It looks like everybody in the county had the same
idea that we had in coming to the flea market. I never
realized there were this many people in Laurel County and
it looks like most of them are here," Suzanne said.
"Refresh my memory, Rose. Why did we come?"

Rose looked over the crowds of people then said to her
friend, "We came here to get some fresh air, to let Daniel
run and jump and shout and to maybe find some things for
the clinic walls."

"Hey, so we really are working! I feel better now,"
Suzanne admitted.

"Oh, smell that heavenly smell!" Rose exclaimed in
delight. "Wood smoke! I love it. It ranks right up there
with lavender, roses, honeysuckle, and apple blossoms!"

She drew in a deep breath. "There's nothing better on a cold night than the sounds and smells of a crackling wood fire."

"Uh, that may be a personal observation," Suzanne said with a giggle. "On a cold night I, myself, am pretty fond of cuddling up with one Dr. Bennett Gardner."

"You're not fooling anybody," Rose said. "You're fond of cuddling with one Dr. Bennett Gardner whether it's cold or not."

Suzanne and Rose followed Daniel into a tent that all but busted its seams with displays that were designed to attract children.

Barbie Dolls, doll houses, doll clothes, cars, trucks, toy soldiers, cowboys, horses, games and books beckoned to the young flea market visitors who gladly pulled their parents in for a closer look.

Daniel moved slowly through the toys, picking up and replacing one after another until a train on a colorful tabletop caught his eye. Lionel's Mighty Sound of Steam Allegheny Train chugged around a winding track, delighting the boy with its realistic, intricate detail and chugging motion.

The heavy duty die cast engine and tender climbed hills and wound its way through the miniature train station and village pulling a hopper, gondola, a variety of boxcars and a caboose. The working locomotive sounded off with a realistic train whistle.

Daniel watched the train, entranced by the motion, color, and by the automated arm push levers that rerouted the train to an alternate track.

"This is going to make Santa's job really easy," Suzanne remarked. "Maybe I better ask him to bring two train sets, one for Daniel and one for Bennett."

"I'd be happy just asking for one," Rose replied. "Maybe I'll change my mind about the wood smoke being my favorite winter thing when Jan returns and we get married."

She nodded at Daniel whose enthusiasm over the train was fun to watch.

Something unseen and unbidden prompted Rose to confide to Suzanne "I just hope that Jan and I are as in love and happy as you and Bennett. I know lots of married people but none of them are as close as you two."

Rose fell silent as if deep in thought. "Suzanne, I love Jan too much to risk failing him as a wife. What's your secret? What's the magic between you and Bennett? What does it take to have a love like yours?"

Suzanne moved closer to Daniel. The crowd inside the toy tent was getting bigger

"Rose, there are probably as many answers to that question as the number of people you could ask but for me and Bennett, a few things come to mind."

"The first is trust. If you can't trust your partner 100% then your marriage is doomed."

"Next is respect. Bennett and I respect one another, always. Sometimes we don't agree and at those times, we talk. We're lucky. Too many people talk *at* one another. Bennett and I have learned to talk *to* one another."

"People tend to blurt whatever pops in their heads then after they've had time to think about it, they wish they hadn't. We also make snap judgments. We say things that have no basis in truth, but originate in our own imagination. In one of my psych classes they called this Stinking Thinking."

"For example, my friend, Laura, dated this guy. From the start she called him Shep although his name was Samuel. When she introduced him to her family as Shep he yelled "My name is Samuel, not Shep!""

Alone on another occasion, she called him Shep and he exploded. "You call me Shep because Samuel isn't good enough for you!"

"Laura said his words stunned her. She had never done anything to make him believe that but the conversation ended right there. They never talked about it. And she never knew why he said it or felt it."

"If they had discussed it, she would have told him that it was Shep that she fell in love with. It was Shep that called her every day, Shep that wrote her notes and poetry, Shep that said he loved her and couldn't wait to marry her. It was Shep that shared her love of gardens and growing things. And it was Shep who gave her the one cherished gift that changed her life forever."

"Laura never called him Shep because he wasn't good enough. She called him Shep because in her heart she believed there was no one better."

"Rose, whatever you do, talk with Jan. If Laura and Samuel had talked with one another their lives would have been different."

"And acceptance is a really big consideration. If you love someone, you don't try to change them. You accept them the way they are. You accept everything about them. You don't try to rearrange his life with his furniture and he doesn't try to turn you into Suzy Homemaker when your talents lie elsewhere."

"Trust me, Rose, it hasn't always been smooth sailing for Bennett and me. I'm hyper-sensitive. I cry at the drop of a hat. Things that most people let slide off their backs, I take to heart."

"At first, when Bennett hurt my feelings, I reacted like a wounded animal. I ran away and hid. Bennett didn't like that. He feared saying anything to me that I might take as criticism. We refused to talk and went to our separate corners."

"But again, we were lucky. We cared enough about one another to analyze our problems and to find ways to solve them. I looked at myself through Bennett's eyes. I didn't like what I saw so I took steps to change."

"Instead of being hyper sensitive, I came to accept Bennett's advice in the way that he intended it, to help me, not to hurt me."

Suzanne raised a finger. "And, there are two sides to this story. Bennett Gardner used to be rigid and demanding. It was his way or else. He could make a big deal out of something as simple as folding underwear wrong side out. He didn't put them on right side out or, God forbid! Just refold them himself. No, he had to point out to me that I folded them imperfectly!"

Suzanne made a face. "Am I wrong here? Is folding underwear wrong side out that big a deal? I mean, really, if he cared about me, how important would that be? Sometimes I'm concentrating on other things. I don't fold the laundry perfectly or I start the dishwasher too soon, or I don't put the knives in the end pocket of the dishwasher or I fold the wet towels that he would spread out to dry."

"Rose, I never expected my domestic talents to win Homemaker of the Year. I didn't play house as a child, I played hospital and I never thought I would marry a micro-manager, but in the beginning, Bennett Gardner was a micro-manager!"

"When he was in the service they noticed too. He told me that they said of him "There's the Air Force way and then there's the Gardner way.""

"But we both know that we aren't going to change. We are what we are, we are who we are. Bennett and I have learned to talk and we've learned to compromise. We accept each other as we are."

"I married him because I love him. He married me because he loves me. Our love is unconditional. That's why it works."

"Suzanne, how did you know? How did you know that Bennett was the one? What made him different from the others?"

"For me it was easy. While there were plenty of guys that I could have lived with, could have gotten along with, I knew in my heart that there was only one that I couldn't live without. And that was Bennett."

Daniel squealed with laughter and reached to touch the moving train.

"Rose, you think we're going to get out of here without a new train set?" Suzanne asked. She lifted Daniel's chin with her finger and then signed to him "Want some juice?"

Daniel nodded.

Suzanne reached into her bag, retrieved a cup of juice and gave it to Daniel who made short work of it. He drained the cup in a couple of gulps and then returned it to Suzanne.

"Ah, I get it," she said. "This little boy had rather watch the train than drink juice."

"He's too smart for a four-year old," Rose said and then screamed.

A big man dressed in dirty jeans, a ragged denim shirt and manure-encrusted barn boots snatched Daniel. He lifted the boy to his shoulder and squeezed him.

"Put him down!" Rose demanded.

"Get away from my son!" Suzanne shouted. She threw the bag off her shoulder and pulled Daniel from the man's arms.

"SlappinClap ain't gonna hurt him. He's knowed Daniel longer'n you. Besides, Daniel ain't yer son! He's Daniel Ruddy's son and he's gonna be comin' to live with me and his daddy and his baby brother here!"

The woman nodded to the baby that she carried in a soiled blue blanket. The woman herself was dressed in a dirty white blouse, too tight pedal pushers and scuffed boots. Her hair looked stringy and unwashed.

The man beside her that she called SlappinClap looked like he could use a shower too.

"What do you mean, he's Daniel Ruddy's son?" Suzanne demanded. "Mr. Ruddy signed away his parental rights and we have the court papers to prove it!"

"Them papers don't mean nothin'. Daniel's lawyer done told him Daniel's gonna get little Daniel back 'cause nobody told him no better than to sign them papers!"

"Daniel loves his little boy and he wants him home with us and his baby brother here!"

Suzanne fought hard to keep her composure. "Who are you? Who is this man?" She demanded.

"I'm Melinda Walker. This here's my brother Lenny but we call 'im SlappinClap."

The woman glanced to her brother and said in a mocking tone "Give him a minute, you'll see why. We's here to find us a camera. My Daniel needs one."

Melinda poked a finger at Suzanne. "Yer married to the doctor what come to our place when Baby Daniel here was born and there's another doctor what lives with you too."

"Daniel Ruddy is in jail!" Rose spluttered. "He can't possibly want Daniel. Even if he did, he can't care for a child while he's in jail!"

"Co..., county," *slap*! "Pay five hun..., hundred," *clap* "Dollars every mo..., month for Little Daniel!" The man that Melinda had introduced as her brother, Lenny, said.

A firestorm flashed from Suzanne's eyes. "Is that what this is all about? Daniel Ruddy's had a sudden change of heart because somebody told him that he can collect five hundred dollars from the county every month for Daniel?"

Melinda said to Lenny in a threatening tone "You shuda kept your mouth shut, SlappinClap Daniel ain't gonna like it that you told!"

Lenny tried to get close to Daniel but Suzanne would not allow it.

Melinda nodded to the four year old. "You might as well let SlappinClap hold him. Daniel loves SlappinClap. They been friends fer a long time. We was friends with his mother, Mary, too."

Suzanne fought back tears. This couldn't be happening. This woman had to be mistaken. No court would take Daniel from her and Bennett and return him to a man who didn't want him, didn't want anything but the money. It couldn't happen.

Suzanne consoled herself by repeating the words in her mind. *It can't happen. It won't happen.*

She held Daniel away from her so that she could see his face. "Friend?" She said and signed to the little boy at the same time as she nodded to Lenny.

The four-year-olds' look of sheer delight answered Suzanne's question. A smiling Daniel reached his arms to the big man who took him and held him close.

"Suzanne, we promised the guys that we'd be back for lunch. We need to go now if we're going to make it," Rose said.

Suzanne blinked at Rose in confusion. She didn't remember saying any such thing to Bennett and Mustafa.

303

"Oh!" After a moment Suzanne realized that Rose was trying to find a way to extricate herself and Suzanne from this unsettling encounter.

Suzanne watched Lenny and Daniel play together for a little longer before she replied "You're right, Rose, we better get going!"

"Uh, Melinda, and," Suzanne began, but interrupted herself to look at the girl.

Melinda was so young. She wasn't much more than a baby at age fourteen and yet she envisioned a future with Daniel Ruddy and his two sons, four-year-old Daniel and his infant brother Daniel who Suzanne estimated couldn't be more than a month old.

Suzanne shook her head to remove the vision that flashed through her mind, a vision of poverty and squalor.

Any misguided soul who entertained the notion that Daniel Ruddy would be a good provider, a good husband and a good father was in for some serious disappointments.

Both Melinda and Lenny were poorly dressed. They were beyond dirty, filthy would be more honest. Suzanne wondered how Melinda planned to pay for a camera and why a camera?

Surely, with a new baby, Melinda had far more pressing needs. A new baby blanket would be a good start.

Suzanne could not see how the baby was dressed as he was so tightly wound in the blanket.

She could not inject her and Bennett's Daniel into this vision.   She would not.

"Uh, Melinda, Lenny, we have to go now," she said and waited for Lenny to release Daniel.

When Lenny did not let the boy go, Suzanne repeated "Lenny, would you please give Daniel to me?   You're welcome to come and visit anytime you like.   I think you know where we live and you've been by the clinic, too, haven't you?"

Lenny nodded. He liked Suzanne and Rose.   He didn't have many friends and he would like for them to be his friends.   He hugged Daniel one last time and then, making it plain that he was reluctant to do so, he returned the little boy to Suzanne.

Having Daniel back in her arms sent a wave of relief through Suzanne.   She caught Rose's eye and smiled.

"B…, bye, Daniel!   Le…,"! "Lenny loves Da…, Daniel!"

"And just don't you worry none, SlappinClap'' Melinda vowed. "You ain't gonna need to go visit him 'cause Daniel's gonna be home soon with me and you and his daddy and his little brother!"

Suzanne squeezed Daniel a little tighter and then, with Rose, walked away at a faster pace than normal.

Chapter Twenty-Four

S&S Horse Farm
Widows Hollow, Kentucky

Jimmy Joe scanned the faces before him with an intent that he didn't like to admit even to himself. He was looking for an arsonist. Family members, neighbors and ranch hands had gathered at his request near the front barns of the S&S Ranch, his family's thoroughbred farm.

Jim Johnson sat on the tailgate of his pickup with Jimmy Joe's younger brothers, Willie and Buddy.

Jimmy Joe's younger sister, Olivia, sat on a hay bale with Jim Johnson's younger twin sisters, Lucy and Lottie.

Mose Tate and Kenny Simpson also sat on hay bales that waited to be tossed into the stalls of some of the finest horseflesh in Titus County, Kentucky.

"I'm pretty sure that all of you know why I asked you to meet me here this morning," Jimmy Joe began. He didn't like what he had to say. It made him feel uncomfortable. He made a face, cast his eyes to the ground and shook his head.

"The fire department has finished investigating the fire. We lost the back stables, the storage barn, the silos and a couple hundred acres of alfalfa."

"The only reason we didn't lose all the horses in the back stables and everything else is because me and Willie and Buddy just happened to return from the Louisville auction and saw the flames."

"While all of this is bad enough, it gets worse. Chad Walker, the Titus County Fire Marshal, said that the fire was arson. Someone set it intentionally."

Jimmy Joe heard the chorus of gasps.

"Who would want to do such a thing?" Mose Tate cried. "Ain't a body in this county what don't love your sister and your family, Jimmy Joe! There ain't a one of 'em what wouldn't give the shirt off'n their back if you was a needin' it!"

Deep frown lines embedded themselves in Mose's thin face. "This don't make no sense. Hit don't make a bit of sense at all!" Mose repeated and then spat a stream of brown tobacco juice from the corner of his mouth.

"Has anybody associated with our farm made anybody mad? Have we had any complaints, any disgruntled buyers, sellers, riding students, boarders?" Jimmy Joe's eighteen-year-old sister, Olivia asked.

Being the youngest of the McKinley siblings and Rose's only sister, Olivia made up in determination what she lacked in family seniority and experience.

Dressed in jeans, gleaming mahogany boots, a crisp burgundy checked shirt and fringed leather vest, she spoke with a confidence that showed in her face and announced itself in her voice.

Born with hair so blonde that it was almost white, Olivia had changed over the years. Her fine, cotton-colored hair had turned black, a thick mass of shining ebony that now hung past her shoulders, framing her pale face and her beautiful, large doe eyes.

Having been raised from age 4 by Rose, Olivia shared characteristics with her elder sibling. She sounded like Rose too.

Olivia scanned her brothers' concerned faces, those of her neighbors and ranch hands, and the faces of her best friends from childhood, Mama John's twins, Lucy and Lottie.

"I can't believe this fire was arson, but if it was, we will find the guilty party or parties and we will bring them to justice!" Olivia exclaimed, her eyes flashing.

"To hurt our family or any property of the S&S Ranch is to hurt our neighbors and our community."

Distracted by his digging at something in the hay-strewn path with the toe of his boot, Olivia glanced to Jimmy Joe, frowned, and then continued. "And I think you all know how we feel about that!"

"We know all right!" Lucy replied.

She reached behind her head to tighten the bright paisley scarf that she wore wrapped around her hair. She and Lottie had chosen to dress alike today in denim bell bottoms, poet shirts and vests, something they had mostly avoided since childhood.

Both Lucy and Lottie with their coppery chocolate skin had porcelain faces with deep set eyes, prominent cheekbones, and delicately carved features. The two stood exactly five feet, ten inches tall and possessed a beauty that never failed to turn heads.

Lucy nodded to her twin. "I, we, remember when Pick, Rose, was little. She was only five when Stump came running to our house carrying her. Blood gushed from her head. She was bleeding so bad Lottie and I both cried. We were sure she was dying."

"Drunk boys from the city had gotten lost in the hollow. They saw Pick-- I'm sorry, family, I just can't get used to calling her Rose!" Lucy exclaimed, directing her gaze to Buddy and Willie, and then to Jimmy Joe whose grin prompted her to cross her eyes and make a face.

Jimmy Joe burst into laughter at Lucy's unexpected antics.

When the laughter subsided Lucy continued. "Those city boys laughed at her. They called her White Trash and Hillbilly. Even though she was only five Rose threw a rock at them. She yelled at them and told them they didn't belong in Widows Hollow and to get out." Lucy shook her head. "Those boys were full grown and she was so little. She could have been killed."

Lottie nodded, sharing the memory with her twin.

"Rose," Lucy continued, nodding in triumph at getting the name right, "has been protecting this community and everyone in it ever since."

"Does everyone here agree that we won't stop until we find out who tried to burn down the S&S Ranch and harm the McKinley Family?"

Everybody in the circle nodded and declared their resolve to help find the arsonist or arsonists.

Jimmy Joe squatted to pick up the shiny gold object that he had uncovered with his boot. He held it up for everyone to see. "Anybody recognize this? It's a gold initial that looks like it belongs on a woman's necklace or bracelet. "

"What's the initial?" Lottie asked. She scooted from the hay bale to get a closer look.

"It's an *M,* and its stamped 18 carat," Jimmy Joe replied.

"It could mean something, "Olivia commented. "But 18 carat gold is pretty common for the women that visit here. I think maybe we all assumed that the arsonist was male but isn't it equally possible that a woman set this fire?"

Olivia's question sparked a buzz of speculation and comments. Most agreed that they hadn't considered the possibility that a woman had set the fire.

"Let's not jump to conclusions here!" Jimmy Joe insisted. "Any woman visiting the ranch could have lost this. There's no reason for us to believe that this charm off a necklace or bracelet belonged to the arsonist."

"Olivia, there was this one guy, Mr. Brondyke, he's one of the boarders. He complained when we told him his horse colicked. But we called the vet and he came right out and took care of it. Mr. Brondyke seemed to be O.K. after that," Mose Tate said.

Kenny Simpson recoiled the rope that he had been using to drop loops over a barrel.

"Horses are going to colic, Mose. It wasn't anything that we did and I'm pretty sure Brondyke wasn't upset enough to try to hurt us or burn the place down," Kenny replied.

"Can anybody think of anything, anything at all that might have created an enemy of this farm?" Jimmy Joe's face was all business, his voice sharp.

"Everybody please think. Was there anyone who said our prices are unfair? Were there any complaints about the boarding, about the way we treat horses, the training, the hands, or any of us?"

"Whoever set this fire poured an accelerant around the silos and then they trailed it to the stables. If me and Willie and Buddy hadn't shown up when we did, this ranch and everything on it would be gone. Until we find out who set this fire, we can't afford to take any chances."

Jimmy Joe glanced at his watch. "We're going to have to have around the clock security. We can take turns and do it ourselves or we can hire an outside firm."

"Since this is our family farm and everybody here has a stake in it either as owners or employees, I'm asking you how you think we should handle it."

"I don't know about the others, but I'd feel better if we take turns watching ourselves," Olivia said.

Lucy flashed a hand through the air. "Me and Lottie agree with Olivia. We'd rather do it than have outsiders that we don't know come in here, even if they are professionals."

Kenny wagged his head and said with a laugh "As usual, we all agree. Jimmy Joe's right, we do have a stake in this farm. I'm just hired help but this farm means everything to my family."

"This farm changed our lives. It changed this whole community and I for one sure won't mind giving up a few hours to see to it that these horses and this property are safe."

"I'm with you on that, Kenny," Jim Johnson added. "And I don't think anybody here's just an employee. We've never been treated like employees. Jimmy Joe and Rose and the rest of the McKinley's have always treated us like family and in my mind, family sticks together."

Jimmy Joe caught Jim's eye with a nod and then looked around again at the faces of his family and friends. "So we all agree. We take turns watching out for the farm?"

Everybody nodded, confirming Jimmy Joe's words and then the gathering of friends and ranch hands broke into the lively and boisterous give and take that marked their closely held bonds.

"Olivia, I've got to get to a meeting with some subcontractors in Ashford. "If you have time after class maybe you and Lucy and Lottie can come up with a schedule."

"We'll have it for you this evening Jimmy Joe," Olivia promised.

"Add my name to it too because I'll do my part even though," he removed his hat and swatted it at Buddy and Willie, "it's you and my younger brothers who run this show while Rose is out of town."

Willie grabbed Jimmy Joe from behind in a bear hug. "We run it when she's in town, too," he said with a laugh.

"You wish!" Olivia cried. "All you two do is play with the horses and pretend to be cowboys. Me, Lucy, Lottie and the hands do the real work."

"Really?!" Buddy countered. "We didn't see you out here busting ice last winter so the cattle and horses could have water."

"No, and you won't see me out here this winter, either! We have to leave something for you guys to do!"

"Hey!" Jimmy Joe yelled. "Why don't one of you overworked administrators answer the phone? It's ringing in the stable."

"I'll get it!" Olivia volunteered. She jumped from the hay bale and, brushing hay from her backside, headed for the stable.

The friends and neighbors of Widows Hollow and the Samuel L. Simpson Memorial Ranch, known as the S&S Ranch, continued their playful exchanges.

Mose and Kenny, along with Willie, Buddy, and Jim Johnson, lifted hay bales and scattered hay in the rows of stalls that stretched down each side of the main barn.

"Buddy, what are we gonna do about that burned out alfalfa field? You want us to replant it this morning?" Kenny asked with a grunt as he stood from a squat with one end of a heavy hay bale in his hands.

"Yeah, we need to but I think maybe we need to get those stalls rebuilt first. If all of us drive our trucks we can get most of the materials we need in…, Olivia! What's wrong?" Buddy yelled.

Olivia cried so hard that she stumbled from the stable. Her tears blinded her.

Buddy's easy-going smile vanished. He hurried to his sister. "Olivia! What is it? What's happened?"

"Jimmy Joe! Willie! Buddy! Oh, my God!" Olivia cried. "Oh my God! How are we going to tell her? I can't tell her!" Olivia covered her face with her hands and wailed.

"Tell who what?" Buddy's heart thumped in his chest. He had never seen his baby sister cry like this and he didn't like seeing it now.

"What are you talking about? Who's upset you like this? Who called?"

In long, determined strides Jimmy Joe strode past the others to his sister. He placed his large hands on her shoulders.

"Tell me, Olivia!" He barked.

Olivia wrapped her arms around her brother. "It was Klaus that called. He called, he called to tell us that Jan's been killed in Vietnam!"

"What?" Jimmy Joe pushed his hat off his forehead. He looked at his sister in stunned disbelief. "That can't be! Olivia! That can't be right!"

Heartbroken, Olivia continued, her words mixed with sobs "Klaus said Army officers came to his ranch with a letter from the state department. The letter said that Jan's dog tags were found in the Quang Tri Province in the jungles just south of the DMZ. The village woman who turned them in to the Americans found Jan's tags beside the body of another American soldier."

Jimmy Joe swiped at his tears. "Jan's body?"

Olivia shook her head and burst into renewed sobs.

Tears fell from Jimmy Joe's eyes as he held his baby sister. After a few minutes he pulled a card from his pocket and handed the card to Kenny.

"Kenny, will you call this number? Ask for Mike Stauffenberg. Make my apologies and cancel this appointment, please."

With his eyes fixed on the ground, Kenny took the card and nodded.

One by one, Jim Johnson, Mose Tate, Kenny Simpson, Willie, Buddy, Lucy and Lottie formed a close circle around Olivia and Jimmy Joe. With their hearts breaking and with their arms around one another the friends and neighbors of Widows Hollow did what they had done all their lives. They cried together and shared one another's sorrow.

"Melinda, dang it all, why'd you have to drive this broken down jalopy here to git me? Couldn't you find somethin' that would run all the way to Boyd County and back?"

"Daniel, Honey, this was the best I could do. It got me here, didn't it?"

"Well, Honey!" Daniel shouted the word with sarcasm "That and a plug nickel ain't gonna get us back to your place! And if you think I'm walkin' from Boyd County, Kentucky to Laurel County, West Virginia, you're crazier than I thought!"

"Well, maybe it just needs a battery," Melinda suggested, seemingly unruffled by Ruddy's loud words and temper.

"Well maybe it just needs a battery! Or a transmission! Or an alternator! Or a starter! Or a danged-gone engine!" Ruddy mimicked her with sarcasm.

"Or maybe I need me a woman with enough smarts that she ain't gonna show up to fetch me out of the pokey in some broken down crate that ain't even gonna get us out of the danged parking lot!"

Ruddy glared at Melinda and growled. "Why don't you just cool yer heels here while I go find us a ride?" Then he stomped off without a backward glance.

"I ain't stayin' here!" Melinda yelled.

"I ain't slowin' down, I ain't lookin' back and if you can't keep up, that's your problem! And my business is my business! You don't see nothin', you don't hear nothin' and you danged sure don't go spreadin' it all over two counties, you got that?" Ruddy yelled.

"A'course I got that!" Melinda replied, her voice calm and steady as ever.

Ruddy put a hand to his eyes to shade them from the sun and then looked in four directions at the landscape that framed the acreage around the Boyd County Jail.

"I need to git up high so's I kin see," he said and took off climbing through the briars, boulders and scrub pines that hedged the ridge behind the jail.

Ruddy climbed and clawed his way to the top of the ridge. "Ain't this a shame!" He complained. "I just git sprung from being in jail fer three months and here I am crawlin' up a ridge like I ain't nobody and ain't got no more smarts than you!"

"I'm sweatin' and I'm thirsty and if you was anybody with any sense we'd a done been at yer place by now!"

Ruddy sat on a boulder and took in the scenery below.

There was a small Main Street with a hardware store, a post office, a drugstore, a diner and a gas station that served the locals as a garage.

Beyond Main Street and the horizontal and vertical patchwork of nearby streets, the population thinned out with dirt roads that led to scattered farms.

Ruddy watched with interest as a farmer and his wife backed a pickup from beside their barn, turned, and headed off down the dirt road that led from their farmhouse.

What he watched with greater interest was the 1960 DeSoto Adventurer that the couple had left sitting unattended beside the barn. The car's shining burgundy body, long tail fins and wrapping of gleaming chrome were something to behold.

"Now, that's more like it!" Ruddy cried. He turned to Melinda. "If yer comin' with me, you best be ready to run 'cause I'm hot steppin' it out of here and I ain't wastin' no time about it!"

He pointed to the DeSoto. "You see that car down there? That's our ride!"

Chapter Twenty-Five

"So do you think any of the locals will show up for Mustafa's grand opening?" Rose posed the question to Vena with a glance and then she narrowed her eyes in a scowl as she searched among boxes, tubes and bags that cluttered the floor and the counter in the clinic's reception area.

"I've lost my pocketknife again. Anybody seen it?" She asked on an exasperated sigh. "I need it to open this box."

Although Vena had stopped by just to say hello and to deliver messages from Reverend and Janice Hobson, Rose and Suzanne had wasted no time in recruiting her to help stock the shelves.

They had opened and shelved boxes of drug samples, cases of baby formula, gauze, Band Aids, latex gloves and other various and assorted items that physicians require in their day to day practice.

Shoving aside boxes in her search for Rose's knife, Vena replied over her shoulder. "It's hard to say, Rose. People in Appalachia have always been a different sort. They don't forget their roots and no matter what outsiders and the rest of the world think of them, mountain people are proud."

"Their pride comes from their long and sustained history of being self-sufficient. It's a tradition and a way of life that mountain folk hand down to their children. Most outsiders have misguided notions concerning Appalachia's people."

"Outsiders got their notions from what they saw on television in the sixties where a parade of politicians, presidents, would-be presidents, movie stars and glory hounds came here to tell the world about the poverty of Appalachia."

"They came in limousines with film crews and body guards making promises and talking about change and improvements, about literacy programs and making things better," Vena stopped midsentence. "Here's that knife you're looking for, Baby," she said and handed Rose the knife.

"Thanks Vena. I've worn my fingernails to nubs opening boxes."

Vena continued. "But as soon as the cameras stopped rolling all of them high-falutin' folks returned to their Washington, D.C., and Hollywood, California cocktail parties and they took their promises with them."

"Oh, they got what they come after all right. One after another they gave interviews telling tales of squalor, illiteracy, unemployment, mental illness and drug addiction problems that plague the people of Appalachia. They got talk shows, headlines, and some of them, like then Senator Kennedy, got votes."

"Everybody that watched the nightly news from California to Florida knew that forty eight percent of the households in Appalachia had incomes that fell below the poverty line."

"What they didn't know and weren't told," Vena said, emphasizing her words, was how the first people came to Appalachia."

"Nobody mentioned how the ships that arrived on these shores arrived here filled with prisoners, prisoners of the British Crown."

"The king found that keeping prisoners is expensive, even for royalty, so he emptied his prisons of blacks, whites, and children. He put them on ships bound for America and when the ships arrived here some of the prisoners escaped. Black slaves, white slaves, debtor slaves, they all escaped off the ships with one thing in mind—freedom."

"Mind now," Vena became animated, telling the story with great passion.

She wagged a finger at Rose and Suzanne. "Those runaway slaves didn't come with wagons loaded with household goods, guns, sacks of wheat, flour and sugar. No. They come with nothing. They knew nothing about farming, about raising a garden or keeping pigs or cows or chickens."

"Those determined souls settled in these mountains and hollows with nothing but hope and a prayer to be free."

"With their bare hands and little else, they built homes, raised families and they didn't ask nothing from nobody. That's why yet today lots of these mountain folks won't ask for nor accept charity. They're too proud."

"Miss Suzanne." Vena looked across the room to where Suzanne scraped tape from the new windows before she washed them. "Do you mind if I blow up one of these for Mr. Daniel?" Vena waved a latex glove in the air. "My little ones used to get the biggest kick out of playing with these things."

"You go right ahead Miss Vena!" Suzanne replied with a laugh. "I'm sure Mr. Daniel will love it!"

Rose leaned against the counter. She watched Vena blow up the glove, tie it and then bounce it in the air.

The bouncing balloon caught Daniel's attention and distracted him from his play. He had squeezed Snidely Whiplash into the front seat of a Tonka truck which he placed across his train track. He waited for the train to circle around the track, approach, and then collide with the truck. The collision bounced Snidely in the air and sent Daniel into fits of laughter.

With Snidely clutched in one hand Daniel raced across the room. Laughing loudly he batted Vena's balloon back into the air.

Rose laughed at Daniel and Vena. "You two are clearly having too much fun! What do you say, Suzanne, let's play too!" She invited.

Rose then grabbed a glove from the box and huffed air into it. She tied the glove-balloon and then swatted it toward Vena's balloon. "Bet I can float mine higher than yours!" She cried with a giggle.

"You think so, do you Miss Rose?" Vena replied. "We'll just have to see about that now, won't we? I'll get me another balloon since Mister Daniel took mine."

"So it's a competition, is it? I'm in!" Suzanne cried. She swiped an arm across her forehead and lay the knife she used for scraping the tape on the window sill. With a childlike giggle she grabbed a glove for herself and inflated it.

Laughing and giggling like children, Rose, Suzanne, and Vena swatted, batted, and bounced the glove balloons.

Daniel chased them all while at the same time doing a fair job of keeping his balloon in the air.

Vena swatted her balloon with a powerful swat, aiming for a collision with Suzanne's balloon. The balloon veered across the room and disappeared into the small foyer at the front door.

"Ha! Missed me!" Suzanne cried.

"Not for long Miss Suzanne; I've had a lot of practice at this!" Vena replied with a laugh when her balloon sailed back into view seemingly having reversed itself.

Clearly delighted and squealing with laughter, Daniel batted his balloon and chased the others.

Suzanne swatted her balloon at Daniel when the little boy's smile vanished. Ignoring the balloon, he ran to Suzanne, his face frightened--twisted with a look of panic.

"Well looky here Melinda!   It looks like our Danny boy has made hisself some new little friends!" Daniel Ruddy Senior exclaimed.

Reeking of alcohol and tobacco, Ruddy swept into the room with a cigarette in one hand and with a camera in the other.

He wore a dirty denim button up shirt that wasn't buttoned, filthy, threadbare jeans and boots that were caked with mud and straw and manure.

Melinda wore a wrinkled housedress that needed washing, grimy white socks and dirty tennis shoes.

Her blonde hair was pulled back in a ponytail and the baby that she carried by the car seat handle was wrapped in a familiar stained blue blanket.

"Mister Daniel, you can step outside to smoke.   This is a clinic and there is no smoking in here!" Vena announced with a scowl.

Daniel stuck the cigarette in his mouth, drew in a lungful of the tobacco and toxins and then spewed it into the air.   With his eyes fixed on Vena he handed the cigarette stub to Melinda and chucked his head in the direction of the front door.

Like a well-trained lap dog Melinda took the cigarette from Ruddy and threw it outside.

"We ain't interruptin' anything important, are we?" Ruddy asked with a sneer. He frowned at Suzanne who had scooped up Daniel.

Daniel put his head on Suzanne's shoulder, turning away from his father and Melinda.

"Somebody's gonna have to teach that boy some manners!" Ruddy growled. "His mother never did teach him nothin', nothin' what would make a man out of him nohow!"

"You will not speak ill of the dead, Mister Daniel Ruddy, it will not be tolerated here! Daniel's mama, Mary, was my friend, you best keep that in mind!" Vena cried, glowering at Ruddy.

Ruddy shot a glance at Melinda. "But me and his new mama, Melinda here, we're gonna change that!" Ruddy strode across the room and behind Suzanne so that he could see Daniel's face.

"I'm yer daddy, boy and you'd best get used to it! And I'm gonna teach you to show some respect real quick, you understand me boy?" Ruddy yelled at Daniel.

Clearly shaken and uncertain what to say or do, Suzanne frowned at Ruddy and clutched Daniel tighter.

"Of course he don't understand you Mister Daniel Ruddy, he can't hear you!   Or have you forgotten that Daniel is deaf?"   Vena demanded.

She and Rose stepped together to Suzanne's side, putting themselves between Ruddy and Suzanne.

"What business you got coming in here, lickered up and stinkin' of tobacco and barnyard manure?"   Vena cried. Obviously fearless and refusing to be intimidated by Ruddy, she wagged a finger in his face.

"You ain't got no right coming in here, you got no right being around this boy at all seeing as how you signed over your rights to be his daddy and gave him to Miss Suzanne and Mister Bennett!"

"But Daniel didn't know no better 'cause he didn't have himself no lawyer!" Melinda cried in Ruddy's defense. "He didn't know what he was doing when he signed them papers.   He never had no notion of giving up his boy!"

"Me and Daniel and this baby and his brother, we's family now and ain't nobody gonna say different. Daniel's lawyer done told us that we is gonna get Daniel back!"

"We've heard this before," Suzanne said, directing a frown at Melinda.

"Melinda's right, Missy! I got myself a lawyer, a good lawyer and he done told me that since I wasn't in my right mind, I was all confused-like and didn't nobody tell me my rights, and I didn't know what I was a'doin when I signed them papers, the law's gonna give me my boy back!"

"That's impossible! It can't be true!" Suzanne exclaimed.

"And just how do you plan to support him Mr. Daniel?" Vena demanded. "You ain't never had no job as far as I can recollect and little boys need a home and food and clothes! How are you planning to provide that? You can't support yourself much less two babies and a woman!" Vena declared, her eyes fiery, her temper flaming.

"The State of West Virginia's gonna give us five hunerd samolians ever month!" Ruddy retorted, puffing out his chest like a Banty rooster.

"That's right," Melinda cried. "They's gonna give it to us on account of Daniel's deaf and dumb!"

Suzanne spluttered. "Deaf and dumb? Deaf and dumb!" She cried, trying hard to control her temper.

"But that ain't all!" Melinda continued, oblivious to the effect her words had on Suzanne.

"Me and Daniel and our boys, we's all gonna be rich soon because their daddy's got hisself a plan that's gonna make us more money than any of these folks in Wolf Laurel Creek's ever seen!"

"Ain't that so, Honey?" Melinda asked. Without a glance at the baby inside the car seat, she swung the seat from one hand to the other and smiled at Ruddy.

"Will you shut up!" Ruddy growled. He looped the camera strap around his wrist and dangled the camera from the strap. He snapped his eyes to Daniel who clung to Suzanne with his face buried in her shoulder.

"Melinda here wants a family picture and I ain't plannin' to have one showin' nothin' but Googly Finger's backside!" Ruddy exclaimed. He glared at Suzanne and then pulled a crushed red and white pack of Winston cigarettes from his shirt pocket and lit one.

"Mister Daniel Ruddy you take that cigarette outside right now. You hear me!" Vena demanded.

Swinging the baby in the car seat like it was a pocketbook, Melinda stepped closer to Suzanne. "That's why we come here, to take some pictures and to learn real good how to use Daniel's new camera," Melinda gushed. She reached a hand to the little boy on Suzanne's shoulder and rubbed his back.

Suzanne stiffened. She kissed Daniel's cheek and his forehead.

"This here new camera's gonna make us rich," Melinda continued, nodding to the camera that dangled from Ruddy's wrist.

Daniel's gonna take some very special pictures for the *National Enquirer* and they's gonna pay us a lot of money for 'em!"

Vena slapped her hands on her hips. "And just what kind of pictures is Mister Daniel going to be taking that's going to make you all this money?" She demanded, looking from Melinda to Ruddy.

Daniel suddenly lifted his head from Suzanne's shoulder. He looked into her face and shaped a capital letter *L* with his fingers and then continued spelling.

"He's spelling Lenny," Vena said with a shake of her head. "This boy has always loved Lenny. No doubt he's wondering why Lenny isn't with Melinda. Lenny and Melinda were always together when they saw my Daniel."

"Ain't that just like a little googly-fingered freak! He don't miss his daddy or his mama or his new baby brother, he just misses the other freak in the family, Wolf Laurel Creek's most famous retard, Slappin Clap"

"That's enough!" Suzanne shouted. "I think it's time for you to go! We've asked you not to smoke in here and I won't have you saying such vile and horrible things in front of my son!"

"You may not have respect for anyone or anything but I won't have you demeaning Lenny in front of Daniel. Lenny is a kind, decent man and Daniel has every right to love him!"

"The little freak don't even know what I'm talkin' about Missy! He...."

"Do not underestimate Daniel! He can read lips now and he gets better at it every day! He's remarkably intelligent and he's the faster learner we've ever seen! He deserves opportunities, opportunities that Bennett and I can give him! If you care one bit about this precious little boy, you'll back off and leave him alone!"

"You ain't the only one what kin give him opportunities! Money can buy anything and me and Melinda here, we'll have plenty of it and soon!" Ruddy replied.

He walked up to Daniel. "So Little Freak Boy, you kin read lips, huh? Well, read this. Come to daddy, boy!"

The look on Daniel's face broke Suzanne's heart. She felt his little body tense as he again buried his face in her shoulder.

"Hold this!" Ruddy snapped. He unwound the camera strap from his wrist and slapped the camera in Melinda's hand. Tossing his lit cigarette on the floor, he jerked Daniel from Suzanne's arms.

Suzanne shrieked.

"Leave him alone!" Rose cried and grabbed for Daniel.

Belligerent and bellowing, Ruddy shoved Rose backward.

Rose tried to catch herself but failed. She fell hard to the ceramic tile floor.

"Come here Daniel!" A deep masculine voice commanded.

Quayle Johnson, his eyes blazing with fury, snatched Daniel from Ruddy. He returned the trembling child to Suzanne and then grabbed Ruddy's arm and twisted it behind his back.

"The lady asked you politely to leave but I'm going to insist!" Quayle growled. With one hand he pinned Ruddy's arm behind his back and marched Ruddy, cursing and kicking, out the door.

Melinda watched in dismay. Pointing her dirty hand with its chewed fingernails at Quayle she cried "You shouldn't have done that, Mister!"

"Daniel don't like being shoved around!" She glanced at the whimpering baby in the car seat and then added "He'll get you for it. Daniel will get you good!"

Paying Melinda no mind, Quayle reached his hand to Rose and pulled her to her feet.

With a glance at Melinda he said "Maybe so Little Lady, but right now it might be best if you go and see after him. He's had too much to drink and he doesn't need to be driving."

Chapter Twenty-Six

"Rose, are you all right?" Quayle asked. He had pulled her from the floor and his hands remained on her wrists.

"I'm fine," she replied, flashing a smile beneath her green eyes. "Nothing hurt but my dignity."

The hard lines in Quayle's face softened. "That Ruddy character is out of control. You ladies need to be careful. He might be harmless when he's sober but he's not sober now and it's anybody's guess what he might be capable of."

Quayle watched Ruddy and Melinda pull out of the parking lot. Despite being obviously drunk, Ruddy was at the wheel.

"That shiny car that Ruddy's driving tells me there's a good chance that he's a thief," Quayle said, smiling at Rose. "But of course I could be wrong. I guess it is possible that they saved up some money and bought it."

He inhaled deeply. Rose smelled of lavender. Her ginger colored hair was in a ponytail and she was dressed in a plain white tee shirt and jeans. Her shirt was dappled with brown spots from her window washing.

Quayle dropped his eyes to Rose's feet and then shook his head. Why did he suppose that she might be wearing shoes? He had never known anyone who insisted on having bare feet like Rose McKinley.

It wasn't exactly warm out and the clinic's tile floor had to be at least a little cold. But that didn't seem to matter to Rose. She might have come in to the clinic in shoes but Quayle had learned through their numerous encounters that it was equally possible that she had left them at home.

"No sir, Mr. Quayle," Vena snapped. "You're not wrong! Mister Daniel Ruddy never worked a week in his life!"

"Hey little boy, are you and Snidely ready for a snack?" Suzanne asked Daniel while at the same time signing the words. She hugged the little boy close, kissed his cheek and then released him.

With Snidely wrapped around his wrist Daniel ran across the room gathering the glove balloons. One by one he batted them in the air.

"Suzanne, are you all right?" Rose asked. "I can't believe they keep showing up, insisting that the court is going to return Daniel to his father."

Suzanne hugged Rose. "Yes, I'm all right. But I can't say that they don't upset me. When I think about Daniel being with those people, living in the conditions that they must live in, it breaks my heart."

"And that Ruddy! He doesn't even try to hide his contempt for Daniel. There's no doubt in my mind that this little boy's life will be miserable if he is returned to his father and Melinda. I can't imagine how he would suffer!" Suzanne turned away from the others to wipe her tears.

After a moment she straightened her face and smiled. "Rose, Vena, Quayle, anybody up for some fresh coffee? We have celery, peanut butter and crackers, apple slices and grapes. It's a five star buffet so if anybody's hungry help yourselves." She took the coffee canister from a cabinet and filled the filter with coffee.

"I pass on the buffet," Quayle said. "But fresh coffee sounds great."

Suzanne filled the coffee maker with water. "And by the way Mr. Johnson, you're becoming quite the regular around here. What brings you to our fine almost-finished medical clinic today? Have you retired from the railroad?"

"Not hardly," Quayle replied with a laugh. "I've accumulated a little vacation time and find that I much prefer spending it here with you delightful ladies rather than home alone or in a hotel room. I have a housekeeper and gardener that look after my homes so I really don't need to be there."

"Homes?" Rose asked and batted a balloon back to Daniel.

"No big deal," Quayle replied. "I have a house in the mountains here and a log cabin in the Cumberlands pretty close to the Tennessee/Kentucky line."

Rose let her eyes wander to Quayle. She looked as if she didn't see him, but rather looked right though him. After a moment she addressed Vena who had returned to stocking medical supplies.

"Vena, you've lived here all your life. Do you think there's any chance that the court will give Daniel back to his father?"

Vena left off opening boxes and storing items for a minute. Her smile vanished beneath the brows that she squeezed together in a frown. "I have to be honest with you Rose, I wish you hadn't asked me that question." Vena darted a glance to Suzanne who added grapes to a plate that she made for Daniel.

Suzanne set the plate on Daniel's play table and signed to the little boy that it was time for his snack. She opened a carton of juice for him, settled him in his chair and then returned her attention to Vena.

Vena began with a sigh. "The State of West Virginia is very protective of its population. So many young people grow up and leave the state looking for a better career and better educational opportunities than those they can find here."

"The state tries to hold on to as many of its citizens as it can so in a typical custody case where one parent is from West Virginia and the other is from another state, the court will frequently rule on the side of the West Virginian."

Suzanne's moan prompted Vena to quickly add "But not always. The court does consider all the relevant facts, and Suzanne, in this case, those facts clearly favor you and Mister Bennett."

"Thanks for that Vena, but I can't get the thought of losing Daniel off my mind. "I couldn't stand seeing him taken from us, but just as bad is knowing that losing that sweet, precious little boy would break Bennett's heart. There's no way I'm going to have one minute's peace until this is settled once and for all."

"Come here my love. I'll give you one minute's peace!" Bennett called from the doorway.

"Something smells heavenly!" Rose cried.

Bennett and Mustafa banged through the door carrying bags of burgers and fries in each hand. They deposited the bags on the counter and then spilled the contents from the bags.

"Rosie, single patty, no cheese, lettuce, tomatoes, pickles and mayo. Vena, single patty, cheese, lettuce, tomatoes, pickles and mayo. Suzanne, single patty, lettuce, tomatoes, onion, and mustard."

"Moose, you have your own, and Quayle, double patty, cheese. The rest is pot luck because it was strictly guess work. Oh, and fries all around," Bennett announced. He kissed Suzanne's cheek and then gleefully crammed a handful of fries in his mouth.

Suzanne brushed a kiss on Bennett's cheek and snatched fries from his hand. "You brought Quayle a burger and fries? How did you know he was here?"

Bennett raised his brows and twisted his mouth in a quizzical look. "How does anybody know anything in Wolf Laurel Creek? We didn't get through the door at Austin's until the locals were telling us that "The Train Man" was at the clinic.

"Good thing, too," Bennett quipped, biting into his burger. "Me and Moose just picked up a trailer load of mulch and a zillion landscape items. It's good to know that the Train Man's here to help!"

Quayle took another bite of his burger. "No problem, glad to help."

With lunch finished everyone returned to their chores. Rose and Suzanne cleared away the lunch clutter.

The men gathered outside to discuss the landscaping.

Rose tossed paper plates and bags into the trash and wiped down the counter. Sweeping bread crumbs and French fries into her hand she commented "Can you believe it, the clinic's official ribbon-cutting and grand opening is in two weeks? Is it possible that time has passed so quickly?"

Suzanne spit on a paper towel and wiped at the yellow mustard stain on her shirt. She shook her head and replied "Not to me, Rose. It seems like only yesterday that you arrived here from Widows Hollow and then, then," Suzanne fell suddenly silent, seemingly lost in her thoughts.

"The flood?" Rose's words triggered an avalanche of visual images that paraded themselves into hers, Suzanne's and Vena's minds.

Rose washed out Daniel's cup, dried it and replaced it in the cabinet. "Even the flood seems like a long time ago. If it weren't for the constant reminders, the devastated landscape, the broken and grieving families and the lost way of life that scars and will continue to scar every survivor in this community, the flood too, would seem like nothing more than a distant memory."

"In two weeks?" Suzanne repeated the words like she had just heard them for the first time. She collected empty packing boxes and carried them to the door for the men to load and haul off.

"Even though we're planning to keep it casual, more like a neighborhood get-together than a ribbon cutting, we still have plenty to do and a lot of details to attend."

"Printer first, maybe?" Rose said. She shot her arm in the air, and with a burst of laughter, caught Daniel's flying Snidely.

Suzanne and Vena clapped. "Way to go! Great catch Rose!"

Daniel continued in his favorite pastime of the moment, watching Snidely go airborne when Daniel's train and his Tonka truck collided. The child laughed with glee and ran to Rose to retrieve his beloved Snidely.

Rose returned the toy. On impulse she grabbed Daniel up and hugged him with a fierce hug. She signed "Aunt Rose loves you Daniel," and then immediately felt an overwhelming sadness.

For Daniel's sake she did not allow the tears that demanded release to flow. But the feeling of sadness was not so easy to control. It lingered and that bothered Rose. She released the giggling boy back to his play and returned to her chores.

"Suzanne, think we need to make a list?" Rose asked over the snapping sounds of the cardboard box that she broke down.

"Couldn't hurt. It might keep us from forgetting something important," Suzanne replied. She rummaged through a drawer in search of a tablet and pen.

"So, where do we begin? The printer's going to have to have some lead time so maybe we should start there. What do we want to have printed?" She asked, looking to Rose and Vena.

Suzanne waited while Vena tore heavy plastic from the new reception room chairs. "Vena, how should we do this? Send personal invitations, post flyers, mail announcements? You're familiar with the accepted protocol here in the valley so jump right in here, please."

"I believe I would go with all of the above Miss Suzanne," Vena said with her good-natured laugh. "I would send personal invitations to friends and patients that you've already seen, to the drug and medical supply vendors, and to the local doctors and hospitals so they know you're in the area."

"It might be good to mail announcements to the local residents and to post flyers at the community centers, churches, local businesses, you know," she said with a shrug of her shoulders.

Susanne bent over her writing. "Okay, no problem. Unless of course, not having any addresses might be a problem."

Vena wagged her head and laughed. "That sure ain't no problem. I've been doing this for the schools, the churches, the community centers, new businesses, and most anybody else that needed it for longer than this old memory of mine can recollect. I got all the addresses you'll need at home."

With a wink to Suzanne Vena added mounds of plastic to the boxes that waited at the door for disposal. "How about I bring them with me tomorrow?"

"Tomorrow? Hey!" Suzanne cried in delight. "Does that mean you're volunteering to help us out here again tomorrow?"

Vena squashed the plastic into the boxes. "I guess I am," she replied. "I'll help you every day as long as you need help. That way I'll be on hand when the printer's done so I can add your announcement of the clinic's opening to my scrapbooks!"

Daniel suddenly pushed his chair away from his play table. Running to Vena he hugged the woman's legs with his little arms and raised his face to her beaming face. He squashed his four fingers against his thumb and grinned.

Vena raised a hand to her mouth. "Oh, you sweet baby! You sweet, sweet baby, Daniel! Vena knows what you're saying. You remember, don't you baby? You're wantin' this old woman to make you some brownies, aren't you Sweet Baby?"

Vena spelled *b-r-o-w-n-i-e-s-* with her fingers.

Daniel hugged her legs tighter and grinned.

Vena scooped Daniel up and kissed his cheek. "You know you're gonna have them brownies tomorrow, don't you Daniel? Vena can't say no to Daniel. Vena can't never say no to her angel boy."

Rose glanced at Vena as if Vena had zapped Rose with a cattle prod. *Angel Boy.* Goose bumps stormed across Rose's arms. *Angel Boy!*

Don't say that! Don't call him Angel Boy, Vena! Rose's mind screamed. She felt her heart race and her stomach churn. Her mouth went dry. She sought Daniel with her eyes. *No! It can't be true! You're in danger, Daniel! Mortal danger!*

Chapter Twenty-Seven

Fearing that the others might feel her panic Rose fled to the bathroom. Alone in the privacy she prayed "Lord, this is Rose, the same as Pick that you knowed from when I was a young'un in Widows Hollow."

"We always been close, you and me, Lord and you told me all my life what was happenin' before it happened. I got the message you just sent, Lord, the message you sent about Daniel!"

"It can't be, Lord! It can't be! I know you don't mean no harm to that little boy! Tell me what to do! Tell me what to do to see that that little boy is safe and that he grows up to know you and love you like I do."

"Suzanne and Bennett got their hearts wrapped around Daniel, they love that little boy like he's their own. I know you don't mean to take him from them, so please Lord, show me what to do to see to it that Daniel's safe."

"And Lord, if you don't mind my askin', send your fighter angel, Michael, to stay with Daniel and protect him until the danger passes. You said in Matthew 7:7 that if I'm askin', I'm receivin', and Lord I'm askin' now! I'm prayin' in the name of the One who came to save us all, Amen!"

Rose wiped her face. She felt surprise that it was so wet with tears. She was glad that she and Vena had stocked the bathrooms. She took a hand towel from the dispenser and dried her eyes and face.

Suzanne and Bennett were already upset enough, fearing that they might lose Daniel, so Rose determined that it would be best that she not share this revelation with her friends.

Vena loved Daniel too. In fact, she had loved Daniel longer than any of them because she had known him longer. Rose didn't want to frighten Vena either so that left no one.

There was not one soul with whom Rose could share this nightmare. She looked in the mirror at the sad eyes that stared back at her.

She had learned the hard way that carrying a burden alone always made the burden heavier. But she would carry this burden alone. She would gladly carry it for Daniel.

And she would trust God for His promises. She had asked for Archangel Michael's protection over Daniel so she knew for certain that it would be Michael himself, the leader of God's angels, whom watched over and protected Daniel.

"Even so," she said to her image in the mirror "It's gonna be awful hard for me to let that little boy out of my sight." She tried a smile in the mirror to see if she could summon one and then she left the bathroom.

Suzanne and Vena arranged chairs along one wall of the reception room.

Rose looked for Daniel. He wasn't at his play table. He wasn't chasing glove balloons.

"Where's Daniel?" She asked, acutely aware that her heart rate had sped into the red zone.

"He went with Bennett and Quayle to get some more mulch. Why?" Suzanne asked with a curious glance.

Rose raced to the window. "They took my truck?"

"Yes. Why? Rose, what's going on?" Rose had Suzanne's attention now. Suzanne knew Rose McKinley better than anyone else alive with the possible exceptions of Mama John and Rose's siblings. Something was wrong with Rose. Suzanne could feel it.

"Rose, are you going to tell me what's going on?" Her concern showed in Suzanne's eyes.

"Uh, um, nothing," Rose said without looking at Suzanne. "Could I borrow your van? I need to run an errand."

Rose didn't like this, she didn't like being dishonest for any reason. God wanted people to be honest and she always tried to be; but this wasn't a lie. Not really. She did have an errand to run. She had to find Daniel. Quick.

Suzanne studied Rose for a minute. She felt certain there was no errand that Rose needed to run. But Rose was not given to deceit. Suzanne had been close friends with Rose long enough to know that if Rose said something, you could bet your life on it. Suzanne smiled. "My keys are on the counter. Will you be long?"

"No, I don't think so," Rose replied. "Can I pick up anything for anybody while I'm out?"

"Nothing for me," Suzanne replied.

"No, thank you baby, I don't need a thing," Vena said and then on impulse, she squeezed Rose with a hug.

Rose grabbed Suzanne's keys and disappeared out the door.

Through the window Suzanne watched Rose back out and drive off toward town. When Rose was out of sight

Suzanne remarked to Vena. "That was weird. Something's up with Rose."

Vena peeled a strip of cellophane off a chair leg. "What makes you say something like that Miss Suzanne?"

"Rose and I have been friends for years. I know her better than I know my own sister. Something's bothering Rose and for whatever reason she chooses not to share it with us."

Rolling it in her hand, Vena made a ball of the cellophane. She fired it at the growing pile of cardboard and plastic by the front door before replying to Suzanne.

"Maybe it's just something the child feels she needs to study on. You never know; she might see fit to tell us about it when she gets back." The gentle, warm smile that wreathed Vena's face accompanied her words.

Suzanne puffed her cheeks and spewed a deep breath. "You're probably right, Vena. Rose isn't one to keep anything to herself for too long. I'm probably just being silly." Suzanne looked at the unopened boxes, at the growing pile of trash by the front door, and at the floors that would have to be cleaned.

"I better get my mind back on this clinic's opening or it's going to open with no invitations, no guests, no food and no drinks."

Vena laughed and shook her head. "Now Miss Suzanne, don't you go and be getting carried away. We both know that ain't gonna happen."

The women turned to the sound of a vehicle arriving in the parking lot. "Hey, maybe she's back already and we won't be guessing any longer," Vena said with a laugh.

"That would be gr...!" Suzanne's smile vanished. Goose bumps prickled her arms. No! No! No! Her mind was spinning.

The grand opening wasn't for two weeks and yet through the window she watched all of Rose's siblings pile out of Jimmy Joe's truck and not one of them was smiling. Suzanne's heart sank.

"Jimmy Joe, Willie, Buddy, Olivia!" She hugged them each in turn as she called their names.

"Vena," Suzanne said with an unshakeable feeling of dread that caused her voice to crack. "Vena, these are Rose's brothers, Jimmy Joe, Willie and Buddy and this is her baby sister, Olivia."

Jimmy Joe smiled. His 6'1" frame stretched straight and rigid from beneath his black Stetson. He wore a crisp long-sleeved white shirt with a black leather vest, jeans and boots that were polished to a shine.

Willie, with his blue eyes and ebony black hair smiled a smile that sank his dimples deep in his cheeks.

Buddy, as always, shied a little and hung close to his older brothers. Both he and Willie wore black Stetsons, plaid western shirts and boots that shined like Jimmy Joe's.

Olivia towered over Willie and Buddy. At 5' 10" and reed thin, she could have easily been mistaken for a model.

Set in her flawless face of olive skin, Olivia's blue eyes sparkled in deep and noticeable contrast to her mass of thick hair that hung to her waist in cascading waves, shining like black silk.

She was dressed in light blue pedal pushers with a matching sleeveless shirt and cardigan. The light blue flats she wore looked like they had could have been died to match her outfit.

"For you, from Mama John," Olivia announced. She handed over to Suzanne a basket that was filled with Mama John's fried chicken, potato salad, green beans and with bags of Mule's famous Kentucky jerky.

Holding the basket in one hand, Suzanne pulled Vena closer with the other. "Family, this is our friend and neighbor, Vena Thompson."

The newly introduced friends exchanged hugs and friendly greetings while Suzanne looked on with a sinking feeling of horror. They shouldn't be here, she insisted to herself. Something's wrong. They know the grand-opening is in two weeks and they all have very busy schedules.

Suzanne fought hard now to prevent a domino-effect from spinning off the rumbling in her stomach. Tears leaked from her eyes. She clutched Vena's arm and scanned the four newly-arrived faces. "Jimmy Joe, what's wrong? I'm about to lose my composure and maybe my lunch. What horrible news have you come to deliver?"

Olivia met Suzanne's eyes and burst into tears. "Where's Rose?"

"She, she said she had an errand to run. She left a few minutes ago to go to town." Suzanne replied, so frightened she was certain that she couldn't breathe.

Olivia wept openly.

Buddy stepped to Willie's side and slipped his arm around his brother's shoulder.

With a single finger Jimmy Joe pushed his Stetson off his forehead. He cut his eyes to Suzanne and reached for her at the same time.

"Believe me Suzanne, we didn't want to come. But none of us could not come. We had to be together for Rose's sake. She's going to need all of us now," he said, looking from Suzanne's anxious eyes to Vena's anxious eyes.

"We don't want to deliver this news any more than you want to receive it because we know it's going to destroy our sister, her future, and her dreams."

Jimmy Joe, with determination, had set his jaw but despite that, his lip quivered. Tears fell from his eyes.

"Yesterday the Army informed Klaus that Jan is dead. His dog tags were found in the jungle just south of the DMZ."

Jimmy Joe swiped at his tears with the back of his hand. "The village woman that found his tags and turned them in to the Army said there was no body.   She found the tags in a jungle area where there's lots of wild life.   Any number of creatures could have, could have…."

Olivia rushed to Suzanne.   The two fell into one another's arms and wailed.

After a few moments Suzanne sniffled.   She raised her wet eyes to Jimmy Joe's wet eyes.   "Oh my God Jimmy Joe!   How are you going to tell her?   How are you going to tell Rose!" She repeated.

"She told me just last week that she dreamed that Jan had been captured but that he had escaped and was on his way home.   She believes that!   Rose is certain of it!"

"We know," Jimmy Joe replied, his face a reflection of misery. Rose told Mama John and Mama John told Olga."

"Olga." Suzanne repeated the word. She yanked tissue from a box on the counter and patted her face. "We've got to straighten up before Rose gets back. I don't want her to think that she's walking into a funeral!"

"Oh, Lord help me! " The stricken look on her face confirmed that Suzanne couldn't believe she'd said what she had said.

"Rose doesn't deserve this! It's so unfair! She's the most loving, giving, most incredible woman I know!" Suzanne sobbed.

"Lord help me! I've got to pull myself together before she returns!" Suzanne cried. Again, she patted her eyes, sniffled and straightened her shoulders.

"Vena, I'm sorry we're all such a mess, but we are Rose's family and we know what this is going to do to her."

"Don't you be a wastin' your time apologizing to me, Miss Suzanne! This old woman understands. I'm praying right along with the rest of you for Miss Rose--that our Good Lord will comfort her."

Suzanne and Olivia hugged Vena. "I love you Vena Mae Thompson!" Suzanne vowed.

"Thank you Miss Thompson," Olivia added.

"That's Vena, Sweet Child," Vena said, turning her soft brown eyes to Olivia.

"I haven't known your sister Rose very long, but I love her just the same. She's a fine, fine woman. All the folks in this community have come to love and respect her, too."

"Olivia, how is Olga?" Suzanne asked, gathering wads of tissue in her hand. She disposed of the tissue and then wiped the counter with disinfectant.

"Olga's not well at all, Suzanne," Olivia replied, sniffling. She pulled tissue from the box, wiped her face and then continued. "She's had bleeding ulcers for a while now. The doctors want her to have surgery but Olga refuses. She won't leave the house, refuses to see anyone, and has become very ill and reclusive."

"Klaus is going out of his mind with worry. And now, bless his heart, the poor man is beside himself. He is convinced that the news of Jan's death will push Olga over the edge and that soon he'll lose her too."

Suzanne met Olivia's eyes at the same time as Olivia burst into renewed wails. The two women embraced, pulled more tissue from the box, and then continued their sobbing in one another's arms.

Rose drove slowly through the communities of Wolf Laurel Creek. Without realizing that she did so, she shook her head at the strange, scarred landscape.

One side of the river boasted a dense population with a row of undisturbed houses where homeowners busied themselves with maintenance of one sort or another while on the other side nothing remained of the former neighborhood but a solitary tree or an overgrown lawn.

The piles of smoldering, stinking debris had been transformed into ash heaps and then churned into the ground by the clattering machinery of the National Guard.

Rose reached a hand to her stomach. The gnawing in the pit of it had returned. With a start she realized that she was driving past the site where once had stood Daniel's home.

What if she hadn't ignored Corporal Connor's demands that she not enter that house? What if they had not found and rescued Daniel?

Rose's pulse responded with a quickening as though it had read her thoughts. *Danger.* The word forced itself in her consciousness. *Danger!*

"Michael! Uriel! Archangels of the heavenly host! I know you can hear me! I know that if I am asking, I am receiving. Please protect that little boy! Protect Daniel with all the powers of Heaven!   Where is he?   Where is Daniel?   I've got to find him now!"

Despite the rough road and despite being jostled about in the minivan Rose pressed the accelerator to the floor.

Chapter Twenty-Eight

Rose scanned both sides of the road. Bennett and Quayle had taken her pickup with a trailer behind it to get more mulch for the landscaping.

Bennett had insisted that Daniel needed to get outside for a while so Daniel had gone along with Bennett and Quayle.

Her truck would be easy to spot, Rose felt certain. She tried to second-guess Bennett. Would he stop anywhere other than the garden supply or local nursery? Rose made a face. She didn't know if there was a garden supply or nursery in Wolf Laurel Creek.

Did such businesses exist here or was she looking for a private farm and some enterprising farmer who supplemented his income selling nursery items and mulch?

Rose had no idea. Maybe she could stop at Austin's and see if the folks who had lived here all their lives could help her.

Bennett scooped a shovel full of mulch from the steaming mound and tossed it onto the thin layer of mulch on the trailer floor.

"I don't know about you Quayle, but I think maybe we shouldn't have been so macho, insisting that we could load this stuff ourselves."

"For ten bucks more Farmer Joe would have filled and emptied his front loader a few times, this trailer would be loaded, my back wouldn't be cursing me and we'd already be outta here!"

Bennett leaned on his shovel and wiped sweat from his forehead. "But no, here we are, winded, sweating and stinking and we aren't anywhere near finished loading this stuff!"

"Buck up, Bennett. It's not that bad," Quayle said, laughing. "Besides, those love handles you've got look a lot like the ones I have so we obviously need the exercise!"

Quayle removed his grey Stetson. "This is West Virginia, Doc. Where's that hearty pioneer spirit?" He asked, wiping his forehead with his arm.

Raising a hand to his eyes, Bennett squinted to a sloping rise behind them that was dotted with barns and silos. "I think it took off down that path there with Daniel! He's wandering a little too far out so I better go and fetch him."

Quayle glanced at the mountain of mulch and at the mostly empty trailer. I'll come with you. I need to stretch my legs," he said and dropped his shovel beside Bennett's shovel.

"I'll give him five if you give him five," Bennett said, reaching for his wallet.

A grin played about Quayle's mouth. "Oh, so now I'm a partner in this clinic adventure?" He quipped. He gladly pulled out his wallet and slapped a five in Bennett's hand.

.

"But of course! Didn't Moose tell you?" Bennett replied, laughing.

They paid the farmer who pocketed the bills and fired up his front end loader.

"Hey, where is he?" Bennett cried.

"Who?"

"Daniel! I don't see Daniel!" Bennett's eyes went wild. He pointed to the path behind them. "He was following that path up the hill just a minute ago!"

Both men tore off running in the direction that Daniel had gone.

"Daniel! Daniel!" Bennett shouted, and then swore under his breath. "Will I ever get it through my head that he can't hear me?"

"Yell anyway. Somebody will hear us!" Quayle cried. He kept pace with Bennett who ran uphill surprisingly fast.

The two men reached the top of the hill breathless and panting.

"Daniel!" Bennett cried, sounding very much like a man with a sob in his throat. He sprinted to the little boy, wanting to grab him up in his arms and hold him, to reassure himself that Daniel was all right. But Bennett refrained.

"You're pale as a ghost!" Quayle remarked. He knit his brows and fixed his eyes on Bennett. "Are you all right?"

Bennett wiped his face on his shirtsleeve. "Yeah Quayle, I'm all right now. I guess I hadn't really given a lot of thought to how much that little boy means to me. Thinking just for a minute that I had lost him...." Bennett couldn't hide his tears. He didn't try.

"I want to grab him now but he's having too much fun throwing rocks in that fish pond!" Bennett blurted with a laugh.

"I know I should stop him," he said and raised sheepish eyes to Quayle. "And I will in a minute. But right now, I just want to watch him and hear him laugh. God, I love hearing that little boy laugh!"

"I know what you mean," Quayle said. "I have a son. It wasn't easy raising him and working my *CSX* schedule. I missed a lot, ball games, recitals, holidays, birthdays, but I always tried to let him know that I loved him, let him know that I cared and wanted to be with him."

"I tried to teach him that he didn't have to prove anything to me. I didn't care if he could hit a ball or score a touchdown or make straight *A*'s in school. I just wanted him to be himself and to do what he enjoyed doing."

"When we did have time together, I told him how important it was to treat everybody else the way he wanted to be treated. If he does that, I think he'll live a good life."

Quayle and Bennett suddenly burst out laughing.

"That's my boy!" Bennett cried.

Daniel threw a rock in the fish pond with enough force to splash water from the pond and into Daniel's face. It was Daniel's comical look of surprise that had prompted the men to laugh.

Bennett untucked his shirt and wiped the water from Daniel's face with his shirttail. "Whatever works, huh?" Bennett quipped.

"Yeah, that's one of the first lessons we learn with our kids, isn't it?" Quayle said. "My son's grown now. He grew up to be a fine man. I don't take any credit, he did it himself and I couldn't be prouder. We're still close. Even though I don't see him as much as I'd like to, we've remained close."

"He always loved animals, brought home every stray he ever ran across so it was no surprise that he wanted to become a vet. He worked hard at it and now he has his own practice in Ashford, Kentucky."

Quayle fell silent for a moment and then said "I wonder how different it all would have been if, like Daniel, my son couldn't hear or speak."

Bennett picked up a rock and chunked it into the pond, surprising Daniel who turned and grinned at Bennett.

"That smile of his melts me every time!" Bennett exclaimed. "And as for how different things might have been if your son could neither hear nor speak, I can't say. But for Daniel, they won't be all that different."

Bennett picked up another rock and at the same time as he did it, Daniel turned to look at him.

"I swear this boy has some kind of intuition that offsets his hearing loss!   Some of the things that Daniel does are just plain uncanny!"

"He knows it if Suzanne and I get crossways for one minute.   It's like he's super-sensitive.   He knows our moods better than we do and he reacts to them, always."

"We're learning from him.   Neither one of us let little things bother us anymore.   They're not worth upsetting him."   Bennett fell silent and watched Daniel play for a moment.

"And his intuition extends further than just around me and Suzanne.   Daniel sums up people in a blink.   He's outgoing and friendly with almost everyone but once in a while he comes across someone that he doesn't trust for whatever reason.   He lets us know this when he shrinks away from them because he hides behind me or Suzanne."

"Daniel can read people like that.   Suzanne and I can't do it so we always go with Daniel's reactions."

"We're going to give this little boy every advantage we can give him.   Suzanne and I are going to enroll Daniel in the West Virginia School for the Deaf and Blind in Romney," Bennett said.   He added with a laugh "We're going to enroll all of us!!"

Quayle cast Bennett a quizzical look. "All three of you? You and Suzanne are going to school with him?"

"Well, sort of. It's a long story," Bennett replied and glanced at Daniel. "Uh oh! Pointer finger, up, tip of second finger touching nose, somebody has to pee!" Bennett announced.

Bennett headed for Daniel. "All this water's getting to him. I hope Farmer Joe has a bathroom or an outhouse or something."

Quayle exploded with laughter. "You city boys are hilarious! Tell me why he needs a bathroom or an outhouse? We're in the country and there's nobody around but me and you and some pissed off fish!"

"Let the kid do what comes naturally. There's a forest over there if hiding him behind a tree would make you feel better."

Bennett shook his head and laughed. "Suzanne's gonna kill me! But when he pees in the middle of a mall or something I'm gonna tell her it's your fault!"

Bennett took Daniel by the hand and walked the short distance to a copse of white pines. When they returned shortly Daniel was all smiles.

Suddenly, Daniel tapped his wrist and then smacked his right fist with his pointer and second fingers extended into the open palm of his left hand.

"*Lost?*" Bennett signed and then repeated "Lost what?"

Daniel smacked his wrist again and raised his anxious little eyes to Bennett.

"His little toy, that ugly little rubber toy he wraps around his wrist and takes everywhere," Quayle said.

"Snidely?" Bennett asked darting his eyes between Quayle and Daniel.

Daniel nodded and pointed to the pine copse.

"What are you grinning at country boy?" Bennett shoved Quayle with a playful shove. "Come on. This was your idea! Let's go find Snidely."

With Snidely safely wrapped around Daniel's wrist, he and Bennett and Quayle walked back down the hill to the mulch mounds.

"Think we've goofed off long for Farmer Joe to have that trailer loaded?" Bennett asked, casting a sideways glance at Quayle.

"Probably!" Quayle replied. "If not, I'm sure we can find something to do that will make us look reasonably busy."

"My kind of guy." Bennett cracked.

Daniel pulled on Bennett's pants leg and, with a look of urgency, raised his face to Bennett's.

"Hey, what is it, Son?" Bennett asked, signing at the same time.

Daniel fisted his left hand, stuck his right thumb in the hole of his fist and pulled his thumb down.

Quayle roared with laughter. "I don't claim to be able to read sign language but I think even this old country boy can read that!"

"Yep!" Bennett replied. "My boy's gotta poop and there's no way I'm taking him behind a tree for that." Smiling a mischievous smile he added "But of course, Quayle, being the country boy that you are, you may want to."

"Whoa!" Quayle threw both hands in the air. "I pass. How about I square us up with Farmer Joe and meet you at the truck?" He pushed his hat back off his forehead and added, with what good country folk would call a possum grin "But ya'll have a good time now, ya hear?"

Bennett took Daniel by the hand and headed off. He shook his head and muttered "And they turn him loose across the country in big trains."

Rose hurried from Austin's with a map and directions to the farm and nursery where she would likely find Bennett and Daniel.

Reverend Hobson and his wife Janice were having lunch at Austin's. Sid Triplett, the owner of the farm and nursery that Rose was trying to find, was their personal friend and a member of their church.

Rose left the parking lot feeling encouraged. At least now she could find Daniel and see for herself that he was all right. Farmer Joe's nursery was about ten miles away.

Rose drove faster than she would normally drive. The gloomy apprehension that shadowed her refused to leave her alone.

Upon exiting the washboard ruts of Wolf Laurel Creek and turning at last onto the smooth asphalt of county roads, Rose heaved a sigh of relief.

"Ahhhh!" She cried out. With a grimace she reached a hand to her back where a sudden sharp and vicious pain stabbed at her. The pain felt so sharp it brought tears to her eyes.

"No!" Rose cried. "No!" She raised her eyes to Heaven. "This ain't my pain, it's his! Lord, git me to Daniel!"

Fearing that her heart would thump out of her chest, Rose pushed the accelerator to the floor. The map she held in her hand shook with her trembling.

"Up this road for a mile, turn right, I'm there!" Rose dropped the map to the floor board so that she could concentrate on the unfamiliar road. She made the right hand turn and almost cried with relief. There was her truck with the trailer behind it loaded with dark mulch.

Where were Bennett and Daniel and Quayle? Rose pulled up alongside her truck and waited. In a minute she saw Bennett and Daniel exit what looked like a big red barn.

Hand in hand the two walked toward her. Daniel carried a bright red balloon on a string. The balloon was imprinted Farmer Joe's.

"Hey there!" Bennett called to Rose. "Don't tell me you women don't trust us to bring home the mulch!"

Rose laughed. "No, nothing like that!" She said, searching Daniel's face. The child was all smiles, bouncing the balloon and clearly enjoying himself.

"Where's Quayle?" Rose asked.

"He should be here," Bennett replied. "Daniel had to go potty and Quayle was going to settle up with Farmer Joe so we can get back to work."

An image flashed across Rose's mind. "No!" she cried. Frantic, she pushed open the door and ran to the back of the loaded trailer.

Chapter Twenty-Nine

The news that Bennett had blurted into the phone less than an hour ago had rattled Suzanne to her core.

She had wasted no time in locking up the clinic and with Vena driving, led a fast moving parade of friends and family members fifteen miles through the communities of Wolf Laurel Creek and into the crowded lot of Laurel County General Hospital where they looked for parking spaces.

The back of the five story flesh colored brick building butted against a mountain giving the illusion that the stark, oblong structure was three-sided.

The building had what passed as a portico in the front, dead center, but little else inspired images of caring medical practitioners in a comforting, healing environment.

"This place looks like something I saw as a kid in the television series *Nightmare Theater*. It looks more like a prison or an asylum than a hospital," Suzanne said with a shiver.

"Don't let the looks of this old building fool you, Miss Suzanne. They've got some mighty fine doctors in here. You'll see. Your friend will get the best of care. He's gonna be all right. Me and the Good Lord done discussed it."

"What's the matter? Why are you looking at me like that?" Vena asked with a troubled look.

"It's just that, that telling Rose about Jan is going to be hard enough, but telling her about him here, in the middle of another emergency, it just seems so wrong!"

"Vena, I almost feel like we're all under a curse of some kind!" Suzanne's face was taut with stress.

"Bennett and I are being threatened with losing Daniel. Jan's been killed in Vietnam--we still have to tell Rose. And now this! Why? How do we make sense of it?"

Vena lay a comforting hand on Suzanne's arm. "I can't rightly answer that Miss Suzanne, all I know is that the Good Lord knows what He's doing. He won't ever give us more to handle than we can bear. Everything will be all right, I'm sure of that."

Vena found a parking space, pulled into it, and then she and Suzanne hurried from the car.

Suzanne glanced across the parking lot where Mustafa climbed from his truck, and where Jimmy Joe, Olivia, Willie and Buddy piled out of Jimmy Joe's pickup.

"Rose is going to know that something is wrong the minute she sees them!" Suzanne cried. She angrily wiped at the tears that fell from her eyes.

Vena walked around the car and took Suzanne by the hand. "Come on, Miss Suzanne, straighten your pretty face. Rose is gonna need us now. We got to be strong for Miss Rose."

Jimmy Joe and his siblings waited under the portico for Vena and Suzanne.

Mustafa held the door and then entered the hospital behind Vena, Suzanne and the McKinley family.

Jimmy Joe asked directions to the emergency room and then led the way down corridors that bustled with visitors, people in wheel chairs, physicians that scanned charts as they walked and with medical techs who transported patients on rolling beds down the hallway.

Jimmy Joe spotted his tall, beautiful sister with her unmistakable mass of fiery hair and her fine, milky-skinned face that was dotted with freckles. She fed coins into a vending machine and then withdrew a paper cup filled with coffee.

Rose turned from the vending machine with the coffee in her hand. *Jimmy Joe? Olivia.... Willie....and Buddy....* Rose blinked.

Why were her siblings here? Why were they all here? They knew the clinic's opening was two weeks away.

Rose looked from Jimmy Joe to Olivia and from Olivia to Willie and Buddy. Rose could find not a hint of a smile among them. Rose let the cup fall from her hands.

"No! No! No!" She screamed. "Please God, no!"

"Oh my God!" Suzanne cried and burst into tears. She clutched Vena's arm.

Vena burst into tears.

"Rose! Rose!" Jimmy Joe and Olivia cried. Weeping, brother and sister broke into a sprint. Jimmy Joe reached her first. Pulling Rose into his arms, Jimmy Joe whispered through his tears. "Rose, I'm so sorry! I'm so sorry! If I could make it go away, make it not be true! We're here for you Rose, we're all here for you!"

Bennett, dressed in a hospital gown and his jeans, bolted from a restroom holding Daniel by the hand. Seeing nothing but sobbing humans he looked in dismay to Suzanne.

"What's going on Suz? Did somebody die?"

Suzanne shrieked.   She pulled a hand to her face, nodded to Bennett, and then darted her eyes to Rose. Jimmy Joe, Olivia, Willie and Buddy.

Bennett felt confused.   His face showed it.   Jimmy Joe.   Olivia.   Buddy.   Willie.   Somebody did die.

"No!"   Bennett cried.   He snapped his head to Suzanne. "Jan?" He mouthed the word in denial. Impossible.

Suzanne's nod confirmed it for Bennett.   Jan Vandeventer was dead.

"Oh my God!" Bennett cried.   He felt a tug on his hand.   It was Daniel.   Everyone in close proximity to the child was crying.   The little boy looked from face to face and all that he could see was sadness and weeping.

Daniel's lip quivered.   He dropped his head.   He began to wail.

Bennett scooped Daniel up and hugged him close. "Hey Little Buddy, it's all right.   I know you don't understand why everybody else around here is crying, but it's all right Son. Mommy and Daddy are right here.   We love you Daniel and it's all right."

With Daniel on his shoulder Bennett reached for Suzanne.   He hugged her close.   He kissed the top of her head. "God, I am so sorry about this, Suz! What happened? When? Do Klaus and Olga know?"

Suzanne nodded. "They know," she said, trying hard not to sob. "And it's killing Olga. Klaus is afraid he's going to lose her too."

Vena, as heart-broken for Rose as the rest of those present, had also been weeping. She dried her eyes, managed a smile for Daniel and reached for him.

"You come to Vena, Sweet Baby. Tanzy's on her way," Vena spoke and signed the words to Daniel. She continued. "She's bringing your little friends, Marty and Augustus and you're going to go to Vena's house and play with them like little boys are supposed to."

Vena raised her eyes to Suzanne and Bennett. "That is, of course, if it's all right with your Mama and Daddy."

Daniel's face lit up with smiles for at that same moment, Vena's eighteen-year old daughter, Tanzy, came through the glass double doors of the hospital's emergency entrance.

Marty and Augustus, the two little boys that accompanied Tanzy, broke into a run, heading for Vena and Daniel.

Daniel's smile stretched wider with his obvious joy at seeing his little friends.

Suzanne and Bennett gave him their undivided attention as Daniel spelled with his fingers *Tanzy, Marty* and *Augustus.*

Marty carried a blue Matchbox Car Official Collector's Case filled with little die-cast cars.

He opened the case and held it for Daniel who giggled with delight and selected a blue and white Ford Mustang and a red Volkswagon Beetle convertible.

"He'll be a lot happier playing with his friends than he is here in the middle of all this sorrow," Suzanne said with her eyes on Bennett's eyes.

"I agree," Bennett said. "Vena's offer sounds great to me. He hugged Vena and then he and Suzanne hugged and kissed Daniel.

Tanzy, an elegant young woman who appeared to be about 5' 2" with copper skin and a glowing face that was set off with finely chiseled features and smiling, golden eyes, hugged Vena.

"Mama, I made a pot of chicken and dumplings and some brownies. Don't worry about the boys. I'll feed them and bathe them and put Daniel in a pair of Marty's pajamas. You just take your time and be with your friends."

Vena kissed the young woman's cheek. "Thank you my sweet baby. I'll be along shortly. Don't forget to say your prayers with the boys."

"I won't, Mama," Tanzy promised.

Vena smiled and waved at her departing daughter and the three little boys.

"If you will excuse me, I think this old woman needs to go and have a talk with the Lord. There's a chapel down the hall there," Vena said. She hugged Bennett and Suzanne and then departed with the sound of muted footsteps.

Suzanne smiled a weak smile at Bennett. "I think maybe I'm feeling a little overwhelmed. First Jimmy Joe and the family showed up with the news about Jan, and then we got your call that somebody had stabbed Quayle."

"More like somebody tried to slice him in two!" Bennett snapped with a frown. "Quayle was closing up the trailer and paying Farmer Joe while I took Daniel to the bathroom. About that time, Rose showed up. She just happened to walk to the back of the trailer where she found Quayle."

Bennett squeezed Suzanne a little tighter. "If she hadn't shown up when she did, there's a good chance that Quayle would have bled to death."

"Suzanne pointed to Bennett's chest and the hospital gown that he wore. "Is that what happened to your shirt?"

Bennett looked at the gown and then nodded. "Tourniquet. Quayle never saw his attacker. Whoever it was came up on him from behind. They must have used a machete or something close. No pocket knife or even kitchen knife for that matter could have done so much damage."

"Quayle's attacker just missed Quayle's spinal cord by a hair. He stabbed him and then ripped his weapon across Quayle's back to his side. Pretty horrible. Quayle's been in surgery for a while. It's too soon to know the extent of the damage, but I can tell you this much, whoever did this is a monster!"

"Has the world gone mad?" Suzanne asked. "First someone tries to burn down Rose's horse farm and now somebody tried to kill Quayle. I don't understand it, I don't understand it at all."

"Did Quayle say anything? Does he have any idea who did this?"

"No, my love. Quayle fell unconscious about the time Rose found him. He never said anything to her."

"Bennett!" Looking frantic, Mustafa ran toward Bennett and Suzanne. "You must please come quickly, please. He hear Rose cry. He try to get up!"

"He? Who?" Bennett frowned. He placed a hand on Mustafa's shoulder. "Take a minute and catch your breath, Moose."

"Mister Train Man. Mister Quayle!"

Bennett's look was incredulous. "Quayle is trying to get up? How is it that he's even awake! Isn't he sedated? I can't believe he's out of surgery already!"

"Yes! I do not know how he is awake already. He no listen to Mustafa. He no listen to anyone!"

Bennett brushed Suzanne's forehead with a kiss. "Suz?"

"Go with Mustafa, Bennett. Take care of Quayle. I'll stay with Rose and her family," Suzanne said. She returned his kiss and then watched him depart with Mustafa.

Chapter Thirty

"Whoa there, Country Boy! Where do you think you're going?" Bennett demanded.

Quayle sat upright near the edge of the hospital bed. "Help me get this darned rail down so I can get out of here!" He barked.

"That ain't gonna happen, Bubba!" Bennett exclaimed. He bumped the rail release lever with his knee and dropped the bed rail. He placed a hand on each of Quayle's shoulders and tried to force the man back against the pillows.

"Don't you see that red stuff all over those bandages? You've likely already busted some stitches and you can't afford to be doing that, man! You want to live to see the sunrise? You better get yourself back in that bed and act like a man who is lucky to be alive and not like an idiot!"

"Get out of my way, Bennett! I heard her crying. What's wrong? Did somebody hurt her? Help me up, please! I've got to get to Rose!" Quayle spoke with desperation. His eyes were pleading.

"You're not going anywhere, Brother! You can't help Rose and the last thing she needs today is more bad news. So you just be still and let me see how much damage you've done!"

"Moose, see if you can get the surgeon back in here. I don't know what's been cut where but he's doing some serious bleeding."

"Bennett, get out of my way!"

"Quayle, settle down damn it! Rose just learned that her fiancée, Jan, is dead. Her three brothers and her sister drove here from Widows Hollow, Kentucky, this morning to deliver the news personally."

"As you might imagine, Rose isn't taking it very well. That's why she's crying. And that's why there's nothing you can do about it!"

"Oh, my God!" Quayle exclaimed. "Bennett, help me get out of here!"

"Quayle, think about what you're saying man! Rose just learned that all her dreams are shattered, that the future she's waited for years to share with Jan will never be. Rose is hurting as much as a human can hurt right now and there is nothing any of us can do about it!"

"If you run out of here and rip your stitches out, that won't help her. It won't do anything but make her feel guilty that you hurt yourself because of her!"

"And in this small community people talk. Most everyone knows that Rose has a fiancée in Vietnam and they're going to wonder how you fit into this picture with Rose. Let that sink into your thick skull for a minute!"

Quayle exhaled a deep breath and winced, in obvious pain. He looked at Bennett and then hung his head.

"You're right Bennett. I'm sorry. I know you're right. It's just that, that I heard her scream. And then I heard her crying! She was crying so hard! I just wanted to get to her. To protect her. To make the crying stop! Is that so bad? Am I wrong?"

The hard lines and the angry scowl disappeared from Bennett's face. "Quayle, I know those feelings. Trust me, I know exactly how you feel," Bennett said and then shook his head.

He glanced again at Quayle and seeing the misery in the man's eyes, Bennett's compassion returned. "You're in love with her, man!"

"Bennett, believe me, I didn't mean to be!" Quayle reached a hand to the blood soaked bandages. His pain was getting worse. He needed to be sleeping in a medicated sleep, not sitting up having this conversation.

"I mean, I kept my distance. I stayed away from her. I respected her relationship with Jan and I never treated her like anything other than the lady that she is!"

Quayle's eyes softened. "I like talking to her. She doesn't have a pretentious bone in her body! What you see is what you get--she apologizes to no one."

"She's headstrong as a Kentucky mule and she's not likely to take orders from anyone. And at the same time she's so sensitive I think even the flowers and the trees conspire to protect her."

Quayle wiped at a trickle of blood that oozed from his bandages. "I don't have to wonder what she's thinking because Rose has no problem being blunt! She's honest and open and she expects honesty in return."

"You don't have to explain Rose to me, Country Boy! Suzanne and I both fell in love with her a long time ago." Bennett gently touched Quayle's bandages. "Now come on, let me help you back into bed. You're going to have your hands full in a minute with one angry surgeon."

"No, Bennett. I'm gonna head on out of here anyway. I never did have much use for these places."

Bennett shook his head. "You are one hard-headed country boy. Do you have anyone at home who can keep an eye on you?"

"No and I don't need anybody!" Quayle huffed.

"Oh yes you do Mr. Johnson! If you're gonna insist on leaving here, I'm gonna insist that you come home with us. Me and Moose and Suzanne too, for that matter, can sew you back up. We can also keep you out of trouble since you're so hard-headed. With Jan gone, Rose is...."

"Hold on, Bennett!" Quayle grabbed Bennett's wrist, his eyes blazed with anger. "Rose was in love with Jan Vandeventer. He's all she talked about. If you think I'm glad he's gone, you need your head busted! He made her happy and that made me happy! That's how love works!"

"You want the best for the person you love, even if it means that you're the odd man out! And in this case, that was me, but I dealt with it! You think I liked hearing her cry? I hated it! If I could blink and bring Jan back, I would! I'll never get the sound of her crying out of my head! I never want to hear her cry again!"

"Hear who cry?" Quayle's surgeon asked. Entering the room at a brisk pace, he frowned at Quayle's blood soaked bandages.

Looking past the surgeon as if they hadn't seen him, Quayle and Bennett looked to the figure who stood in the doorway.   It was Rose McKinley.

Chapter Thirty-One

One week later

"Where is God? Where is He?" Suzanne screamed. She cried so hard that she could barely navigate across the parking lot of the Laurel County Courthouse.

"I can't handle this Bennett! I can't! It's so wrong! How are we going to tell that precious little boy that he has to go live in that filthy squalor with his so-called daddy and Melinda?"

Suzanne's voice was loud and she didn't care. Neither she nor Bennett had been prepared for the stunning events that had just taken place in Judge George C. Thompson's courtroom in the Laurel County Courthouse of Laurel County, West Virginia.

"Bennett, Suzanne, I am so sorry! I, we, all assumed that Daniel Ruddy would show up here today with a court appointed attorney. That attorney would predictably go through the motions as the law of the State of West Virginia demands."

"We assumed that because he was court-appointed, that he would present Ruddy's case with all the enthusiasm and legal expertise of an overworked and underpaid civil servant who wanted nothing more than to get through the hearing as quickly as possible and return to his golf game!"

"I for one am still thunder-struck! How did Ruddy manage to retain one of Laurel County's most aggressive and expensive family attorneys?"

"Ruddy has no job, no money, and apparently, no relatives. How could he possibly have come up with a twenty-five hundred dollar retainer for Attorney Wesley Morrison in less than a week?"

"More than that, how is it that Morrison just happened to be available for Mr. Ruddy? I'm very familiar with Morrison's calendar. He's always booked at least six months in advance! There's no way he just happened to be available when Ruddy called."

"I don't care about his attorney or about how Daniel Ruddy did or didn't pay for one!" Suzanne cried. Her face was red and swollen. The tears had started when Judge Thompson read his decision and they hadn't stopped since.

Bennett had tried every way he knew to calm and comfort her but Suzanne refused to be calmed or comforted.

"The only thing I care about is Daniel! And we have one hour to turn him over to Wesley Morrison who will then take him to Daniel Ruddy who has just been granted full custody and control of OUR little boy!"

"I can't believe it! Morrison made it look like Daniel was in danger because he was with us! Because he was with Bennett and Quayle when Quayle got stabbed! How did this get so twisted?" Screaming her words, Suzanne threw her arms in the air. "There's nothing right about this! How could Morrison possibly make Ruddy look like the more qualified parent?"

"Bennett! I can't do this! I can't watch Morrison trot off with Daniel!" Suzanne clutched her husband. She buried her face in his shoulder and sobbed.

"Isn't there something you can do, Drake? Isn't there some way to reverse this ruling?" Bennett demanded. He opened the door to the minivan and attempted to help Suzanne inside.

Suzanne balked. She pushed Bennett aside so that she could address Drake to his face. "There's got to be something you can do! There's got to be! Daniel's life will be nothing but a nightmare if he lives with those people! They don't love him, they don't even want him! They just want the money the state will pay because Daniel has physical challenges! We'll be happy to pay the guy the five hundred a month if we can just keep Daniel!" Suzanne's eyes were pleading. Tears dripped off her cheeks.

Looking anything but happy, Drake shook his head. "I'm sorry Mrs. Gardner but Morrison relied on West Virginia law to win this one."

"Ruddy is a citizen of West Virginia and the child was born in West Virginia. You and Mr. Gardner are Kentuckians and your home is in Kentucky."

"Judges tend to go with the residency law, but not always. In this case, I think Judge Thompson's personal friendship and regular golfing outings with Morrison helped swing the decision in Ruddy's favor. I know that's no comfort to you, but it's more than likely the truth."

Drake glanced at his watch. "If you folks are going to have any time at all to say good-bye to Daniel, you better get going."

He shook his head and said with downcast eyes "I'm so sorry. Please believe me, I never dreamed the decision would go this way! If there is any way to reverse this ruling, I won't stop until I find it."

"I took this case personally because I have two sons and I was and am convinced that Daniel deserves the life that you two could give him." Drake shook hands with Bennett who quickly turned again to help Suzanne into the minivan.

Bennett closed the door. "Drake, something's got to happen! For Daniel's sake, something has got to happen that will return him to us! In my life I've never prayed a whole lot and I admit it. I do believe there's a God and I do believe that He won't let this little boy down. I equally believe that me and God will be doing a lot more talking from now on."

The two men shook hands.

"Thank you, Counselor," Bennett said. "Sometimes we can't win 'em all but we know you did your best. Suzanne and I both appreciate it and if you do find a way to get us our boy back, please let us know."

"You can count on it, Bennett."

"What?" Rose cried from the kitchen door.

"What?" Quayle echoed Rose from his reclining position on Mustafa's sofa where, at Bennett's insistence, Quayle had been for the past week.

Quayle had protested admirably, but Bennett won this one, refusing to allow Quayle to go home alone because Quayle's wounds were too serious.

The most minor exertion on Quayle's part could rip out his stitches and cause further damage.

"But that's impossible!" Rose cried, incredulous. "How could any judge give Daniel to them?"

Quayle winced. Trying to push himself upright on the sofa was more painful than he anticipated.

"I don't know Rose, but he did! Where's Daniel?" Suzanne asked tearfully.

"He's sleeping. He and Snidely and their cars have been keeping Quayle entertained. Daniel was exhausted."

"Bennett?" The question mark in her eyes dissolved in Suzanne's tears.

"Yeah, let's," Bennett's voice failed him. He gave his head an angry shake and then, with a nod to Suzanne, managed "Let's wake him up."

"You wake him," Suzanne said. She dropped her head and burst into tears. "I'll, I'll, gather his things."

"Oh, Suzanne!" I am so sorry!" Rose cried. "Is there anything I can do?"

"Only if you can blink me back to yesterday and tell me this would never happen!" Suzanne removed tacks from the signing chart that hung on the door and bellowed.

"Rose, I can't take lying here useless as a stump. Is there anything I can do?" Quayle's voice was deep and determined.

"No, Quayle. Thank you. We just need to get his things together," Rose replied. She and Suzanne headed for separate rooms to pack Daniel's clothes and toys.

Don't cry! Do not cry! Bennett ordered himself. He climbed the stairs like a condemned man. *Little buddy, we don't want to do this. But nobody gave us a choice.*

Bennett eased open the door to the room that he and Mustafa had transformed into Daniel's room.

Daniel slept curled in the fetal position in Mustafa's antique iron bed.

With his heart already broken beyond repair, Bennett tried to ignore the soft, childlike sounds of Daniel's breathing.

The incredible little boy slept peacefully, snuggled under a handmade quilt that depicted Thomas Train and his train yard friends. Snidely Whiplash lay grinning on Daniel's pillow, sprawled out in Daniel's curls.

Bennett crept to Daniel's bedside.

Daniel's eyes flew open. With a smile that stretched across his face Daniel threw off the quilt and reached his arms to Bennett.

Bennett choked. He raised his eyes to heaven. "Help me out here, I can't do this! Don't let him see me cry, please!"

Daniel sprang to his feet. He bounced on the bed, waiting to jump into Bennett's arms.

A single tear fell on Bennett's cheek.

Daniel looked up into Bennett's eyes. The little boy's lip quivered. He touched the corners of his eyes with his pointer fingers and then dragged his fingers down his face.

Feeling that his heart would burst, Bennett raised his eyes again to heaven. "Yeah, Midget, Daddy's crying."

"Moose! Moose!" Bennett yelled.

Mustafa burst into the bedroom. "Yes, Bennett, what is?" Mustafa asked.

Bennett wiped his eyes. "Moose, help me out here. We have to say good-bye to Daniel and I'm trying not to break his heart. I'm not having much success. I've made him cry and making him cry was the last thing I wanted to do."

Mustafa glanced at Bennett at the same time as more tears trickled from Bennett's eyes.

Mustafa grabbed Snidely from Daniel's pillow. He took the doll, opened its arms and pretended that Snidely was striking Bennett.

Daniel laughed and grabbed the doll from Mustafa.

"Thanks Moose," Bennett said. He sniffled and then headed downstairs with Daniel in his arms.

The stack of boxes near the front door caught Bennett's eye, boxes that were filled with Daniel's things. Bennett looked from the boxes to the clock on the fireplace mantel. According to the clock he and Suzanne had fifteen more minutes with Daniel. There wasn't a dry eye in the house except for Daniel's eyes.

Suzanne and Rose put on their happy faces for the little boy but the faces didn't last long. Their smiles fled when Daniel looked into the corner for his play table and basket of toys. The play table and the basket of toys were gone. Daniel frowned.

He looked at the back of the front door. The colorful American Sign Language chart was gone. He glanced into the kitchen and to the refrigerator. The sign language chart was gone from the refrigerator too.

Bennett squeezed Daniel tighter.

Suzanne took Bennett's arm and she hugged Daniel.

"Rose, Moose, somebody, please go get the quilt off Daniel's bed. Vena made that quilt for him. He loves it and he'll be more comfortable if he has it," Bennett said.

Rose, Mustafa and Quayle headed for the stairs to get the quilt.

Daniel pushed away from Bennett. With his beautiful, innocent blue eyes he stared into Bennett's and Suzanne's eyes. He fisted both hands, pushed his thumbs between his pointer and second fingers and shook his hands.

Suzanne let out a yelp. Tears pelted her cheeks.

Bennett strangled on a sob.

Signing, Daniel had asked *Where toys*?

Fighting to form a smile, Bennett said and signed to Daniel "Mommy and Rose packed them for you little buddy. You'll have all your toys with you and maybe you can share them with your baby brother."

Tears slid from Daniel's eyes. He leaned into Bennett's shoulder and wrapped his little arms around Bennett's neck.

Suzanne and Bennett hugged the little boy, held one another and tried not to howl.

Rose and Mustafa and Quayle descended the stairs.

Quayle carried the quilt that Rose had removed from the bed and had neatly folded. He looked from Bennett to the stacked boxes at the door and then gently placed the quilt on top of the stack.

At the same time as Quayle turned from the door, somebody knocked.

"No!" Suzanne cried. "Not already! Bennett! Bennnneeet!"

"Suz! Suzanne!"

Rose and Mustafa had joined Bennett and Suzanne with their arms about their shoulders, hugging Daniel, and sobbing.

Quayle pulled open the door.

"Hello! I'm Wesley Morrison, here to return the child to his rightful father per Judge Thompson's orders. I assume that the child is ready," Morrison barked and raised cold, steely eyes to Quayle.

Quayle, who fought the inclination to kick the door shut in the smug attorney's face, instead shoved open the screen and slammed a box packed with Daniel's belongings into

Morrison's hands. "Here, make yourself useful!" Quayle said with no hint of a smile.

"The child's name is Daniel! It's Daniel!" Bennett cried.

"Bye little boy, Mommy loves you Daniel, Mommy will always love you Daniel!" Suzanne whispered through her sobs. She hugged Daniel one last time and kissed him as her tears mixed with his on his cheeks.

Mustafa hugged Daniel. He kissed his cheeks. "Good-bye Midget. Mustafa love you always too."

Rose wagged her head in despair. She shook her head to dislodge her tears. She wrapped Daniel in her arms and kissed his cheeks. "Good-bye precious little baby. I love you Daniel."

Turning to the door, Bennett lifted Daniel higher on his shoulder. Morrison had returned from loading the last box in his flashy 1972 red and white Mark IV Lincoln.

Bennett approached the door with Morrison on the other side. He scowled at Morrison who made it clear that he had no intention of being detained.

Bennett pulled Daniel to him. He hugged the little boy as tight as a grown man can hug a child without causing injury. He ran his hand over Daniel's curls and said to him

"Good-bye little buddy. Mommy and Daddy love you. We didn't do this, Daniel, but we couldn't stop it, either!"

Bennett's voice broke. Sobs punctuated his words as he spoke and signed "We love you Daniel, we will always love you Daniel. Little Buddy, I'm so sorry about this! I am so sorry about this Daniel!"

Quayle stepped next to Bennett. "Here Bennett, let me be the one," he said and gently pulled Daniel from Bennett's arms.

With a howl of grief and unabashed sobs Bennett released Daniel to Quayle.

Quayle stepped quickly to the door. He pushed the screen open with his foot and handed Daniel to Morrison who refused to take the little boy into his arms.

"You take care of this little boy and you make it plain to them that they better take care of him, too!" Quayle exclaimed with a threat in his eyes.

His voice softened. He fought to maintain his composure. "Bye Daniel. Train Man loves you too."

Daniel pulled his hand from Morrison's. He ran to the screen and pressed his face against it. Tears streamed down his face as he spread his fingers in a five-hand. He tapped his thumb first against his chin and then tapped his thumb against his forehead.

Suzanne screamed. "Bennett!   Oh my God, Bennett!
He's crying.   Daniel's crying and he's signing *Mommy!*
Daddy!"

Chapter Thirty-Two

"Ladies, there's entirely too much sadness in this house! How are we supposed to plan a party when everybody's walking around like there ain't no God in Heaven and there ain't no hope for anyone here on this Earth!" Vena demanded, pointing her ink pen at Suzanne and Rose who sat on the sofa across Mustafa's living room from Vena.

The women had been making a final list of things to do in preparation for the clinic's grand opening.

A soft smile played about Vena's mouth. "Vena knows it's some hard times we're dealing with now but the Good Lord don't never close no doors without He opens a window!"

"I miss that little boy just as much as you do, Miss Suzanne. And Miss Rose, I know the heartache of losing a loved one, too."

"But moping around here and feeling sorry for ourselves ain't gonna get Daniel back home and it ain't gonna bring back Mister Jan either!"

Vena's smile grew wider. "So how about I'll make some fresh coffee and we'll all gain a few pounds eating some of my Mississippi Mud brownies?   They were Daniel's favorite."   Vena corrected herself "They *are* Daniel's favorite!"

Upon hearing Daniel's name Suzanne looked like she might burst into tears.

"Ain't no need in your crying and carrying on and messing up your make-up Miss Suzanne!   The reverend's wife, Janice Hobson, and Judy Connors will be here shortly."

"Daniel ain't dead, he's just gone for a while and his Aunt Vena ain't gonna pretend that he is dead by refusing to speak his name!"

"Look at us!   What a sorry sight!   Daniel would be plumb scared if he could see us now.   We look like them ghosty people what hangs out in the graveyards and in them scary movies what young folks is so crazy about watching!"

Vena's words worked their magic.

Suzanne and Rose appreciated that Vena departed from her educated, erudite speech and into a mountain slang that better served her purpose in resurrecting her friends from the depths of their depression.

Suzanne straightened her face. She offered a smile to Vena and Rose. "Ghosty people, huh?"

"That's right!" Vena exclaimed. She stood to her feet and said with a wave of her hand "Come on you two. Let's get that coffee perking. The ladies will be here in a minute!"

The three friends reconvened around the table in Mustafa's kitchen. Hot coffee steamed before them next to plates that held the crumbs and chocolate frosting smudges from Vena's Mississippi Mud brownies.

Suzanne grinned a mischievous grin. "Vena, I need this recipe. If I make these brownies for Bennett one time then I can use them later for blackmail!"

Vena focused her attention across the table and on Suzanne who was dressed in denim bellbottoms with a long-sleeved red and white print shirt and a red vest. She wore her long black hair pulled back behind a red headband.

"And tell me now, Sweet Child, why would you want to blackmail Mister Bennett?"

"I don't know that I would, but the recipe would be nice to have handy just in case," Suzanne said with a giggle. She took another brownie from the platter in the middle of the table. "Anybody want to share this one with me?"

Vena looked to Rose who shook her head and waved her hands. "One's enough for me. I'm afraid if I eat another one I may not stop!"

Vena reached her open palm to Suzanne who placed half a brownie in it.

Suzanne bit into the brownie. "Has the sheriff gotten any leads on who may have stabbed Quayle? I heard the guys talking about it before they left for the clinic but I didn't catch whether or not the sheriff had any suspects."

Suzanne dragged her finger through the chocolate frosting that remained on her plate and then sucked the chocolate from her finger. "Rose, you were there so soon after it happened. You never saw anyone or anything that looked suspicious?"

Rose sipped her coffee and then replaced her cup on the table. "No. And I can't remember why I even went to the back of the trailer."

Looking like she was lost in deep thought Rose got a far-away look in her eyes. "It was a very strange morning.

Remember. The three of us were working at the clinic and I left right after Bennett and Quayle took off with Daniel?"

Suzanne and Vena nodded.

Again Rose fell silent for a moment and then "I left because my intuition insisted that Daniel was in danger. I was desperate to find him and to perhaps intervene, to maybe prevent whatever it was that intended him harm."

Rose dragged down one corner of her mouth and, with a napkin, wiped at some coffee that had spilled on the table.

"You know me and my intuition. It's like a silent and invisible guide. It's been with me for as long as I can remember and it was always something that I could rely on no matter what."

"Sometimes it floats into my mind like a thought or idea from out of nowhere, other times it shows up in my dreams."

Suzanne ate the last bite of her brownie, caught Vena's eye, and raised a hand. "I can testify to that! Bennett and I and most of the people in Widows Hollow have experienced Rose's intuition more than once."

Suzanne darted her eyes from Rose to Vena. "Rose McKinley's intuition saved more than one life in Widows Hollow."

"At age sixteen she argued with Dr. Stephen Stalworth, a former colleague of mine and Bennett's, and over Stalworth's very loud protests, Rose saved a baby's life."

"Rose!" Suzanne slapped an open palm on the table top. "Is it possible that these things happened so long ago? Has it really been years?" Suzanne asked with an incredulous look.

Rose shook her head. "I know. Time seems to have taken wings. And things are different now. I think that maybe my intuition is slipping."

"Last week when I felt so certain that Daniel was in danger, nothing could have stopped me from finding him. Turns out Daniel wasn't the one in danger. It was Quayle. He's the one who came close to dying that morning."

Rose frowned. "Maybe it's more than my intuition that's slipping. Before Jimmy Joe and the rest of my family showed up here with the news about Jan, I assured Olga that Jan was all right, that he couldn't be dead because I dreamed that he was all right."

Frowning, Rose squeezed her brows together. She said in a faltering voice "I guess my dreams are failing me too."

Vandeventer Farms
Ashford, Kentucky

Margaret Olliphant flitted about dusting and tidying the Vandeventer home. Although Olga had made it quite plain that she wanted no visitors, would receive no guests, and would not speak with anyone on the phone, Margaret had refused to be denied. After all, Margaret's mother, Katharine, was Olga's oldest and dearest friend.

It was no secret throughout Ashford's glittering social circles that Margaret had had a crush on Jan that began in high school and had continued through college.

Jan's courtship with Rose McKinley and his subsequent engagement to her had dashed Margaret's hopes of a future with Jan so she had entered into a marriage that had quickly failed.

Like most of her privileged peers Margaret had not learned of Jan's death via the grapevine nor through personal contact with his family.

Margaret had learned in headlines that had blazed across the front pages of the Ashford News Sentinel that Klaus Janssen Vandeventer Jr., the son and sole heir to the Vandeventer Farms Estate of Ashford, Kentucky, had been killed in combat in Vietnam.

Margaret had allowed herself to cry, to grieve for a future that now, for certain, would never be.

Her grief had been tempered and somewhat mitigated by the knowledge that in addition to herself, that horrible white trash hillbilly from Widows Hollow, one Rose McKinley, would equally never have the honor of taking the name Vandeventer in marriage.

The knowledge had fortified Margaret's opinion of herself. With Jan's death, there was no longer an engagement, so, to Margaret's mind, her standing in the Vandeventer family circle had advanced.

Rose McKinley was no longer the daughter-in-law to be. Rose
was no longer anything but an undesirable upstart, a usurper who had never belonged anywhere outside the *vile holler* that had spawned her.

Margaret smiled, comforting herself. She was here in Jan's home while that probable heathen, Rose, was off somewhere doing God-knows what in some God-forsaken place in West Virginia. *This* Margaret had learned through the grapevine.

But Margaret was here, free to roam from room to room, to handle any of Jan's personal items that she cared to hold or to keep.

Margaret strode to the oversized mirror in the foyer. Preening before it, she smiled at her image that the mirror returned.

She ran her hands down the lean figure that was dressed in brown pinstriped wool pants, bell bottom with cuffs of course, and a brown silk polka dot blouse with a sleeveless white angora vest.

The red silk necktie that she wore tied loosely about her neck looked fabulous. Earlier, at lunch at Jack Fry's, the scarf had worked like a magnet drawing looks of envy from both the district's well-heeled tourists and its celebrity diners.

Margaret returned to the living room and passed through it to the study where her eyes fell on a photo of Jan and Rose.

Rose was wearing a cap and gown. The smile on her face looked like the smile on the face of a thoroughbred owner whose horse had just won the Derby.

"Why wouldn't she smile?" Margaret asked herself aloud. "She's wearing Jan's ring and holding his...."

"Mama, you call Rose, please. Tell her that my Olga needs her." Speaking in a rasp, Klaus patted Mama John's arm. Gone were the vibrant good looks, sparkling eyes and jovial smile that friends and associates had always recognized and loved as trademark Klaus Vandeventer.

Klaus looked old and gaunt and beaten.

He clung to the stair rail as if his doing so would prevent him losing his balance. His skin sagged from his bones giving him the appearance of one who had lost too much weight too fast.

The eyes he turned to Mama John with his request were lifeless and dull. He descended the stairs from his and Olga's bedroom with Mama John who carried a tray laden with gold-rimmed china and a dinner that looked like it hadn't been touched.

"The doctor insists that Mama must have surgery but she refuses!   Mama said she vill nod go until she first speaks with Rose."

Klaus took the tray from Mama John. "I vill vash dese, if you vill please call Rose."

Mama John felt a sadness that weighed heavily on her. Klaus was breaking her heart.

Margaret intercepted Klaus and Mama John at the bottom of the stairs.   She beamed a smile for Klaus.

"Klaus! I won't hear of you washing dishes!" Margaret snatched the tray from Klaus before the man could protest.

She shoved the tray at Mama John. "The maid can wash them," she remarked. "I'll make that call for Olga."

Klaus dragged his weary eyes to meet Mama John's eyes.

"Margaret! Mama John is no maid. She is our friend. She will call Rose as Mama has asked."

Klaus looked from the tray in Mama John's hands to Margaret.

Margaret followed the man's eyes with her own. "Oh!" she exclaimed with a blush rising to her cheeks. Without looking at Mama John, Margaret took the tray and vanished with it into the kitchen.

Klaus removed a white Stetson from a wall hook by the back door. He slapped the hat against his legs and then pulled it on.

"Mama John, after you speak vid Rose, vill you please stay close with Mama? I check on horses, I vill nod be long."

The sympathy and compassion that Mama John felt for Klaus ran root deep and it welled up from her heart. The man was doing all that a mere human could do to hang on to his family and to his life.

In better times, Klaus would select one of his wool, straw or leather Stetsons, dust it against his legs, pull it on with a bit of showmanship, a bit of a swagger, and then sail out the door with a playful wink to lose himself in his barns and stables and pastures among magnificent animals with bloodlines that were the envy of nations and kings.

Klaus did not sail out the door today. There would be no light-hearted whistling from the barns or stables. He would perform his chores with a heart heavy as chains, his joy was gone, his future questionable.

Mama John wagged her head. "Mister Klaus, ain't no need for you to be a worryin' and you ain't got to be in no hurry! You just go on and take your time. You enjoy seein' to them fine horses. You know this ole woman be seein' to Miss Olga. Don't you worry none for her, Miss Olga's gonna be just fine!"

Watching the man retreat like he carried all the weight of the world on his shoulders, Mama John felt a pang of guilt. *Would Miss Olga be just fine?*

Mama John shook her head. That answer was No! Without an almighty miracle of some kind, Miss Olga would most certainly not be just fine.

Mama John softly closed the door and headed for the study to call Rose.

Chapter Thirty-Three

"Let's give ourselves a hand ladies. We did it!" Vena exclaimed. She moved an armful of bags from Mustafa's kitchen table to a chair.

She and Rose and Suzanne had been shopping and running errands all day and had just returned to Mustafa's.

"I don't know about you two," Rose said "but I don't think I could have made it through another store. My feet are protesting. Loudly. They want out of these shoes!"

And as was her habit, Rose kicked off her shoes and then placed them beside the bottom stair of the staircase.

Vena carried a steaming cup of coffee to Mustafa's kitchen table and then seated herself with Rose and Suzanne.

"Got your lists handy?" Vena asked, referring to the remaining list of things that had to be done for the clinic's grand opening.

Suzanne read from her list. "I mailed the invitations. Janice and Reverend Hobson are spreading the word through the church.   Judy and Azle Connor are reminding the guardsmen and their families."

The three women checked the items off their lists.

"I've got the scissors and the ribbon at my house. Folks from the paper will be there to take pictures and to print the story," Vena said.

"I posted notices on the store fronts of the local businesses.   The notice is here in today's paper too," Rose said, tapping the folded newspaper that lay on the table.

"I put on a pot of Bennett's favorite chili this morning and it sure smells good!" Suzanne said.

Rose sank a corner of her mouth and narrowed her eyes in a mock scowl, pretending to scour the notes before her. "That's not on my list," she said, laughing.

"It's not on mine, either," Vena added.   "But that chili sure does smell good!   My mouth is watering already!" She glanced at Suzanne.   "You are planning to make cornbread to go with that chili, aren't you Miss Suzanne?"

"Cornbread?" Suzanne made a face.   "Uh, no! Miss Vena!   For Suzanne to make chili is to stretch Suzanne's culinary skills.   Making cornbread falls outside my very limited cooking boundaries." She laughed at the face that Vena made and then remarked "Bennett and I eat crackers with chili."

"Crackers!" Vena shook her head in mock dismay. "Um, um, um, Chile! You ain't in no city now Miss Suzanne, you in mountain country, in West Virginia. West Virginia girls don't be eatin' no crackers with they chili!"

Vena wagged her head. "Mountain girls eats West Virginia Cornbread with they chili and we ain't shy in addin' jalapenos to the recipe!"

Suzanne wagged her head, mimicking Vena. "Then you just be my guest Miss Vena! Mustafa's kitchen is your kitchen! What do we need for Miss Vena's West Virginia Cornbread?"

The ringing phone interrupted their conversation.

With her empty coffee cup in hand, Suzanne crossed the kitchen to the phone on the counter. "Hello? Hello Mama John, how are you?" A smile lit Suzanne's face upon hearing the voice of her sweet friend. "Yes, she's right here. Love you too, hang on, I'll get her." Suzanne held the phone to Rose.

Rose took the phone and walked with it into the living room. After a brief conversation she returned to the kitchen and replaced the receiver.

Rose refilled her coffee cup and, turning from the counter, she bit her lip. "Mama John said that she tried to reach us all day but she got no answer."

"Klaus asked her to call. He said that if Olga doesn't have surgery very soon, there's a good chance that her bleeding ulcers will kill her. Mama John said that Olga's doctors are very concerned. They feel certain that her life is in danger if she doesn't heed their advice."

"Mama John also said that Klaus is giving up. He can't talk Olga into the surgery and the poor man doesn't know what else he can do."

"Rose, I'm so sorry to hear this!" Suzanne exclaimed. "How can we help? What are you going to do?"

Rose looked at the concerned faces of her two friends. She inhaled a deep breath and then she replied. "I'm going to go home. To Widows Hollow. Now."

"Rose! You can't leave now. You were up early this morning. We've been running around all day and you must be exhausted. You don't need to try to drive home now. At least take a nap first, then go if you must."

"Suzanne, I appreciate your concern but Olga's running out of time. I can't wait."

"Are you going to try to talk her into having the surgery?"

"No."

Suzanne's surprise at Rose's answer showed on Suzanne's face. "Why not?"

Rose answered with downcast eyes and with quiet resolve. "Because Olga won't survive the surgery. She doesn't want to survive the surgery."

"But what choice does she have?" Suzanne asked in alarm. "If the doctors say that she won't survive without it?"

Rose's green eyes bore into Suzanne's eyes like lasers.

Suzanne sucked in a sudden breath. She had seen that look on Rose McKinley's face more than once.

"Don't take this personal Dr. Gardner, but doctors have been wrong before!" Rose sucked in another breath and vowed "And the one thing I am sure of is that Olga Vandeventer *will* survive!"

Suzanne fanned her face with her hand. "Whew! I felt the heat from that one! When you're serious, you're serious, aren't you lady?"

Suzanne turned her wrist so that she could see the face of her watch. She frowned. "It's almost five thirty and it's getting dark out! Where did this day go?"

"Come on ladies, if we're going to make cornbread, we better get it made," Rose said. "It won't take long so I'll help you before I go. The guys are going to storm in here any minute and if I know your husband, Suzanne, he's going to be starving!"

"Speaking of," Vena said. She peered through the window at Bennett who parked in the drive and then raced across the lawn.

"He must be really hungry," she remarked. "Or in a real hurry!"

Bennett slammed through the door and into the kitchen. "Suzanne, Rose, Vena, come on! Get in the van! "

"What? Bennett!" Suzanne didn't like the look on her husband's face. "What's going on? What's wrong?"

"Suz, please, you girls get in the van! There's no time to lose!"

"Bennett!" Suzanne grabbed his arm.

"Come on, Suzanne! Daniel's in danger!"

The three women piled into the minivan where they were met by Mustafa and Lenny Walker. Both men sat grim-faced and silent.

More confused than ever, Suzanne demanded an answer. "Bennett, what's going on? Why is Lenny here?"

Bennett didn't answer. As soon as the door slid closed, he stomped the accelerator and pushed the minivan as fast as it would go over the washboard ruts and gaping crater-holes of the roads that took them higher and higher into the mountains of Laurel County, West Virginia.

"Lenny showed up at the clinic to tell us that Ruddy and his girlfriend Melinda took Daniel and their baby up the mountain to take pictures of the blue people.   They think they're going to get rich selling the pictures to the *National Enquirer.*"

"Oh, bless Jesus!" Vena cried. "There ain't a soul in Wolf Laurel Creek that don't know about them blue people up on that mountain!   The smart ones know, too, to leave them alone!"

Vena's words tumbled out in a rush. "Silas Fuquay and his brothers and kin will shoot anyone who trespasses on their property!   They don't see it as being lawless or mean, they see it as protecting their families!"

"This isn't a game with mountain people.   Privacy and property rights are about life and death.   Mister Daniel Ruddy has no idea what he's getting himself and that poor girl and those babies into!"

"Bennett, can't we go any faster?   We've got to get there before Ruddy!" Suzanne cried.

Chapter Thirty-Four

Silas Fuquay, the big blue man dressed in overalls and a white tee shirt, stood with his *1960 Remington Fieldmaster 574* 0.22 rifle tucked under his arm with the barrel pointed to the ground.

Anger sharpened his voice. It pronounced itself in the steeled lines of his face.

"You should'na come here! You ain't got no business bein' here!   We put up them signs to tell looky-lous like you to keep out and stay away!   But you didn't pay them signs no mind, did ya!"   The man pointed an accusing finger at Ruddy and Melinda.

He swiped a huge paw across his face. "You come sneakin' up here near dark thinkin' nobody's gonna know you're here a' lookin' to make easy money takin' our pictures and sellin' 'em like me and my family ain't nothin' but a circus come-see!"

"Why couldn't you just leave us be? That's all we ever asked of anybody! How am I gonna live with this now?" He demanded.

The big blue man shook with sobs. "I ain't never meant to hurt no baby!"

"Daddy! Why ain't he wakin' up? I wanna play with Daniel. Why ain't he wakin' up?"

The big man sniffled. He wiped his face on his shirt sleeve and called out to his wife. "Mary Nell! Come get Elizabeth! Take her inside. She don't need to be here. She don't need to see this!"

The man scooped up the little girl and pressed her head against his shoulder, instinctively shielding her from a vision that no child should carry in their memory.

Dressed in a yellow flowered dress and with her long blonde hair in a single braid down her back, Mary Nell, the little blue woman, appeared, barefoot and soundless.

She glanced at the still, ashen face of the little boy, at his reddish blonde curls, curls that remained wet with perspiration from where he had been running, running to find Elizabeth when the shot rang out.

His face was pale, his lips blue. A cloth diaper bound the bright red wound in his right shoulder where Fuquay's 0.22 shell had blasted him.

He hadn't heard the shouts. "Daniel! No!" Or the gunfire. And the impact of the bullet had dropped him. Hard. On his back.

"He ought to be covered," Mary Nell Fuquay said. She removed her sweater, knelt beside the child and gently covered his little body.

She took Elizabeth from Silas and then, holding Elizabeth by the hand, she left as silently as she had arrived.

"Hello! Hello! Mr. Fuquay, this is Dr. Gardner and Dr. Dhingra. My wife, Lenny Walker, and two friends are with us. We're here to see about Daniel. Can we come up? Please. We mean your family no harm."

Fuquay removed the battered hat from his head and waved it in the dusk.

His younger brother, Ampshel, hidden by boulders and shrubs, read the signal from across the yard where, silent as a fog, he had observed everything.

Ampshel shouldered his .12 gauge Winchester and moved to intercept Bennett and company.

"Come on up," Fuquay directed in a flat voice, a voice that was barely audible up close much less over mountainous acres of boulders and undergrowth.

Bennett and company moved, as quickly as the uneven and rock-strewn terrain allowed, to Fuquay, Ruddy and Melinda.

"Hit was an accident! I never meant no…," Silas began.

But Bennett interrupted. "No!" He roared. The man crumpled to his knees and tried to make sense of what his eyes signaled to his brain. *He's dead. Daniel is dead.*

Sobs exploded from the man. They convulsed his body as Bennett reached a trembling hand to touch the little figure that lay still and unresponsive beneath Mary Nell Fuquay's sweater.

Suzanne had prepared herself. She was ready to find Daniel shaken. She was ready to find him frightened, confused and crying maybe. But she was not prepared for this.

"NO! God, please, no!" Suzanne's shrieks ripped through her husband, through Rose and Vena who clutched one another, their faces awash in torrents of tears, and through Lenny Walker who intertwined his hands behind his back and tearfully sought solace and his sister's hand.

Mustafa, standing apart from the others, watched in silence.

After a few minutes Bennett raised his tear-streaked countenance to Ruddy.

"May I?" He asked, indicating that he wanted to remove the sweater from Daniel's face.

Wet-eyed and mute, Ruddy nodded.

Bennett carefully removed the sweater. Seeing that precious little face again, that face that he had come to love, that face that had lit up his life like nothing else since Suzanne, Daniel's little face that had now fallen silent, his small, slender body soaked in blood, his shoulder wrapped in a bloody diaper…. Bennett howled in his grief.

"Daniel, I'm so sorry little buddy! I'm so sorry that I wasn't here to protect you, to keep you safe. I failed you buddy and I'm so sorry!"

Wailing, Suzanne lost her strength. Her legs buckled under her and she fell beside her husband. "He can't be gone, Bennett! He can't be! My heart is so broken, I can't stand it! You know how much I loved that little boy!"

Bennett's tears came in a flood. He squalled and held Suzanne. "I know Baby, I know. We both loved him more than words can say."

Mustafa approached. He squatted behind Bennett, rested a hand on Bennett's shoulder and kept his silence.

Bearing witness to such grief, and wracked themselves with sorrow, Rose and Vena held one another and squalled.

"What? What did you say?" Rose released Vena and searched the woman's face.

Confused, Vena replied through her tears. "Rose, Baby, I didn't say anything."

Rose spun to Bennett and Suzanne. "He's not dead! Daniel's not dead!"

"Rose!" Bennett yelled.

"Check his pulse, Bennett! He's not dead!"

Bennett reached for Daniel's wrist, wrapped his fingers around it, and after a moment, turned an angry face to Rose.

"Rose, stop it! He has no pulse! Suzanne can't take anymore!"

Marching to Bennett, Rose shoved the man. "Move!"

"What?"

"Get out of my way! Daniel's not dead but he will be if we don't do something now!"

Not daring to argue with the authority and the certainty in Rose's voice, Bennett and Suzanne scrambled out of the way.

Rose knelt beside Daniel. She put her head on his chest. She felt for a pulse. Bennett was right. There was none.

Very gently Rose turned Daniel on his side. With the heel of her hand she smacked him up high in the middle of his back.

Daniel remained still and lifeless.

"Come on Daniel!" Rose commanded. She smacked his back again with all the force she dared.

Daniel coughed and choked. His eyes flew open. Something that looked like a marble flew from his mouth.

"Daniel!" Suzanne and Bennett shouted the name as one.

Bennett reached to pull the child into his arms, but, remembering that he had no rights, he quickly withdrew his hands.

Bennett swept his eyes to Ruddy and spoke in a breathless rush. "We've got to get him to a hospital. My wife and I and our friend there, Mustafa, are doctors."

"It would be best if one of us stays with him to try to stop the bleeding. We'll go with you, you come with us; however you want to do it. But there's no time to waste. He's not out of danger, not by a long shot."

Keeping his eyes on the ground, Ruddy said "You take him with you. Me and Melinda, we'll follow you."

"Mary Nell! Elizabeth! Come out here quick," Silas yelled.

"Lookit! Lookit him! He ain't dead. Sweet Jesus, Lord! He ain't dead!" Weeping and smiling, Silas gathered his tiny blue wife and his little blue daughter in his arms.

The big blue man laughed through his tears. "I ain't kilt no baby! Thank you, Jesus, Lord! I ain't kilt no baby!"

Though desperately concerned for Daniel, Bennett could hardly contain the joy that sang in his heart as he lifted the little boy in his arms.

"Moose, do you mind driving?"

"Moose drive. No problem," Mustafa replied, happy himself to see Daniel once again in Bennett's arms.

Despite the single tear that leaked from his eyes and the incredible pain that he had to be enduring, Daniel smiled for Bennett. "Daddy," he said, mouthing the word.

"Yeah, Midget, Daddy!" Bennett replied, wishing with all his heart that it was true.

"But I'll take anything I can get and for the moment, I'm happy and thankful to be holding you in my arms.

Mommy and Daddy are gonna make you all better, promise."

Suzanne leaned from the back seat with a hand on Bennett's shoulder. "I feel like God has plugged a big hole in our hearts, Bennett. I can breathe again without sobbing."

"I agree, Suz. Maybe Ruddy will at least let us be part of Daniel's life. I'm grateful that he let us drive him to the hospital."

After a very fast trip over grueling terrain, Mustafa arrived at the hospital. He looked to Bennett.

"Just pull up to the *ER*, Moose. He's lost a lot of blood and we don't know how long he was deprived of oxygen."

The women piled from the back of the minivan.

Suzanne pulled open the door for Bennett who exited with Daniel in his arms.

Once inside the emergency room Bennett shouted. "Get a gurney over here. We need a surgeon! This little boy is four years old. He's got a .22 slug in his shoulder."

Bennett glanced at Daniel. "He's lost a lot of blood and he was unconscious for an hour maybe. We thought he was dead because he had a jaw breaker lodged in throat, choking off his oxygen."

Bennett continued with Daniel pressed close to Bennett's chest. "His name is Daniel Ruddy. His father will be here in a minute to sign whatever you need, but in the meantime, this little boy needs a surgeon now!"

Suzanne held Bennett's arm and with Bennett, looked into Daniel's face. The little boy's eyes were closed. Blood continued to ooze through the makeshift bandage that Silas had tied around his shoulder.

Rose said in quiet tones to Suzanne "I'm going with Vena to the chapel." She added with a smile "Don't look so grim, Suzanne. Daniel's going to be just fine. Promise."

Daniel Ruddy Senior burst through the double glass doors of the hospital emergency room.

Melinda followed. Behind her, Lenny hurried to keep up. He carried the baby in the baby's car seat, and cradled him with all the tenderness that Lenny could manage.

"Ruddy, they need permission to take care of your little boy," Bennett said. "That lady there has some papers for you to sign." He nodded to the young woman who picked up a clipboard and pen and offered them to Ruddy.

Bennett sought Suzanne's eyes. "And if it's all right with you, Suzanne and I will take care of the bill."

Suzanne nodded. With an anxious face and hopeful eyes she watched the gurney for any signs of movement from Daniel who remained still and with his eyes closed.

Ruddy walked to the counter and took the clipboard. With clipboard in hand, he seated himself.

Melinda and Lenny took seats next to Ruddy. Melinda read along over his shoulder, pointing and advising as Ruddy scanned the page and filled in the required information.

When he came to the *parents of a minor* section he filled in his name as father.

He read to the line that said mother and then Ruddy allowed his eyes to wander to Bennett who had covered Daniel on the gurney and who was now engaged in anxious conversation with the surgeon.

Ruddy looked at the little curly-haired, sheet-covered figure on the gurney and then at Melinda.

You're no Mary Ruddy, that's for sure. Mary had been petite and pretty. She was soft-spoken and she had taken impeccable care of herself, of him and of Daniel. She had been a good cook and had always maintained their home in immaculate style.

And she had loved him.

Despite his hateful, selfish ways, Mary Ruddy had loved him, Patrick Daniel Ruddy Senior.

Mary Ruddy had tolerated his drinking, his womanizing, his angry and frequent eye-rolling contempt for her, and for her unquestioning acceptance of everyone. Of everything. Of damaged people and kids with their garden variety of challenges, kids like their own son, Daniel.

And Lenny with his irritating slapping and clapping. Of adverse circumstances that would set Ruddy to cussing, kicking at walls, and then running out the door seeking his own personal comforts.

Ruddy squeezed his brows together. He couldn't remember the last words that he had spoken to her. They were probably hateful, though.

How had he reacted upon hearing that she was dead? That she had drowned in their home, on their bed, more than likely trying to save their son Daniel?

Ruddy shook his head. He couldn't remember reacting at all.

He had accepted the news that his wife, Daniel's mother, a good, kind, decent, well-respected woman, had died alone –protecting their child--in a nightmare that would haunt the people of Wolf Laurel Creek West Virginia for generations to come.

And he had said nothing. Had done nothing. The news hadn't touched him. Couldn't touch him. Maybe he did have a heart somewhere, but if he did, it was buried deep.

Survival, self-preservation, they're born of instinct. Animals survive.

But love, compassion, understanding, caring. Ruddy didn't seem to possess these attributes. They required nurturing, tending, unselfish, conscious effort.

Ruddy dropped his head a little. He let his eyes sneak to Melinda. But it wasn't Melinda that sat next to him.

It was Mary. Smiling as always, she reached her small hand to his face. "It's all right Daniel, I forgive you."

Daniel Ruddy howled. Tears erupted from his eyes. He threw the clipboard from his lap and then raced madly out the hospital doors.

Chapter Thirty-Five

"I don't know about you Miss Vena, but if we don't have God's attention by now we may never get it!" Rose declared. She rubbed her backside and gave Vena a cockeyed grin.

"I hear you, Child! And I don't mind telling the Good Lord how grateful I am that He saw fit to bless our church with padded pews! This hard wood becomes really *hard wood* after an hour or two."

"I agree with you on the padded pews," Rose said, laughing, and then her expression turned troubled. "You think everything's all right?"

"I surely do!" Vena replied. "And unless I'm wrong in my thinking, you do too! The Lord does work in mysterious ways. I can't figure why he would give little Daniel to Bennett and Suzanne and then snatch him back and then allow that little baby to get shot."

"I had to do some powerful praying when we thought that baby was dead!" Vena exclaimed. She allowed her eyes to rest on the wooden cross that hung on the wall in the front of the small chapel.

"I was mad at God. And I told Him so. I didn't see no reason at all why He would take that precious baby. No reason at all." Vena's eyes softened. "And now look, our Daniel ain't dead and he never was! And I'm questioning our Lord God of all creation!"

A huge smile wreathed Vena's face. "Praise God! He forgives us sinners! He allows us to question Him. He allows us to get mad at Him! And He loves us just the same!"

"And you want to know if I think everything is all right?" Vena grabbed Rose by the shoulders and gently shook her. "Of course I think everything is all right! God knows what He's doing even when Miss Vena Mae Thompson don't!"

"And come Sunday mornin', I'll still be grateful for them padded pews when I'm sitting on one, praying for forgiveness!"

"Maybe you better save me a seat," Rose said. "I wasn't too happy with God either. I hated seeing my friends so torn up. I thought they lost Daniel twice in one week and I couldn't bear it."

"If all the children on this planet could have the love that Suzanne and Bennett have for Daniel, there would be nothing but happy children."

"Bless God, I pray we see that day, Rose."

"I think we will Vena. I think we'll see it soon."

Rose turned from Vena to look at the cross on the wall. A smile crept over her face as familiar voices sounded in her mind, the voices of her parents, Isabel and Joseph McKinley. They sang Isabel's favorite hymn, "How Great Thou Art".

Rose looked back at the cross and quietly began to sing.

"Oh, Lord my God, when I in awesome wonder consider all the worlds thy hands have made. I see the stars. I hear the rolling thunder, thy power throughout the universe displayed. Then sings my soul, my Savior God to thee! How great thou art! How great thou art! Then sings my soul, my Savior God to thee. How great thou art! HOW GREAT THOU ART!"

Vena looked stunned. "Rose McKinley, how did you possibly keep such a secret from me?"

Rose smiled a tiny smile. "What secret?"

"Your voice! Child, there ain't no voice in the Heavenly Choir what could sing better than that. I still got goose bumps! Get me to a phone! I be callin' the reverend to tell him that we got us a soloist for Sunday morning!"

Vena wagged her head and then added with a chuckle "And I'll be tellin' him not to be surprised if, while his soloist sings, she sprouts wings!"

Rose hugged Vena and laughed. "Let's go check on Daniel. Maybe we'll have some news by now."

The two women started for the door.

"I'm sorry. I didn't meant to startle you." The deep masculine voice coming from the chapel doorway was Quayle Johnson's voice.

He stood ramrod straight, dressed in his black Stetson, starched black denim shirt, jeans and Lucchese full quill ostrich boots.

Stepping through the chapel doors, he swept the Stetson from his head, freeing thick, shoulder length silver hair that he wore tied in a ponytail.

"How are you Mr. Johnson?" Vena greeted the man with a smile and then added "If you and Rose will excuse me, I'm going to go find some coffee and check on our baby."

"Vena, you'll let me know if…."

Vena waved a hand. "If he's chasing balloons down the hall? Of course I will, Baby."

With a deep sigh Rose watched her friend depart and when Vena was out of sight she turned to Quayle.

"You have a way of showing up when you are least expected," she said. "Don't tell me the Austin grapevine is broadcasting again."

"Hardly," Quayle replied with his blue eyes, sharp and observant, locking onto Rose's green eyes.

"It was the Laurel County Sheriff's grapevine, actually. They stopped by with some news and with other things of interest."

Rose pulled her hands to her face. "They found your attacker?"

"So it would seem," Quayle replied. He frowned. "All things considered, this isn't happy news."

"What do you mean?"

"A few weeks ago, a farm couple in Boyd County, Kentucky, reported their burgundy and chrome 1960 Desoto Adventurer stolen."

Quayle glanced to the chapel doors and nodded. "That automobile is in the parking lot of this hospital. One of the owner's Civil War sabers—with my blood on it-- is in the trunk." Quayle glanced at the rows of pews. "Rose, do you mind if we sit?"

"Oh, of course not! I'm sorry, Quayle, I forgot that you're still recovering from the attack."

After they seated themselves Quayle replied "I'm probably about ninety-nine percent recovered but I don't want to push that last one percent."

"And that's likely a good thing," Rose said in agreement.

Quayle continued. "There was a camera in the car and it had some interesting photos in it. Some of the photos were blurry images of what looks like blue people, it's hard to tell. The shots were made without a flash in what appears to be sunset or something other than full sun."

Rose inhaled a sharp breath. "Quayle, do you mean, it was? We know who took those photos of the Fuquay Family. We were there. That's when Daniel got shot! Daniel's father took those photos!"

Without thinking, Quayle rested a hand on Rose's knee. "And that's what makes this so difficult, Rose. Somebody took photos of me and Daniel and Bennett loading mulch at Farmer Joe's."

"There's enough evidence in the car and in the camera to prove that it was Daniel's father, Daniel Ruddy, Sr., that attacked me."

"Quayle!" Rose cried in dismay. "What are you going to do?"

Quayle did not answer immediately. He seemed intent on searching Rose's face. "Rose, are you all right? Everybody's been concerned about me and now about little Daniel. How about you? Who's concerned about you? Does anybody ask if you are all right?"

Quayle's question startled Rose. She stammered. "Of…, of course. Why would anybody ask about me? I'm fine. They have good reason to be concerned about you and about Daniel. I have good reason to be concerned about you and Daniel."

Quayle lifted a brow. Beneath his neatly trimmed salt and pepper mustache, a smile played about his lips. "About me?"

Rose felt heat rise to her cheeks and knew they had turned crimson. She pulled her long copper hair over her shoulder and twisted strands in her fingers. It was a habit from childhood, something that Rose did when she felt awkward or ill at ease.

The fire in her eyes returned. Rose straightened her back. The slight movement of her jaw indicated that she gritted her teeth, a movement that did not escape Quayle's notice.

"Don't take that the wrong way, Mr. Johnson! Yes, I am concerned about you, you've become a good friend over these past few weeks and I would be lying if I didn't admit that I was worried about you."

Quayle was enjoying this. He wanted to smile but, discretion being the greater part of valor, he decided against it.

Rose continued. "A weaker man would not have survived that attack. It could have been fatal in multiple ways!" Rose allowed her face to relax. Her smile returned.

"Bravo! That was an admirable job, Ms. McKinley." Quayle's smile stretched wide across his face.

Rose looked stunned. "What do you mean?"

"I asked about you, how you are doing. You managed to turn the conversation to focus on me."

Rose became suddenly aware of Quayle's hand on her knee. She could feel the heat of it through her jeans. His hand was more like a paw, huge, bigger than Jan's hand. He should move it. She wanted him to move it. Or did she?

"What?"

He had said something and she had missed it.

"So now, I ask again, how are you? How are you handling your loss? Have your plans changed? And is there any chance perhaps that you will remain here in West Virginia?"

Rose answered quickly, maybe too quickly. "I haven't given it much thought, really."

She looked to the chapel doorway. "We need to go and check on Daniel. And speaking of changing the direction of a conversation." Rose stared into Quayle's eyes. "You never said what you plan to do about Mr. Ruddy."

"Ah, that, Ms. McKinley." Quayle had never known anyone to direct a conversation away from themselves like Rose McKinley. *Why was she avoiding his questions about her future plans? What was it that she did or did not want to say? Would he ever know?*

Quayle stood after Rose. He followed her down the carpeted aisle to the chapel door. "I'm going to drop the charges. I'm a believer in second chances. Even though he nearly killed me, the man was drunk. I don't believe that Daniel Ruddy is a serial killer or that he poses a threat of any kind to society."

Rose had stopped walking. Quayle had her full attention.

Chapter Thirty-Six

"I believe Ruddy needs to stop drinking. The man must have skills that he can use to try and build a life for those two boys and for this Melinda, the very young woman who is apparently going to raise them."

"From what I know, any boy who grows up in these parts learns a lot of things in a lot of ways. They learn everything from building and gardening to bee-keeping, raising chickens, pigs, horses and cattle, wood working, furniture making, engineering, pretty much anything they want to learn."

"Every country boy I know in West Virginia can take apart any car and can put it back together again. Ruddy must have skills of some sort. He just needs to use them."

Quayle tried to continue but was prevented. Feeling like a schoolboy with his first kiss, he couldn't find his tongue.

Rose had reached for his hand. She held it now.

Rose was tall and elegant. But in Quayle's eyes she was small and fragile. She was breakable, could shatter with a look or a word.

How did he know this? How could he possibly know this? Because Quayle Johnson paid attention. Perhaps he paid too much attention to Rose McKinley.

He had tried not to, but how many times every day did he find that his mind had wandered to her? Where was she? What was she doing? What was the distance in miles between the two of them?

If she needed him, how long would it take for him to get to her? Would she ever need him? Or the more honest question was, would she ever let him know that she needed him? Quayle knew that answer. And he hated it.

Rose continued as if nothing had changed, as if she wasn't aware that she held his hand.

"Quayle, even if you drop the assault charges Ruddy could still be locked up for a long time for stealing that car. There's nothing you can do about that." Rose said the words with the sudden realization that Quayle's blue eyes penetrated her green ones.

"Maybe not. But I might know someone who can," Quayle replied. His smile had returned and with it a look of mystery.

"Let me guess, you're best friends with the sheriff?" Rose blurted.

"No, I'm friends with Isaac Ramsey."

"Isaac Ramsey?" Rose's eyes were questioning. ""Who is Isaac Ramsey?" She asked. She liked having to look up to Quayle when she talked. She didn't do if often for Rose was taller than most of the people in Widows Hollow, Kentucky and in Wolf Laurel Creek, West Virginia.

Quayle felt the heat of her hand in his. It was distracting at the least.

"Isaac Ramsey is a collector. He collects American Civil War memorabilia. He has an impressive collection of muskets, rifles, revolvers, swords, sabers, Bowie knives, grenades, you name it." Quayle winked.

"He even has a couple cannon. He has a pretty impressive Civil War library, too, loves history and he's read every book that he owns."

"Does he work for the railroad?" This was an assumption on Rose's part. She knew that Quayle had started his career with *CSX* early and that the schedule he kept pretty well limited his social life. Quayle didn't have the time or the opportunity to meet a lot of people.

Quayle's dimples sank deep in his face. "No, Isaac is a farmer. He's also my cousin and he happens to own the 1960 Desoto that Ruddy stole. He's on his way here now."

Rose made a face. "You didn't recognize your cousin's car when Ruddy drove it to the clinic?"

"No, my love, Isaac buys and sells cars like farmers sell produce. I wasn't aware of this most recent purchase."

Quayle was however, acutely aware of the fact that he had just called Rose McKinley *My Love.*

Rose pulled her hand from Quayle's. She brushed her hair from her shoulders and stared into his eyes.

"You asked me before if I was all right. No! I ain't all right. I try not to think about it because if I do, I might be like one of your cousin's grenades that somebody's pulled the pin on and it's ready to explode!"

"I'm hurting so bad I can hardly breathe but I can't let on!"

"I have friends that need me, friends that have had their hearts torn out. Friends that thought they had a little boy and then they didn't. And then they thought they lost the little boy again, for good this time."

"I have another friend in Kentucky who might be dying. She could be dead this minute for all I know. She called for me and I have to go, but first I had to know that Daniel's all right."

"There is a pain that nobody can tend. Words can't help. Tears can't wash it away."

Rose bit her lip. The tears started. "It's a pain that pricks your heart when you least expect it. It wakes you in the darkness and makes you grab your pillow over your face so that others won't hear you cry."

"It makes a liar out of you. You tell your friends you're tired or that you have work to do but the truth is that you have to hide. You have to escape and be alone because this pain is going to splash from your eyes. It's going to bust out of your throat. You know it but there's nothing you can do to stop it!"

Rose squeezed her eyes in anger. Tears slid down her cheeks. "There is nothing you can do with this pain but carry it! And I've carried it since the day Jan kissed me good-bye and left for Vietnam."

"It got heavier when they told us Jan was missing."

Rose, don't cry! Please don't cry. If only I could grab you and make the pain go away! I want to, Rose. I want to so bad!

Rose sniffled. "And now, I ain't sure how I'm even walking. I should be crawling! The pain is too heavy!

It's breakin' me but I ain't supposed to break! I ain't no hillbilly, I'm a survivor! I am Rosemillion McKinley, daughter of Joseph and Isabel McKinley, mountaineers and survivors!"

Anger blazed in Rose's eyes. She doubled her fists. "And McKinleys don't break!"

"And I held your hand for a minute because I thought that maybe, maybe the pain would wait, wait until I could get out of here, wait until I could get alone so the tears could drown me and make me blind, so the pain could beat me to my knees and make me scream!"

"But it ain't waitin'! Jan may be gone from this Earth, but he will never be gone from me! He's right here. I can see him, I can feel him. And he will never leave me, because just like I carry the pain, I will carry Jan!" Rose thumped her heart with her hand. "I will carry him right here!"

Rose looked at Quayle with a look that he would never forget in this lifetime. Her words wounded him. He *felt* them.

"I'm sorry Quayle. But I ain't your love. And I know you didn't mean nothin' by it, but I had to say it so that it's settled once and for good. You're my friend and that's enough."

Speechless, Quayle watched Rose's transformation, her instant metamorphosis.

She scrubbed the heel of her hand over her face, patted her eyes and then she looked up at him with a look that was as serene as a mountain lake on a spring morning.

The pain had vanished from her face. The tears were gone from her eyes. She captured his heart with an impossible smile and invited "Now let's go check on Suzanne, Bennett and that little baby."

Feeling like he'd just been hit by a freight train, Quayle followed Rose in silence. *How does she manage to leave me speechless? This woman makes me feel things that I didn't know I could feel.*

Rose inquired of a nurse who directed Rose and Quayle to Daniel's room.

Bennett and Mustafa stood outside the door talking with the sheriff and with a man that Rose didn't recognize.

"Cousin," Quayle said with a nod to the stranger.

"You can't stay out of trouble, can you Quayle?" The stranger, a short, smiling man with black hair, a matching mustache, and with the look of a well-fed farmer, grabbed Quayle's hand and shook it in greeting.

"Isaac Ramsey, Rose McKinley. Rose, this is my Cousin Isaac," Quayle said, introducing the two.

"I'm pleased to meet you Miss McKinley," Isaac said with a nod.

"And I, you," Rose replied and then turned her attention to Bennett.

Bennett pulled Rose to him. He hugged her tight. "Our boy is going to be just fine! They got the slug out of him and said that he should recover completely. Rose, we are so grateful! If you hadn't acted…. He might, he might have…."

Rose pressed two fingers to Bennett's lips. Her smile could not have been brighter. "Sshhh. He's all right. That's all that matters. I want to see him for a minute before I go. Is that all right?"

Bennett nodded. "Just so you know, Ruddy's in there. In handcuffs. So don't be surprised."

"Suzanne and Vena?"

"Right there." Bennett pointed to the two women who walked toward them carrying vending machine pastries and coffee.

Suzanne's smile was angelic. "You heard? He's all right! He's going to be just fine!"

Vena quipped "All that time we spent on them hard wood pews paid off!"

Laughing, Rose hugged Vena who returned Rose's embrace with loving warmth.

"I'm so happy for you, Suzanne! And I'm so grateful to God!" Rose said, opening her arms to her friend.

Wreathed in smiles and then taken with sudden giggles, Suzanne waved the pastry. "And of course, he's hungry! Let's go feed him, shall we?"

Rose was delighted to find Daniel awake and alert. Despite his grogginess from the pain medication and the after effects of the anesthesia, his little eyes lit up when Suzanne entered the room.

She wasted no time breaking off pieces of the sugary pastry and feeding them to Daniel.

Daniel's love for Suzanne was obvious to everyone in the small, crowded space of his hospital room.

That included Melinda who sat nursing the baby in the room's only chair, Lenny, who glued himself to Melinda's side as always, and Ruddy who stood at the foot of the bed with his hands handcuffed behind him.

Rose walked to the bedside. She gently kissed Daniel on his forehead. "I love you Daniel. Aunt Rose is so happy to see you. You're gonna be all better soon but Aunt Rose has to go now."

"You ain't his aunt!" Melinda huffed from her chair.

The woman's words startled Rose. "Oh, of course not. I just meant that, that, I love him too!"

"And who asked you to butt into my business?" Ruddy barked at Melinda.

"Where's that sheriff?" He barked at Rose.

"He's right outside the door in the hall," Rose replied, apparently unruffled by Ruddy's rudeness.

"Would you ask him to come in here?" The sharpness had gone out of Ruddy's tone, the hardness out of his face. He looked like a contrite school boy.

"Sure," Rose replied.

Bennett, Mustafa, Quayle, and Ramsey followed the sheriff into the room.

"What can I do for you, Ruddy?" The sheriff asked. "This is your party."

"Seeing as how you're the law, can you take down what I got to say?"

"What, you want me to make out your last will and testament, something like that?" The sheriff asked. His belly shook with his derisive laugh.

"Something like that," Ruddy replied.

Suzanne produced a tablet and pen from her pocketbook. She gave them to the sheriff.

With a rare calm on his stubbled face and with a distinct sadness in his eyes, Ruddy nodded first to Bennett and then to Suzanne. "You take him," he said. Then he scowled. "I can't even remember your names."

"Bennett Gardner."

"Suzanne Gardner."

"Well Bennett Gardner and Suzanne Gardner, you take my boy. You take Daniel. And you keep him. I don't deserve to have him!"

Ruddy swung eyes that were heavy with guilt to his son.

The little boy took another bite of the pastry while keeping his eyes on Suzanne. He trapped her wrist with his small hand before she could return it to her side.

"Damn!" Ruddy swore. In anger he lifted a shoulder to wipe tears from his eyes. "Me and my stupids nearly got him kilt! The best thing I can do for my little boy is give him to you."

Speechless, Bennett and Suzanne exchanged glances.

"If I was to really love him, and God help me, I do! I'd give him to you so he can have better'n what I could give him. I ain't no fit daddy for no kid but maybe I can change that."

"I know I ain't got the patience or the smarts to raise Daniel like he's gonna need. His mama, Mary, she could of done it, but not me."

"Daniel, what are you saying?" Melinda demanded. "What about the money? If you give that kid to them, we won't get the money!"

Daniel turned on Melinda. "I don't care about the damn money, Melinda!   Daniel's more important than the damn money and for the first time in my life, I'm trying to do the right thing!"

With an anxious look Ruddy glanced to the little boy in the bed. "I'm sorry Daniel, I didn't mean to yell like that!" Tears coursed down Ruddy's cheeks.   "See what I mean?" He yelled in anger.   "I can't even get it in my head that he don't hear me and I never bothered to learn that finger googling that his mama used with him."

Ruddy slid his red eyes from Suzanne to Rose.   "And maybe it's as much for her as for Daniel that I'm doin' this. Maybe this one time Mary might of been proud of me." Ruddy's voice broke.

"Watchin' you folks and how you see to one another, how you hug and hold hands, and carry on, I ain't never seen that much."

"Ain't never been around folks what cared about one another. Pretty much raised myself with an old she-wolf dog out in a barn. "

Ruddy met Quayle's eyes for the first time. "And I'm sorry for what I done, Mister. I know it ain't no excuse, but I probably wouldn't a done it if I hadn't been soused and madder'n a Jap at everthing in the world! I deserve to be locked up for the rest of my life."

"If I could take it back, I would, but life don't work like that, does it?" Ruddy's dark eyes seemed to fill with genuine sorrow.

He hung his head and then added in a quiet voice "I'm glad I didn't kill you. I never meant to kill nobody."

Ruddy addressed Ramsey. "And I'm sorry too, for stealing your car. But I just got out of the slammer and I sure as hell wasn't gonna walk a good hundred miles from Kentucky to West Virginia in the dad-blamed heat!"

Ruddy turned his attention to the sheriff who had listened without interrupting.

"Sheriff, if you'll draw up some papers that'll do until the judge can make it stick, I hereby give my son, Daniel Ruddy Junior to Bennett and Suzanne Gardner. This time it's for keeps and it's forever. And I'll get me a lawyer that says so, too."

He looked from Bennett to Suzanne. "You two take him and raise him like he deserves. Let me know from time to time that he's doing all right, will ya?"

Ruddy wiped his tears on his shoulder. He tilted his face to the ceiling. "There, Mary, I done it!" He broke into sobs. "And I'm so sorry Mary that you was alone, you was alone in that flood. I shuda been there, damn it! I shuda been there!"

Bennett crushed Suzanne to him. Trying to contain his excitement and his voice, he said in low tones "Baby, did I hear him right? Midget is ours?"

Suzanne squeezed Bennett's hand and nodded through her tears.

"Mustafa glad for you. And for Midget," Mustafa said and clapped a hand on Bennett's shoulder.

"Maybe when I get out of the slammer this time I'll find me a job and learn to be a good daddy. I'm wantin' to try." Ruddy met Bennett's eyes. "Maybe the day'll come when your little boy will be proud of me."

"Ruddy! About you getting out of the slammer," the sheriff barked the words in his toughest-sounding voice.

He stepped behind Ruddy, inserted the key in the handcuffs and turned it. "You're out now. Mr. Isaac Ramsey has dropped the grand theft auto charges and Mr.

Quayle Johnson has dropped the assault/attempted murder charges."

"What?" Ruddy's voice was sharp. Demanding. Every eye focused on him.

The man eyed the sheriff and blinked in disbelief. "They dropped the charges? For the knifin' and the car?"

The sheriff bobbed his head up and down. He fastened the handcuffs that he had removed from Ruddy's wrist to the sheriff's belt.

"You're still gonna have to go before the judge to see if the state's willing to drop the charges." The sheriff pointed to Ramsey and to Quayle. "And because of these good folks, I'm inclined to bet that he will. But in the meantime, you're free to go."

The sheriff slapped Ruddy's back. "Consider this your second chance, Ruddy. Don't blow it!"

Suzanne let go Bennett's hand. She approached Ruddy, wrapped her arms around him and hugged the startled man. "You won't blow it, Daniel. We know you won't! Thank you! God bless you!"

Lenny circled behind Suzanne and Bennett to Daniel's bedside. He kissed the little boy on the forehead. "Ca..., can I come see him?" He asked, raising his shy eyes to Suzanne.

"Yes, Lenny, yes. Of course you can!"

Bennett took Ruddy's hand in his own. Pumping it, he said "Thank you Daniel. Take care of that baby. Make him proud."

"I swear to God I'm gonna try," Ruddy replied. He turned to Melinda. "You coming?"

Melinda passed the baby off to Lenny. She stuffed baby items in a bag and then she hurried after Ruddy, who, on his way out the door, cast a fleeting glance at the curly haired little boy that had fallen asleep in the bed.

Chapter Thirty-Seven

Rose, not wanting to wake him, kissed Daniel on the forehead and lightly touched the little boy's hand. "Bye sweet baby. Aunt Rose loves you and I'm happy that you're home to stay. Mommy and Daddy will take good care of you while I'm gone," she whispered.

She drew in a deep breath and opened her arms to the two women who had so closely shared her life in Wolf Laurel Creek. "Vena, Suzanne, I feel like I'm running out on you. There's so much yet to do and I enjoy helping but Olga can't wait any longer."

She hugged the two women in turn and said with a smile at the handsome man who leaned near the door with his feet crossed at the ankles and with his arms crossed over his chest "Quayle offered to drive me home so I guess I better get going. I'll call and let you know that I arrived safely and we'll stay in touch concerning Olga."

"You go on and take care of your friend, Rose, Baby. We'll miss you but she needs you now," Vena said.

"Rose, please be safe, especially on that highway out there! Drive with one eye on the rear view and watch the logging trucks!" Suzanne did a good job of keeping it light and cheerful until a single tear escaped the corner of her eye.

She clutched Rose close and hugged her tight. "It's going to feel so strange, waking up without you here! Coffee, alone." Suzanne smiled through her tears. "It won't be the same!" She said and swiped at her cheek with the back of her hand.

She sniffled, straightened her shoulders, and said with a half-hearted laugh "I'm not going to do this! I wish you could leave in the morning or at least get a nap first. But we know you, Rose McKinley."

"And we love you," Bennett added. He stepped to Rose's side and wrapped her in his arms. "We know you well. Where Rose goes, miracles seem to follow. You'll be fine," he said. He glanced at his wife and added with his typical Bennett Gardner laugh "I'm not so sure about Suz."

"She'll be fine, too," Rose said. "She has that beautiful little boy to keep her company and to keep her busy."

Bennett's smile fled. His eyes watered. "Rose, thank you for him!" Bennett swiped at his cheek with his crooked finger. "We wouldn't have this little guy if it wasn't for you, for your miracles, for your magic!"

With Suzanne's hand in his, Bennett looked at Daniel sleeping peacefully in the hospital bed. Bennett pulled Suzanne to him. "He really is ours, Suz! I think I'm the happiest man alive!"

He turned again to Rose. "You better scoot if you're gonna go! You go and take care of Olga. Give everybody our love and we'll see you soon one way or another."

"Bye," Suzanne and Vena said.

"Thank you Rose for help Mustafa. I appreciate," Mustafa said. He hugged the girl and then released her.

"I'll be fine," Rose said. "Love you all."

Quayle stepped aside to let Rose go before him and then he followed her from the room.

Unhappy that the short trip had ended so quickly, Quayle pulled into Mustafa's driveway. He unfolded his lanky frame from his pickup and then headed around to the other side to open the door for Rose.

He furrowed his brow and said with a frown "Do you have to leave now? Can't you wait until the sun is up at least?"

Rose's expression was apologetic. Her hair fell off her shoulders and down her back as she lifted her face to his.

Her green eyes with their endless depth held mysteries, mysteries that Quayle wanted to discover, mysteries that he wanted to discuss with her while holding her hand, while sharing a meal, or while watching her laugh.

"As much as I'd love to, Quayle, I can't. Besides, it wouldn't do me any good. I won't be able to sleep and I need to get to Olga as soon as I can."

Have I memorized his face? How is it that I know it so well? I know his smile, that he lifts the left corner of his mouth. His eyes are blue as the morning sky over Widows Hollow, his dimples remind me of laughing children. And his voice is comforting.

Rose acknowledged this truth with a start. *It's deep and masculine. Deeper than Bennett's or Mustafa's or Jan's.*

And it makes me feel safe.

"But what can you do?   You say she refuses to have the surgery that could save her life."

What?

Rose waited for her subconscious to retrieve Quayle's words.   She had missed them.

Quayle's mouth asked the question about Olga but his heart said something different.

Rose, I want to touch you so bad.   I want to hold you and never let you go.   Maybe if I give you enough time, you'll change your mind.   Maybe, after you've had time to help his mother and time to grieve for Jan, maybe then...."

Rose startled Quayle by taking his hands in her own. "Quayle, you've become a good friend and I appreciate it. Thank you for bringing me home but it's getting late.   I need to pack a few things and then be on my way."

Rose pulled door keys from her pocketbook.

Quayle glanced at the keys.   And hated them.   *That's my cue to leave.*

Rose's plans to quietly pull into her drive, check out her home, barns and stables, and then run to pick up Mama

John didn't exactly happen as she had envisioned them happening.

The normally quiet and vacated ridges and ruts of Widows Hollow were unusually busy this morning.

Friends and neighbors that Rose hadn't seen for months showed up in the strangest places.

They sat in cars, on fences, waved from rotting, abandoned barns and from *John Deere Tractors* in fields that didn't need plowing or harvesting.

A smile flickered across Rose's face. Mama John. She must have told them that Rose was coming home. No matter, Rose decided.

It felt good to be home, good to wave to neighbors that she had known all her life, good to know that the tight-knit community that she had grown up in hadn't changed in heart over the years although it had changed in appearance.

Rose turned into the winding, tree-lined drive that led past her pastures and her grazing herds of world class thoroughbreds. For fun she pressed harder on the accelerator, challenging the horses on the other side of double rows of white wooden fences to a race.

Rose pulled up on the circular brick drive in front of the house. She scrambled from her pickup and ran up the brick steps. She had her keys in hand and felt surprise that the door wasn't locked. In fact, it was open.

Rose's heart raced. None of her siblings' cars or trucks were in sight. And nobody but one of them should be in the house or should have left the door open for any reason.

Rose inhaled deeply. Something smelled so good. *It smells like….*

"Rose, baby, is that you?"

"Mama!" Rose cried in glee. "I didn't expect you to be here! I thought I was gonna pick you up at your house!"

Rose ran into Mama John's arms. She hugged the old woman with a fierce hug. "It's so good to see you! I've missed you so bad. I ain't never spent so much time away from you in all my life."

"It's good to see you too, Rose, Baby," Mama John said. "We all been missing you and wondering when you'd be getting back home."

"Well, it would not have been today if you hadn't called, that's for sure." Rose said. She darted her eyes about the house and walked from the living room past the dining room and into the kitchen.

"Mama!" Rose cried with a gasp. "You been cooking all night?"

Mama John wagged her head. "Oh, not me, Baby! I fried up some chicken and made you some potato salad that I know you love so well. But the rest of this," Mama John said and waved her hand over a table that was loaded with bowls and plates and jars and baskets that were filled with salads, vegetables, cooked meats and canned delicacies.

"The neighbors brought the rest of this. They're so glad you're back, baby. They just wanted to say welcome home."

"They come one after another'n carryin' plates and bowls and pots to my house so I called Jimmy Joe. He told me to come on over here and wait fer you to git home. The neighbors been showin' up here all mornin'! They love you, girl!"

Rose beamed. She picked up a piece of Mama John's fried chicken and bit into it. "How is Olga?"

The smile vanished from Mama John's face. A sadness worried her eyes. "That's another reason I'm here, Rose, Honey. We need to go on now. Olga's bad off. She's worse than I let on 'cause I didn't want you hurtin' yourself tryin' to get here too fast."

Rose snatched up a napkin and wrapped the chicken in it. She took another and wiped grease from her face and hands.

"Let's go."

Chapter Thirty-Eight

Rose was not prepared for the shock that was Klaus Vandeventer. The man who opened the door to her and Mama John was a shadow of the vibrant, handsome man that Rose had known before.

Klaus had lost so much weight that he looked skeletal. His eyes were sunk in his face and he seemed to have aged well beyond his years.

He wore a light blue long sleeved denim shirt, dark blue cashmere vest, and jeans that he had cinched with his belt to keep them from falling off.

Rose hoped that her shock and dismay in seeing Klaus in such bad shape would escape the man's notice.

"Rose! You are here finally! My Mama ees so sick! She ask for you Rose, she need you here wid her."

Smiling a rare smile, Klaus hugged the girl. "You vill make my Mama better. I know you vill," he said with a meager spark of confidence in his dulled eyes.

Rose's heart ached for the little man. His voice seemed to have aged too. It sounded foreign and strange to her.

"Mama John, thank you. Thank you for calling Rose and for coming vid her dis morning. Come now, please. Come up and see Mama."

Klaus started for the stairs with the two women when the doorbell rang.

"Mr. Klaus, you take Rose and go on and see Miss Olga. I'll get that door and tidy up a bit down here," Mama John insisted.

"Thank you, Mama," Klaus said. He took Rose by the hand and, together, they climbed the stairs.

Mama John answered the door to Margaret Olliphant who blurted "I swear, if I didn't know better I'd think that you've moved in here!"

"What can I do for you Miss Margaret?" Mama John asked without her typical smile or enthusiasm.

"Well, you can invite me in so that I can take these flowers up to Olga. My mother sent them with instructions that I am to deliver them to Olga myself."

"Mr. Klaus don't want nobody disturbing Miss Olga right now. She has a visitor, a somebody that Miss Olga invited."

"And who would that be?" Margaret demanded with a flash of anger. She shoved past Mama John and cast a resentful glance up the stairs.

"Miss Margaret, that ain't none of my business. My business is to see that Mr. Klaus and Miss Olga have their time like they asked." Mama John pointed to the study. "You can wait in the study if you've a mind to."

"Fine!" Margaret huffed. "And since you insist on keeping me waiting, I would like a cup of coffee. Nothing too strong. Two sugars and cream." She tossed the words over her shoulder, stormed to the study, and pulled the doors closed behind her.

Klaus opened one of the polished oak double doors to the bedroom where Olga lay sleeping. A smile brushed his lips as he stepped aside to allow Rose entrance ahead of him.

Rose squeezed Klaus's hand and then quietly crossed the plush mauve carpet to Olga's bedside.

A tray laden with fresh fruit that was cut into bite size pieces and a bowl of homemade soup remained untouched on the table nearest the bed. Wads of tissue and medicine bottles littered the pink marble table among gilt-framed photos of Jan.

Rose could see nothing against the mounds of down pillows but bed linens and Olga's long blonde hair. A pink sheet and burgundy down comforter hid Olga's face.

Klaus pulled back the sheet and said in the quietest voice "Mama. Mama. Rose is here Mama. She is here to see you."

Olga remained motionless and asleep in the bed.

"Mama," Klaus repeated.

After a moment Olga turned from her side to her back in the bed.

Klaus reached for his wife and lifted her higher on her pillows.

For the second time in five minutes, Rose felt shock and dismay.

All this worry and stress over Jan and Olga had taken a toll on Klaus. It had affected the man in every way, not the least of which was his appearance.

But if it were possible, Olga looked worse. This creature bore little resemblance to the woman that Rose had known and loved.

"Rose," Olga whispered and reached for her. The skin on Olga's arms looked like parchment, her fingers were cold and skeletal.

"Olga!" Rose reached for her friend and squeezed the frail woman with affection.

Olga patted the bed and reached for Rose's hand. "Come, sit with me," she invited. "I am not doing well, Rose. My heart is broken without my Zhan. I have not even his body to bury here at his home," Olga confided with sobs that came quickly.

Rose was desperate to help her friend, to banish her torment, to ease her pain. But Rose felt torn and conflicted.

How could she confide to Olga what she felt in her heart to be true without perhaps giving Olga false hope? That's the last thing Rose wanted to do and yet how could she stand by and watch Olga grieve herself to death without cause.

How could she tell Olga that she, Rosemillion McKinley, did not believe that Olga's son and her own fiancé, Jan Vandeventer, was dead?

If Jan was dead, she, Rosemillion McKinley would know. She would have felt it the moment he died for at that same time, a part of her would have died too.

That's how it worked in Rose's world. Attachments were more than words. They were more than made and kept or broken promises. They were bonds, living bonds that transcended time and space and known human capacity.

Rose's life had not been ordinary. Her beliefs were not ordinary. These were truths that she had learned to accept in silence.

At times messages came to Rose like mental teletype. They insisted their way into her mind as thoughts, unbidden, uninvited, but distinct, determined.

At other times, like with Vena yesterday, when Rose believed that Vena had spoken to her--Vena had not spoken but Rose had heard the words *He's not dead.*

And although Rose could neither see nor identify the speaker, the words, nonetheless, had proven true.

Messages came to her in dreams. It didn't matter if humans lied by commission or by omission, Rose's dreams told her the truth.

The Army said that Jan Vandeventer had been killed in Vietnam.

Rose's dreams told her that Jan was alive. And unlike Olga, who grieved his death, Rose refused to believe it.

And Olga was dying.

Rose had a decision to make and no time to think about it. Her mind warned, *Don't give Olga false hope.* That would be cruel beyond measure.

But her heart said *He's alive. He's coming home and you know it.*

And the litany of what-ifs showed up to taunt her, to make her fearful, to cause confusion.

What if you're wrong? What if people hear about it and call you a fool? Do you want to take that chance? Suffer the consequences? The derision? The gossip and the disparaging looks?

And of course, if she was wrong, there would be condemnation.

"She's a know-it-all. She thinks she's so smart. Olga's in the ground because of her!"

Rose bit her lip and glanced at Olga. Olga was dying. Without her beloved son, Olga wanted to die.

"But I ain't gonna let you! Jan's coming home, Olga! And you're a mess! You don't want him to see you like this do you? You're gonna get out of that bed. You're gonna eat some breakfast and get a bath. We're gonna put you on something pretty and we're gonna get you all better!"

"Rose! Rose, vat are you saying?" Klaus looked apoplectic. "You must not say this to Mama!"

"Klaus, run a bath for Olga. Help her bathe, wash her hair. I'll find her something pretty to wear."

Klaus had to scoot out of the path of his dogs. Both Annie and Maverick had been napping across the room from Olga. Now they nudged Klaus, yelping like puppies demanding treats.

Klaus stared at Rose and did not move.

She walked to the closet, opened the door, and began inspecting garments one by one.

She glanced to the bed and to Olga and then chose pink silk pants with a matching silk shell and cardigan.

"Here, Klaus. Olga will look beautiful and she'll feel better in these. You run the bath. I need some Vaseline. Can you tell me where to find it?"

Klaus wrinkled his brow. "Vaseline?" He managed to repeat, but did not move.

Rose frowned. "If you aren't going to bathe Olga, I will. But I could be making medicine that will heal her ulcers."

Olga spoke in a quiet voice. "Klaus, help me to bathe, please. We must do as Rose says."

Klaus pulled a hand to his face. Olga hadn't spoken that many words in months.

Whatever it was that motivated Rose was contagious. The dogs felt it. Olga felt it.

Klaus shook off his doubt. "I ged Vaseline for you, Rose. I bathe Mama."

Rose carried the pink outfit to the padded bench at the foot of Olga's bed. She lay the garments on the bench and said to Klaus as he passed "Is there any goldenrod in the greenhouse?"

The tiniest little laugh burst from Olga's throat. A smile followed the laugh, a genuine smile. "Do not ask Klaus about Olga's greenhouse. He does not know."

"Hey, is that a smile I see?" Rose asked, pointing to Olga's face.

"You say my Zhan is coming home! Olga smile always if my Zhan is coming home!"

"Well, you can keep smiling, Olga! We're gonna get rid of those ulcers, too," Rose said with an emphatic nod.

Klaus returned with the requested Vaseline and placed the jar in Rose's hand.

Rose nodded to the jar. "We're going to use a little bit of this and a little bit of the Good Lord's goldenrod. And after Olga is bathed and dressed, she's going to eat some real food," Rose added.

She pulled open one of Olga's dresser drawers and selected undergarments for her friend. "Mama John's downstairs so you know she's getting some of the best home-cooking in Kentucky ready for you."

Rose lay the undergarments that she had selected for Olga on the bench beside the pink outfit. "So here you go, here's everything you need to get dressed. And since Klaus is going to help you, I'm going to go find some goldenrod so we can get rid of those ulcers."

"I'll take this tray with me, Olga," Rose said. She picked up the tray with the untouched food on it and then headed for the door. She wasn't sure but she thought she caught a sparkle in Klaus's eyes.

Wagging their tails with great energy, both Maverick and Annie followed Rose. She skipped down the stairs, feeling certain for the moment at least, that she had done the right thing in telling Olga that Jan was alive.

"You two aren't fooling anybody," she said to the dogs. "You know I'm going to the kitchen and that Mama John's in there. You two think you're gonna get some treats, don't you?"

Rose pushed through the kitchen door with her two four-legged friends following. She placed the tray on the counter and grabbed Mama John.

"Guess what, Mama, Olga's up. She's getting bathed and dressed! Klaus can't believe it. He says she hasn't smiled or laughed in so long that he can't remember!"

"I know that's right, Baby," Mama John replied. She looked at the tray of untouched food that Rose had brought down. "Now if you can just get her to eat, you'll have yourself a miracle!"

Rose smiled a smile that lit up her face. "Oh, she's gonna eat all right Mama!"

Mama John's smile vanished. She turned to Rose with her brows knitted and with her lips in a straight line.

"Rose Baby, what did you tell Olga? You didn't tell her that Jan's coming home, did you?"

"I did, Mama."

Mama John took Rose's hands in her own and squeezed them. "Rose, Honey, I know you mean well, but what's gonna happen to that poor woman when Mr. Jan don't come home? We got to think on that, Baby!"

"Mama, he is coming home. I know he is!" Rose pointed to Rose's arms and said with a laugh. "Look at them! Goose bumps! I get them when something is right. They're my confirmation."

"Rose, Baby, it's just that, that…, it's dangerous to give somebody hope when we can't rightly say for sure they should be hoping. I know you want Jan to come home, I know you want to be right. But what we want and what we can prove are two different things. I don't think we should tell Olga that Jan's coming home if we can't prove it, that's all I'm saying Baby."

Rose locked her green eyes onto Mama John's brown eyes. "Mama, what is faith? What did you and my mama teach me?"

"We taught you straight from the Lord's own word in Hebrews 11:1-- *Now faith is the substance of things hoped for, the evidence of things not seen.*"

"That's right, Mama, and I ain't never forgot it. I got faith, faith that Jan is coming home. I got so much faith that this very day I feel like singing."

"It's been a long time since I felt like singing. It's been a long time since I felt like smiling. But today is different. Today I feel like singing and laughing."

Rose grabbed Mama John and hugged the dear woman in a bear hug. "And I feel like eating some of whatever it is that you're cooking!" Rose vowed. She inhaled deeply of the tantalizing aroma that filled the kitchen. "It smells heavenly."

She walked nearer the oven and sniffed the air. "Mama, are you baking bread too?"

The corners of Mama John's mouth swept upward. "You know I am, Baby!"

"Can't wait!" Rose exclaimed and then she pointed to Annie and Maverick.

Both dogs yelped and wagged their tails with enthusiasm. "They can't wait, either," she said, laughing.

Rose gave Mama John a peck on the cheek. "I'm heading for the greenhouse to get some goldenrod."

She added with a smile as big as a full moon over the Cumberland Mountains and with a sparkle in her eyes "I have faith that Olga's ulcers are going to be healed and that she's going to be good as new in no time."

Rose started for the door but turned to the dogs. "You two stay put. I don't want you wrecking Olga's greenhouse."

Ignoring Rose's command, the two dogs followed her, yelping and running in circles between Rose and the horses that whinnied and bobbed their heads on the other side of the fence as Rose passed.

Rose stopped for a minute to watch the horses play and then she returned to the business at hand which was mixing medicine for Olga.

Rose loved Olga's greenhouse, had been enchanted by it the first time she had seen it.

Flowers held a special meaning for Rose. Her mother, Isabel, had loved them, had loved them so much that she had made up a fairy tale about them, a fairy tale that she had called Rosemillion.

Rose wished that Isabel McKinley could have known something other than hard times, wished that Isabel could be here now, wished that she could have known Klaus and Olga and Jan.

Rose pushed open the door to the greenhouse. In an instant the memories enveloped her, the smell of the fragrant flowers, the pungent soil, and the mossy brick of the wishing well.

He had been here with her. It was here in this greenhouse that he had touched her for the first time, and she had doubled her fists, threatened him, dared him to think that he could have his way with her because he was the spoiled rich son of famous parents and she was a penniless nobody from Widows Hollow.

He had laughed and his laughter had further angered her. But then..., but then he had invited her to sit with him beside the wishing well, to sit and talk with him with his beautiful smile, his irresistible dimples, his sandy blonde hair that fell over his unforgettable blue eyes when he worked or rode one of his horses.

484

She had ached for Jan for months and now, being here in his home, in his mother's greenhouse where his memory was so alive, so fresh, and so *real*.

Rose wasn't going to do it. Not today. There would be no tears today. But Rose couldn't stop them. Had she made a mistake? Had she given Olga false hope? Was Jan dead?

Would the citizens of Ashford be right when they called her arrogant? When they would point at her and accuse her "You think you're so smart! Now see what you've done! It's your fault, your fault that Olga's dead!"

"You couldn't leave well enough alone! She could have had surgery but you prevented it! You never one time encouraged her to follow her doctors' advice, no! You knew best!"

"How does it feel now? You'd be better off if your life had never changed, if people continued to call you Pick--if you were still penniless and illiterate."

"Maybe then you would have done no harm. Maybe then you would have kept your opinions to yourself and she wouldn't be dead!"

Rose wiped at the tears that blinded her. She couldn't think about it now. It was too late. She had to find that goldenrod, mix the medicine, and make Olga better.

Rose looked beyond the rose bushes and the lavender. She looked for tall, slender plants for she knew that goldenrods grew to be as tall as four to five feet and that their bright yellow color was hard to miss.

Rose looked over the rows and rows of plants and then she cried out "Who am I kidding? Who am I to play God?"

Rose crumpled to her knees with her face on the ground. "Lord! What have I done? I didn't mean to hurt no one! You know I wouldn't hurt Olga. I love her! Just like I love her son! I didn't mean no harm, Lord! Help me! What do I do now?"

"What do I tell Olga and Klaus and Mama John and all them others what believe my words? What do I say to them? Tell me Lord. I ain't got no notion what to do, what to say. I need your help, God! I need it now!" Prostrate, with her face in the dirt of Olga's greenhouse, Rose sobbed.

"Get the goldenrod. It's on the farthest row, between a dogwood and a silver leaf maple."

Rose felt like she had been zapped with high voltage electricity. The goose bumps that confirmed her questionable beliefs marched over her arms now like a determined and well-regulated militia.

She picked herself up from the dirt and headed for the back of the greenhouse at the same time as the dogs cut loose, barking in high-pitched, excited barks.

In their hurry to return to Mama John's cooking, Annie and Maverick knocked over pottery, plants and garden tools.

***

Margaret stormed from the study and into the kitchen. "I have never heard such a racket in all my life!   Whatever is wrong with these dogs?"

She glared at Mama John.   "If you were as concerned for Olga as you would like for us to believe, you would do something to quiet these dogs!"

"Miss Margaret, I…," Mama John's words were lost on Margaret who had turned her attention to the sound of the doorbell.

Barking louder and with a greater urgency than before, the dogs raced to the front door and to the repeated sound of the bell.

"That's probably my mother, wondering why Olga hasn't called yet to thank her for the flowers that you have prevented me from delivering!" Margaret huffed and then stomped off to answer the door.

Mama John wagged her head and remained in the kitchen.

Margaret pulled open the door, prepared to enter into a tirade about how Mama John had refused to let her go up and see Olga and how the hateful woman had made up some story about Olga having a visitor whom Olga had invited.

When her eyes fell on the caller, Margaret stood for a moment, motionless, with a look of miscomprehension.

When her brain correctly signaled to Margaret what her eyes had perceived, Margaret bolted out the door.

"You? It's really you! You're home! Oh, my God! I am so happy! I can't believe you're home!" She squealed.

Margaret grabbed the gaunt figure. Repeating as if in a delirium "Oh, my God, it is you! You're home! Thank God, you're home!" She threw her arms about his neck and kissed the man.

Not anticipating Margaret's show of affection, the soldier staggered backward. With an unsmiling face he asked "Where are my parents? Where is Rose?"

Margaret look stunned.   Wasn't he happy to see her?
Why didn't he say so, after all she was *here.*

"What?"

"Where are my parents?   Where is Rose?" He repeated
with the same unsmiling face.

"Why, Rose is gone," Margaret stammered.   "She's
been gone for the longest time, off somewhere in West
Virginia.   But Mommy and I, we've been here, taking care
of your mother.   Jan, she's so sick!   And she won't see
anyone but us!"

Jan's eyes remained dull and lifeless, his face
expressionless. Dressed in his Army fatigues and holding a
camouflage duffel bag, he remained outside the door.   He
dropped the bag only to return the greetings of the noisy
dogs that yelped and licked at him, happy to see their
young master home at last.

Jan looked over the bounding dogs to a flicker of a
fiery-red something that burst into the living room with
anything but an elegant and ladylike entrance.

Jan could not identify the object of his interest,
Margaret blocked his view.   With his eyes straining to see
past her, Jan pressed a single finger to Margaret's waist and
then applied sufficient pressure to signal to the girl that he
wanted her to step aside.

With an indignant huff, Margaret turned to see what Jan clearly wanted to see.

Having cleared a path and with his unimpeded vision focused beyond the foyer and across the living room, Jan Vandeventer smiled a smile that neither Rose nor Margaret would ever forget.

There she stood, holding a drooping bunch of flowers. Dirt clods or something that looked like dirt clods clung to her wildly disheveled hair, to her shirt, her pants.   Her bare feet looked as though she might have been, perhaps, playing in the mud.

The flowers flew and the girl ran!   Unabashed, unapologetic, dirty, muddy and rumpled, Rose flew into Jan's arms.

Jan caught her up and despite the dirt on her face and the dirt clods in her hair, he covered her mouth, her face, her heart with his kisses.

Rose returned Jan's kisses with all the fire and passion that a once in a lifetime love could ignite.

She laughed and cried and kissed him over and over and then she caught a glimpse of Mama John.

The beloved woman stood in her God-bless-you-God triumph, waving her hands to heaven and bawling.   All the doubts that had plagued her such a short time earlier had fled.

Feeling their eyes on her, Mama John looked up to Jan and Rose. Her face was transformed into a picture of pure joy as she bounded across the room as fast as her feet would move.

With Rose and Jan wrapped in her arms, Mama John kissed them both time and again. Ain't God good? Ain't our God good?" She cried.

"Bless God, Mister Jan, you're home! And you ain't dead like they said. And your sweet mama...."

"Zhan!" Olga shouted his name from the top of the stairs where Klaus held her close to prevent her falling.

"My Zhan!" Olga cried again. With her beautiful blonde hair shining down her back and herself glowing in the pink silk outfit that Rose has chosen for her, Olga opened her arms to her boy.

With Rose's hand in his, Jan raced up the stairs to his parents.

"Mama!" He shouted and lifted Olga off her feet to spin with her in his arms. He hugged her and kissed her. "Don't cry, Mama! I'm home! Please don't cry!"

"Papa! I am so glad to see you, Papa!" Jan gushed and greeted his father with hugs and kisses. Jan looked down the stairs to Mama John. "Do you know how long it's been since I had a home cooked meal? And is that a home-cooked meal that I smell in my kitchen?"

Beside herself with happiness, Mama John replied. "You just come on down here and see for yourself Mister Jan!"

Jan grabbed Olga in his arms. "We're coming!" He replied. Jan descended the stairs carrying his weeping and laughing mother.

Klaus followed with an arm about Rose. With his knuckles, the little man wiped his tears as he, too, laughed and wept.

Chapter Thirty-Nine

One week later

Vena Mae Thompson did the honors. She snapped the yellow ribbon in two and then, with Mustafa, Suzanne, Bennett and Daniel, she smiled for the cameras.

It was official, Mustafa's Wolf Laurel Creek Clinic was open for business.

The turn-out was far greater than anyone had anticipated. Visitors from as far away as Charleston had stopped by to offer their good wishes.

The local neighbors and friends had shown up in smiling swarms and Widows Hollow, Kentucky, was very well represented.

Jan, Klaus and Olga fell in love with Daniel on sight.

Jan smiled at overhearing his mother's remark. "He reminds me of my Zhan. Maybe after we plan a wedding, we can soon plan a baby shower. I am ready for grandson. Klaus is ready for grandson."

Rose winked at Olga. "Or granddaughter," Olga added with a giggle.

In just one short week, Jan, Olga, and Klaus had all gained weight with Mama John's home cooking.

Olga had dutifully followed Rose's instructions and had rolled Vaseline in her hand to the size of a pea. This she mixed with the goldenrod flower, and swallowed at least three times a day.

Olga's physicians were skeptical but the test results were conclusive. Olga's ulcers were indeed on the mend.

Jimmy Joe, Jim Johnson and their younger brothers kept the hot dogs and burgers coming while Olivia and her best friends, Mama John's girls, Lucy, Lottie, Peach and Jasmine served drinks and desserts.

Dr. Bennett and Dr. Suzanne Gardner helped field questions about the new clinic and the new doctor in town, Mustafa, "Moose" Dhingra.

It quickly became apparent that Dr. Dhingra would be known to the Wolf Laurel Creek Community as Dr. Moose.

Azle and Judy Connor stopped by to chat with Suzanne about the West Virginia School for the Deaf and Blind that she and Bennett and Daniel would be attending in Romney as soon as Mustafa's clinic was fully staffed and operational.

Reverend Darryl Hobson and his wife Janice assured Mustafa that he had the full support of their church and of the local community.

Word had spread throughout the valley that Dr. Moose was associated with a string of medical miracles. The locals would have no problem putting their trust in this foreign-born doctor.

Mary Nell and her husband, Silas Fuquay, sent a card. They would have loved to attend the opening but, all things considered, felt that it would be best for all concerned that they did not.

Attorney Thomas Drake stopped by with a leafy dieffenbachia and adoption papers bearing the raised seal of the State of West Virginia that declared Drs. Suzanne and Bennett Gardner to be the legal forever parents of one young Daniel Bennett Gardner.

Frank and Ellie Perkins brought Mustafa a beautiful handmade quilt and then lingered to tell the story of how Dr. Moose and his friends had saved Frank's life.

One late arriving guest who turned heads and hushed conversation was the Train Man himself, Mr. Quayle Johnson.

Dressed in his favorite black Stetson and black Lucchese deer calf boots, Levi jeans, dark denim shirt and black leather vest, Quayle cut an impressive figure as he made his way through the crowd of well-wishers and to Rose and Jan.

"So we meet at last," Quayle said with a friendly nod to a smiling Jan Vandeventer. Quayle accepted Jan's hand and returned his firm handshake.

"Good to meet you Mr. Johnson," Jan said. "I've heard a lot about you and some of your adventures here in West Virginia. I want to personally thank you for taking care of Rose and for looking out for her in my absence."

"I know that it was lonely for her and it had to be a little frightening, too. I'm glad you were here for her. She's very fond of you," Jan said with a laugh "and she doesn't mind telling me so."

Jan took Rose's hand in his and kissed it. "Anytime you're up near Ashford, please be our guest. We'd love to have you." He winked at Rose. "And maybe, after the wedding, she'll let me sneak off and do some fishing."

Rose blushed. "Maybe," she said and then smiled. "Letting you two go off and do anything might require some serious consideration, all things considered!"

Jan and Quayle laughed.

"So you folks will be leaving soon?" Quayle asked, his eyes on Rose.

"In the morning we'll be returning to Widows Hollow," Rose replied.

"That soon?" Quayle asked. He knit his brows and found it difficult to hide his disappointment. Hearing that Jan Vandeventer had been killed in Vietnam and then hearing that he was alive had been one thing.

But seeing the tall blonde man with his striking good looks, undeniable charm, and international fame with Rose on his arm, beaming like a new bride, was another.

Rose caught Quayle's eye. Her eyes had never looked greener. Her smile had never been brighter. And her words had never made him feel more desolate.

"I came here from my home in Kentucky to help my friends open this clinic. The clinic is open. "Now it's time for me to return home to Widows Hollow."

www.ingramcontent.com/pod-product-compliance
Lightning Source LLC
Chambersburg PA
CBHW071629260626
47170CB00001B/23